CA

These are the stories of the... force including a supercar... cruiser, and destroyer. And... blistering reality of intern... Explosive.

CARRIER...The smash debut thriller about the ultimate military nightmare: the takeover of a U.S. Intelligence ship.

VIPER STRIKE...A renegade Chinese fighter group penetrates Thai airspace—and launches a full-scale invasion.

ARMAGEDDON MODE...With India and Pakistan on the verge of nuclear destruction, the Carrier Battle Group Fourteen must prevent a final showdown.

FLAME-OUT...The Soviet Union is reborn in a military takeover—and their strike force shows no mercy.

MAELSTROM...The Soviet occupation of Scandanavia leads the Carrier Battle Group Fourteen into conventional weapons combat—and possibly all-out war.

COUNTDOWN...Carrier Battle Group Fourteen must prevent the deployment of Russian submarines. The problem is: They have nukes.

AFTERBURN...Carrier Battle Group Fourteen receives orders to enter the Black sea—in the middle of a Russian Civil war.

ALPHA STRIKE...When American and Chinese interests collide in the South China Sea, the superpowers risk waging a third World War.

ARCTIC FIRE...A Russian splinter group have occupied the Aleutian Islands off the coast of Alaska—in the ultimate invasion on U.S. soil.

Don't miss these CARRIER novels—
available in paperback from Jove Books.

Titles by Keith Douglass

THE CARRIER SERIES:

CARRIER
VIPER STRIKE
ARMAGEDDON MODE
FLAME-OUT
MAELSTROM
COUNTDOWN
AFTERBURN
ALPHA STRIKE
ARCTIC FIRE

THE SEAL TEAM SEVEN SERIES:

SEAL TEAM SEVEN
SPECTER
NUCFLASH
DIRECT ACTION

Keith Douglass

JOVE BOOKS, NEW YORK

CARRIER

A Jove Book / published by arrangement with the author

PRINTING HISTORY
Jove edition / June 1991

ISBN: 0-515-10593-7

Jove Books are published by The Berkley Publishing Group, 200 Madison Avenue, New York, New York 10016.
The name "JOVE" and the "J" logo are trademarks belonging to Jove Publications, Inc.

PRINTED IN THE UNITED STATES OF AMERICA

10 9 8 7 6 5

CARRIER

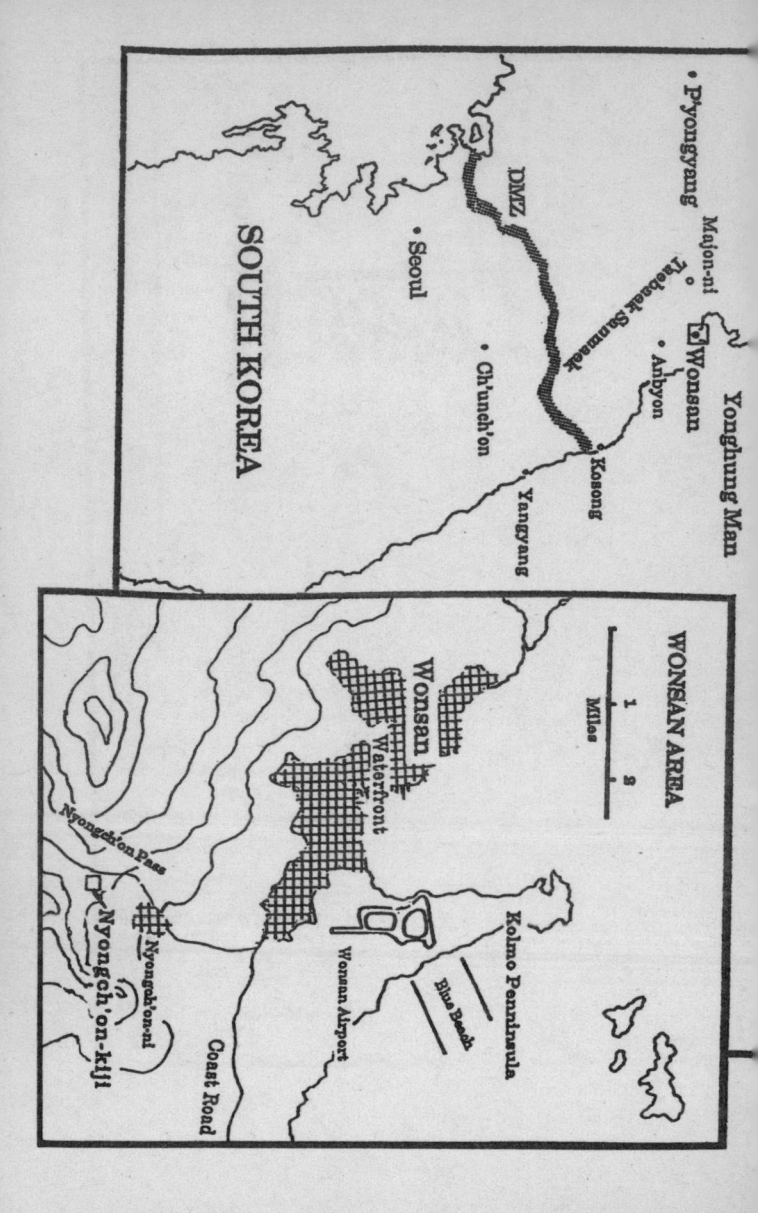

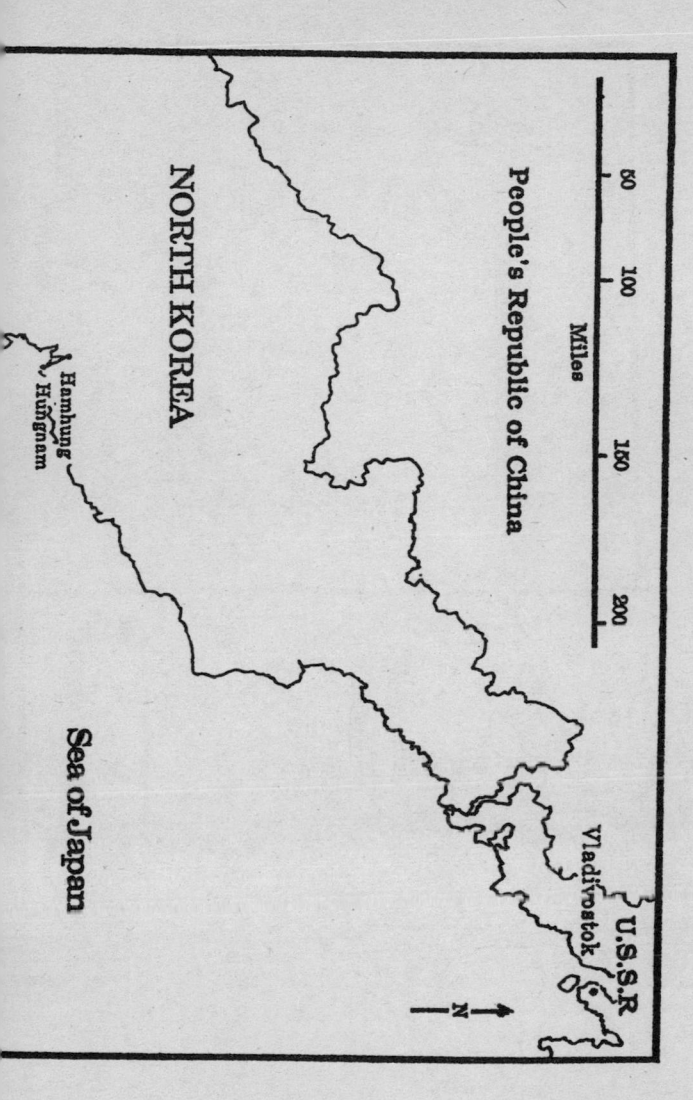

PROLOGUE

"Two bogies, Captain! Airborne, bearing two-five-niner, speed five hundred knots, closing."

Captain Gerald K. Gilmore leaned across the shoulder of the young radarman first class, his frown lengthening as he studied the radar screen. "Altitude?"

"Right on the deck, sir. I keep losing them in the wave clutter."

Chimera's exec edged closer, studying the hash of glowing fuzz scattered across the screen. "Damn, skipper. They're coming straight across the line!"

Gilmore nodded. "Sound general quarters, Will. Let's not take any chances."

"Aye, Captain." The exec's finger was already coming down on the panic button. A raucous clamor shrilled through the ship. He brought a microphone to his lips. "Now General Quarters, General Quarters! All hands, man your battle stations."

"Helm, come to zero-niner-five and bring her up to full throttle."

Through the deck, Gilmore felt the steady *chug-chug-chug* of *Chimera*'s diesels increase in tempo, felt the heel to port as she went into her turn. *Chimera* was ancient even by Navy standards, built on an LST hull first laid down nearly fifty years before. She was weathered and sea-battered, and only small bits of white relieved her steel-gray monotony: the shallow, sky-staring dish of a satellite downlink and the designation RL 42 picked out in fresh paint at bow and stern. She was a lot newer inside, packed keel to masthead with the latest generation of advanced electronics. *Chimera* was a spy ship, designed to eavesdrop on conversations

1

beyond the horizon. If this *was* an attack, she wouldn't stand a chance.

Gilmore picked up a telephone handset and punched in some numbers.

"Wilkinson," the voice on the other end announced. Commander Jake Wilkinson was *Chimera*'s chief spook, the officer in charge of the fourteen officers and enlisted ratings who worked down in the spy ship's "SOD-hut," carrying out their electronic eavesdropping on the airwaves.

"Captain speaking. Our friends out there are getting pushy."

"We're monitoring them down here, Captain. Spin Scan-B radar emissions. Probably MiG-21Fs."

"Is the line to Fort Meade open?" He was referring to the satellite-relayed teletype link through which they fed their scavenged data to the National Security Agency headquarters in Maryland.

"Affirmative, Captain." Wilkinson's curtness bordered on bad manners. The strain between the "real Navy" and the spooks on an intelligence vessel such as *Chimera* was always a problem, to the point where it was sometimes difficult to tell who was really in command.

At sea, in combat, that was deadly.

"You might let them know what's going on, then, and keep the line open."

"We're feeding them sitrep updates every fifteen minutes, Captain. We'll keep you informed."

"Very well." He replaced the handset, then paced back to the bridge radar station. "What about our shadows?"

"Still there, Captain. Range three miles . . . just inside the twelve-mile limit." *Chimera*'s "shadows" had paced the intelligence ship off and on for the past week, sometimes visible, sometimes not. The best guess by the spooks was that they were North Korean patrol boats shepherded by something big. The escort was probably a *Najin*-class frigate, one of the four largest warships in the KorCom inventory. They were as big as *Chimera* but a hell of a lot better-armed.

Gilmore strode to the starboard bridge wing, bringing his binoculars to his face and scanning the vague, pearly light illuminating the sky between cloud deck and horizon to the east. The coast, the Korean Naval vessels, all were invisible in fog and distance, but the bogies were coming from *that* direction. . . .

The alarm continued to shrill. Below the bridge, crewmen

spilled onto the deck, pulling on life jackets and battle helmets as they ran to their stations in a tumble of practiced confusion. *Chimera*'s armament consisted of two quad-mounted 40-mm antiaircraft guns in well mounts, one at the bow, the other aft, along with four heavy machine guns. He watched a machine gun crew snapping belts of ammo into the breech blocks and jerking back the levers to charge the weapons.

"Fifteen miles off the coast, Captain." Lieutenant Commander William Kingsly's face mirrored what Gilmore was feeling inside. "We are clearly in international waters. Do you think it's an attack?"

The Captain lowered his binoculars and looked at the exec. "I don't know, Will. Maybe they're just testing us. But no way I'm gonna let them pull another *Pueblo* on us." The fate of the Pueblo—also an intelligence-gathering vessel—had been heavy on everyone's minds since they'd been ordered to these waters the week before. The U.S.S. *Pueblo* had been in this same area when she was captured in 1968.

Pueblo's captain hadn't even tried to resist, though, had left the canvas covers on his machine guns. Gilmore was dammed if he was going to surrender *his* command without a fight.

Gilmore raised his binoculars again. He saw nothing. . . .

No! *There!* A pair of black specks, low above the gray, white-capped water. "Targets, Mr. Kingsly," he told his exec. "Bearing two-six-oh." The specks swelled visibly . . .

. . . and exploded over the ship at mast-top height. Gilmore flinched and ducked, the reaction instinctive. The bridge windscreen rattled and the deck shuddered as though *Chimera* had just run aground. A thundering sound followed those twin, death-gray shapes; it shook the ship and assaulted Gilmore like a physical blow. He found himself staring into twin orange eyes of flame as the combat jets cut in full afterburners yards above the surface of the sea, pulling up and around, turning . . . turning . . .

As the thunder faded, he was again aware of the shrilling of the General Quarters alarm. The approach of the jets had been so fast, so shockingly sudden, that the crew was still running to battle stations.

The fighters were back, bow on and low above the waves.

"They're firing!" Gouts of white water exploded on either side of the bow. The geysers walked aft until a shell slammed into *Chimera*'s hull like a jackhammer. Gilmore had an instant's horror-frozen glimpse of a sailor pitching back, his dungaree shirt

exploding in tatters and crimson mist. Explosions flashed and
shrieked, savaging the forward deck, parting the railing, slamming into the hull. . . .

"Captain!" the radarman screamed. "Surface targets changing
course! They're closing, speed thirty knots!"

Gilmore fought the sense of unreality which had closed around
him. "Mr. Kingsly! Are our colors raised?"

"They are, Captain." The exec showed his teeth, a humorless
smile. "There's no mistake this time."

There'd been speculation that the Korean Communists had
initially thought *Pueblo* was South Korean when they attacked
her.

Gilmore nodded. "Send out an SOS, Number One. Give our
position, and tell them we are under attack."

Damn! *Chimera* was lucky when she could manage eleven
knots, and these bastards were running her down at thirty.

An intercom buzzed, and Gilmore picked up the handset.
"Bridge. Captain."

"Wilkinson, Captain. Just thought you'd want to know. They're
fingering us with Kite Screech."

Kite Screech was NATO code for a certain type of Soviet
fire-control radar. The Koreans had it, were probably using it to
aim the 100-mm guns on that frigate.

Things could get grim very quickly now.

"Thank you. Are you in contact with Fort Meade?"

"Negative, Captain. No contact."

"No contact! Why?"

"Beats me, Captain. We're checking. We may have an equipment failure here . . . or the SOBs may be on their coffee break.
No way to tell if they got our message or—"

Thunder filled the bridge again as the two North Korean MiGs
roared straight toward *Chimera*'s bow, guns sparkling. Stanchions
on the middeck helipad spun away, followed by fragments of deck
plating as 23-mm shells chewed into the ship. A crewman running
down the starboard side gangway skidded and fell, his legs
pulped. Another sailor stooped to help, was hurled over the side.

Then the jets passed low above *Chimera*'s masts in a savage
thunder which shook the entire ship.

Water exploded forward, a towering pillar of white reaching as
high as the bridge. For a moment, Gilmore thought the MiGs had
dropped bombs . . . and then another white pillar erupted close

to port and he realized that *Chimera* was under fire, *cannon* fire from an enemy warship.

A third round struck somewhere behind the bridge, and the shock knocked Gilmore to the deck. Glass shattered in the bridge windscreen. There was a rending crash as the whaleboat close by the starboard wing of the bridge was slammed against the ship's hull. It took Gilmore a long second to recognize the high-pitched keening he heard.

Someone was screaming.

He looked down at the intercom handset he still held, blinking at it. The line was dead, useless. Carefully, he placed it back in its cradle.

How can I save my ship? How can I save my *men*?

The next shell missed, geysering close to starboard. The one after that struck amidships, between the bridge and the helipad, a shattering explosion which flung antenna leads and deck plates, stanchions and piping, high in the air. Flames boiled from a broken fuel line, sending a black and ugly clot of smoke past the bridge.

Above the roar of explosions and fire, above the screams of the wounded, Gilmore heard the rumbling search of the MiGs returning . . .

. . . and then what was left of the bridge windscreen burst inward, filling the air with knife-edged shards of glass and the whip-crack of exploding shells. The helmsman jerked back from the wheel, half of his head gone in a spray of bone chips and blood.

Smoke fouled the air. Gilmore lay sprawled on the deck with no memory of how he'd gotten there. "Someone get on the wheel!" he snapped. "Get—"

He stopped when he saw Kingsly. The exec was on the deck three feet away, most of his face blown away.

Oh, *God* . . . !

He tried to rise, tried to get his legs under him, and failed. Something was wrong. He couldn't *see*. . . .

"Captain Gilmore! Captain Gilmore!"

Gilmore blinked his eyes open, groggily aware that he must have passed out. How long . . . ?

A young lieutenant knelt over him, his uniform blackened with soot, tears streaking his face. "Captain, please!" Somehow, Gilmore managed to prop himself up on his elbows, to look down at the gash in his thigh, at the spreading crimson pool on the deck beneath him. He felt weak and very cold. "What . . . ?"

He tried to remember the lieutenant's name. Novak, that was it.

"Captain! They're coming aboard, sir! What should we do?"

Coming aboard? Who . . . ?

Distantly, he heard the chatter of automatic weapons fire, the shouts of voices, *foreign* voices.

Not on my ship!

"No . . . surrender . . ."

But somehow, Gilmore knew it was already too late. Through the open way to the starboard bridge wing, across a hundred yards of gray water, he could see the knife-lean shape of a North Korean frigate, could see the forward turret trained on *Chimera*, and the boats in the water loaded with armed men.

He must have been unconscious longer than he'd realized. Strange, but he couldn't feel the wound at all. He'd heard that that happened sometimes, but he'd never quite believed it.

God! He was so *cold*. . . .

"Take . . . command, Lieutenant . . ."

But he saw only fear in Novak's eyes, fear and incomprehension.

Then Korean soldiers in mustard-colored uniforms appeared in the door, brandishing AKMs, and Gilmore knew that he'd lost.

Chimera had never really had a chance.

CHAPTER 1

1345 hours
Tomcat 205, off the Korean coast

"Tango Seven-niner, this is Rodeo Leader. Say again your last."

Golden morning light exploded through the canopy of the F-14 Navy Tomcat, riding high about the overcast which blanketed the western arc of the Sea of Japan. Lieutenant Commander Matthew Magruder, "Tombstone" to his fellow officers of the Vipers, VF-95, wasn't entirely certain he'd heard the order right the first time.

"Rodeo, Tango Seven-niner," the radio repeated. "Come left to two-eight-seven and go to buster."

"Copy, Seven-niner," he replied. That was what he thought they'd said. Now what in the hell . . . ? "New heading two-eight-seven buster. Coyote, you copy?"

"Copy, Boss." The voice of his wingman, Lieutenant Willie Grant, sounded a lot more carefree than Tombstone was feeling at the moment. "We're with you."

A glance to the right showed Coyote's F-14 off Tombstone's starboard wing, the early sun edging the aircraft's sleek gray hull with quicksilver. He could make out the masked and helmeted heads of Coyote and his backseat RIO easily. Tombstone's wingman looked across the gulf between the two aircraft and shook his head slowly back and forth in an exaggerated, rueful gesture.

"Tango Seven-niner, Rodeo," Tombstone said. "What the hell's going on?"

"Hang tight, Rodeo. Will advise. Please comply, two-eight-seven buster."

"Roger, Tango Seven-niner. Rodeo coming to two-eight-seven."

Tombstone brought his stick left, nudging the Tomcat onto the new heading, and pushed the throttles forward to full military power. He felt the familiar shudder, the drag of acceleration as the twin GE engines shoved the aircraft toward the sound barrier.

West, toward Wonsan. Why? The two Tomcats were on BARCAP—Barrier Combat Air Patrol—maintaining their station at angels thirty some three hundred miles in advance of their carrier group. Somewhere ahead, less than a hundred miles distant now, lay the coast of North Korea, an unseen, menacing presence. To the north, closer even than the U.S.S. *Thomas Jefferson*, lay the Soviet Naval base at Vladivostok. Flying west toward Wonsan, Tombstone felt like they were heading directly into a dragon's gaping jaws.

"Hey, Tombstone!" The voice of his Radar Intercept Officer, Lieutenant j.g. Dwight "Snowball" Newcombe, sounded a bit shaky over the intercom, but that could have been the effects of the mild buffet as the Tomcat trembled at the spearpoint of its own vapor trail. "Tombstone, what's goin' on, anyway?"

"Damned if I know, Snowball. They'll tell us when they want to, I guess."

The buffet increased until they passed Mach 1, and then the rise was silk smooth and silent, arrowing through an endless blue heaven above a ruffled cloud deck that boiled and churned beneath the Tomcat's keels. Twin aircraft shadows raced ahead of the F-14s, rippling across the uneven surface of the clouds.

"Rodeo Leader, Rodeo Leader, this is Tango Seven-niner."

"This is Rodeo Leader. Go ahead, Seven-niner."

"Be advised that we have airborne targets, bearing two-seven-seven your position, range one-zero-four."

"I got 'em, Tombstone!" Snowball called. Magruder heard the young RIO's breath rasping over his earphones, his breathing quickening. "Confirmed two-seven-seven! I make it . . . two targets. Looks like they're vectoring for us."

"Keep on them, Snowball." He opened the radio frequency. "We copy, Seven-niner. Have two bogies on scope. What's the gouge, over?"

"Rodeo, Seven-niner. Wait one."

He waited. The "gouge," Navyese for hot information, was obviously being withheld for the moment. The tension was palpable, a smothering closeness in the F-14's cockpit.

Tango Seven-niner was a Navy E-2C Hawkeye a hundred miles behind them, one of the five twin-engined radar planes of

VAW-130 flown off the *Jefferson* to provide long-range radar surveillance for the CBG . . . and to provide up-to-the-minute tactical information for carrier group and fighters alike during combat.

Combat. Behind his oxygen mask, Tombstone's mouth went dry. Somewhere up ahead, just over that white sea horizon, an unfriendly someone was scrambling MiGs, and the two Tomcats were hurtling to meet them at better than Mach 1.5.

"Hey, Tombstone!" Coyote called. "Think they're sending us in to hassle the November Kilos?"

"More likely they're sending us in to hassle *us*," he replied. He hoped his voice sounded as confident over the air as Coyote's did. His heart was hammering in his chest, beneath the snug pressure of his harness. He shifted to intercom. "Talk to me, Snowball. What are our friends doing up there?"

"Still closing, Tombstone! Range niner-three. And we're picking up all sorts of radar crap from up ahead. Broad band. They're watching us. . . ."

"Rodeo Leader, this is Homeplate. Rodeo, Homeplate. Do you read, over?"

"Read you, Homeplate." Here it comes, he thought. Homeplate was the call sign for the *Jefferson*. The voice, static-ragged, was Commander Marusko's. The Commander Air Group, better known as CAG, was overseeing the mission from the electronic arena of the *Jeff*'s Combat Information Center.

"Rodeo, we've got a problem. One of our ships has been reported under attack off the Korean coast. We've been directed to investigate."

"One of ours?" Tombstone wondered if they meant one of the ships of *Jefferson*'s carrier battle group. None of the CBG's escorts was anywhere near the Korean coast, however, and that was sure as hell where they were headed now. "Which ship?"

"Rodeo, be advised ship in distress is U.S.S. *Chimera*, ARL 42, over."

Which made things even more confusing. ARL was the Navy designation for a small repair ship, probably a converted WW II landing ship held together by rust and good wishes. What the hell was an ARL doing alone off the coast of North Korea?

"Ah . . . copy, Homeplate. Understood." There was no use trying to get more information out of CIC, not when eavesdroppers might be listening in.

The thought of eavesdropping reminded Tombstone of another

attack on a Navy ship in these waters, some twenty-five years earlier.

Could *Chimera* be a spook ship? It was possible. Spook ship or not, Washington wouldn't be happy at the thought of another *Pueblo* incident. The capture of an American spy ship by the North Koreans in 1968 was still widely viewed as a classic failure of American will.

"Tango Seven-niner will vector you on radar target at coordinates three-three-niner, zero-one-four. Be advised hostiles may be operating in area. Homeplate out."

Advised . . . right. Right now, the two Tomcats were flying into the dark, with no clear idea of what to expect. If *Chimera* was a spy ship, there was precious little F-14s could do about it, advised or not.

"Tombstone, Coyote. Sounds like we're gettin' into deep spooky shit here."

"Could be, Coyote. Tell you what. Let's take 'em down on the deck. I'm starting to feel a bit chilly up here, aren't you?"

"Copy. Rodeo Leader, that's affirmative. After you."

The two Tomcats edged forward into a shallow dive, plunging into misty twilight. Clouds closed around the plastic canopies, shutting off the morning sun like a door. Moments later, they broke through the floor of the clouds and into the dim clear air between cold gray sea and leaden gray ceiling at thirty-five hundred feet. Magruder could see whitecaps on the water, a tatter-edged choppiness ruffling the smooth swell of the ocean. The two F-14s continued to descend until they were two hundred feet above the water, burning through the gray sky as they chased Mach 2. Tombstone felt a bit safer, knowing he'd just compounded the problems of any North Korean radar operators trying to sort his flight out from the clutter of wave caps and spume.

"Tombstone!" his RIO shouted into the intercom. "Two bogies just became four! They're havin' a party over there!"

"And we weren't invited. Maybe we'll get to crash their little party, Snowy."

"If you say so, Mr. Magruder." Tombstone heard the tightness in his RIO's voice. Snowball Newcombe was a nugget, a rookie posted to the Tomcat's backseat in keeping with the Navy's policy of teaming new men with experienced officers.

That, Tombstone thought, made him the experienced officer, the old hand who knew what he was doing. At the moment he didn't feel experienced, though, just old. . . .

1350 hours
CIC, U.S.S. *Thomas Jefferson*

Three hundred miles east of the two Tomcats, the U.S.S. *Thomas Jefferson*, CVN-74, newest of America's nuclear-powered carriers, plowed steadily through gray seas. Over one thousand feet long, with four and a half acres of flight deck and carrying some ninety aircraft, she and her sister *Nimitz*-class carriers were by far the most powerful warships history had ever seen. The *Jefferson* and her five escorts comprised Carrier Battle Group 14, a Naval force wielding power unthinkable only forty years earlier.

Within *Jefferson*'s bowels, on the O-4 level starboard, was the red-lit dimness of her Combat Information Center. Commander Stephen Marusko leaned over a console and scowled at the demon-green eye of a radar screen displaying a real-time feed from Tango Seven-niner, the Hawkeye orbiting between the CBG and Rodeo, the carrier's far-flying scouts.

"We're gettin' a ton of ground clutter here, Mr. Marusko," the first class radarman sitting before him said. "But the gomers must be scrambling everything they got."

Marusko nodded as he picked up a microphone. "Admiral? CAG, in CIC. Looks like it's breaking."

The reply was a voice of hard gravel. "You're ready to launch?"

"Four aircraft on Alert Five, Admiral. Call sign Backstop."

"Right. I'm on my way." The admiral sounded like he'd been rubbed raw.

Hardly surprising, Marusko thought. Admiral Magruder knew that his nephew was flying CAP.

More than once, Marusko had felt caught between the two Magruders: Matt, the young skipper of VF-95, and Rear Admiral Thomas J. Magruder, CO of CBG-14 . . . the younger Magruder's uncle. Hangar deck scuttlebutt had it that Tombstone Magruder owed rank and career both to the influence of the CBG's admiral.

That was one opinion Marusko could not share. He'd seen young Magruder fly, had been the one to recommend him for the skipper's slot when VF-95's last boss had exchanged his squadron for a billet with United Airlines. A recent graduate of the Top Gun school in Miramar, Tombstone Magruder was without doubt one of the hottest aviators on board *Jefferson*, a guy who wouldn't need his uncle's political influence until he struck for admiral himself a few years down the way.

But there were times when Marusko wondered just how closely young Magruder's high-powered relative looked after his dead brother's son.

His scowl deepened with the thought. Korea was getting hot again. The police-action war of the early fifties had never ended, never for real. Both Koreas had been armed camps since the armistice, the south supplied by the United States, the north by the Soviet Union and, to a lesser extent, by the PRC.

A steel door at the end of the darkened compartment opened. "Admiral on deck," the watch announced, but the men bending over CIC's radar displays remained unmoving, their faces stage-lit by the green and amber smears on their screens.

Marusko indicated the screen he'd been watching. "They're trying to jam us, Admiral, but it looks like they've got at least ten in the air. Rodeo is sixty miles out and on the deck. They'll be over *Chimera*'s last plot in two minutes."

Admiral Magruder gave a small sigh. "We'd better get Backstop airborne, CAG," he said slowly. "Our people are pretty naked out there."

"Aye, sir." Marusko reached for a telephone handset. The orders from Washington, relayed down the line through the Commander-in-Chief, Pacific, and the 7th Fleet, had directed the admiral to vector a combat air patrol over *Chimera*'s last reported position. It was the admiral who'd elected to put the battle group on alert . . . and mount the Alert Five as backup. Now he wanted the backup launched as added insurance.

"And keep me posted," Magruder added. "I want to know if those NK bastards even give a sour fart in our direction." He jerked his head sideways, indicating the flag bridge. "I'll be topside, waiting for Washington to make up their goddamned minds." He patted for the omnipresent pipe resting in the pocket of his khaki uniform shirt and rolled his eyes toward the overhead. "God only knows what'll happen when those bureaucratic bastards put their oar in. Call me if there's a change."

"Aye aye, sir."

The admiral appeared to be carrying a weight slung across his shoulders as he turned away, and in that moment Marusko decided that he wouldn't exchange places with Pops Magruder for anything on God's green earth.

Sometimes, the price was just too damn high.

1355 hours
Flight deck, U.S.S. *Thomas Jefferson*

Lieutenant Edward Everett Wayne, call sign "Batman," shifted in his seat, trying to work the cramp out from under his left shoulder blade. He'd been on Alert Five—sitting in the cockpit of his F-14, ready to launch from *Jeff*'s number two catapult on five minutes' notice—for the past hour and a half.

His point of view from twelve feet up gave him a splendid panorama of the carrier's flight deck, of the other three Tomcats set and ready for launch, of the crewmen in their color-coded shirts milling about in what looked like confusion but was actually a precisely choreographed ballet. Beyond, endless gray ocean merged with soot-gray overcast. Up there above that lowering ceiling was air and light and the golden glory freedom of airborne speed . . . he wanted to *go!*

Batman twisted far enough around to the right so that he could glimpse *Jefferson*'s Pri-Fly, the glassed-in structure overlooking the carrier's flight deck from high up along the inboard side of the island. The shadowy figures glimpsed there gave no indication that launch was imminent or even that they would launch at all.

His RIO grinned at him past the tangle of cables and equipment separating their ejection seats. Lieutenant Kenneth Blake's helmet was decorated with stars and bore his call sign, "Malibu," picked out in red. "Holy hemorrhoids, Batman," the RIO said, bantering. "I think I'd rather be surfing."

Batman Wayne chuckled. "I just wish they'd get this show on the road!"

As if in answer, his radio headset crackled in his helmet. "Backstop, Backstop, this is CAG. Time to wake up out there and earn your pay. Immediate launch. You are clear for engine start."

About damn time, Batman thought, fastening his mask across his face. "Roger, CAG. Let's go for it. Starting engines."

The Tomcat's port engine thundered to life, followed a moment later by the starboard. Outside, the deck crew completed their last-minute checks. "AWG 9 light is out, circuit breakers OK."

A green shirt standing off the port side of the aircraft held up a signboard on which he'd scrawled the numerals 66,000, and Batman nodded confirmation. The exchange was crucial, since the catapult officer had to make certain the catapult was set to deliver steam enough to hurl 66,000 pounds of Tomcat and fuel to a take-off speed of one hundred seventy miles an hour. A pair of red shirts scooted from beneath the wings after a final check of the ordnance slung there.

Batman grasped the stick, moving it forward, backward, left, and right, murmuring the traditional "Father, Son, Holy Ghost" mnemonic as he did so. Next he moved the rudder pedals with his feet, first left, then right, finishing the litany with "Amen." Outside, a pair of yellow shirts watched the aircraft's control surfaces and signaled thumbs up. Everything was working properly.

"All set, Malibu?"

"We've got the green light. Go for it!"

Batman glanced back over his right shoulder at the carrier's flight deck island. The green light there showed he was clear for launch. The voice in his headphones confirmed it. "Backstop Leader, you are go for launch. Good-bye and good luck."

"Copy, Homeplate." He opened the throttle to full afterburner, dumping torrents of raw fuel into the twin infernos in the aircraft's tail. He saluted the yellow-shirted launch officer, confirmation that they were ready to go. The launch officer gave a final all-round check, then executed a ballet-perfect gesture, leaning over and to the side, one leg extended, touching the deck with his hand. Somewhere out of sight, a catapult officer's finger came down on a red button, releasing an avalanche of steam against a huge piston buried beneath the flight deck. . . .

A giant's hand closed over Batman's face and chest, squeezing. He kept himself hunched forward, the better to keep his eyes on his instruments in the critical first seconds of launch. His eyes felt flattened in their sockets. The sharp rattle of wheels on steel below blended with the shriek of engines behind as sound, sight, and sensation were compressed into a single, nerve-jarring event. They hurtled forward. . . .

And sailed an instant later into comparative silence, a gentle feeling of sinking as the acceleration which had slammed the Tomcat from zero to one-seventy in two seconds flat died.

"Good shot!" Batman radioed, announcing that he had control of the aircraft and was airborne. The Tomcat seemed to hang in midair off the *Jefferson*'s bow for one dizzying instant, then began to pick up speed. The shock of catapult's launch was replaced by the gentler surge of acceleration as the fighter began to climb.

Voices buzzed over his headset, announcing a second Tomcat airborne, then a third, then a fourth. Air Ops began feeding him vector information. Batman noted the figures, but automatically, without real interest. His attention, his heart was on the sky as the *Jeff*'s bow dwindled astern and the universe became nothing but sea and sky and airplane. His Tomcat was moving now, wings folding back along her flanks as she leaped toward the cloud deck, plunging into the leaden, prison-wall barrier between him and the crystal blue beyond. It turned dark, and then he was bursting through into morning light, free of the ship, free of the world, hurtling north toward Mach 1.

1355 hours
Tomcat 205

Tombstone eased back slightly on the stick, bringing his nose up as gray water whipped past a scant hundred feet beneath his feet. This should be the place. . . .

He glanced to starboard at Coyote, who shook his head and gave an elaborate shrug. They'd reached their destination but the spook ship was nowhere to be seen.

"Anything, Snowball?"

"Clutter, Tombstone. Damn, lousy clutter. I think they're jamming us!"

"Easy does it, son," he said. He didn't like the urgent shiver that edged his RIO's voice. "Everything's green."

"Yeah, but it's gettin' worse, Mr. Magruder! I don't think—"

"Try to get through it. Ho, Coyote!"

"Copy, Tombstone."

"Coming right to triple zero."

"Triple zero it is. Mind the sharp corners."

"Tango Seven-niner, this is Rodeo," he called. "On target and no joy. Bogie dope! What can you give us, over?"

"Rodeo, this is Tango Seven-niner. We're picking up heavy jamming, broad band. Suggest new heading, one-eight-zero."

"Rog, one-eight-zero. You copy that, Coyote?"

"Back the other way. Lead the way, Boss."

"Here we go." They began their turn. "Tango Seven-niner, this is Rodeo. Confirm ROEs, over."

There was a pause as his question was relayed back to the CBG, which by now was below Tombstone's radio horizon. The ROE—Rules of Engagement—for his patrol had been set for Hotel-Two: fire only if fired upon. It was the worst possible situation for a fighter going into possible combat since it meant the other guy had a free first shot.

His compass reading steadied on one-eight-zero, due south. He could hear the rasp of Snowball's heavy, rapid breathing in his headset. "Right, Snowball. Keep your eyes peeled now for—"

"Skipper!" Snowball's call was a ragged burst of noise over the intercom. "I got 'em! I got 'em!"

"What . . . ?"

"Bandits, Mr. Magruder!" His voice was urgent. *"MiGs! MiGs! MiGs!"*

CHAPTER 2

The MiGs dropped like hawks stooping on their prey, four silver-gray aircraft with backswept delta wings. Tombstone had only a glimpse of the odd-looking cone-in-open-cylinder cowlings before he was on the radio. "Tango Seven-niner! Blue bandits! Blue bandits!" The code phrase had origins in the air war over Vietnam, identifying the attackers as MiG-21s.

"Four blue bandits, three o'clock and high!" Coyote echoed.

"Punch it, Coyote! Go to burner!"

"I'm out of here!"

Tombstone hauled back on the stick and his Tomcat clawed for sky, twin-throated torches of flame stabbing aft as he kicked in the afterburners. Down on the deck was no place for a dogfight, not if he expected to keep his airplane in one piece. MiG-21s had been around since the years right after the Korean War, but the modern versions were fast and mean, able to better Mach 2 and as good at dogfighting as any fighter in the sky. His instant's glimpse had caught sight of the pair of air-to-air missiles slung under each wing.

"Rodeo Two! Rodeo Two!" The sky went gray as they plunged into the cloud deck. "Where are you?"

"Right with you, Boss, at your five!"

"Level at nine point one!"

"Rog!"

They burst through the cloud deck and into the light. Heaven arched above him, achingly beautiful. At ninety-one hundred feet, the twin-tailed Tomcats rolled into level flight and turned west, away from the Korean coast. They were close to the twelve-mile limit here. Most likely the MiGs had been buzzing them to scare them off, and yet . . .

"Tally-ho!" Coyote called, the warning for enemy in sight. Like silver arrows, the four MiGs snapped up through the clouds a mile to the east.

"Got 'em, Coyote. Talk to me, Snowball!"

"Yeah! I have them!" the RIO yelled. At this range the heavy jamming would have little effect and his backseater would be able to tag them on radar. "Bearing two-three-five, range twelve hundred . . ."

There was a flash and an unraveling thread of smoke.

"Launch! Launch!" Coyote yelled.

The surprise was almost paralyzing. For all of Magruder's hours of training, his eight weeks at Top Gun school, the concept of someone actually *shooting* at him seemed too strange to be believed.

The paralysis lasted only fractions of a second. "Tango, Tango! We are under fire. Engaging!" The air-to-air missile swept up from the cloud tops, moving too quickly for the eye to follow. "Coyote! Break right! Break right!"

"Rog!"

That single launch might have been an accident . . . or the result of inexperience. A mile was long range for a decent heat-lock, and with a broadside shot at the Tomcats, there was little hope for it to latch onto the hot flare of a fighter's tailpipes. The latest intel stressed that the North Koreans were still using old-style Atolls, missiles which had to be looking up the enemy's tailpipe to get a lock. If G2 was right, the November Kilos had just thrown away their first shot.

But then, Intelligence had been wrong before.

By breaking right, both F-14s had swung to face the oncoming missile. That would break the lock, unless the Atoll was an upgraded all-aspect heat-seeker like the deadly AIM-9Ls slung beneath his own wings.

Tombstone watched the oncoming MiGs and turned cold.

Those pilots were not inexperienced. There was nothing he could point to, no specific clue which gave it away, but Tombstone knew aircraft and he knew good pilots. There was something about that rock-steady, welded-wing approach which told him that these four MiG drivers, at least, were the North Korean's first team.

And that meant . . .

"Right break, Coyote! Break, break, break!"

"Rog, Boss!"

Tombstone was already leaning on his stick hard to the left, cutting away from the oncoming missile as Coyote broke in the opposite direction. If the pilots were good, he had to assume the decision to fire was good . . . and that meant an all-aspect missile at least as sharp as his own AIM-9Ls.

"Hang on!" he yelled to Snowball. "I'm gonna make you bleed!"

Hard maneuvers by the Tomcat driver, felt more in the backseat than in the front, had more than once burst blood vessels in his RIO's nose, and his words were less threat than warning. The G-forces piled on as the Tomcat twisted away in a seven-G turn, then slipped into a dive to pick up speed.

He'd lost sight of the Atoll, already past him by now. The question was whether it could turn tightly enough to stick with one of the Tomcats. "I can't see it!" Snowball yelled. "I can't see it, man!"

"Forget it!" If the heat-seeker hadn't hit them by now, it wasn't going to. "Stay on the scope! Tell me what the bandits are doing!"

"Closing! Range seven hundred!"

A close-knit pair of shapes rocketed past, silver against deepest blue, and Tombstone caught a glimpse of the red star painted on each of the Korean fighters' tails. The enemy formation had split, two and two, and suddenly the sky seemed to be filled with aircraft, rolling, twisting, and jockeying for position. His first assessment had been right. These fighter jocks were *good* . . . and he and Coyote were in for a rough time.

The enemy was too close now for the Tomcat's radar-guided Sparrows, which suited Tombstone perfectly. To guide them to their targets, the Tomcat had to fly his own aircraft straight and level and pointed at the enemy, which struck Tombstone as a silly way to enjoy a dogfight. Besides, the Sparrow had been dogged by problems since its inception, and he didn't trust the missile to hit anything it was aimed at.

The four AIM-9L all-aspect Sidewinders slung from his wings, though, those were something else again. Given the choice, Tombstone always preferred a Sidewinder kill.

"Rodeo Two! Rodeo Two! Coyote, you've got a pair closing on your six!"

"Rog, Tombstone. I see 'em!"

"Hold on. Ready to break right, on my word. I'll brush him off!"

"Pedal to the metal, man! This guy's all over me!"

"Break! Break!"

Coyote's F-14 sheered off sharply to starboard, the MiG on his tail hauling back in an attempt to hold the turn. Tombstone dropped in behind one MiG, leading him, too close now for missiles. "I'm on him! Going for guns!" His finger closed on the trigger, and tracer rounds drifted like glowing, angry hornets toward the MiG-21.

"Tombstone!" Snowball called. "They're behind us! *Behind us!*"

MiG cannon fire floated above his canopy, each round an orange-white flare hanging a few yards above his head and drifting closer. His initial surprise swallowed now in icy detachment, his hands and mind guided by training and countless hours of practice, he dropped his Tomcat's nose, plunging forward and down, knowing that if he twisted left or right one wing would snap up into that deadly train of fire.

Ahead and to the left, he could see the MiGs on Coyote's tail breaking left and right as Coyote hauled back and climbed, twisting his aircraft into a three-quarters turn and rolling out in an Immelmann which carried him clear of the immediate threat. Another burst of 23-mm cannon fire probed past his right wingtip.

"Coyote! Where are you? I need a brush-off!"

"Copy, Tombstone. Cavalry to the rescue!"

Since Vietnam, American Naval aviators had trained and refined the "loose deuce" formation for dogfighting, a system allowing far greater flexibility than the old wingman-on-his-leader concept. There were greater dangers . . . but advantages as well. A pair of aggressive pilots could confront a traditional wingman pair with two dangerous attackers instead of only one.

But the odds here were still two to one, no matter what tactics the Americans employed. Two MiGs clung to Tombstone's tail, following him down toward the cloud deck. Tombstone kicked the throttle, going to full burner, and the Tomcat lunged forward like a living thing. The MiGs lagged but kept on coming.

"Tombstone! Tombstone! I've got a set! Hit the brakes and get clear!"

"Rog, Coyote! Take your shot! Take it!"

He feinted left, then broke hard right, killing his burner and dragging back his nose until he felt that first mushy sensation that warned him of a stall. Two MiGs dropped past him like stones, one to the left, one to the right. Tombstone pushed his nose over again, working now to win back the speed he'd lost.

"I'm on the left one," Coyote called. "Fox two! Fox two!" The cry was a warning they'd launched the heat-seekers.

For a long moment, Tombstone hung suspended in the sky, his eyes following that twisting, flaming point of light as it raced toward its target. The MiG was turning hard now, aware of the missile and throwing everything he had into a frantic break high and left. The Sidewinder closed the range in a steady march.

Then the burning flare of the heat-seeker merged with the MiG, eating its way up his jet exhaust. The explosion, even though expected, was startling, a blossoming fireball of orange and black which seemed to unfold, layer upon layer as the stricken plane disintegrated in flame and spinning, burning chunks of metal.

"Yow! Splash one MiG!" Coyote called.

"Great shot! Watch your six, now!" Another MiG was closing, dropping onto Coyote's tail.

"I see him!"

"I'm on him!" Tombstone rolled to port and kicked in afterburner, hurtling down across the sky, the Tomcat's wings folding back like the wings of a diving eagle. The MiG drifted across his forward field of vision, left wing high as it angled away from him, intent on Coyote's aircraft. He toggled his fire selector to Sidewinder, listening for the steady tone in his headset which told him the missile had a solid target lock. There! He pulled back on the stick, leading slightly to compensate for the target's hard turn without breaking his lock. "Fox two! Fox two!"

With the warning, Coyote's aircraft broke left and rolled in a split-S maneuver to port. The MiG followed, the maneuver dragging the MiG's tail around to give Tombstone a better shot, straight up the NK's tailpipe.

His finger closed on the trigger and he felt the shooshing lurch of the Sidewinder arrowing off its rail. He followed the missile's flight as it closed on its target, a bright orange-white flare of light which dwindled, trailing smoke, closing . . . closing . . .

An explosion filled the sky as the rear half of the MiG erupted in a cloud of burning debris. Tombstone watched the nose of the aircraft twist into a fiery plummet. There was a tiny flash, and a moment later the pilot's canopy blossomed. "Splash another one!" he announced. "Score tied, Coyote. One and one!" He turned in his seat, searching the sky. Two down, two to go . . .

The remaining two MiGs were dwindling into the distance, running for home.

"Tally-ho, Tombstone! Two gomers at one-niner-three! I'm on 'em!" Coyote's Tomcat twisted right, angling toward the fleeing MiGs.

Magruder almost ordered Coyote to hold position. Those MiGs had a long head start. This close to the Korean twelve-mile limit, he didn't want to risk breaking the ROEs by crossing that invisible barrier in hot pursuit.

But there was another danger as well. They'd been vectored to this spot in the ocean to locate an American ship, a ship somewhere down there beneath that unbroken floor of snow-wisp clouds.

"Copy, Rodeo Two. Hold the fort while I drop to the deck. I want to find our people."

"I hear you, Stoney. Mardi Gras and me are gonna make the score two-one while you're loafing."

"ROEs set to Hotel-Two," Tombstone reminded him. "Don't cross the line."

"Copy, Boss."

"You still with me, Snowball?"

"Y-yeah, Tombstone. But check your fuel!"

He glanced at the gauge. They were down to less than four thousand pounds of fuel. Dogfighting and full burner on those twin GE engines gulped down JP-5 at a prodigious rate. He checked his clock and felt a dull thump of surprise. The air battle had lasted less than six minutes.

"We've got time." The Tomcat was already pulling negative Gs as it nosed over and dropped toward the clouds. "The *Jeff*'ll be sending us a Texaco."

Once more between sea and clouds, Tombstone pulled up, leveling off at five hundred feet and angling southwest toward the coast. Radar interference had slackened, and Snowball reported two large, strong targets close together in that direction.

"Tango Seven-niner, this is Rodeo Leader. We're tracking two surface bogies, bearing two-zero-three, range about four miles. Do you have them, over?"

"Rodeo Leader, Tango. Affirmative." They triangulated the position of the targets. The two were well inside the twelve-mile limit, on the surface and moving slowly west. One of those blips had to be the *Chimera*.

"Homeplate, Homeplate, this is Rodeo Leader." The people in

Jefferson's CIC were following the situation as it was relayed to them by the high-flying Hawkeye. "Request permission to cross the line, over."

"Rodeo Leader, this is Homeplate. Negative. Break off and return, over."

"Homeplate, Rodeo. Believe *Chimera* inside twelve-mile limit, repeat, inside twelve-mile limit. Request permission to overfly, over."

"Rodeo, Homeplate. Denied. RTB immediately."

And that, Tombstone reflected, was most distinctly that. RTB . . . Return to base. He brought his Tomcat into a shallow climb, as Snowball searched for Coyote. He should be off to the northwest, no more than four or five miles away. . . .

"Rodeo, Rodeo, this is Tango Seven-niner. Be advised, we have bogies bearing three-two-one, your position."

"Snow?"

"Got 'em, Mr. Magruder. They're all over the place! I see six . . . no, eight . . ."

Heedless of fuel, Tombstone went to full burner and blasted back up through the clouds. Sunlight dazzled from the blue glory of the sky, a panorama of eerily peaceful beauty. He rolled the aircraft, the sun dazzle in the cockpit replaced by shadow as the Tomcat went belly-up.

"Rodeo Two, Rodeo Two! Do you copy, Coyote?"

"I got 'em, Tombstone." Coyote's voice was charged with excitement or fear. "Your ten o'clock, and high. God damn, where'd *they* come from?"

He saw them then, a ragged line of dots against the western sky. For one hopeful instant, Tombstone wondered if they might be friendlies off the *Jefferson*. But no . . . not from *that* direction.

"Negative on IFF," Snowball said. "Tombstone, let's get *out* of here!"

He hesitated.

"Skipper," Snowball insisted. "We *gotta*! Our fuel's goin' critical!"

"Not without Coyote and Mardi Gras!" Just where the hell were they, anyway?

1405 hours
Tomcat 207

Coyote heard the eerie, high-pitched warble in his headset which told him his aircraft had been tagged by someone's radar weapons lock.

"Tone!" he yelled to his RIO. "I got a tone! Shit, Mardi Gras, where are they?"

"On our ass, Coyote!" said Lieutenant j.g. Vince Cooper, "Mardi Gras" for his New Orleans hometown. "There's a million of 'em!"

"Shitfire! We're goin' ballistic!"

The Tomcat kicked him in the small of the back as he went to full burner, then rocketed past twenty thousand feet in a chest-crushing climb that made his eyes blur.

"I see 'em, Coyote! Five o'clock and low!"

Coyote looked aft. He saw a deadly white line drawing itself across the sky, the contrail of a radar-homing missile. He punched the Tomcat's chaff dispenser, then twisted away from the missile to give it a smaller radar profile.

"Bandits! Bandits!"

They were climbing to meet him from the cloud deck far below. He counted three . . . no, four. He checked the missile again and saw it still arcing toward him, undeterred by the rapid-fire barrage of chaff.

"They're locked on us, man!" Mardi Gras yelled. "They're locked on us!"

"Good night, Mardi!" Coyote killed the afterburner, then snapped the Tomcat into a wingover which sent the heavy aircraft plunging toward the cloud deck in an inverted dive. They fell for a mile through clear cold air before he hauled back the stick and kicked in full burners once more. Fuel was becoming a problem, but bingo fuel was a worry he would gladly live with later . . . if they survived the next sixty seconds.

The Gs built up as he continued to pull out of the inverted dive. He felt his mask, his skin dragging at his face as they pulled eight . . . nine . . . nine point five Gs. He felt the odd mixture of light-headedness and crushing weight. The Tomcat was easily capable of pulling Gs enough to put both Coyote and Mardi Gras to sleep. The trick was to pull *just* enough to stay awake, to stay in control.

His vision distorted, blurred by a nebulous disk of black fog as though he'd stared hard into the sun, then looked away. The blackness spread . . .

. . . and he came out of the dive, pulling up at nine thousand and continuing to climb as he rolled upright. "Mardi Gras! Are you with me?"

No answer. His RIO was out for the count. He continued his

climb with a half roll to starboard, searching. Where was that damned gomer missile . . . ?

The explosion came like a hard punch to his stomach, slamming him in his seat, then forward against his harness in a vicious one-two jolt.

He glimpsed silver fragments of high-tech aircraft hurtling past his canopy, felt the off-center surge as fuel ignited in a fireball a few feet behind him. What was left of the Tomcat rolled to the right as white flame swallowed the sky.

Coyote was functioning on pure, raw instinct as he reached down between his legs, grabbed the black and yellow ejection loop, and yanked it toward him. There was no time to think as ejection charges blew the F-14's canopy up and back. A second blast rocketed his seat up the rails and into cold blue sky, followed an instant later by a third explosion which sent Mardi Gras hurtling from the cockpit as soon as Coyote's seat was clear.

The ejection slammed Coyote's tail like a hard-swung baseball bat. Wind smashed against his face and chest. His head whipped to one side and he felt himself flung against his harness. He was tumbling. For a moment, he glimpsed his F-14 suspended above him, sleek nose protruding from a devouring monster of flame, the empty cockpit staring down at him like a huge, blind eye.

Then he was clear of his seat, falling through space with the clouds rising like a glaring snowfield to strike him in the face.

His parachute opened with a yank that whipsawed his body around, feet down, a sensation at once terrifying and wonderful, as though God himself had plucked Coyote from above. It felt as though he were whooshing skyward again, but that was illusion. He looked up to check his chute and was rewarded by what was at that moment the most welcome sight in the universe—the full, undamaged expanse of his white canopy blocking his view of the sky.

Dropping through the clouds was like entering a heavy fog. Then he was in the clear again, the water rushing up to meet him.

Grasping the beaded loops at the waist of his life jacket, Coyote jerked them out, then down, and was rewarded by the hiss of gas inflating the vest. His feet hit the water with a jolt, and an icy shock engulfed him. Working on automatic, his hands fumbled at the Koch fittings which secured the parachute to his harness as he broke the surface. He took a breath and choked on salt water. His mask was filled with water and he tore at it, yanking the straps free and gulping cold, wet air.

He could still die very, very easily, if the parachute dragged him down, if the shrouds tangled his arms and legs before he could get free . . . if no one could find something as small as a man adrift in a wide and empty sea.

A stiff wind was blowing the chute clear as he finally freed the harness fittings. Gently, he reached down and pulled some shrouds clear of his legs, letting the canopy collapse downwind as he worked his way free. He felt the stiff collar of his life jacket pressing against his neck, holding his head above water as he bobbed in the icy gray sea.

There was no sign of Mardi Gras.

Only then did Coyote realize how very much alone he was.

CHAPTER 3

"Tango! Tango! Rodeo Two is down!" Tombstone had seen the explosion as he clawed for altitude above the cloud deck, but he was so far away that he'd lost sight of Coyote as he hauled the Tomcat around to close with his wingman's aircraft. With mounting desperation, he searched the sky, praying for even a glimpse of parachutes.

"Tango, this is Rodeo Leader! Rodeo Two is down. I've lost him, over."

"Copy, Rodeo Leader. What's the situation with your bandits, over?"

Tombstone put his F-14 into a shallow port turn. "Situation clear, Tango. I think the bandits have decided to get out of Dodge, over."

"Copy, Rodeo Leader. Be advised, help is on the way. Call sign Backstop, four aircraft, ETA mikes one-three."

"I've got them on my scope," Snowball reported. "Bearing zero-eight-four, range one-seven-oh miles. The bad guys are breaking off and heading west."

More than likely, the North Koreans had picked up the incoming flight of Tomcats from the *Jefferson* and decided a one-for-two kill ratio for the day was just fine. Rodeo had been jumped at close range, but in a situation such as this, the incoming F-14s could mark targets and launch long-range Phoenix missiles from well over one hundred miles out. The MiG pilots knew that and would not care to linger.

"We've got them, Tango," Tombstone reported. "And the bandits are definitely running for home. Over."

27

"Copy, Rodeo. Can you orbit your station to cover Rodeo Two, over?"

Tombstone checked his fuel again, the scowl behind his mask deepening. There was no escaping the grim reality of those numbers. "Negative, negative, Tango. I'm going to be burning fumes in a minute."

"Understood, Rodeo Leader. Homeplate advises that a Texaco is on the way."

"Texaco" meant one of *Jefferson*'s four KA-6D tankers, an aircraft designed for air-to-air refueling operations. But he wouldn't be able to wait for the tanker to come to him. He would have to leave *now* if he wanted to rendezvous before his tanks went dry.

"Tango Seven-niner, this is Rodeo Leader. I'm going to have to boogie now to make it to the Texaco."

"Copy, Rodeo Leader. The word from Homeplate is: break off and RTB."

"Affirmative, Tango. Rodeo Leader, RTB."

But there was time for a quick check first.

The Tomcat stood on its portside wing and dropped, arrowing down into the clear, cold space between clouds and sea. The swells and whitecaps of the ocean surface whipped past as he brought the aircraft level at five hundred feet and throttled back. His Tomcat's wings extended, reaching forward as his airspeed fell.

"This is Rodeo Leader, switching to SAR frequency," he reported. In the backseat, Snowball clicked the F-14's radio over to the search-and-rescue channel and began sending out a call.

"Rodeo Two, Rodeo Two, this is Rodeo Leader. Do you copy, over?" Tombstone, listening in over his own headset, heard the empty hiss of static, felt tightness in his chest.

"Rodeo Two, Rodeo Two, this is Rodeo Leader. Do you copy, over?"

The silence stretched on through the crackling static.

1406 hours
Flag Plot, U.S.S. *Thomas Jefferson*

The radioman raised one hand to his earphones, narrowing his eyes as he listened to words filtered through static. "One aircraft down, Admiral. No chutes. Rodeo Leader is still calling on the SAR frequency."

"Damned idiot," Admiral Magruder muttered. "Didn't CAG flash him an RTB?"

"Yes, sir. I guess he's stretching it a little."

"I'll stretch *him*." The words sounded angrier than he'd intended. He was feeling an inner, guilty tug of relief that his nephew had come through the dogfight in one piece, and he was covering his emotions with an acid manner. A yeoman handed him a mug of black coffee from the Flag Plot mess. He kept his face impassive as he raised it to his lips, sipped it, accepting its scalding heat. "What about his wingman?"

"There's been no more contact with Coyote or Mardi Gras, Admiral. Backstop will be over that area in another ten minutes now."

"Captain on deck," a marine sentry announced. Magruder glanced up, acknowledging Captain Fitzgerald with a nod and a tight smile.

"Hello, Jim."

"Admiral." Fitzgerald's voice was tight, rigidly in control. "What's Tango Seven-niner say about our gomer friends?"

"Seems they've had enough. Hightailing back to Wonsan and a nice, safe bed."

The captain nodded. He looked worried—for his ship, for his men. "So. What now, Admiral?"

"We've engaged." He sighed. The responsibility was a yoke across his shoulders. Fitzgerald wasn't the only one who was worried. Magruder's responsibility extended to five other ships of the carrier group besides the *Jefferson*.

Worse, what he did or didn't do in the next few minutes might well start a war—a *real* war.

Magruder turned to his chief of staff, who stood nearby. "Brad, get me CINCPAC. Secure net. FLASH for Admiral Bainbridge."

"Aye aye, Admiral."

Flag Plot grew quiet. The seizure of a U.S. ship on the high seas was an act of piracy by international law, but now the situation had escalated drastically. Shots had been exchanged between the military forces of two countries. The dogfight off the Korean coast might well touch off a domino-chain of events which would end . . . where?

Tensions in East Asia had been running high for weeks. Rioting students in the streets of Seoul, calls by the United Korean Democratic Faction for a withdrawal of American troops from South Korea, a steady barrage of propaganda from the North

Korean leadership in P'yongyang, all had served to create the hottest world crisis since the Gulf War. The clash of political wills between Washington and P'yongyang could have far-reaching implications. By attacking American aircraft over international waters, Kim Il-Sung had just raised the ante in that eyeball-to-eyeball poker game. It was time to see him, and raise.

"I have CINCPAC on the secure net, Admiral." Magruder accepted the red phone.

Jefferson's captain looked as though he wanted to say something more but seemed to think better of it. "I'll be on the bridge, Admiral."

"I'll keep you posted, Jim." He brought the phone to his ear and pushed the handset button. "This is Admiral Magruder, sir. We have a situation here. . . ."

1407 hours
In the Sea of Japan

Coyote spat brine and fought for air as he rode the swell. The skin along the angle of his jaw already felt raw where the collar of his life jacket ground against him with each surging mountain of cold, dark water. A wave passed and he rode the slope of water into the trough. Momentum carried him down, plunging his head for one icy instant under water, and he felt the shrill jangling of panic in the back of his mind.

The shock of ejection, of hitting the cold water, had left him stunned, his thinking cloudy. Somehow, Coyote pushed the panic aside. Survival now depended on a cool head, and on his training.

His life raft had deployed from his seat on impact and inflated automatically. He managed to throw himself across the side and cling to it, gasping for breath. A SAR radio was strapped inside a vest pocket of his life jacket. Coyote pulled it free and opened the channel.

There was a hiss of static, and then he heard Tombstone's voice, faint and faraway, but clear despite the slap and slosh of water against his raft. "Rodeo Two, this is Rodeo Leader. Do you copy, over?"

"Rodeo!" he called. His mouth filled with salt water again and he choked. He spit, drew a wet and ragged breath. "Tombstone! This is Coyote!"

"Rodeo Two, this is Rodeo Leader!" Tombstone's voice crackled with excitement, as though he'd been calling for long minutes with no answer. Coyote's own emotions soared as well. "I hear you, Coyote! Are you okay?"

Coyote did a mental inventory. He could move his feet . . . both arms. He felt bruised from head to toe from his rough ride during the ejection and numb . . . numb from cold more than anything else.

"I'm okay!" he called back. He managed to roll the rest of the way into his raft. "Wet, but okay!"

"That's great, Coyote. SAR's on the way."

"Roger that." It would take time for the rescue chopper to reach him, but at least he was in contact with friendly forces. He'd be warm and dry on the *Jefferson* before lunch.

The thought of food brought a sour taste to his mouth, an unpleasant twist to his stomach. Oh, God, he thought. Don't let me be seasick . . . !

"Coyote, give me thirty seconds of beeper."

"Rog." He shifted the selector on his radio. After a minute he switched back to the voice channel.

"We've got you, Coyote," Tombstone said after they'd re-established contact. "You're south of us."

But how far? "Copy, Leader. Do you want smoke?"

"Not yet, Coyote. Let's make sure we're in the same county before you pop your flares. Do you see Mardi Gras?"

"That's negative. Do you have him on radio?"

"No joy, Rodeo Two. But we're looking."

Coyote thought he heard a distant growl now, a far-off and muted thunder that might be almost anything. He fumbled at his life vest, checking by touch that his flares were in easy reach. He didn't want to show smoke until Tombstone was closer . . . and he'd need to save one for the search and rescue helo when it arrived.

Only then did the real danger of his situation hit him. He was in contact with friendlies, but the nearest ship of *Jefferson*'s battle group capable of launching a search and rescue helo was still a couple of hundred miles to the east at least. SH-60B Seahawks had a top speed of 145 mph, which meant he was going to be bobbing around in frigid water for hours before a helo could get to him.

And the cold was already penetrating his flight suit. He was shivering as he spoke again. "Rodeo Leader, Rodeo Two. It's going to be a while before anyone gets here."

"No sweat, Coyote. We'll mount CAP for you until the SAR helos get here."

"Copy, Tombstone. Uh . . . what's your fuel look like, over?"

There was a long pause, and Coyote's worry grew. "We've got enough to find you first, Coyote. Stay cool."

Stay cool, yeah. Very funny. Coyote twisted, trying to face the rumble of sound he could now hear quite plainly. The movement brought with it another cold slap of water, the biting taste of salt. "Tombstone, you've got to be running pretty lean right now. Better break off and RTB."

"Copy, Two. A Texaco's on the way."

Yeah, and you'll never make rendezvous if you don't break off and didi for the *Jeff*, Coyote thought.

"Rodeo Leader, this is Rodeo Two," he said after a long, cold moment. "Listen, Stoney, with this cloud ceiling you're never going to spot me down here." He felt the hard truth of those words even as he said them. He'd overflown pilots down in the water before. Glimpsing something as tiny as a raft in the middle of all that water was next to impossible despite dye markers and signal flares; it got worse when low clouds kept you close to the sea. Even idling along with the wings full out, a Tomcat simply could not move slowly enough to give her crew a decent look at the water. He swallowed, tasting salt. "Suggest you break off and make for Homeplate. I'll be okay."

This time, Tombstone's hesitation seemed to drag on forever. "Rodeo Two, Leader. I . . . yeah, you're right. If I lose this airplane, we're going to have some very sore taxpayers on our case. You sure you'll be okay?"

"Affirmative, Rodeo Leader. I'll put on some light music, relax a bit—"

"Copy that, Two. Listen, you'll have Backstop overhead in . . . ten minutes. They'll orbit until the next relay gets here. It shouldn't take more than an hour or two for the SAR boys to get here. Think you can hold out that long?"

"No sweat, Tombstone. Tell 'em to keep me a warm spot by the fire." He listened again. Was the thunder closer now? He couldn't tell.

"Put your radio on beeper, Coyote. I'll tell 'em you're waiting. See you at home!"

"Roger that. See you . . . back home."

Home. The word brought a rush of thoughts, of memories, and the nostalgia was so surprising it momentarily crowded out of his mind thoughts of survival, of cold, of being abandoned in this vast expanse of water. For a moment, he could see Julie's face as clearly as if he could touch her. She was in San Diego now, with Jimmy.

Something caught his vision, tugging at his awareness just as he slid down the back slope of another ocean swell. What was it? Helplessly, he waited out the approach of another swell, felt himself rising . . . rising . . .

At the peak of the wave, he strained his eyes toward the something he'd glimpsed before and felt a thrill of recognition. A parachute! At first he thought it might be his, but then he realized the lines were still caught on something, that the canopy was still partly inflated and billowing in the stiff, chill wind.

Mardi Gras! That was his chute! After setting the radio to send out its steady, homing *beep-beep-beep*, he secured it to a strap on his shoulder, then began paddle with clumsy strokes toward the chute. It was at least a hundred yards away, and he lost sight of it every time he slid into the trough between one wave and the next.

But if he could reach Mardi Gras, the job of the search and rescue choppers would be one hell of a lot easier. Grimly, he kept stroking and slowly closed the range.

Yes, the thunder definitely sounded a little louder now.

1415 hours
Tomcat 232

Batman Wayne looked from side to side as his Tomcat roared low over the Sea of Japan. The ocean was gray and empty, with a heavy swell under a stiff northeasterly breeze. "Well, are we getting closer or what?"

"Try south," Malibu replied from the fighter's backseat. "Uh . . . make it one-eight-five. We're close, but I don't know how close."

"Can you get a triangulation with the other aircraft?"

"Affirm. We've got him to within a couple of miles. Wait one."

"Rog." Batman dropped to four hundred feet, trying to focus on the water rushing past his aircraft's belly at better than three hundred knots. He was ashamed of himself for snapping at Malibu, but the pressure was on for some high performance. MiGs he could handle, he thought, but how the hell was he supposed to spot a couple of guys swimming in all that ocean? The string of beeps his RIO was listening to would vector them in. The only question was how long it would take.

"Surface contacts," Malibu said. "Three miles, bearing two-five-oh. Inside the line."

"Shit. Maybe Homeplate'll let us go have a peek. Raise 'em, will you?" Batman wanted to concentrate on flying, on the gray swell of sea and whitecap below.

"We'll have to go through Tango," Malibu replied. "Too low to hit the *Jeff* . . . Tango Seven-niner, Tango Seven-niner, this is Backstop. Do you copy, over?"

"Backstop, Tango Seven-niner," the familiar voice answered. "Go ahead."

"We have multiple surface targets at two-five-zero, range three miles. Request flyby, over."

Batman shut out the radio chatter as he brought the Tomcat around in a low, slow turn, wings fully extended, streamers of white contrail blasting from the trailing edges in the humid air. Far to the east, sunlight spilled through a rare break in the cloud deck, then flashed from an aircraft canopy. That would be his wingman, Nightmare Marinaro, quartering another piece of the ocean. The other two aircraft of Backstop Flight were searching behind them, further to the north.

Even with the damned beeper, this was going to take some looking. The fact that the invisible line marking North Korean territorial waters now lay only a mile or so off his starboard wing didn't make it any easier. What if Rodeo Two had gone down on the wrong side of the line?

"No go, Batman," Malibu said over the Tomcat's ICS. "We're stuck with the ROEs."

"Aw, shit!" Batman replied. "They already shot one of our people down! We gotta go through that ROE crap every time we meet gomers?"

"Don't take it out on me, amigo! I'm right behind you, all the way."

"Yeah." Batman stifled the surge of emotion—it wasn't anger he was feeling so much as excitement, a keyed-up, high-pitched eagerness to come to grips with an unseen enemy. There were *MiGs* out there, damn it, and he wanted one so badly he could taste it.

That realization only fanned the flames hotter. Every aviator in the Navy lived his whole career for one thing, and one thing only . . . the chance to come up head-to-head with an enemy MiG, to engage in combat and prove that mix of skill, training, and ego which made a combat fighter pilot.

It wasn't that he'd forgotten about Coyote and Mardi Gras. He hadn't . . . *couldn't*. But pilots went for unscheduled swims in the peacetime Navy too. It was a part of duty aboard a carrier that every aviator trained for . . . and kept as far to the back of his thoughts as was possible. Ditchings happened.

Turning and burning with real live MiGs, now, that was something else! The last time an American aircraft had tangled with MiGs had been during the Gulf War, and the dogfights over Iraq had been Air Force victories, more often than not. But how he would have liked to have been a part of *that* set-to!

Lieutenant Edward Wayne was a victim of one of the paradoxes of modern Naval service . . . especially service with a carrier air wing. He'd spent eight years of his life so far training for only one thing: meeting an enemy pilot in air-to-air combat and shooting him down. It wasn't that he wanted a war; nobody did. But air-to-air combat, *real* combat, and not the mock dogfights aviators engaged in with one another on an almost daily basis, was the crowning test of any fighter pilot's career.

And Tombstone and Coyote, those lucky sons-of-bitches . . . it had been handed to them on a plate!

He dropped the Tomcat a little lower, his eyes watering as he tried to focus on the water rushing past, searching for smoke, for parachutes, for *anything*. "Ho, Malibu," he said. "How about doing the radio for a while? Maybe he'll tune in."

"Sure thing, man. Rodeo Two, Rodeo Two, this is Backstop. Rodeo Two, this is Backstop. . . ."

CHAPTER 4

Coyote was exhausted. The struggle to make his way toward the other chute through the heaving sea had left him so tired he could hardly move his arms. After almost fifteen minutes of paddling, he still wasn't sure whether he was getting closer to Mardi Gras . . . or whether his RIO's chute was dragging Mardi Gras closer to him.

"Mardi!" he shouted. Water slapped him in the face again and he spat it out. "Mardi! You okay?"

There was no answer, no indication that Mardi Gras was even there, that he was still connected with his chute. Somehow, Coyote found the will to keep going. His hand closed on wet nylon and he began pulling hand-over-hand, dragging fistfuls of guideline as he pulled himself and the raft past the collapsing parachute and toward the dark form he could now see each time it rode to the top of another ocean swell.

Vince Cooper's helmet was blue with white stripes, the call sign Mardi Gras picked out in red letters on either side of the visor knob. The RIO's head sagged back against the collar of his life jacket, completely limp with the roll and swell of the waves. Unconscious, Coyote decided. Their life preservers were designed to inflate automatically when they hit salt water. Fortunately, Mardi's had functioned as advertised.

"Mardi! It's gonna be okay!" He dragged himself closer. "You hear me, Mardi?" His hand closed on Mardi Gras's life preserver, dragging the bobbing form against his body. "It's gonna be okay, Mardi! Just . . ."

Mardi Gras's head lolled sideways with sudden movement, and

36

Coyote saw the shattered side of the helmet, the crimson color staining the water. He pulled Mardi Gras partway onto the raft, clinging to him as he searched for signs of life.

Coyote could feel the sickly crackle of bone fragments grating as he touched the RIO's head. Mardi Gras was dead, the left side of his skull crushed within the damaged helmet. "Oh, God, Vince!" He peeled off one of his gloves, probing his RIO's throat searching for a pulse. "Don't die on me!"

For the first time in some minutes, Coyote was again aware of the deep-throated rumble of an engine in the distance. Numb with cold and exhaustion, with one arm still thrown across Mardi Gras's chest, he fumbled with his free hand for a flare. His radio squawked, the words thin and indistinct. He couldn't reach it, not and still hold onto Mardi. No matter. They sounded close now. They'd see his smoke. The rumble was too throaty and deep to be jet engines. It was more like the heavy *thud-thud-thud* of a helo. Hell, that was fast work. If the SAR helo could pull them from the drink in time, they might still do something for Mardi back on board the *Jeff*.

By feel, he found the end of the flare for day use and twisted savagely at the cap. Red smoke spilled from the end, boiling across the water in a thick, churning cloud. With the last of his strength, he waved the smoke marker back and forth. Where was the helo? The engine noise was much closer now . . . and behind him.

"They'll have us back aboard *Jeff* in no time, Vince!" he told his RIO. Clinging to the man's body, he twisted around so that he could watch the helicopter's approach.

The shock of recognition brought bile to his throat.

It was not a helicopter approaching him with the deep-throated growl of triple diesels, but the angled gray bow of a missile boat. The turreted, automatic 30-mm gun on the forward deck, the huge, blunt canisters on either side housing Styx anti-ship missiles identified the craft as a Soviet-built Osa I.

The flag whipping from its mast was North Korean.

Coyote clung tighter to Mardi Gras's body, still unwilling to accept his friend's death, unwilling to accept the gray specter which was drawing closer now on throbbing, idling engines. North Korean seamen were lining the Osa's rail, AKM rifles pointed directly at Coyote.

"Oh, Vince," he said softly. "We are in one hell of a world of shit. . . ."

1445 hours
Tomcat 205, one mile abeam of the U.S.S. *Thomas Jefferson*

"Rodeo Leader, charlie now." The voice of *Jefferson*'s Air Boss sounded over Tombstone's earphones, signaling him to leave his holding pattern ahead of the carrier. He brought the stick over, dropping the Tomcat into a 4-G turn. He throttled back until the engines were barely idling and popped the speed brakes to further slow the craft. At 300 knots, the F-14's computer decided to slide the wings forward.

Normally, Tomcat pilots overrode the automatics and kept the wings folded back, holding that a wings-forward position made them look like a goose as they went into the break. This time, though, Tombstone left the wings forward. He was angry and he was worried, and somehow the aviator's concern with looking good on the landing simply didn't seem as important as it did normally.

"We are now in goose mode," Snowball said from the backseat. "Training wheels activated."

Tombstone ignored him and concentrated on the turn. His left hand flicked the control to lower his landing gear. At 230 knots he dropped the wing flaps, slowing the aircraft still further as he maintained the turn. His eyes flicked to the console. Rate of descent . . . 600 feet per minute. Turning at 22° angle-of-bank. Range from the ship now three-quarters of a mile. He was coming up on *Jefferson*'s wake now, sweeping out of the turn and lining up with her flight deck from astern. The carrier was plowing northeast into the wind at twenty knots. The swells had gotten stiffer in the last half hour, and Tombstone caught a glimpse of white spray bursting over *Jefferson*'s bow. From here he could make out the squat tower of the ship's Fresnel landing system, the "meatball" on the carrier's port side which let him judge his glide slope.

He called the ball. "Tomcat Two-oh-five. Six point four, ball." That told *Jefferson*'s landing signals officer—the LSO—that he had the meatball lined up, and that he had sixty-four hundred pounds of fuel on board. He'd not taken a full load from the KA-6D, since he needed only enough to get back to the ship. Excess fuel would have to be dumped before landing anyway.

"Roger ball," the LSO replied over his headset. "Deck going down. Power on."

In these rough seas, *Jefferson*'s deck was heaving up and down, changing altitude beneath Tombstone's wheels by ten feet with the passage of every wave. The LSO's warning let him increase speed enough during the last second of his approach to keep from touching down short on the deck. Tombstone caught his breath and held it. It was in these critical seconds that the LSO would wave him off if he'd screwed it up.

Large as she was, *Jefferson* never looked tinier to Tombstone than when he was dropping toward her deck for a trap. The deck was rising now to meet him . . . fast . . . faster. As the wheels touched steel he shoved the throttles forward; if his tailhook missed the arresting wire, he needed full power for a "bolter"—a touch-and-go that would send him off the forward deck and around for a second pass.

The hook caught hold with a savage jolt that flung Tombstone against his shoulder harness. "Good trap!" he heard over his radio, as he brought the throttles back and the whine of the engines dropped in pitch. Ahead of his aircraft, a yellow-shirted deck director waved a pair of wands, guiding him onto his taxi pass. He backed the F-14 slightly to spit out the wire, then folded the Tomcat's wings and crept forward, following the yellow shirt.

He'd already killed the engines in the designated space when he realized something was different. As the F-14's canopy raised up and he pulled the oxygen mask clear of his face, he saw that there were more men than usual gathering about the aircraft . . . and more were arriving second by second. Normally, the color-coded crewmen seemed segregated, each with their own kind, but now purple-shirted fuel handlers mingled with red-shirted ordnance-men, shoulder to shoulder with green-shirted hook and catapult men, safety monitors and corpsmen in white, crew captains in brown. The noise which assaulted his ears as he unfastened his harness and hitched himself up was deafening. Chief Walters, 205's crew chief, unfolded the ladder from the Tomcat's side and was there to congratulate Tombstone as he stepped from the cockpit and onto the deck. "Welcome home, sir! Number one job! Number one!"

"Thanks, Gabe."

The crowd was all around him, pounding him on his back. A red-shirted ordnanceman beamed up at him. "We got us a MiG, didn't we, Commander?"

"We sure did," Tombstone replied. He tried to grin and failed. He felt keen disappointment. He'd just experienced what every peacetime Navy aviator dreamed of, engaging MiGs air-to-air and scoring a kill, but worry about Coyote and Mardi Gras dampened his joy.

Besides, Coyote had made a kill as well.

But the enthusiasm of the flight deck crew was wildly contagious. Those men regarded the MiG kills as no less theirs than his. He found himself laughing despite the pain as he and Snowball were hoisted high and carried in triumphant procession toward the carrier's island.

If only Coyote and Mardi could have been there to share it.

1455 hours
Pri-Fly, U.S.S. *Thomas Jefferson*

"Admiral on deck," a seaman barked out, as Magruder stepped across the hatch combing and into the glassed-in brightness of Primary Flight Control. Captain Fitzgerald was there, the inevitable blue ball cap with *Jefferson*'s name and number inscribed on it low over his eyes, an unlit cigar clenched in his teeth. He was looking through the windows aft, watching the flight deck where a rainbow of colored shirts was closing in on the pilot and RIO who had just made their trap.

Fitzgerald turned and met Magruder's eyes. "Your boy's done well for himself, Admiral. A goddamned hero."

"That he has, Captain." Inwardly, he wondered what he should say . . . or should not say. More than ever, Magruder questioned the wisdom of allowing Matthew to be stationed aboard *this* carrier, out of all the carriers in the Navy.

He knew Matthew had the same questions. Having an admiral for an uncle could cause more problems than it was worth.

"You look worried, Admiral. What's the gouge?"

Magruder sighed. Better to say it right out. "I've already talked to CAG. Backstop is RTB. And the carrier group is to stay put for the time being."

Captain Fitzgerald was silent for a long moment. Behind him, through the Pri-Fly windows, Magruder could see one of *Jefferson*'s angels, a rescue chopper holding station half a mile off to port. That was routine during launch and landing ops, a safety net against the chance that a plane might have to ditch. So many flight op procedures were designed to safeguard the men who launched, flew, and recovered the carrier's planes, to give them the best possible chance of returning from a mission alive.

Magruder's words might well have just condemned Coyote and Mardi Gras to death. He couldn't escape that fact . . . but it was damned hard to look at it too.

"Washington?" Fitzgerald asked. There was the slightest curl to his lip as he spoke the word.

Magruder looked at his watch. "Fourteen fifty-six," he said. "They've been in the water for almost an hour. Backstop lost the beeper signal forty minutes ago. How long do you think they'll survive in that cold water, Captain?"

Fitzgerald's cigar worked up and down in his mouth, the muscles in the lean face working furiously. "I'd say we still have to give it a try, Admiral. We can't just leave our boys out there, can we?"

Magruder looked away as he handed a teletype printout to Fitzgerald.

The reply to his call to CINCPAC had been routed back down the line with startling swiftness. Admiral Bainbridge had assured him that the Joint Chiefs were closeted with the President at that very moment, discussing this latest twist to the Korean crisis.

In the meantime, though . . .

Jefferson's carrier battle group consisted of six ships spread across nearly one hundred miles of ocean. Closest to the Korean coast was the *Spruance*-class destroyer *John A. Winslow,* now steaming north some forty miles west of the *Jefferson.* Even at top speed, it would be hours before the *Winslow* could launch her two Sea Kings, hours more before the helicopters would reach the waters where Rodeo Two had gone down.

They'd be better off getting help from the Republic of Korea. The ROKs kept helos—Blackhawks and Sea Kings—stationed at Yangyang and Kangnung on South Korea's east coast. Hell, they might even have a few up at Kansong, and that was only seventy-five miles south of where the action was. Seventy-five miles was thirty minutes for a Blackhawk. They could have *been* there already!

Fitzgerald looked up from the teletype. "Washington is sitting on the ROKs?"

Magruder nodded. "Somehow, they seem to feel the North Koreans are going to feel *threatened* by a fleet of South Korean helicopters coming at them up the coast." He gestured at the message. "Quote, it is imperative that no actions which can be construed as deliberately provocative be taken, unquote."

Commander Wheeler, *Jefferson*'s Air Boss, looked up from his chair across the compartment. "And shooting down one of our Tomcats isn't provocative," he said in disgust. "Shit."

Magruder ignored him. "We've been ordered to hold our position while the Joint Chiefs study the situation," he said quietly. "We're too far out to launch a SAR of our own, and a sortie by the ROKs is out of the question. I'm afraid we've lost our people."

"You want to explain that to our aviators?" Fitzgerald asked. The faces of the other officers in Pri-Fly wore the shock which the Captain's words lacked.

"Want to? No. But there's not a hell of a lot else to do, is there? Except wait for CINCPAC and the Joint Chiefs to get off their asses and make up their minds."

"We'll be sitting out here until this time next year."

Magruder walked over to the window and looked down on the aft flight deck, forty feet below. The procession of deck crewmen had vanished with Tombstone and Snowball beneath the overhang of the island's superstructure. Matthew would be coming up shortly. The Admiral had passed the word for his nephew to meet him here.

The Air Boss walked over to stand beside him. "Pardon me, Admiral, but we can't leave those boys out there."

"What do you want me to do, Commander? Invade North Korea?"

"If that's what it takes." The muscles at his jaw worked for a moment before he added, "Sir."

There was a stir of emotion by the Pri-Fly entry, and Tombstone walked in. Lieutenant Commander Pete Lepke, the Assistant Air Boss—"mini boss" to *Jefferson*'s aviators—was the first to shake his hand. "First class, Matt."

"Thanks, Pete." Tombstone turned to face Magruder and Fitzgerald. "Admiral. Captain. Reporting as ordered."

The admiral couldn't look at Matthew Magruder without seeing the boy's father—his brother. Tombstone was tall for an aviator, as tall as Sam had been, with the same unruly brown hair, the same dark eyes. The somber, almost brooding features which had given the boy his running name were Sam's too.

"So you chalked one up for the wall at Miramar?" the admiral asked. There was a wall in a passageway at the Top Gun school at Miramar where the dates of Navy air-to-air victories are recorded on red-painted silhouettes of the kills. "Well done, Matthew."

"Thank you, Admiral. Is there any word yet about Coyote and Mardi Gras?"

The admiral kept the smile frozen in place. The older man shook his head, a slight, jerking movement. "Negative, Matthew. Backstop lost the SAR beeper forty minutes ago." He paused, unwilling to say the rest. "I've ordered Backstop RTB."

"For God's sake, why? Coyote is still alive out there somewhere! I talked to him!"

Admiral Magruder looked away. "They're out of range for SAR helos. And we're being dangled by those bastards in the five-sided squirrel cage."

"The Pentagon? What—"

"It's a touchy situation, son," Captain Fitzgerald said. He gestured with the teletype flimsy. "Coyote may have gone down inside North Korean territorial waters."

"So? They shot him down. They shot first. We go in and get him."

"I wish it were that simple," Admiral Magruder said. "But with tensions running as high as they are up here, the word is to play it with a low profile. No hostile acts."

"It was the NKs who started with the hostile acts, damn it!" He caught a warning glint in his uncle's eye, and stiffened. "Yes, sir."

"I know how you feel, Matthew, but right now our hands are tied. There's a chance the North Koreans picked him up. If so, it will be up to the State Department boys to get him out, not us."

"And if the November Kilos didn't pick him up?"

The admiral walked over to one of the windows. A rainbow of colored shirts spilled across the flight deck a telephone pole's length below. A pair of F-14s were being nudged into position on catapults two and four. Green shirts ran the cat shuttles back, locking them in place to each aircraft's nose gear as steam boiled from the deck around them. "Then it's probably too late already. That water out there is damned cold."

"Yeah," Tombstone said after a moment's silence. "And the water's not the only thing that's cold. Sir."

He turned and strode from Pri-Fly. Admiral Magruder could feel the younger man's anger like a white heat.

CHAPTER 5

Tombstone spent the next hour surrounded by sea and sky on Vulture's Row, the railed walkway high up on *Jefferson*'s island, trying to come to grips with the knowledge that Coyote wasn't coming back. The sight and jet-engine shriek of Batman and the other Backstop aircraft coming in for their traps onto *Jefferson*'s stern were like nails driven into the coffin.

They'd lost Coyote.

Numb, he made his way down the number two island ladder and into the gray maze of passageways and corridors branching out beneath the flight deck. His destination was the mess area known as the dirty shirt wardroom. In the formal wardroom below the hangar bay he'd be expected to change into the uniform of the day, but things were more relaxed here. He was still wearing his flight suit, and he felt sticky, dirty, and ripe enough to peel paint off a passing battleship, but his squadron was still on alert, and he didn't want to risk the luxury of a shower and a clean uniform. Not yet.

He was stopped along the way by an explosion of noise from the VF-95 ready room. "Tombstone!" Batman Wayne and Malibu Blake burst from the open doorway, still wearing their flight suits and carrying their helmets.

"What happened out there?" Tombstone said, cold fury moving beneath the words. "How'd you guys lose the Coyote?"

"Take it easy, Stoney," Batman said. "We didn't lose him. He just stopped transmitting." Other officers stepped into the passageway behind him. Lieutenant Gary Ashly, "Dragon," gave Tombstone a tight grin.

"Congratulations on your kill, Tombstone! Nice job."

Dragon's RIO was Lieutenant Commander Henry Whitridge. He took a hard look at Tombstone and shook his head. "Lay off the guy, Dragon. Can't you see he's shot?"

Malibu seemed to read the misery in Tombstone's face. "Look, Tombstone," he said. "We're all real sorry about the Coyote and Mardi. I know you guys were close—"

"That has nothing to do with it!" The words were out before he could stop them, driven by the pent-up anger and frustration he felt inside. He reined himself in, looking from Batman to Malibu and back. "Coyote and Mardi Gras were two damned good men. I hate the thought of losing them . . . that's all."

But he knew that that was a lie as he said it. He'd flown with Coyote before, off the *Kennedy*, and before that they'd been stationed together at San Diego Naval Air Station. Both of them had dated Julie Wilson until she finally decided to marry Coyote, and then Tombstone had been best man at their Navy wedding.

"You know, Stoney," Whitridge said. "We all miss those guys. But we can't bring 'em back. All we can do is go back in, right?"

"Snoops is right," Batman said, using Whitridge's running name. "Rack 'em up and zap a few black hats for Coyote and—"

"Damn it. Wayne, I don't want to hear your damned hotdogging patter!"

He turned away and strode off, lifting his feet as he stepped through the knee-knocker partitions where bulkheads crossed the passageway. After a moment's silence, he heard a burst of laughter from behind.

"Ah, he'll be okay," he heard Batman say as the officers filed back into the ready room. "Just shook, is all. Man, I hope those gomers come out again. I just wish I could've had one of 'em in my sights—"

Tombstone walked away, feeling as though he'd lost his brother. It wasn't that his running mates were insensitive, he knew. Sometimes it was the bravado, the aviator's mystique of *the right stuff*, that helped a man handle sudden death. Or maybe the idea of Coyote's death hadn't touched them yet, hadn't sunk in.

Coyote, *dead*. He forced himself to face that word, to say it in his mind. And how would he ever know for sure that Coyote's death had not been his fault? He, Tombstone, had split the formation after the first dogfight. It had been his command responsibility, his decision.

And Coyote was dead because of it.

The question gnawing at his thoughts now was, would he be able to make that kind of decision again? As squadron commander he would have to, but could he? It was possible that they'd be in combat again within the next few days in the skies over Wonsan.

He didn't know. The uncertainty was as keen an agony as the loss of his friend.

2130 hours (0730 hours, EST)
Cabinet Room, the White House

The President of the United States had been up the entire night. His Chief of Staff had pulled him out of the formal reception for the OAS representatives early the previous evening, and he'd been on the firing line ever since.

He sat at the end of the long hardwood table which dominated the Cabinet Room. The other men who ringed that table had also been at it all night, and they looked it. Most had abandoned suit jackets or uniform coats for shirtsleeves, and the room's ventilation system was having difficulty with the cigarette smoke collecting under the ceiling's soundproofing tiles. The Secretary of State looked worried; the Director of Central Intelligence looked tired. Most of the others showed varying mixtures of fatigue and worry as each came to grips with this latest piece of bad news from the Far East.

At the far end of the room, a Pentagon action officer tapped a pointer against a series of photograph enlargements mounted on cardboard and propped up on easels. The pictures were almost abstract, black disks flecked with white and cryptically annotated with meaningless letters and numbers.

"We have here repeaters off the radar screens pulled from the Hawkeye's transmissions and downloaded to the NSA at Fort Meade," said the officer, a lieutenant colonel in an immaculate dress uniform. Like most Pentagon briefing officers, he had the good looks and articulation of a TV news anchor, but this one at least seemed to know what he was talking about. "As you can see here . . . here . . . and here, *Chimera* was being almost constantly shadowed by what we presume was a North Korean task force, a frigate and eight to twelve light patrol craft. At zero-seven-thirty-six local time—that was seventeen-thirty-six hours last night—two military aircraft provisionally identified as MiG-21Fs of the North Korean air force strafed the *Chimera*. At the same time, the Korean Communist surface units closed in." The pointer moved, touching featureless blobs of light. "We see them here . . . and here.

"At zero-seven-thirty-nine local, Fort Meade received a portion of a message by teletype, indicating that *Chimera* was under attack. The message was interrupted. It is possible that the sending antenna was damaged or destroyed."

One of the men at the table shifted uncomfortably, then removed his glasses and polished the lenses with the end of his tie. Secretary of State James A. Schellenberg had already made his position quite clear. A military response in this crisis was the last thing the United States wanted at this time. "Excuse me, Colonel, but, ah, there was nothing to indicate that this, uh, *Chimera* was *destroyed*, was there?"

"If by 'destroyed' you mean sunk, no, sir." The action officer shuffled the stacks of photos to reveal a new series. "Okay, fifteen minutes later you can see this large Korean vessel—radar intercepts indicate it to be a *Najin*-class frigate—moving close alongside *Chimera*. Here, they get so close that the two blips merge into one.

"At eleven-fifty hours local time, we have two blips again, underway at eight knots and moving toward Wonsan, some twenty-four miles to the west." He lowered the pointer and turned to face his audience. "We can only assume, Mr. President, gentlemen, that *Chimera* was boarded by hostile forces and taken by force into Wonsan."

"Taken by force," the President repeated. He watched as the action officer gathered his photographs. "Options, gentlemen," he said at last. "Give me options."

General Amos Caldwell, Chairman of the Joint Chiefs, looked up from the yellow tablet on which he had been making notes. "How many options are there in a situation like this, Mr. President? Seems to me we simply can't allow this deliberate and premeditated provocation to go unpunished."

"Are the Joint Chiefs in full agreement on this?"

"I would have to agree with General Caldwell, Mr. President." Admiral Fletcher T. Grimes was Chief of Naval Operations, a crusty, lantern-jawed man who twenty years before had commanded an aircraft carrier in the Gulf of Tonkin. "This is the *Pueblo* all over again. We can't let those bastards get away with piracy, damn it!"

"So? What are we going to do about it, Fletch?"

"We have a carrier battle group less than twelve hours from Wonsan. *Use* it!"

"How?"

"Air strikes . . . backed up by amphibious landings, if necessary. The Marines in Okinawa are on alert already. If we show the KorComs we mean business . . ."

"I'd go one further, Mr. President," Caldwell said. "This calls for full-scale intervention, right down the line. Army. Air Force. Special Forces . . ."

"Invasion."

"We'll look pretty damned silly if we don't use *every* means at our disposal to bring about a resolution of this . . . this crisis, Mr. President. These people mean business. I suggest we show them we mean business as well."

"Good God," Schellenberg said. "Don't you think we ought to take the diplomatic approach first? The days of head-to-head military confrontation are over!"

"Who says?" The Director of Central Intelligence leaned forward at the table, hands clasped. Victor Marlowe, head of the entire American intelligence community, had personally brought word of *Chimera*'s capture to the White House the night before. His voice carried a quiet, almost bantering tone which fooled no one at the table. They all knew how important *Chimera* was to him. "Mr. Secretary, you know as well as I do that gabbing with those people isn't going to get us anywhere."

"How do you know unless we try?" George Hall, the White House Chief of Staff, said from the other side of the table. "Mr. President, this could really backfire on you in the polls. There's time for a military option later."

"I'm aware of the polls, George," the President said. "Let's leave them out of this for the moment."

"It's not just politics, sir. Korea was not a popular war in 1950, and it won't be popular with the people now."

"Popular!" General Caldwell scowled. "Since when are issues like this settled because of their *popularity*?"

Ronald Hemminger, the Secretary of Defense, smiled. "You haven't worked inside the Beltway long, have you, General?" There were subdued chuckles from around the table. General Caldwell was new to the position, having received his appointment to the JCS after his predecessor's recent retirement. His intolerance for Washington politics was well known.

"But he's right, you know," the CIA Director said. The

bantering was gone from his tone now. "We let the KorComs get away with *Pueblo* in '68. They held our people . . . what? Eleven months? We let the Iranians get away with the embassy seizure, and they kept things boiling for four hundred forty-four days! This is a chance for P'yongyang to dirty our faces on every front page in the world."

"Hell, you're just pissed that they snatched your spook ship," Schellenberg said.

"That has nothing to do with it. They've snatched close to two hundred *Americans*! You want to see them paraded on the evening news every night for the next year or two? You want another Lebanon? Mark my words: we let them get away with this, they'll be all over us. A military option is our *only* option here!"

The President looked at the Secretary of Defense. "Ron, what do you think?"

Hemminger looked unhappy. "Protest at Panmunjom won't win us a damned thing, Mr. President. Hell, every year or two some KorCom border guard kills one of our people on the DMZ. We protest, they counter-protest, we take it up with the Military Armistice Commission, and nothing gets done. This'll be the same goddamned thing. But a military assault . . . Shit, we're gonna have to cover our asses until we know how the Russkies are gonna react."

Phillip Buchalter, the President's National Security Advisor, shrugged. "What are we gonna do, hit North Korea with trade sanctions?"

No one bothered to laugh. The United States already had no direct contact with North Korea at all.

"There are ways of dealing with them," Schellenberg said "Ways short of starting a war. We could approach them through a third party which has diplomatic relations with P'yongyang. The People's Republic of China, for instance."

"That'll look just great in the *Washington Post*," the DCI said. He turned to face the President. "You wanted options, Mr. President. Well, you've got plenty of them, soft to hard." He began ticking points off on the fingers of his left hand. "We bring the matter up at the next MAC meeting at Panmunjom. We put through a formal diplomatic protest through another government . . . the PRC, or a clear neutral like India or Sweden. We hit 'em with carrier air strikes at selected targets, try to shake 'em up. B-52 raids mounted out of the ROK, same thing. Covert ops . . . use Delta or someone to go in and bring our people out." He held up a sixth finger on his other hand. "We send in the Marines." He opened all of the fingers on both hands. "Or we hit 'em with every goddamned thing we have. Full invasion."

"Hell, Vic," Schellenberg said. "Why'd you leave out nuking the bastards?"

"Be serious."

"No, *you* be serious! Good God, what do you want, a new Korean War?"

"I wasn't aware that the old one was over," said Grimes.

"We go in full-scale and we'll never be free of it! And the Russians, man, the Russians! We have half a dozen new trade or disarmament treaties on the line right this minute, and they'll all be up for grabs if something like this blows up!"

"Speaking of treaties, we could have some real trouble with Tokyo over this," Buchalter pointed out. "Our basing agreements with them clearly prohibit our launching offensive missions from their territory."

"Wonderful," the defense secretary said. "Three squadrons of Falcons in Japan, and we can't use 'em."

"There's always South Korea," Marlowe said. "*They* won't mind rubbing North Korean noses in it."

"You really do want a war over there, don't you?" Schellenberg said wonderingly. "Haven't you guys at Langley heard? The Cold War's over!"

"And haven't you people at Foggy Bottom heard there are American lives at stake here? I'd like to get our people back, damn it, and talking Kim Il-Sung and his cronies to death is not going to do it!"

The battle positions around the table were being drawn along predictable lines. The DCI wanted *Chimera* back and wanted to avoid the sort of intelligence tarpit they'd been trapped in during the Iran crisis. State wanted a political settlement. There were disarmament treaties and foreign obligations which would be jeopardized by a fresh round of military saber rattling. Defense was worried about the Russians. The Navy wanted to use the carrier group they already had in the area. The Chairman of the Joint Chiefs wanted a full invasion with combined arms.

The President was himself an old Navy man, and his own, deep-down gut feeling was to send in the carrier group. The threat of carrier-borne airstrikes against North Korean targets—oil tank farms, military bases, airfields—might be enough to make them back down.

"Here's the way we'll play it," he said at last. The bickering around the table ceased at once, each head turning to face the President. He looked at the Director of Central Intelligence. "Vic, we can't go into this blind. I'll want you people to step it up with the intel. We have to know where our people are being held and what the North Koreans are up to."

"Yes, sir."

He turned to the Defense Secretary. "Ron, I think we can raise the alert status for all our bases over there without stirring up the Russians much. Or the Japanese."

"The Russians will up their status too, sir, but . . . I guess that's all we can do."

"Not quite." The President looked at the CNO. "Fletch, I want you to cut orders for the *Jefferson*. I want them and the Marines in position to do something ASAP. What have we got in the way of covert capability out there?"

"We could have a SEAL team on board the *Jefferson* in eighteen hours."

"Mr. President," General Caldwell said, "under the circumstances, wouldn't it be prudent to put the entire military on alert, sort of start things rolling?"

The President sighed. "I want to avoid an all-out invasion, Amos," he said. "You're right, of course. At least you can put the 82nd on alert, start getting ready to go in if we have to. But I think I want to gamble on the Navy for this one. They're there, and they're ready. If they can't handle it, we'll have to work some other angle."

Schellenberg started to say something, but the President held up his hand. "All of this is just in case, gentlemen. I won't mind at all being all dressed up with no place to go on this one . . . but I sure as hell don't want to be caught naked if the doorbell rings."

As the Security Council meeting broke up, it struck the President just how much was riding on the carrier group commander. That poor SOB may just find himself on the point of the spear, the President thought. And I thought *my* job was a bitch. . . .

DAY TWO

CHAPTER 6

The briefing room was called Civic. The name was a Navy contortion of CVIC, CV being the designation for carrier, and IC standing for Intelligence Center. It was a long room aft of Flag Plot with the ever-present grays and off-greens of Navy-painted steel bulkheads relieved by an oil painting of the U.S.S. *Thomas Jefferson* at one end. Framed prints along other walls depicted scenes from U.S. Naval history: the *Constitution* and the *Guerrier*, the *Kearsarge* sinking the *Alabama*, the sailing of Roosevelt's Great White Fleet, the firing of the first salute to the U.S. flag, F-4 Phantoms dueling MiGs over Quan Lang. A projection screen mounted on the wall and folding chairs facing a podium gave it the air of an elementary school auditorium.

Admiral Magruder had called the meeting for all squadron commanders, and Marusko was there as CAG.

The *Thomas Jefferson* carried ten squadrons in her air wing—CVW-20—a total of eighty-six aircraft and over twenty-eight hundred officers and men. The realization that he was in command of that wing still took Marusko by surprise from time to time. The acronym CAG, for Commander Air Group, was a holdover from the years prior to 1963 when the term for an aircraft carrier's striking arm was changed from "carrier air group" to "carrier air wing." Marusko had often gotten a laugh with his explanation of the term, insisting that no self-respecting aviator could go around calling himself *CAW! CAW!*

He watched the other officers walking in. They were young, most of them, with that curious, bright-eyed mixture of arrogance and aggressiveness which made a good carrier fighter pilot. He saw Matt Magruder enter, talking with Marty French, the skipper of VFA-161. The way he was moving his hands, stiff-fingered, one just behind the other, left no doubt that he was describing his dogfight to French. You could *always* tell a fighter pilot by the way he used his hands to tell a story.

Commander Richard Patrick Neil trailed in after the squadron skippers. A short, slightly built Boston Irishman from Admiral Magruder's staff, Neil was Carrier Group Intelligence Officer and head of *Jefferson*'s threat team. He came in carrying a slide projector which he proceeded to set up on a stand at the back of the room.

It would be Neil who would conduct the major portion of the briefing, Marusko thought. He didn't particularly like Neil. The man had a grating personality and the irritating habit of always being right, but he'd be the one to best present the spooks' view of the current mess. Several others of the admiral's staff were present as well. A yeoman chief was in one corner, taking notes. A transcript of this briefing would be heloed over to each of the other five ships in the CBG.

"Attention on deck!" Every man in the room came to his feet as Admiral Magruder strode in, walking briskly toward the front of the room.

"As you were," he said before anyone was fully at attention. There was a scraping clatter of feet and steel chairs as the officers took their seats. The admiral took his place behind the podium.

"Very well, gentlemen," Admiral Magruder said as the noise died away. "All of you know by now that yesterday afternoon a patrol from VF-95 was vectored to a point just off the North Korean port of Wonsan. Washington didn't give us much to go on at the time, but the word was that one of our ships was in trouble there.

"Our aircraft did not locate the ship, but they did come under fire from North Korean aircraft. One of our planes was shot down. Commander Neil will fill us in on the background. Commander?"

"Thank you, Admiral." Neil signaled to a staff lieutenant to dim the lights, then switched on the projector. A political map of Korea flashed onto the screen, a blunt, indented finger dangling south from the Asian mainland. It was color-coded, red for the People's Democratic Republic—the PDRK—in the north, blue for the Republic of Korea in the south, sundered by the zigzag of the DMZ.

"Korea, gentlemen, the Land of the Morning Calm," Neil said. His voice was high and had a faintly nasal quality underlying the flat, New England twang. He sounded self-assured and somewhat detached, as though he were briefing the men on a routine Naval exercise. "A little background for those of you who don't know their history. After World War II, the country was divided between Soviet and American occupation forces. Korea became, in effect, two countries, the People's Democratic Republic north of the 38th parallel, capital at P'yongyang, and the Republic of Korea in the south, capital at Seoul. In 1950, the PDRK invaded across the 38th parallel. That, of course, began the Korean War."

"Korean Police Action," someone in the front row said. Several men laughed.

Neil ignored the correction. "As far as the PDRK is concerned, the Korean War never ended. They've wanted to . . . their word is *liberate* the south ever since, but they haven't been able to so long as we've been backing the Seoul government.

"Now we come to the events of the past several weeks. Those of you who read the newspapers know that there's been considerable saber rattling from both P'yongyang and Seoul. The President has called on both sides for restraint, but the shouting's been too loud lately for anyone to hear appeals for moderation. As a precaution, the President ordered our carrier group into the Sea of Japan last week. The 9th Marine Expeditionary Brigade in Okinawa was put on alert, and an ad hoc MEU was prepared for possible deployment. The PDRK has responded by calling for the withdrawal of all foreign forces from South Korea, to allow the Koreans to settle their own 'internal' problems.

"The CIA feels that the escalation in tensions is being deliberately orchestrated by P'yongyang for a purpose, we're not sure why. It was decided that more intelligence on the Communist forces, deployments, and intentions was needed."

The slide projector went *chunk-clunk*, and the map was replaced by a beam-on shot of what Marusko thought must be one of the ugliest-looking ships afloat.

She'd been designed as an LST. The designation stood for Landing Ship, Tank—a World-War-II-era transport vaguely reminiscent of an oil tanker, long, boxy and flat, with the superstructure and bridge set far aft in order to make room for the tank deck forward. Before completion, her builders had changed their minds and rebuilt her as an ARL, a landing craft repair ship. From blunt stem to squared-off stern, her long forward deck was crammed with a tangled clutter of struts, fittings, masts, booms, and aerials. A raised helicopter landing pad had been dropped onto the deck halfway between the superstructure and the bow almost as an afterthought. The bridge was flanked by whaleboats slung from davits on either side of the deckhouse. A tripod mast rose abaft the bridge, bearing a large radar dish and an array of exotic antennae. Black-shadowed letters and numerals at bow and stern prominently spelled out *RL 42*.

"This, gentlemen," Neil said in the darkness, "is the U.S.S. *Chimera*, ARL 42. She's three hundred twenty-eight feet long, with a fifty-foot beam and an eleven-foot draft. Top speed eleven knots. She carries a complement of eleven officers and one hundred eighty-two enlisted personnel. The ship was laid down in 1945 as the LST 1156. Today, she is the last World-War-II-era 'T still in service with the U.S. Navy. *Chimera* served as a light repair ship until 1971, when she was finally mothballed at Bremerton.

"In the early eighties she underwent a full refit. The machine shops, foundries, all the inboard repair ship gear were torn out and replaced by the latest in electronic wizardry from our friends at Fort Meade."

That brought a low buzz of murmured conversation from the men sitting in the darkened room. Electronics and Fort Meade meant the National Security Agency.

"In 1985 she was recommissioned as an AGI," Neil continued, "an intelligence collection ship. Six months ago, when the crisis in Korea first began building, she was deployed to the Sea of Japan. Her mission was to remain well offshore, one hundred, one hundred fifty miles at sea, eavesdropping on Korean Communist radio and radar transmissions, recording them for decoding by the NSA. Three days ago, *Chimera* received new orders from the Navy Department. It was felt . . . expedient to move her in close to shore, close enough that she could monitor local tactical radio frequencies. The *Jefferson*'s battle group was moving into the area at the time, and Washington wanted a more accurate picture of what the KorComs were up to."

The slide projector chunked again, and the converted LST was replaced by another map, this one a close-up of the peninsula's east coast. "Here's the coastline we're interested in," Neil said. He used a pointer in the shaft of light to throw a shadow on the screen, a black finger lying across the Sea of Japan. "These are the PDRK's major east coast ports . . . Ch'ongjin up here in the north . . . the Hamhung-Hungnam complex . . . and down here is Wonsan, sixty miles above the Demarcation Line. Wonsan is the principal KorCom port on the east coast.

"I think it's important to point out at this point that *Chimera* was operating in international waters throughout this time," Neil said. "The KorComs have recognized the international twelve-mile limit. *Chimera* was under orders to approach the Korean coast no closer than fifteen miles at any point.

"For reasons which have not yet been ascertained, North Korean forces attacked *Chimera* yesterday morning, beginning at approximately zero-seven-thirty. The attack took place here . . . fifteen miles off the coast, and about thirty miles from the port of Wonsan. Radar intercepts suggest that both air and surface units were involved. One of our Hawkeyes tracked *Chimera* all the way into Wonsan Harbor, and we must assume she is there now."

Neil signaled for the room lights to be brought up and snapped off the projector. He walked toward the front of the room, hands on hips. "Washington, obviously, is concerned. At zero-two-fifty this morning, *Jefferson*'s battle group received orders through CINCPAC and Seventh Fleet to move to a new operational area, centered one hundred fifty miles east of the North Korean port of Kosong. Our orders as of this time are to hold our position, to take no action which will further inflame the situation until Washington can develop a viable strategy."

Someone muttered something near the front of the room, and Neil turned sharply to face him. "You said something, Mr. Greene?"

"Yes, sir," the skipper of VA-89 said loudly. Lieutenant Commander Greene was CO of the Death Dealers, one of *Jefferson*'s two A-6F Intruder squadrons. Marusko knew the man had a reputation as a bigmouth. Loud he might be, and opinionated, but he was a good pilot . . . and a good skipper. "I just said, sir, that we could give Washington one hell of a viable strategy. An A-6 strike on Wonsan would be just about perfect!"

"Right on, Jolly," someone else said. "Bomb the SOBs back to the Stone Age!"

"Which is just what we can't do, gentlemen," Neil said, asserting control once more. "Washington wants to keep a lid on the situation here. The intelligence community just isn't sure yet what the Korean Communist intentions are . . . why they've provoked this crisis."

"Intelligence, right . . ." muttered Steve Murcheson, commander of the carrier's other Intruder squadron, VA-84. Marusko knew what he was thinking. Neil's reference to "the intelligence community" meant the CIA, the NSA, and military intelligence all working together, organizations that had been wrong at least as often as they'd been right in recent years. They'd been great at collecting information, but analysis was weak. Marusko had known cases where field commanders had actually been hampered by too much raw data, with no way to tell what was important and what was not.

And when it came to guessing what was going through the minds of the enemy, well . . .

The younger Magruder leaned back in his seat with his arms folded across his chest. "What I want to know is why we weren't allowed to go in and help the *Chimera* yesterday? If Washington wanted to keep things bottled up, they should have done something to keep the gomers from taking her into port!"

"You got that right," VF-97's skipper said. John "Made it" Bayerly gave Tombstone a cocky thumbs-up. "If we could've gone in across the line, a strafing run or two would've driven off the Korean ships, and—"

"It's a bit late for recriminations now," Neil interrupted. "We just have to play with the hand we've got."

"Some hand," Tombstone said. "Two hundred hostages held in Wonsan. What are we supposed to do, sit here and make faces at the North Koreans?"

"The State Department has initiated action, Commander," Neil said. "While we have no diplomatic relations with the PDRK, we have access through the Military Armistice Commission at Panmunjom. A formal deputation will meet with—"

"A formal deputation?" the younger Magruder exploded. "Those SOBs pirated one of our ships and shot down one of our aircraft! Don't you—"

"Just a moment," Admiral Magruder said, stepping up behind the podium. "May I remind you . . . may I remind *all* of you that it is not the Navy's place to tell Washington what to do. We carry out foreign policy. We don't make it. For now, and until further notice, this carrier group is on hold, to be used if and when the National Command Authority deems it necessary."

Marusko sighed. The magic name of the National Command Authority had been invoked. It would be the President of the United States, working through the Joint Chiefs and State, who would handle the responsibility now.

"Any questions?" Neil asked. His manner made it clear he did not expect any.

Paul Larson raised his hand. The lanky commander was CO of VS-42, *Jefferson*'s squadron of antisubmarine Vikings.

"Commander Larson?"

"Just what are we up against? I've never thought much about the North Koreans as Naval opponents!"

Several members of the audience chuckled. "We shouldn't face too much in the way of direct threat to our carrier group," Neil agreed. "They have four *Najin*-class frigates, one of which was probably involved yesterday with *Chimera*'s capture. Osa missile boats, patrol craft." He glanced at the admiral. "Their primary offensive arm is their submarine fleet, *Whiskey*-class boats, and a few *Romeos*. But they're all diesel jobs, out-of-date and noisy as hell. They won't be a problem."

"What about third parties?" Commander Drexler asked. The skipper of VAQ-143 sounded worried. "Just how big a problem are the Chinese or Russkies going to be?"

Neil gave a small shrug. "Wish we knew. Intelligence doesn't think either Beijing or Moscow is going to come out in support of the PDRK, but at this point, their intentions are anybody's guess."

"There's intelligence again," Murcheson muttered.

"Thank you, Commander Neil," Admiral Magruder said, stepping up to the podium. The look in his gray eyes as he took Neil's place made Marusko think he wanted to head off further comment. None of the aviators in CVIC looked happy, and several wore expressions that were downright belligerent. He remembered an acronym which had made its way through military circles for years, one which had been invented by the raiders who went into Son Tay to rescue American POWs in 1972. Their unofficial symbol had been a mushroom with the letters KITD/FOHS.

Kept in the dark, fed on horse shit. This looked to Marusko like a similar situation, one where American lives were going to be put on the line with inadequate intelligence . . . and possibly inadequate backing as well.

And the skippers of *Jefferson*'s air wing were beginning to feel the same way.

"Gentlemen," the admiral said. "As of now, this carrier group is on full alert.

"Within two hours this command can expect the arrival of a Marine Expeditionary Unit. The *Chosin* and her escorts put to sea from Okinawa last night. They should rendezvous with us by eleven hundred hours this morning, and their presence will give us full amphibious capability, if it becomes necessary to go ashore.

"Our orders are to be prepared to implement whatever policy the National Command Authority deems necessary for resolving this crisis." The admiral's eyes shifted, seeking out Lieutenant Commander Greene. "Obviously, air strikes against North Korean targets are one possible option. I would like to steal a march on Washington and get the planning for such a strike under way at once. Each of you will coordinate with CAG in preparing operational orders for sorties against the North Koreans." A low, chorused groan rose from the seated men. Writing op orders meant hours of paperwork . . . all in addition to their other duties.

Admiral Magruder held up his hand. "We will assume three levels of response: aggressive patrolling, strikes against selected ground targets, and full amphibious operations. CAG will pass out folders with what we know about KorCom radars, SAM sites, and other installations along the east coast.

"It is my intent, gentlemen, to be fully ready to carry out whatever is asked of us." He paused, giving the room one last sweep with those icy eyes. "Dismissed!"

The officers came to attention as the admiral strode past them and out the door.

CHAPTER 7

They pulled him out of the hole in the ground with shouts and curses. His hands were still lashed behind his back, and Coyote could no longer feel his fingers.

It had been a long night, and a cold one. His flight suit was still wet from his inadvertent swim the day before, and crouching in the mud at the bottom of the pit had left him chilled to the very core of his being.

"You come, imperialist damn *sonabichi*!" A rifle butt planted hard against his spine sent him sprawling facedown on the ground. A booted foot caught him in the side, sending a blast of pain through his chest and shoulder. "Up, *sonabichi*! You up!"

"With a kick like that, you oughta try out for the Cowboys," Coyote muttered through clenched teeth. Rough hands grabbed his arms and hoisted him to his feet. Prodded and jabbed by the muzzles of his guards' AK-47s, Coyote was herded toward the low, concrete block building in the center of the compound.

They'd brought him to that building for the first time the previous afternoon. He'd been hauled dripping from the North Korean gunboat which had plucked him from the sea and paraded through the streets of Wonsan while civilians raised clenched fists and chanted unintelligible phrases in which the words "imperialist" and "American" were prominently featured. At some point in the festivities, he'd been tied and blindfolded, slung like a sack of grain into the back of a truck, and transported over rough roads winding up into the mountains which backed Wonsan against the sea.

He was being held in a military base of some sort. Even

blindfolded yesterday afternoon, he'd recognized the growl of military trucks and other vehicles, the measured stamp of booted feet marching in formation, the bark of orders and the answering *whisk-crash* of weapons brought to order arms.

The blindfold had been removed during his first interrogation and his suspicions had been confirmed. This was an Army base, a compound consisting of the drab, utilitarian buildings so prevalent in progressive socialist societies. Many were age-stained, looking as though they dated back to the Second World War. One, a three-story apartment building, was a barracks, Coyote guessed. Beyond the chain-link fence that encircled the compound he could see the ocean, dazzling under a morning sun. He concluded that the base must be located somewhere in the hills south of the city.

Wonsan was squeezed in between the waters of the bay called Yonghung Man and the mountains of Korea's spine. East of the city, a narrow peninsula reached north from the mainland, almost cutting Wonsan off from the sea. Sprawled across the peninsula, only a few miles north of the camp, he could see a large air base; distant thunder echoed among the mountains and in the sky, MiGs on patrol.

Surrounding the city, crowded onto the narrow shelf of land between sea and mountain, was the tangled sprawl of Wonsan's industrial heart. Coyote could see factories, the cranes and smokestacks of shipyards and industrial plants, the wire-festooned masts of high-tension-line towers bringing hydroelectric power in from the north, and the squat, neatly ordered drums of oil storage tank farms. Wonsan was the second-largest city in the People's Democratic Republic of Korea and one of its most important industrial centers. The camp lay at the edge of Wonsan's southern industrial sprawl, near roads and factory chimneys which poked into the hazy air like fingers. Military traffic rumbled along a nearby highway beyond the compound's outer fence, trucks and flatbed trailers carrying antiaircraft cannon.

His inspection of the city and its surroundings was brutally interrupted as a guard knocked him down with an AK butt once more, then kicked him viciously several times in the ribs and thigh. "Up, *sonabichi* dog! You up!"

Yanked to his feet again, he was dragged up the steps in front of the concrete building he'd tentatively identified as a security headquarters of some sort, past a brace of unsmiling guards and into a low-ceilinged passageway that was all gray paint and naked light bulbs. The second office on the right was occupied by a hard-eyed little officer who smoked incessantly and who spoke almost perfect English.

He introduced himself as Colonel Li. The guards made Coyote kneel in the middle of the floor, while the officer rounded the desk and perched on the corner. "Good morning, Lieutenant," he said, taking a pull on his cigarette. "I trust you slept well?"

Coyote did not answer. One of the guards standing unseen at his back kicked him in the hollow of his knee, knocking him to the floor. The other stepped in front of him and kicked him in the face, a light touch which left him blinking away stars. Coyote could taste the salty stickiness of blood in his mouth. He struggled against the ligatures which bound his wrists and elbows. Someone grabbed him by his hair and dragged him upright again.

Li took the cigarette from his mouth, holding it between two fingers. "Name?"

"Willis E. Grant," Coyote replied. He swallowed. The words were muffled through swollen lips and a spreading numbness in the side of his face. "Lieutenant, United States Navy. Service number three-two—"

A rifle butt crashed into Coyote's skull, an explosion of pain which pitched him forward. One of the guards lashed out twice with his foot, catching Coyote in the thigh.

"There are some facts of which you should be made aware, Lieutenant," the colonel said as the guard backed off. "Your country has not declared war against the People's Democratic Republic of Korea. For this simple reason, the rules of war do not apply to you. In the eyes of my government, in the eyes of the world, you are a criminal, charged with various acts of aggression against the People's Democratic Republic, including an unprovoked attack against one of our aircraft."

Desperation clawed at Coyote's reason. "That's bull—"

Another kick silenced him. Colonel Li continued as though Coyote had not spoken. "Your recitation of name, rank, serial number, and date of birth means nothing. Such civilized rules govern the actions of men and officers at war, but this is not war. You are here, you *live* at my pleasure. No one can help you. No one even knows you are here. We could keep you locked away or working at hard labor for the rest of your life, or take you out this minute and have you shot . . . and your people would never know." He paused, drawing a long puff on the cigarette. Coyote watched the tip glow bright orange with a kind of helpless fascination.

"So," Li said after a moment. "You will answer my questions. You will not give me more than what I ask for. You will not give me less." He nodded, and rough hands grabbed at Coyote's hair and hauled him upright into a kneeling position once more. "Now then. Once again. Your name."

"Willis E. Grant."

"Willis E. Grant, you have been charged with acts of sabotage, espionage, murder, and reckless provocation against the People's Democratic Republic. You will describe those activities, and the parts played by ships and aircraft of the United States Navy, in full and complete detail."

"Willis E. Grant. Lieutenant, U.S.N. Service—"

The wooden stock of an AK snapped into the back of his head. Pain jolted through him, leaving him sick and retching on the floor.

"Perhaps," the colonel said, "we are being too lenient with you. We know that your CIA. employs thugs and gangsters of the very worst stripe for their espionage activities. Men such as yourself are far too tough to break under mild questioning such as this. I wonder what sterner measures we could employ in your case."

"You can go—" This time the rifle butt struck his spine just above the thongs which pinned his elbows.

When he was dragged back to his knees, Li made a show of studying a stack of papers in his hand. "You are a spy, a saboteur, and a provocateur. You have been hired by the CIA. to spy on the peace loving People's Democratic Republic. You are also a murderer, having shot down one of our aircraft inside the People's sovereign airspace."

"Screw you!"

This time, he almost didn't feel the pain as they pulled his face off the wooden floor. He felt dizzy, light-headed. He wondered if the goon with the rifle would miscalculate and kill him by mistake.

"Lieutenant Grant, you show an annoying lack of sincerity in these proceedings. I think we shall all be better off if we simply take you out and shoot you." The officer barked something at the guards in Korean. Hands closed around his elbows, yanked him to his feet, and held him upright as a soldier opened the door. His flight boots scraped on the floor as they dragged him out.

In daylight once again, Coyote found himself looking up into blue sky. The cloud deck which had covered the area the day before had broken up. The wind, sharp and biting off the sea, burned like flame through his wet flight suit.

There was a parade ground not far from the headquarters building, a clearing of red clay ringed in by storage sheds and the back of a motor pool garage. One of the sheds had a wall of sandbags stacked up ten feet high facing the courtyard, a lone, head-high stake driven into the mud just in front of it.

They were going to shoot him. The reality of the situation was like a black cloud which overrode the pain, the shock of the interrogator's words, the harsh laughter of the guards as they shoved him upright against the stake, looped a leather strap nailed to the wood around his neck, and pulled it snug.

Coyote had made it through the long and sleepless night before by thinking about Julie, calling to mind her face, her voice, remembering in loving detail each moment he'd shared with her during his all-too-brief leave before reporting to VF-95 at the North Island Naval Air Station at Coronado and flying out to the *Jefferson*. With death a few seconds away, he struggled now to recapture those memories, to hold Julie in his mind as a last conscious thought.

They'd arranged to meet Tombstone in Balboa Park and had a picnic on the grass. Then the three of them had gone to the San Diego Zoo and taken Polaroid photographs of one another mugging in front of the ape house as the yammering howl of a gibbon floated down from the trees behind them.

Later, they'd dropped Tombstone off at the base, then driven north up Highway 5. They'd stopped at a motel overlooking the ocean north of San Clemente, made love on the beach to the rumbling thunder of surf, and watched the sun come up in glory behind the San Jacinto Mountains.

That afternoon he'd reported to Tombstone at Coronado, the scent of Julie's hair still warm in his nostrils.

He found it hard to focus on the memory of her face. It was strange. When he thought of death at all, it was in the context of flying, a flash of exploding fuel and warheads . . . and it was over. Somehow, he'd never thought death would claim him like this, tied to a stake in front of a firing squad, somewhere inside a third-rate, third-world country thousands of miles from home.

The guard gave the strap at his throat a last savage yank, and Coyote gagged against the unrelenting pressure. He was still so weak from repeated beatings that he could barely stand. His knees threatened to give way as the strap tightened.

An officer, a major this time, led two more soldiers onto the parade ground. The soldiers lined up a few feet in front of Coyote, checking their AK-47 rifles with a busy *clack-clack* of sliding bolts. The officer stood to one side, a broad smile twisting his flat features as he raised his hand, palm out. *"Junbenun!"*

The rifles snapped to the soldiers' shoulders, the muzzles three feet away from Coyote's face. He could see their eyes, deadly and glittering on the far sides of each weapon's sights. With something like resignation, he closed his eyes, shutting off the sun, the harbor. . . .

"Chigum!"

The snapping of bolts on empty chambers sounded like the clatter of typewriter keys. Coyote opened his eyes again. The officer burst into screeching laughter. The strap gouged at Coyote's throat, making each breath a struggle.

The officer released the strap and Coyote collapsed to the ground, his arms still cinched behind him, his face pressed down into the wet clay.

Coyote concentrated on breathing, one shaky breath following another. He couldn't say that he'd been *ready* to die, but pain and exhaustion had conspired to rob him of any real interest in living. Now, though, the air was sweet. Relief flooded his body in a rush which actually set the pain at a distance.

He heard the squish of footsteps in the clay and opened his eyes to see a pair of polished black boots inches from his face. "No, Willis E. Grant." The familiar voice of the interrogator sounded as though it were coming from light-years away. "No, I do not think your death will be so easy. We have a very great deal we wish to learn from you, and you will tell us. It may take time, but you may be very certain that you will tell us!"

One of the boots drew back. Coyote saw the blow coming but could do nothing to avoid it. He closed his eyes as the world exploded in raw pain and the taste of blood pumping from his nose. The kick knocked him onto his back, and when he opened his eyes, the sky appeared alive with light and shadow and a roaring in his ears.

The interrogator turned away abruptly. *"Kurul katta!"* he barked, gesturing. Two of the soldiers slung their AKs, then bent over to pull Coyote to his feet. He could feel the blood coating his face as they dragged him off the parade ground. He was led back to the hole and thrown in. He heard the guards laughing as they lowered a wooden grate above him and padlocked it shut.

Then he was alone again, with only memories and fear for company.

0922 hours
112 miles above Wonsan

The KH-12 was the latest in the NSA's long and successful series of imaging spy satellites. In the continuing compartmentalization of U.S. intelligence, any imaging reconnaissance, whether carried out by satellite or by aircraft, came under the code designation KEYHOLE, hence the KH in this satellite's name. Earlier series had included the KH-7, -8, -9, and -11, each remarkably successful, each a jewel of ultra-high technology, of miniaturization, and of the almost magical art of precision lens crafting and scientific engineering.

This satellite was the third of the KH-12 series, launched five weeks earlier from Kennedy Space Center as the top-secret cargo of a DOD space shuttle flight. It weighed twenty-nine thousand pounds, almost a quarter of which was hydrazine fuel which allowed its earthbound masters to change its orbit, permitting its telescopic lenses to focus on selected spots on the Earth's surface. Ultimately, it was planned that four KH-12s aloft at once would give the United States military twenty-four hour, real-time coverage of any place on the planet with twenty minutes' notice, but budget cuts and the changing priorities of a less outwardly hostile world had sabotaged that idea. Still, a new orbit could be calculated and implemented within a few hours, and surveillance of a trouble spot could be carried out once each eighty-five minutes.

Such a change had been carried out the previous day, dropping the satellite from its 175-mile parking orbit altitude to a scant 112 miles above the ground. By expending some of its fuel once during each orbit to correct for the rotation of the Earth beneath it, the satellite could be made to drift over Wonsan once every hour and a half.

At this altitude, the KH-12's long-focal-length imaging cameras and computer-adjusted telescopic mirror had a theoretical resolution of less than three inches, easily enough to read license plates, street signs, and the tail numbers of MiGs. On-board infrared imaging capability let it see in the dark, and radar let it see through clouds and dirty weather, though with much less resolution and more guesswork.

It was the cloud cover which hampered the KH-12 for its first few orbits. On the fourth pass, however, it struck paydirt.

CHAPTER 8

A Marine sentry in full dress uniform stepped through the door. "The President of the United States!" he announced, and the people waiting inside the White House Situation Room came to their feet.

The room was not large—less than 220 square feet—and much of that floor space was taken up by a large teakwood conference table. The rich walnut paneling concealed most of the electronic equipment, terminals, and display monitors which made the Situation Room the White House's central headquarters for crisis management. The far wall, twelve feet wide, was dominated by a floor-to-ceiling rear-projection screen normally masked by a drawn curtain. The curtain was open now, revealing an aerial photograph of a city's waterfront district.

The President took his place at the head of the table, sinking into the plush leather chair. The Air Force officer carrying the "football," the briefcase containing the codes necessary for Presidential authorization of nuclear weapons release, took his accustomed place nearby.

"You've got the pictures," the President said without preamble.

General Caldwell gestured toward the wall screen. "Hot off the wire, Mr. President. Vic just brought them in from NPIC personally."

The recon photo showed an aerial view of a port, of docksides, quays, ships, and small craft, with a crispness and clarity of detail which was astonishing. It was like peering down into city streets from the vantage point of some tall building. From where he was sitting, the President could easily recognize vehicles, stacked crates, ships and boats of all sizes, even people working in the dockyard. Date and time notations in the upper right corner showed that the photographs had been taken only eight hours earlier. They had been uplinked by coded telemetry from the KH-12 to an SDS military comsat in synchronous orbit, then redirected to receiving antennae at Fort Belvoir, Virginia. From there, the signals had been relayed to the National Photographic Interpretation Center, an NSA facility located in an unremarkable six-story building with bricked-in windows located at the corner of M and First streets in the heart of Washington, D.C.

"Don't we have R-T images yet?"

"Not yet, Mr. President," Marlowe replied. "We expect to have real-time coverage later this morning. But this is the first good look we've had at Wonsan." The DCI stood up, taking a pen-sized object from his pocket which he drew out into a two-foot-long pointer. "This is one part of the Wonsan dockyard restricted for military use," he said. He reached out with the pointer, tapping one of several gray cigar shapes. "*Chimera*, Mr. President."

The President studied the photo with interest. It showed an oblique view of the *Chimera* tied up alongside a dock, her ancestry as an LST clearly visible in her bluntly rounded, somewhat box-shaped ends. The designation RL 42 was clear on her hull, and it was possible to pick out individual soldiers standing on her decks and at regular intervals along the quay.

"She's been damaged." There were gashes in her deck, and the tripod mast behind the bridge was lying on its side. One boat alongside the bridge had been smashed, and snaggle-toothed gaps marred the sweep of the bridge windows.

"Yes, sir. She's taken fire from 23-mm cannons and heavy machine guns, as well as several direct hits from a 100-mm Naval gun." The pointer moved to the tangle of piping and machinery between the flat heliport and the bridge. "There is evidence of a fire in this area, probably from a ruptured diesel fuel tank."

"Any sign of the crew?"

"No, sir," Caldwell said. "We've got to assume they were taken off the ship. But whether they're in P'yongyang or still in Wonsan we don't know."

"We'd have heard if they were in P'yongyang," Marlowe observed quietly. "So far, all they're broadcasting is the bare bones . . . unprovoked American aggression, violation of their territorial waters, that sort of thing."

The President looked sharply at Marlowe. "How about it, Victor? Did we?"

"Did we what, sir?"

"Violate North Korean waters. It's happened before." *Pueblo*, he knew, had entered North Korean waters several times before she was captured, though she'd been well outside the twelve-mile limit when she was boarded and taken.

"No, sir. *Chimera* was under strict orders to approach no closer than fifteen miles from the coast. She had good tracking locks on a pair of navigational satellites, and was where she was supposed to be."

"You're certain?"

"Yes, Mr. President." Marlowe used the pointer to touch the screen again at a different place, indicating a second, much larger cigar shape moored to a quay not far from the *Chimera*. "Up here is our real problem. An unpleasant surprise, I'm afraid."

"A North Korean warship?"

Marlowe shook his head. "No, sir. She's *Tallinn*, a Soviet *Kara*-class guided-missile cruiser. Our last report on her was that she was leaving Vladivostok on her way east, probably to Petropavlosk. Evidently, she changed her mind and decided to stop in at Wonsan sometime yesterday afternoon."

"Coincidence?"

"Maybe. Or else her skipper's taking an opportunity to get a close look at the electronics on board one of our AGIs," Marlowe said. "We're not certain how closely the North Koreans and the Russians are cooperating on such matters right now."

The President stared at the Russian ship's sleek and menacing dagger shape for a long moment, then glanced up at one of the clocks mounted in a row along one wall of the room, the one showing Moscow time. A hot-line message had been composed and transmitted five hours earlier. It was eleven-thirty in the morning in the Kremlin now. . . .

"If the Russians are getting in on this . . ." He stopped. "Anything from Moscow?"

"No, sir," Schellenberg replied. "Nothing over the hot line so far but the usual ready code groups. I'd say they're still trying to decide which way to jump."

"Anything more on the Ukraine?"

Marlowe shook his head. "Nothing, Mr. President. Troop movements in L'vov and Chernovtsy. Bases put on full alert at Kiev, Kharkov, a dozen other places. But whether that has anything to do with Korea . . ." The DCI shrugged, allowing the sentence to hang unfinished in the air.

"And if the Russians get a close look at *Chimera*? Any special security threat there?"

"None that we wouldn't have anyway, Mr. President. SOP is to assume that all of *Chimera*'s codes and secret material were compromised as soon as the ship was taken."

"What's more serious is what might happen if you order an attack on Wonsan, Mr. President," Hall said. He drummed his fingers against the polished tabletop, the nails clicking lightly. "Can you imagine the problems if a stray bomb from an American aircraft caught that baby?"

"We'd warn them," the President said. He was thinking of Reagan's warning to the Soviets minutes before F-111s thundered over Libya in 1986. *No* military operation ever went off without a hitch, and with the world situation as unsettled as it was, it was vital that American and Soviet forces not come into direct confrontation, in Korea or anywhere else.

"Okay. So the question still is what to do about it." He swept his gaze across the other people in the room. "And what the Russians will think. Jim?"

The Secretary of State shook his head. "That's still damned hard to say, Mr. President. The Soviets haven't been saying much of anything since the Irkutsk riots. Now, with things getting tight for them in the Ukraine . . . that's Russia's breadbasket, Mr. President. And the curtain is down again."

"I know. I know."

The curtain is down again.

Meaning, of course, the Iron Curtain. When the Soviet Union's empire had begun to crumble, people had celebrated the Cold War's end, a new chance at world peace. Now, the social forces unleashed by *perestroika* and *glasnost* were threatening Mother Russia. Paradoxically, the collapse of Moscow's power structure meant a greater danger for the world than ever. If Russia lashed out in her death throes . . .

"It doesn't look good, Mr. President," General Caldwell said, echoing the President's bleak thoughts. "This whole affair could be a Russian ploy to unite their people in a common cause, to take their minds off shortages of bread and fuel."

"I don't think we need to fantasize about some dark, deep-laid Soviet plan here," Schellenberg said. "They don't want an all-out war any more than we do."

"But they are opportunists, Mr. Secretary," Caldwell said.

"To be sure. They're certainly capable of using the situation to their own advantage. We're going to have to proceed very carefully indeed, measuring each step against how it might be perceived by the Kremlin. I, ah, have to say that the presence of a Soviet cruiser in Wonsan makes things a lot stickier, Mr. President. If you send in aircraft, the Russians might well perceive that as an attack against their assets in the region . . . or they might decide to help the Koreans."

The CNO frowned. "You're saying the Soviets would intervene in Korea?"

"It's a possibility," Schellenberg said, nodding. "It's *also* possible they're getting ready for something bigger." He looked pointedly at the DCI. "Our intelligence hasn't been exactly crystal clear on the point lately, has it? We don't know yet whether these troop movements in the Ukraine mean they're getting ready for more food riots . . . or whether they're setting up to invade Eastern Europe."

"This whole thing could blow right in our faces," the President said. "What is it the North Koreans are after, anyway? Vic, what does the CIA say?"

Marlowe crossed his arms. "All we can offer at this point are guesses, Mr. President. Guess number one is that the leadership in P'yongyang is getting desperate. They see the breakup of the Soviet empire, the internal troubles in Russia and the People's Republic. Remember in Romania in '89? Kim and his cronies must feel pretty damned vulnerable right now, with all their big, powerful socialist neighbors either chucking communism or getting bogged down in their own problems."

"So why provoke us?" Caldwell asked. "I'd think that would just make things worse for them."

"Desperation move, General. If North Korea can paint us as aggressors on Russia's doorstep, maybe they can wheedle a few billion rubles out of Moscow in aid. Maybe they figure that if we attack Wonsan, the Soviets will be drawn in on their side and they'll benefit." Marlowe shrugged. "And maybe the bastards are just gambling that we'll be so concerned about world opinion or Russian reaction that we'll back down. They'd perceive that as a real propaganda coup, a way to prove to the world that their brand of communism still works."

"So we're damned if we attack them and damned if we don't,"

the President said. He leaned back in his seat, fingers drumming on its arms.

"A diplomatic solution is still in our best interests, Mr. President," the Secretary of State said stiffly. "The international repercussions to a military response to the Korean crisis could—"

"*Screw* international repercussions!" Caldwell snapped. "Damn it, Jim, this is no time for appeasement!"

"Mr. President!" Schellenberg insisted, ignoring the general. "I have a meeting scheduled with the Chinese ambassador this afternoon. I have every reason to expect that we can open talks directly with the North Koreans through the PRC's mediation!"

Caldwell opened his mouth as though to say something further, but the President stopped him with a raised hand. "I wanted options, gentlemen. Options, not argument. Mr. Schellenberg thinks we have a possible shot at a negotiated settlement. What else do we have?"

"The 82nd Airborne is on full alert at Fort Bragg," the general said in a crisp, matter-of-fact tone. "Also the 7th Light Infantry and the 75th Rangers. Military Airlift Command is on standby. The Joint Chiefs are working out plans for full deployment out of South Korea. Marine assaults along the coast, airborne landings at P'yongyang, followed up by the infantry. We'll have to assume full ROK involvement, of course."

The image was not a pleasant one. "We'd take a hell of a lot of casualties."

"I don't doubt it, Mr. President." Caldwell looked down at the table. "But we need a strong military response, or these people will know they can do anything to us they want. There's no other *option.* . . ."

Phillip Buchalter cleared his throat. "Not to disagree with the general, Mr. President, but we may have another option. A less . . . radical one." He passed a manila folder down the table. "This came through from the NSC Threat Team an hour ago."

The President accepted the folder and leafed through the papers inside. The Threat Team had been assembled under the auspices of the National Security Council the previous afternoon. The folder contained the summary of a plan for an air strike against North Korea, launched from the carrier battle group already on station and directed at military targets: radar stations, SAM sites, and airfields.

He looked up. "Operation Winged Talon?"

"Yes, sir. Based on proposals put together by the CO of that carrier group we have out there. You'll notice that none of the targets are in Wonsan itself. No chance of hitting that Russian ship. The Threat Team feels that a measured response will convince the North Koreans that we mean business." He glanced briefly at Schellenberg, who was scowling. "It might induce them to negotiate, sir."

"You think so?"

"It may be worth a try." The National Security Advisor seemed unwilling to commit himself. "Certainly, the threat of hitting that Russian ship by accident is quite low. There's also less chance that we'll hit our own people, since they're probably still in the city proper."

"We don't know that," Hall said. "We don't know where our people are being held!"

Buchalter spread his hands. "No guarantees. But it seems like a good bet."

The President studied the report a moment longer. His own gut feeling was to try for a military option. Anything was better than doing nothing.

And yet . . .

"It looks like we're in a holding pattern then," he said after a moment. He looked up at Schellenberg. "Jim, put some of your people to work on the political ramifications of this thing. I want to know how our allies are going to react if we go in shooting."

"Yes, sir."

He slid the folder back down the table toward Buchalter. "Phil, Winged Talon looks good, but it'll have to go on hold, at least for now. We have to give State their chance at negotiation. But pass on your recommendations to the Joint Chiefs." He looked at Caldwell. "General, your plan is on hold too. We've got to get a better feel for how the Russians will react. Agreed?"

"Agreed, Mr. President." He did not sound happy. There was, in fact, a definite feeling of gloom in the Situation Room, a sense that events were drifting beyond the ken of men who were used to being in control.

It was not a pleasant feeling.

1740 hours
Flight officers' quarters, U.S.S. *Thomas Jefferson*

Tombstone lay on his rack, arm thrown over his eyes, trying to sleep. It is never truly *quiet* on board an aircraft carrier. The aviators' quarters were located forward of the hangar deck and immediately below the flight deck. The pounding, hissing, slamming machinery which drove the *Jefferson*'s catapults was located only a few bulkheads away, and the rattle of chains and cat shuttles, the harsh clang of steel on steel penetrated the small room's overhead almost round the clock. During launch operations, it was actually impossible to hold a conversation in the room, so loud was the boiler room racket from the catapults.

The cats were silent for the moment, though Tombstone was aware of the clatter of chains overhead and the periodic roar, screech, and bang of recovery operations aft. Hornets returning from combat air patrol, he decided.

Aviators were used to the noise, of course, and a tired pilot generally had no trouble sacking out. As exhausted as he was, though, Tombstone couldn't sleep. His mind kept going back to yesterday's dogfight, to Coyote's plane falling from the sky over the Sea of Japan, to the promises he'd made to his friend over the SAR frequency.

He gave up and rolled his feet off his rack. His eyes moved across the narrow room to the empty bunk opposite his.

Coyote's.

His roommate and wingman had left his guitar slung from his rack before he left, and it made small, hollow noises as the ship's motion rocked it back and forth. Gear adrift; Coyote would get an earful if the Captain made one of his periodic inspections.

Except that Coyote wouldn't be coming back. Tombstone wondered just when it would be that some Naval officer would come in and pack up Coyote's gear, clean his uniforms and civies out of his locker, pull down the country music group poster taped to the bulkhead, and clear the way for some fresh-faced nugget from the World.

When would they declare Coyote officially dead?

Damn.

Tombstone knew he needed sleep, and he needed it now. This afternoon was prime time, with no duties and no noisy roommates until after chow. Tonight he'd have the duty. CAG had him on the list for standby and Alert Fifteen after 2200, and as sure as he was sitting there, there'd be a scramble. *Jefferson* was cruising slowly at the eye of a political storm; it was silly to think the tensions unleashed by the Korean crisis weren't going to rise, not now, not after yesterday's engagement.

But sleep was impossible.

He rose, splashed water on his face at the stainless-steel basin on the bulkhead, grabbed his leather flight jacket, and left the room. If he couldn't sleep, he could at least lose himself for a bit in sea and sky. All the way aft on the hangar deck, a narrow passageway led from the hangar bay past the ship's engine repair shops to the wide-gaping cavern's mouth which opened across the *Jefferson*'s stern.

This was the ship's fantail. In port, a ladder was rigged to descend from fantail to a floating platform at the ship's stern, allowing the crew to come and go on the liberty boats. Under way at sea, the area was roped off with safety lines, creating a gray-decked pocket of solitude twenty feet above the wash of *Jefferson*'s four big propellers. For Tombstone, it was a place where tension and worry were swallowed by the numbing, rhythmic throb of the engines and the hiss of water boiling into the ship's wake.

Jefferson was cruising slowly eastward now, so the sun was low above the horizon dead astern, a red orb casting ruby reflections across sea and low-lying bands of purple clouds. Korea lay beneath those clouds, one hundred fifty miles distant.

The black silhouettes of three ships stood out in stark contrast against the sky's sunset glory. The largest one must be *Chosin*, he decided, the Marine LPH which had joined the carrier battle group that morning. Beyond her was the LPD *Little Rock* and one of the battle group's frigate escorts. *Texas City* and *Westmoreland County*, the other two ships of the MEU, were out of sight over the horizon.

It was strange to think that the battle group now included almost three thousand U.S. Marines, as well as *Jefferson*'s air wing and the support aircraft on board *Chosin* and *Little Rock*. The carrier group represented a staggering force in terms of conventional arms, yet it was still helpless, dependent on word from Washington to act. Tombstone shook his head. Americans had been captured, had been killed. America ought to hit back.

Yet it all seemed so futile.

A tiny dot in the western sky grew larger. Tombstone gripped the rail, watching as the shape swelled into the blunt, high-winged shape of an S-3A Viking, its huge canopy perched above its nose like a Cyclopean eye. With a rising howl, the Viking rushed toward the end of the flight deck above Tombstone's head, its navigation lights describing brilliant green and red trails in the deepening twilight. He heard the thump of the aircraft's wheels on the steel deck, the rattle and crash of arresting gear snagging the wire, the descending whine as the pilot throttled down after a successful trap.

"Howdy, Commander," someone shouted behind him. "Your uncle's been pushing the ASW patrols."

He turned and found himself face to face with a Navy chief. He recognized the man as part of the deck crew. With over six thousand men aboard the *Jefferson*, the vast majority were strangers with familiar faces.

"Sub hunting," Tombstone replied. He had to shout to be heard above the carrier's wash. Everyone on board agreed that the only North Korean fleet elements which posed any threat at all to the *Jefferson* and her consorts were their *Whiskey*- and *Romeo*-class submarines, and the ASW Vikings of VS-42 had been up and patrolling around the clock ever since yesterday morning. No doubt the Sea King helos off the various carrier group escorts were patrolling vigorously as well.

The chief struck a cigarette, shielding the flame against sea spray and the eddying wind curling past the ship's hull. "That was a great job you did on the gomers yesterday, sir," he said.

"Thanks, Chief." The man had planted himself against the rail and seemed unlikely to move, so Tombstone turned away and headed back for the cavernous opening leading back into the ship. Usually the fantail was a good place to think. But he didn't want a crowd around when he did it.

Thinking . . . that was always a bad thing. In Tombstone's experience, aviators who thought too much about their job, about their friends or families, about their responsibilities, were already as good as dead. Maybe it was time he examined his own future as a Naval aviator.

At the moment, it didn't feel like he had much of a future at all.

CHAPTER 9

Admiral Magruder leaned across the radar operator's shoulder, bathed in the eerie green twilight of *Jefferson*'s Combat Information Center. "How long have they been airborne, son?"

"Almost an hour, Admiral. But they broke off orbiting their base at Vladivostok and set this new course about five minutes ago. One-seven-five, range three hundred. Speed five hundred knots."

Magruder studied the silent sweep of the radar's beam, watching the pulse of light representing a target in the upper left-hand quadrant of the screen. The display was being relayed from one of *Jefferson*'s Hawkeye patrol aircraft, now on station in the darkness north of the carrier some one hundred fifty miles out. The green blip represented a Tupolev Tu-20, a Russian Bear bomber out of the big Soviet fleet base at Vladivostok, and the aircraft's new heading was one which would take it straight over *Jefferson*'s flight deck in less than forty minutes.

Or worse. They'd be in range to launch a shipkiller missile inside of twenty minutes, and they were in position to spot for a sub-launched cruise missile *now*.

Which made Soviet intentions at this point a crucial question indeed.

"Who's up on ready aircraft?" Magruder asked.

"Tombstone and Snowball, Batman and Malibu," CAG replied. "Alert Fifteen."

That meant the pilots and their RIOs were standing by, dressed in their flight suits and ready to scramble for a launch within fifteen minutes.

Tombstone and Snowball. After the scene up in Pri-Fly the day before, he'd toyed with the idea of having Marusko take his nephew off the duty roster for a time, but such an order could have destroyed Tombstone's confidence.

On the other hand, Admiral Magruder had recognized the danger signs in Tombstone during that confrontation. His nephew was brooding, probably wondering if he'd been somehow to blame for Coyote being lost at sea. When aviators started to brood . . . that was when they started to make mistakes.

And there was no room for mistakes in carrier aviation.

All in all, it had seemed best to keep Tombstone in the thick of things, to not allow him time to dwell on his failings.

"Very well," Magruder said, nodding. "Launch the Alert Fifteen."

"Aye aye, sir."

Now his decision was about to be tested. Magruder just hoped to God he was right.

2250 hours
Flight deck, U.S.S. *Thomas Jefferson*

It was dark in the cockpit of his F-14, a pitch blackness relieved only by the red glow from the instrument panel. "Let's have the lights down a bit, Snowy," Tombstone said to his RIO.

The instrument lights dimmed in response as Snowball turned the rheostat control. "How's that, Commander Magruder?"

"Fine. Check your breakers."

"We're all go for launch back here."

In the darkness, it felt as though Tombstone was already somehow isolated from the carrier, suspended in black sky above black sea. But they were still on the carrier's flight deck. Tombstone could feel the ponderous movement of the *Jefferson* as she moved slowly into the wind, and he could hear the familiar clanks and rattles as the deck crew broke down his aircraft, preparing for the launch.

Pastel-colored light stabbed and flashed in the darkness. Yellow lights signaled "come ahead" as the deck crew guided the second Tomcat onto the number two catapult. Blue lights probed flaps and control surfaces as the red lights of ordnancemen checked the F-14's weapon load.

A green shirt to his left held up a lighted board with 66,000 written on it. Tombstone acknowledged by lifting a penlight to the canopy and waving it in a circular motion. There was a final, decisive clank as the hook-and-cat men finished attaching the catapult hook to the F-14's launch bar. He glanced over his shoulder. The launch light on *Jefferson*'s island was still red.

The catapult officer approached the aircraft, holding a green wand in his right hand, a red wand in his left. He waved the green light briskly from side to side, signaling Tombstone to ease his throttle up to full military power. The fighter trembled in the grip of the holdback bar, ready to hurl itself from *Jefferson*'s deck. Tombstone could feel the power building as he moved his stick, checking the controls.

The launch officer signaled with the green light once more, up and down this time. Tombstone shoved the throttles the rest of the way forward, going to full afterburner. The Tomcat strained even harder at the leash, illuminating the deck in pale light as twin streams of fire screamed from the engines, playing against the raised blast deflector behind them.

Tombstone pulled the control knob that turned on his navigation lights, a final signal to the Air Boss and the launch crew that his Tomcat was ready to go. The light on the island turned green.

In one smooth motion, the cat officer dropped to one knee and touched his lighted wand to the deck. . . .

The seat smacked Tombstone squarely in the back as the burst of steam hurled the Tomcat off the *Jefferson*'s number three catapult. He guided the aircraft through that instant of sluggish hold-your-breath as the F-14 hung suspended off the carrier's bow, then felt the outthrust wings take hold and the thrust from the twin engines build. "Good shot, good shot," he radioed *Jefferson*'s flight control. He was airborne. Stars surrounded him as the Tomcat clawed its way into the night sky.

"Good shot." That echo over his tactical net was Batman boosting clear of *Jefferson*'s flight deck right behind him. Tombstone held his rate of climb steady, allowing Batman to close on his position, just off his starboard wing.

"Hunt Leader, this is Hunt Two, coming up on your three."

Tombstone glanced to his right and saw the Christmas tree of green and red nav lights marking Batman's Tomcat. "Hunt Leader to Hunt Two," he said. "Ease off and give me some slack, will you?"

"Roger dodger," Batman replied in his headset. The other Tomcat drifted back slowly, opening the distance between them by a few feet.

Tombstone sighed and eased his own stick a bit to the left, increasing their separation still more. Batman had a reputation as a hotdog, and was probably trying to impress his CO with a dazzling display of precision night formation flying.

How much do I trust this guy? Tombstone wondered. While wingman assignments were never permanent, Tombstone and Coyote had paired up more frequently than otherwise. They'd made a good team, knowing with precision each other's techniques and skill. Batman was relatively new to the squadron. Tombstone had flown with him only three times so far, and never at night.

He pulled his mind away from the thought . . . and away from the twisting, inner longing that it would be Coyote flying off his wing tonight, and not Batman. He had nothing against Batman, nothing personal at least, and yet . . .

Better to concentrate on the mission. He checked his navigational fix again, then opened the F-14's intercom. "Whatcha got, Snowball?"

"No joy on our scope yet, Stoney, but we're still getting a feed from Tango One-three. That Bear's probably about one hundred fifty miles out yet."

"Okay. Keep us vectored on them. Let me know when you get a solid return."

Minutes crawled by in silence. Then his RIO snapped off an excited "Got 'em! Bogie at three-four-niner, course one-nine-five, speed five-zero-zero, range nine-five miles. They're above us, Boss. Angels thirty."

"Right. Pass that to Batman and Malibu. Let's go in for a look."

Long before he sighted the Bear, he could *feel* it, a shuddering, deep-throated rumble below the limits of hearing as the Bear's four massive Kuznetsov turboprops hammered at the sky. He looked up through the canopy, scanning the night. The sky was clear, the stars far crisper and more brilliant than they ever were at sea level. There was nothing . . . no! There! He could just make out the distinctive constellation of red and green navigation lights, the flash of a red anti-collision beacon.

"Tally-ho!" he announced over his radio. "Visual at eleven o'clock high."

"We've got him," Batman's voice replied in his headset.

"Hunt Leader to Homeplate," Tombstone said as he eased into a climb that would take them to thirty thousand feet. His words would be relayed to the *Jefferson* by the circling Hawkeye. "We have visual on the bandit. Closing." He shifted to the aircraft tactical channel. "Hunt Two, Hunt Lead. I'm breaking left and going in for a closer look. You break the other way and take point. You're running interference."

"Rog, Hunt Lead. Count his rivets for us, will ya?"

Tombstone pulled his Tomcat into a shallow turn to port, swinging wide behind the Bear, crossing the bomber's slipstream with a rumbling shudder that reminded him of hitting the rumble strips in the pavement in front of a turnpike tollbooth. Moments later, he drew up alongside the Russian's starboard side.

The vibration was much heavier here, flying behind and below the Bear's two thundering right wing engines. He could still see very little, a blackness against blackness which blotted out the stars, outlined by the pulse of anti-collision lights. He knew the Russians were aware of his presence; they'd have had him on their own radar scopes for some minutes now. But how to get them to—

A light winked on, a tiny sun bathing the Tomcat's cockpit in a silvery glare.

"What in the hell—" Snowball yelled. "Tombstone! I can't see!"

Tombstone held the F-14 steady, turning his head aside and blinking hard to clear the momentary blindness. For an instant he'd thought the Russian bomber had blown up, but he knew now that what had stolen his night vision was a powerful searchlight mounted in the observation blister near the Bear's tail. *Bastards!*

The searchlight moved, shifting a white cone of light back and forth between the two aircraft, briefly illuminating the Tomcat, then swinging up to the Bear's own wing, which materialized out of the darkness ahead like a gleaming fragment of a huge knife. Tombstone could see the silvery arc of one of the Russian's outboard turboprops, could see the markings painted on the backswept wing, a huge red star bordered in white.

Obviously, they wanted him to know who they were.

But what were they *thinking*? This sort of game had been played between Russians and Americans since the first days of the Cold War, and it seemed that the recent thaw had changed none of the rules. In some ways, in fact, the situation now was worse than it had ever been during the seventies or early eighties; at least then, you *knew* what the Russians thought of you.

Gently, Tombstone nudged his Tomcat closer to the Bear's hull.

The searchlight snapped back from the wing and washed across the F-14 again, but he was ready for it this time, narrowing his eyes and looking to one side, just like meeting the headlights of an oncoming car while driving at night.

"Hey, Tombstone," Snowball said. His voice sounded a bit shaky, but in control. "You think maybe they're trying to tell us to get lost?"

"Could be. Let's see if they'll talk to us." Sliding the Tomcat closer to the Bear's fuselage, Tombstone faced the light and held up three gloved fingers. Using exaggerated motions, he repeated the gesture three times.

The searchlight snapped off.

"There's our answer," Tombstone said. "Switch to 333.3 and let's see what they have to say for themselves."

Tombstone held his mask across his face. "Russian aircraft, Russian aircraft. This is Hunt Leader, flying just off your right wing. Do you copy?"

There was a long silence. There were almost always English-speaking personnel on these Bear flights—

"Is Flight Four-one-two speaking, Hunt Leader. Go ahead."

"Flight Four-one-two, this is Hunt Leader. You are on an intercept course with the U.S.S. *Thomas Jefferson*. Please come to course . . . one-five-zero in order to avoid overflying our ships. Over."

"*Nyet*, Hunt Leader. Flight Four-one-two is on routine flight, Vladivostok to Cam Ranh Bay. Is international airspace. As Americans say, 'You go to hell.'"

"That's grade-A bullshit, Stone," Snowball said over the intercom circuit. "He stays on that course, he'll fly smack into South Korea. He's gotta change course sometime soon, and it might as well be now!"

"He just wants to see how far we'll bend, Snowy." Tombstone thought for a moment. There was really very little he could do other than annoy the Bear pilot . . . and risk the mistake which could trigger an international incident. Chances were, the Russian plane *was* on a routine flight to the big Soviet naval base in Vietnam, but they'd have orders to see how far they could press the American carrier group along the way.

He opened the channel again. "Russian Flight Four-one-two, this is Hunt Leader. The U.S.S. *Jefferson* is currently engaged in military exercises in the Sea of Japan and is on full alert. Your aircraft could be in danger if you approach too closely."

"Hunt Leader, are you declaring exclusion zone?"

In times of crisis, in times of war, a carrier group commander might declare an exclusion zone around his fleet. Any unknown aircraft approaching to within, say, one hundred miles could be fired upon. But things weren't that hot, not yet. "Negative, Flight Four-one-two. There is no exclusion zone. What we're telling you is just for your own—"

"*Nyet! Bereegees!*" The burst of startled Russian ended the conversation. Tombstone's thumb hovered above the gun selector switch on his stick. What . . . ?

He looked up and saw a pair of sun-bright flares riding close together and side by side just above the dark shape of the Russian Bear. It took a moment for him to sort out what he was seeing, the twin tailpipes of another Tomcat flying just above the Russian bomber's cockpit. The steady vibration Tombstone had been feeling as his F-14 followed in the wake of the Bear's starboard engines changed. The Russian was throttling down, dropping slightly. Batman's F-14 descended with him.

"Like the man says," Batman's voice said over the channel. "Putting your nose in where it's not wanted could be hazardous to your health!"

"Snowball! Patch me through to that idiot on another frequency!"

"You got it, Skipper."

"Hunt Two, this is Hunt Leader! Break off! Get back out there on point!"

"Copy, Hunt Leader," Batman said, his tone light, almost bantering. "Will comply. Looks like we showed this Bear who's boss."

The Bear continued to descend, still visible only as a black shape with red and green lights at nose, tail, and wingtips. After a moment, the Russian bomber raised its starboard wing slightly and ponderously swung onto a new heading.

"Target is coming to one-five-five, Tombstone," Snowball said.

Tombstone took a deep breath, then let it out slowly. His heart was pounding beneath his harness, and he could feel the slickness of sweat inside the palms of his gloves. The Russian's new heading was five degrees short of the course Tombstone had told him to take, an obvious declaration of "You can't tell *us* what to do." But one-five-five would still take the Bear well clear of the American fleet.

American aircraft would continue to pace the Bear for a time, escorting it out of the area. Judging from past incidents of this sort, Tombstone doubted that the Soviets would try to approach the carrier group again.

The crisis was over.

But not the tension. Tombstone was as angry as he could imagine being, though he kept his voice cool and emotionless as he told Snowball to open a channel to Tango One-three. "Homeplate, this is Hunt Leader. Target has come right to one-five-five. Looks like he doesn't want to play anymore."

"Copy, Hunt Leader," a Hawkeye radio officer replied. "Be advised that Starfire Flight is en route, ETA fifteen mikes. Homeplate says to tell you 'Well done.'"

Well done. Wayne's hotdog stunt could have killed them all. He would have to have words with that boy, once they were back on board the *Jeff*.

CHAPTER 10

0445 hours (1445 hours EST)
The White House Situation Room

"This may be the first good news we've got on this," the President said. He looked up from the report, stamped CRITIC at top and bottom. "The Russians backed down?"

Admiral Grimes grinned without humor. "I'd say, Mr. President, that they got the crap scared out of them when one of our pilots pulled . . . shall we say . . . an unorthodox maneuver."

"And there's been no further attempt to probe our forces?"

Marlowe folded his hands on the teakwood table. "You can bet they're watching closely, Mr. President. Three of their reconnaissance satellites have shifted to new orbits to give them better coverage of the Sea of Japan. But there are no indications that they want a direct confrontation."

The President's eyes shifted to the others at the table. He grinned at the Secretary of State. "Keep that in mind when you talk to the PRC Ambassador, Jim. It looks like it'll be just us and North Korea, with the PRC as go-betweens. Simplifies things, doesn't it?"

"Yes, sir." The secretary scowled. "We shouldn't feel too confident about Soviet motives, though, Mr. President. They've still not responded to our advances."

"Agreed." The President moved his gaze to a new face at the table. Dr. Lee Ann Chu, Assistant Secretary of State for East Asian and Pacific Affairs, was seated across from Schellenberg. She was an attractive, older woman—in her fifties, he guessed. She'd been put in charge of the team studying the political impact of U.S. military action on America's allies in the Far East. "Dr. Chu? I understand you have a preliminary report."

She hesitated, looking first at Schellenberg. There was some unstated struggle there, the President noted.

"Lee Ann's report isn't quite ready yet, Mr. President," the Secretary said. "Her assessment team is still considering the matter."

"Dr. Chu?" the President said gently. "We don't need a formal report. Just tell me what you think. How will our allies react to military intervention in the area?"

Slowly, Dr. Chu removed her glasses, folding them carefully and placing them on the table before her. She met the President's eyes directly. "Mr. President, you can expect the normal round of anti-U.S. condemnations. With the exception of the Republic of Korea, you will find no support, no practical help in this matter at all. On the whole, however, and in the long run, our image will not suffer badly."

Chu went on to discuss each nation in turn, beginning with Japan, pointing out that Tokyo had been pursuing a far more independent course of late and that the Japanese resented South Korea's economic competition. She spoke for ten minutes with authority and conviction. There were no surprises in what she had to say. It was exactly what the President had expected to hear.

He detected, though, that she was holding back, that there was something her boss might be suppressing.

"Thank you, Doctor," he said as she finished. "Is there anything else?"

She hesitated, looking uncertain.

"That will be all, Lee Ann," Schellenberg said. "Thank you."

"A moment, please," the President said, not certain how far he could push. "Dr. Chu, you've discussed the reactions of our friends in the area if we attack. What about those of our enemies?"

"Mr. President—" Schellenberg began.

"My question was addressed to Dr. Chu," the President said brusquely. "Doctor?"

She seemed to reach some inner decision. "Mr. President, the question might better be phrased, 'What will happen if we do *not* attack?'"

"And?"

"The expression 'loss of face' is dated, Mr. President. Its use has certain . . . racist overtones. And yet I must remind you that it is still a valid psychological concept throughout much of the Orient. If you back down before the North Koreans now, you, Mr.

President, will have lost face, before your friends and enemies alike. I urge you—"

Schellenberg interrupted. "What Dr. Chu means, Mr. President, is that an aggressive stance may help us bull through this thing in the short term. But we're going to have to be very careful navigating this minefield for some time to come, and—"

"Since when did I need an interpreter for straight English, Jim?"

"Sorry, Mr. President. The Doctor is new to her job, and—"

"Save it." The President looked from Chu to Schellenberg and back again, scowling. It was clear enough now. Chu's report had held the wrong twist and Schellenberg had been trying to suppress it.

God. Did North Korea's dictator have the same problems with his own advisors, or did he enjoy the luxury of ordering them shot when the infighting got too vicious?

"Dr. Chu, I've already decided that a strong approach is necessary. We have to tell these people we mean business." He looked down the table at Caldwell. "General, as of this moment, I am authorizing a full go-ahead for Winged Talon."

The General nodded. "Yes, Mr. President."

"We'll keep the 82nd and the rest on alert, use them if we have to. But I think a measured response is called for."

"I'll give the necessary orders, Mr. President."

"Excellent." The President looked at his Chief of Staff. "George? We're going to have to prepare a statement for the press. I want Joe brought in on this."

"Yes, Mr. President."

Joseph Collins, the White House Press Secretary, had been kept busy for the past twenty-four hours, ever since the story about *Chimera*'s seizure had broken in the press. Until now his task had been restricted to damage control—denying reports of U.S. military intervention in Korea and insisting that the President was following events in the Far East with grave concern.

The President knew that he would have to start bracing for the storm which would follow *any* decision he made, and the sooner the White House press corps was brought in on things, the better.

He turned back to face Schellenberg, reading the professional hurt in the man's face. There was another problem, bad feelings that would have to be nipped early. "Jim, you still have an appointment with the Chinese ambassador this afternoon?"

"Yes, sir." He glanced at his watch. "Forty-five minutes."

"Good. Keep it." He smiled, turning on the charm which had stood him in good stead in more than one campaign. "You can win them over, get them to talk to us if anyone can. If you can open channels to the PDRK, then Winged Talon is off. You have my word on it." He turned his gaze on the others. "Meanwhile, we keep our powder dry and watch out for minefields. We take those steps necessary to resolve this crisis and get our people back. If they won't talk to us, Winged Talon is on. Agreed?" Briefly, his eyes met the eyes of each of the other people in the room. There was no dissent.

George Hall stirred in his seat. "Mr. President, there remains the problem of the location of our people over there. An indiscriminate strike at North Korean military installations could kill our own people."

"Victor?" He looked at the DCI. "Anything?"

"Not yet, sir. We've got satellite coverage eighty percent of the time now."

"Keep on it, and let me know the moment you've got something solid."

"Yes, sir." He didn't add *of course*, but the words were clear in his tone. We're all getting scraped raw, the President thought. My God, how are we going to win this one?

He wondered what more he could do for Chu. She'd probably been ordered by her boss to tow the party line. Her independence just now might well have ended her career.

He watched as the crisis management team scooped up papers and folders, and decided to say nothing.

0730 hours
CVIC, U.S.S. *Thomas Jefferson*

Admiral Magruder stepped across the cables lying on the deck and found himself a spot out of the way near the bulkhead. *Jefferson*'s Intelligence Center had been cleared of chairs and was now cluttered with the trappings of a television studio: lights, a camera, a handful of seamen in dungarees and chiefs and officers in khaki plugging in power cords and preparing for the morning's broadcast.

A small floating city in her own right, *Jefferson* boasted two television stations of her own, broadcasting regular programs dealing with problems and matters of interest to *Jefferson*'s crew. At need, Captain Fitzgerald or the admiral could address the entire ship's company without the need for assembling them all in one spot . . . an obvious impossibility for reasons of space, work efficiency, and safety.

"Ready to go, Admiral. Are you?"

Magruder turned to face Master Chief Raymond C. Buckley, Jr., a stocky, cherub-faced man who had been in the Navy for twenty-eight of his forty-five years, a high school drop-out who'd joined the Navy at seventeen and found himself a home. Buckley was *Jefferson*'s master chief, the chief of the boat, senior enlisted man on board. More than any other, he acted as intermediary between the ship's enlisted men and her officers.

"Ready, Chief, thanks. You're going to lead off?"

"Just like a game show host, Admiral." He seemed relaxed and at ease. Buckley's face was well known to every one of *Jefferson*'s six thousand officers and men. He hosted the ship's nightly *We'll Sea* program on Channel 1, and he wrote daily articles for the ship's newspaper, the *Jeffersonian Democrat*.

Buckley walked to the lectern and faced the camera. The chief who was serving as director pointed at him as he gripped the lectern with both hands and beamed at the camera. "Goooood morning, *Jeffersons*!" The master chief had adopted as his broadcast trademark PFC Pat Sajak's well-known DJ intro from the Armed Forces Radio broadcasts in Vietnam. Buckley had served in Nam, Magruder knew, ashore at Cam Ranh Bay and later on board the U.S.S. *Constellation*, as had many of the older chiefs on board. It formed a small but important link with other men who had served America's interests in foreign waters.

Magruder did not listen to the master chief's opening remarks. It seemed incongruous, somehow, to be giving *Jefferson*'s crew their orders on TV, orders which could very well lead to their deaths in a very few hours. He looked again at the printout he'd brought with him from the com center, then at the cardboard-mounted photograph which was resting on an easel under the unmoving gaze of a second camera on the other side of the room. Did wars always start this way, with step-by-step events that escalated until there was no longer any way to control them?

"And now, *Jeffersons*, it is my great privilege to welcome the Commanding Officer, Carrier Battle Group 14, Rear Admiral Thomas J. Magruder!"

Woodenly, Magruder walked into the blaze of stage lights, stepping behind the lectern as Buckley moved out of the way. He placed his notes before him, then looked up into the blank, glassy eye of the camera. The red light was on, putting him squarely at the center of attention for several thousand officers and men on board the carrier.

"*Jeffersons,*" he said. It was best, he thought, to tell this one straight, without preamble. "As you all know by now, Carrier Battle Group 14 has been directed by the President to take up station at Patrol Point November, pending further orders. Yester-·day, CBG-14 was augmented by the arrival of MEU-6, comprised of four Marine amphibious ships.

"At zero-five-twenty this morning, we received new orders. They were addressed through the Commander in Chief, Pacific, but the authority comes through the President. I will read you the significant parts."

Magruder pulled his reading glasses from the breast pocket of his uniform coat and perched them low on his nose. "Priority Urgent, to CO, CBG-14, U.S.S. *Jefferson*, on station at Point November.

"One. Carrier Battle Group Fourteen, together with Marine Expeditionary Unit Six, will henceforth be designated Task Force Eighteen. CO CBG-14 is directed to assume overall command TF-18 and of all auxiliary and support forces Oparea November.

"Four. CO TF-18 will make such unit dispositions as are consistent with security of the force. CO TF-18 is reminded of recent hostile KorCom activity in oparea, and urged to take all necessary precautions to avoid unnecessary losses to his command.

"Five. TF-18 will maintain station pending further operational directives of the National Command Authority. TF-18 must be considered to be the primary arm of national foreign policy in the area, and will engage in no activities contrary to national goals or aims.

"Eight. All tactical commands under TF-18, including both Marine and air wing elements, are hereby directed to prepare final operational orders anticipating possible military interdiction at or near the port of Wonsan, North Korea, in keeping with parameters and directives outlined in opplan designated WINGED TALON.

"Nine. Operation WINGED TALON should be considered to be a limited tactical retaliatory strike aimed at securing the safety of U.S. Navy personnel now held by KorCom forces in or near Wonsan, and at securing the release of U.S.S. *Chimera*, seized two days ago in international waters by KorCom Naval and Air Force units. Final authorization for WINGED TALON will be the responsibility of the National Command Authority alone."

Magruder looked up from the paper and into the camera's eye once more. "These orders are signed by Fleet Admiral Wesley R. Bainbridge, CINCPAC. I needn't tell you, men, that they place a heavy responsibility on all of us, on every man in this task force.

"I have here a TENCAP photo which should be of interest to all of you." The camera's red light winked out, and Magruder knew the second camera was on, focused on the photo on the easel across the room. TENCAP—the acronym stood for Tactical Exploitation of National CAPabilities—was a new military adaptation of satellite technology. For the first time, commanders in the field could use their satellite links to call down up-to-the-minute photos from KH-12s directly, rather than waiting for them from Washington.

"What you are seeing, men, is the U.S.S. *Chimera* tied up at a pier in Wonsan Harbor. I'm told this photograph has a resolution of about three inches, which is pretty damn good from over a hundred miles up. You can see soldiers standing on *Chimera*'s deck, wearing steel helmets and carrying AK rifles. There's been quite a bit of damage. One of the whaleboat davits has been shot away, the mast has been knocked over, and there's been some damage to the forward deck and the deckhouse. That blob you see over the taffrail is a flag . . . the North Korean flag, raised in the place of the Stars and Stripes.

"This photo confirms that the North Koreans are indeed now holding our ship and nearly two hundred of our men prisoner, a brazen act of modern high-seas piracy."

The red light flashed on. He was on camera once more. "Task Force Eighteen has been called upon to be the steel behind the President's words when he talks to the North Koreans during the next few hours. He will tell them to release our people and our ship. When the NKs look at us, they'll get a pretty good idea of what will happen if they refuse."

It was hot under the lights. Magruder tried to ignore the sweat trickling down inside the collar of his uniform. "This one carrier battle group carries more firepower than was expended in all of World War II. It serves as a powerful and highly visible instrument of America's political and foreign policy will. The North Koreans are not crazy, and they are not suicidal. I expect that they will listen to reason and give in.

"If they do not, then it is our responsibility to do what Congress and the taxpayers pay us to do . . . defend America's interests wherever in the world they are threatened, defend our people wherever and whenever they are in danger. I know that I can count on each and every one of you to do your duty." He paused. What more was there to be said at a time like this? "That is all."

He stepped back from the lectern, allowing Buckley to take his place. The master chief was speaking as Magruder strode from the CVIC, but he was not listening.

Command responsibility was something Admiral Magruder accepted with the uniform he wore. He'd grown up in a Navy family, he and his brother Sam. Their father had always told them both that command responsibility was something in their blood, that they were *born* to command.

Maybe that was so. His father had served on Nimitz's staff in World War II; his great-grandfather had commanded one of Farragut's monitors at Mobile Bay. The honor, the crisp blue-and-gold glory, of U.S. Naval tradition had been a part of the very air he breathed when he and Sam were growing up in Annapolis, Maryland.

He'd talked a lot about command with Sam, back when they were on those heady first rungs of their careers as Naval officers. "I don't mind the thought of dying so much," Sam had told him once over coffee in the flight officers' mess at Pensacola. "But giving the orders that are going to get somebody *else* killed, that's a real bitch."

Sam had sealed his place in the family's tradition in the skies above the Doumer Bridge in downtown Hanoi, back in the summer of 1969. He was still officially listed as MIA, though the family had long since given up hoping that he was still alive.

His brother's words had come back to haunt Admiral Magruder more than once in the years since then, but now they were taking on an urgency, an intensity unlike any he'd ever known. They followed him now as he hurried down the passageway. A sudden crisis, a set of orders from Washington . . . and he was taking twelve thousand men into combat. The fact that it was what he'd trained to do for so many years, that it was his *job*, meant less than the fact that they were his men.

His responsibility.

Magruder had not told the whole story during his broadcast, and that, more than anything, was what was bothering him. It was true, for instance, that the carrier group carried more firepower than had been expended in all of World War II, but that was counting the nukes stored deep in *Jefferson*'s belly, down in the forward magazine. No way would Washington authorize a *nuclear* strike against North Korea; vaporizing P'yongyang wouldn't solve a thing, and the North Koreans knew that as well as he did. Despite his brave words, Magruder wasn't nearly as certain as he'd pretended to be that the KorComs would back down.

Certainly, no one could count on an airstrike being sufficient in forcing P'yongyang's hand, and it was evident that Washington knew that. The Pentagon was bracing for something more than a quick in-and-out air raid; that much was evident from some of the paragraphs in his orders which he'd not read during the broadcast. Paragraph Seven, for instance, directed him to regard all North Korean ships and aircraft as hostile until further orders, and to take appropriate action as he saw fit.

Paragraph Ten was worse. It told him that a Naval special tactical team was coming in via COD—carrier on-board delivery— sometime after 1700 hours. That meant SEALs, and SEALs meant that someone in Washington was gearing up for the worst, anything from a hostage rescue mission to a full-fledged Marine amphibious assault. There were over twenty-six hundred Marines aboard *Chosin* and *Little Rock*. Suppose Washington decided to send *them* in?

Magruder found himself thinking of the two men shot down off Wonsan two days before, Grant and Cooper. He thought about Matthew's anger and shook his head. If the PDRK didn't back down in the next day or two, quite a few more good men could join them.

Heading back toward Flag Plot, he strode quickly down the narrow, gray-painted passageway, every fifth stride a duck-and-step through one of the openings in the transverse frames the ship's crew called knee-knockers. A sailor approached him coming the other way. Framed by the receding succession of knee-knockers, he looked at first like Magruder's own reflection in a gallery of mirrors. The corridor was so narrow both men had to turn sideways to pass.

The sailor was uncovered and therefore did not salute, but he looked Magruder in the eye as he stepped aside, grinned, and sounded off with a hearty "Good morning, Admiral." Like the majority of the men who served aboard *Jefferson*, he looked painfully young, no more than nineteen. "Sounds like we're gonna kick some ass."

"Damned straight, son."

His men.

His duty.

CHAPTER 11

Tombstone Magruder fed another sheet of paper into the aging IBM Selectric on his desk and began a two-finger hunt-and-peck as he tried once more to write his report on the previous night's Bear hunt. Try as he might, he was finding it impossible to put into words the reprimand he'd wanted to lay on Batman Wayne's record.

He held the same sour-stomached distaste for this kind of administrative work as he had for filling out quarterly fitness reports. A bad word could ruin a promising officer's career forever . . . or at least blight it with personal observations which would follow the guy for as long as he was in the Navy. Magruder was still angry with Batman for his hotdogging with the Bear, but he was less certain now that he should commit that anger to Batman's record. A private talk with the man, maybe a quiet word in CAG's ear in case the situation came up again sometime would be enough.

Besides, in another few hours, Batman might well be in the air facing MiGs, SAMs, and triple A. He'd need all the self-confidence and concentration he could muster.

But *damn*. If someone didn't curb that boy's hotdogging pretty soon—

There was a knock at the door and Tombstone looked up. He'd half expected to see Batman there, but it was Snowball, blinking at him owlishly through his big, round glasses. "Stoney? Got a minute?"

"C'mon in. Make yourself at home."

The invitation was more a matter of polite form than of

practicality. The office was the size of a walk-in closet. The chair and desk, the filing cabinet, the tiny book rack on one bulkhead filled it completely. Fitting another man inside was a logistical problem as complex as moving aircraft around on *Jefferson*'s crowded hangar deck.

Snowball stepped inside the door. "Look . . . I'm not sure how to say this."

"Just spitting it out's usually best. Short and sweet."

"Yeah, I suppose so. Commander, I'm scared."

Scared. The word lay between them, harsh and unforgiving. Tombstone knew he had a problem.

Within the fraternity of aviators and flight officers, admitting to fear was acceptable, but only if it was made in a joking, self-deprecating way. The ego, the *machismo* of combat pilots demanded it. *I'm telling you, boys,* a pilot might say, with the easy grin and down-home drawl of one who has been through it all. *That night trap was so hairy . . . after that bolter I found out why the flight suits they issue us are brown!*

Never, *never* did you simply blurt out your fear. That rule held especially true for aviators, but it applied to backseaters as well.

Tombstone shifted uncomfortably in his chair. "What's the problem? Losing the Coyote the other day? The dogfight?"

"Oh, shit, Tombstone. I don't know. I guess it's a little bit of everything. I was scared the other day, sure, but I figured I could handle it okay. It got me to thinking though." Tombstone waited. Snowball took a deep breath and continued. "It all kind of came apart for me last night, up there in the dark next to that Bear. Look, Tombstone, can I be straight with you?"

"Shoot."

"Mostly I've been worried about flying with *you*."

"Me?"

"Yeah. Ever since Coyote went down, you've been so up-tight . . . hell, everybody knows it. It's like your mind's not really on your flying anymore, and that scares hell out of me! When you tucked in close under that Bear's tail last night, and then when Batman pulled that stunt, man, I thought that was it."

"You came through okay."

"Sure. But it got me thinking, right? It's like . . . like I'm trusting you, trusting the guy up front with my life, know what I mean? I'm married, Stoney. Got married two months before this cruise. Right now, I've been away from her more'n I've been with her. It ain't right for me to smear myself all over *Jefferson*'s roundoff because some other guy's not paying attention! And now the scuttlebutt is we're going up against the KorComs and there's gonna be a fight. Man, I just don't know if I can handle that!"

"Is that all?" He felt ice-cold, as though he'd just been struck.

Snowball looked like he was about to say more, then reconsidered. "Yes, sir."

"You want to swap with another RIO? You're not stuck with me, you know."

"I don't know." He looked away. For a moment, he seemed to be studying the array of papers and notes tacked to the small bulletin board on the office bulkhead. "I don't think it would be any better."

"You want to stop *flying*?" For Tombstone, that was the ultimate impossibility. To give up flying would be like dying.

"No. Yeah . . . aw, shit. Look, Stoney, right now, I'm so screwed up—"

"Damn it, that's *enough*!" Tombstone's palm came down on his desk beside the typewriter, scattering an untidy stack of paperwork. "Listen, mister, I don't give a shit about your piss-ant little problems! You want a shoulder to cry on, go see the chaplain. You don't like my flying, talk to CAG and get yourself assigned to another plane . . . or get yourself grounded, *I don't care!*" Tombstone regretted the outburst at once. It was too late to take the words back, too late to back down, but he could try to control the anger. Who was he mad at, anyway? Snowball? Or himself?

He stood up behind his desk, holding Snowball's eyes with his own, making himself relax. "One way or another, I suggest that you get yourself squared away."

"Y-yes, sir."

Tombstone looked down at his desktop, then picked up a neatly typed paper from among the others scattered there. "Know what this is?"

"No, sir."

"Cut the *kay*-det crap, Snowy. This is an order from CAG, telling me to work out the details for CAP cover for Operation Winged Talon, getting ready for, quote, air operations against North Korean ground positions and air targets in the Wonsan area, unquote. Right this minute, up on the flight deck, they're arming up on the assumption that this thing is a go! Chances are we'll be launching in a few hours, and when we do, it's really going to hit the fan. I don't want you up there if you're going to freeze up on me!"

He saw a spark of anger in Snowball's eyes. "I won't freeze, sir!"

Tombstone sank back into his chair. "Get out of here, then. See CAG if you want a transfer, but don't pester me with this shit, got me?"

"Yes, sir. Aye aye, sir."

Snowball backed out of the office, hesitated a moment, then whirled upon his heel and hurried off down the passageway. A moment later, the doorway was blocked again as Marusko stepped in. "What was that all about? We heard the shouting clear down to Admin."

Tombstone rocked his chair back on two legs, his hands pressed over his eyes. "I don't know, CAG. I probably just screwed it up, that's all."

"Welcome to the club. When will you have that report on my desk?"

He sighed. "What do you want first? Report or opplan?"

CAG grinned. "What's the matter, son? Paperwork piling up?"

"And then some."

"You should see my desk. Okay, the Bear report can wait. From the way your uncle's talking, we're going in this afternoon. An all-squadron briefing's been called for fifteen hundred, so you can figure it for yourself. I'll need the opplan by twelve hundred if I'm going to have anything to show the admiral."

"I love how we fight wars with paper. Okay, CAG. I'll get on it."

"Good. Oh, and Tombstone . . ."

"Yeah?"

"Take it easy on your people. They'll respond to a light hand, voice of experience and all that, right?"

Tombstone drew in a breath. "Aye aye, CAG. You're right."

"That's all, then. See you at twelve hundred."

Tombstone stared at the empty doorway for several minutes more. He really had let his anger and frustration get away from him with Snowball. But what was he supposed to do, nursemaid the whole squadron?

He thought back to his five weeks at Miramar. Top Gun training reached more than the handful of students who attended the school. The idea was to rotate Top Gun grads back to the fleet after they completed the course, where they served as instructors with their squadrons. Tombstone had a regular weekly schedule of lectures in ACM tactics—the high-tech waltz of Air Combat Maneuvers better known as dogfighting.

The drill, as he'd pointed out to several other Top Gun alumni on board *Jefferson*, was to keep a low profile, to not come out and tell the other aviators that he'd been to Fightertown, since that would just breed resentment. It was much slicker, much more in keeping with the aviator's charisma, if he let the information slip out little by little, in the lectures, in the debriefings after missions.

It's all a part of command, he told himself. And damn it all, that's just what I can't handle. Maybe the promotions have been coming a little too fast . . . a little too easy.

He thought about CAG's words. *Your uncle.*

There was no way he could back out now, not just before a combat op, not with every man in the air wing thinking him a coward. Tombstone remembered his own acid reaction a moment earlier, when Snowball admitted he was scared. No. Not like that.

But it was time to admit that he was no leader of men. Maybe it was even a time to find a sane career, one where he didn't have to keep proving himself.

He rolled a fresh sheet of paper into the Selectric and began pecking away.

1030 hours
Vulture's Row, U.S.S. *Thomas Jefferson*

Snowball leaned against the railing and looked down at the flight deck from the railed walkway atop the island. Damn them! he thought. Damn them all!

Among the ranks of Naval flight officers there was a sharply defined sense of *us* and *them*, a camaraderie of mutual respect and fellowship which crossed the lines of rank. Somehow, though, Dwight Newcombe had never quite fit in. He stood out from the others, *different*, as he'd been different from the other kids in school, a loner, always on the outside. His pale and sunburn-prone skin and ash-blond hair had won him the handle Snowball at Pensacola, a hated running name which nonetheless had traveled with him to the North Island Naval Air Base at Coronado, then to his first posting at sea on board the *Jefferson* only five months earlier. Attempts to join the band-of-brothers fellowship had only made him stand out more, had made him feel more of an outsider than ever.

In keeping with Naval policy of assigning experienced pilots to inexperienced NFOs—and experienced NFOs with newbie aviators—Newcombe had been paired with Tombstone Magruder, a Top Gun graduate who'd seemed quieter than the others . . . and more sympathetic.

He'd gotten along well with the guy so far. In the late-night bull sessions in flight officers' quarters, Tombstone had never sounded as though he had something to prove, never rambled on about improbable sexual escapades during some past liberty, never worn the mask of the fearless and invulnerable warrior. For the past several months, Snowball had felt closer to Tombstone than to anyone else on board the *Jefferson*.

But now . . .

His ears caught the faint beat of rotors across the water. He strained his eyes and caught sight of one of *Jefferson*'s helos patrolling off to port. Aft, he could see deck personnel and officers checking the arrestor cables and gathering in front of the Fresnel lens system. A recovery operation then. Somebody was coming in.

Tombstone was carrying a load, Snowball knew. Coyote's loss had been a bad blow to the commander. He'd watched Tombstone change in those long minutes of the flight back to *Jefferson* after that first, terror-laced dogfight two days earlier. But blow or not, change or not, it wasn't right that Tombstone should lash out at him like that.

Pucker factor. It was an old flyer's term, referring to the fear that every aviator felt at one time or another . . . in combat, in a night trap on a rain-swept deck, in the swirl of smoke and flame and noise as the ejection seat kicked you clear of the cockpit. Belonging to the pilots' fraternity, Snowball knew, depended not on the absence of fear, but on the way a man controlled it.

He thought about the confrontation in Tombstone's office. If he quit now, every man in the wing would think he was a coward. Worse, they would feel *sorry* for him . . . or agree with one another that since he never belonged in the first place, it was obvious that he simply didn't have the right stuff.

What else could he do? Go to CAG and ask for reassignment? Who else besides Tombstone would he rather fly with?

His hands closed on the Vulture Row railing, squeezing with his building anger. He would not let this beat him! He would *belong*!

"Now hear this, now hear this," a voice grated over the 5-MC loudspeakers over the flight deck. "Stand by flight deck for recovery operations, COD. That is, stand by flight deck for recovery operations, COD."

Snowball looked aft. It took him several minutes to locate the inbound plane, a speck low above the horizon growing slowly into a recognizable aircraft.

The C-2A Greyhound was designed as a COD aircraft, the acronym standing for Carrier On-board Delivery. Its high wings and two turboprop engines, its odd-looking boom tail with four vertical stabilizers made it a close twin of the E-2 Hawkeye, though a thicker body gave it a heavy-built, stubby appearance, and it lacked the saucer-shaped radar housing above the fuselage. With a range of over fifteen hundred miles, Greyhounds were the principal means of delivering cargo, mail, and personnel to carriers at sea. This flight, Snowball knew, was an unscheduled one. He wondered what it was carrying.

The Greyhound swelled rapidly during the final seconds of its approach, flaps at full and nose high as it roared over the roundoff and dropped to the deck for a perfect trap on the number three wire. A good landing, Snowball thought with the detached interested of a professional. Landing one of those chunky turboprops on a carrier had always seemed more unlikely to him than landing a nimble Tomcat.

Curiously, he watched as the plane backed slightly to spit out the wire, then taxied cautiously past a row of Hornets parked shoulder to shoulder abaft of the island. The Greyhound made a final turn to face away from Snowball. Optical illusion made the spinning propellers seem to reverse themselves as they slowed to a stop.

With a whine, a rear hatch opened in the Greyhound's tail, and a ramp slowly lowered itself to the deck. Before the ramp touched steel, a line of men were filing out of the aircraft. Snowball counted fifteen of them. At first he thought they were Marines, for each wore camouflage-patterned trousers and shirts and had floppy-brimmed boonie hats on their heads. The Navy seabags each man held balanced across his shoulder made him think again. They *could* be Marines, but . . .

Snowball had seen men like that before, during his tour at Coronado: SEALs.

He found himself wondering if those men had ever been in combat. It was likely; SEALs had played an important part in the oil rig raids and recon missions off Kuwait. They might even have participated in anti-terrorist ops, the *successful* anti-terrorist ops that never made the evening news.

Snowball felt a sudden and unexpected lift at the thought, and a new determination. He'd been in combat only two days before, been in combat and come back to tell about it. Training and experience aside, what did those SEALs have that he didn't?

Maybe *belonging* had more to do with his attitude than theirs. He'd *show* them, show them all. He wouldn't quit.

Snowball Newcombe was a flight officer!

CHAPTER 12

Coyote's situation had improved, but not by much. They'd taken him from the hole the afternoon before, questioned him one more time, then marched him across the compound to a long, narrow building guarded by flint-eyed soldiers armed with AKMs.

Inside he'd found the surviving crewmen of the *Chimera*.

He wasn't sure why the North Koreans had herded him into the low, single-storied building with the others. Classes he'd attended during his training on how to survive as a prisoner of war suggested that POWs were nearly always segregated early on, the officers separated from the enlisted men. For some reason, their captors weren't following the usual routine, and *Chimera*'s entire complement was present in the building which the inmates had already named the Wonsan Waldorf.

Of the American spy ship's original complement of 193, 170 were still alive—163 sailors, 7 officers. Coyote learned that 23 men had died, killed outright during the attack or succumbing to wounds during the three days since their capture; 61 were wounded, 18 seriously. Their captivity thus far had been little short of a nightmare, officers and men crammed together into what might have once been a storeroom or warehouse of some kind, with little food, no blankets, no sanitary facilities, and no medical treatment for the injured beyond the most rudimentary attempts at first aid.

Captain Gerald K. Gilmore was one of the wounded. HM/1 Herb Bailey, a hospital corpsman, had sewn up the knee-to-thigh gash in his right leg and stopped the bleeding, but the captain was desperately weak from shock and loss of blood. Infection would kill him and a dozen others in days if they weren't given proper treatment soon.

"The big-bucks question is," one chief petty officer said in a low voice, "whether we'd be better off out there . . . or here."

Fifteen of them were gathered in a circle around the ragged mattress on the floor which served as Gilmore's bed. They were the officers and NCOs who had appointed themselves as the group's escape committee. As soon as he'd been able to prove he was American—an intimate knowledge of Navy slang terms like "slider" and "pogie bait" had quickly established his credentials—Coyote had been invited to join because his pilot training had included such useful tidbits as survival and E&E, escape and evasion.

Coyote glanced away from the circle and down the dimly lit length of the building. The rest of the men were gathered in small groups, talking, sleeping, tending the wounded, or just sitting. At intervals along both of the longer walls, several sailors were positioned as lookouts. They stood on overturned honey buckets, peering out the narrow windows set into the wall high up just under the building's eaves. Their warning that someone was approaching would turn the escape committee's whispered conversation into an animated discussion about girls and improbable sexual experiences. "Getting out won't be easy," Coyote said. "There are several hundred troops here, a battalion at least. The camp is surrounded by a twelve-foot chain-link fence topped with barbed wire."

"Yeah, well, if we *don't* get out," Bailey said grimly, "some of these men aren't going to make it." His hands clenched in front of him, the gesture revealing the man's anger and frustration. "The antibiotics are gone and we're down to dirty T-shirts for dressings. And those bastards won't give me anything better to work with."

A first class radarman named Zabelsky shook his head. "Look, even if we could get out, what would we do? Where would we go? God . . . a hunert an' seventy men, a third of them wounded. Wanderin' around in slope city. What're we s'posed to do?"

"How far is it to the DMZ?" Lieutenant Commander Coleridge asked.

"Maybe sixty miles," Commander Wilkinson replied. "That's straight south, which means climbing the Taebaek Mountains. Follow the coast southeast and it's more like seventy-five miles. Either way, we'd have to walk past half the damned NK Army."

"Shit," someone said. "I read once they've got the fifth largest army in the world."

"Sixth," Wilkinson muttered. "But who's counting?"

"If we could get a radio," Coyote suggested, "we could call for a rescue. *Jefferson* must still be offshore somewhere. If they've moved in closer in the last couple of days, they could pick us up off the beach."

"Fine," a lieutenant said. He had a savage bruise across his forehead, and his eyes were puffy and blackened. "All we need is a radio, the right frequency, a lot of luck, and some way to break out of this hole."

The chief, a machinist's mate named Bronkowicz, looked across the room to where one of *Chimera*'s officers, another lieutenant, sat alone in a far corner. "Hell, I vote we send ol' Grape 'n' Guts over there out to get a radio. I'll bet his slant buddies—"

"Belay that, Chief." Gilmore's voice was weak but held an edge to it which still carried the authority of command. "Lieutenant Novak did what he thought was right."

None of *Chimera*'s people had been willing to talk much about the capture of their ship, but Coyote had gathered that at some point Gilmore had been wounded badly enough that he'd passed command to the only available line officer, a young lieutenant on his first tour of sea duty. Apparently, Novak had surrendered the ship, even ordered the crew not to resist, as North Korean troops had poured aboard.

It seemed the others had already judged him, finding him guilty of cowardice.

Coyote looked away from the solitary figure. He could imagine what it was like, alone on a shattered bridge, the noise, the agony as shipmates died. He remembered his own loneliness when he'd been adrift in the ocean, his horror at Mardi Gras's death.

He tried to imagine what he would have done in Novak's place. Probably pretty much the same thing.

"The way I see it," Commander Wilkinson said, "we're a lot better off here."

Bronkowicz nodded. "That's what I was wonderin', sir. We don't stand a virgin's chance in a Marine barracks out there. They'd run us down before we got two miles."

"It's more than that, Chief," Wilkinson said. "The way I see it, we have two good chances to get out of here. Either Washington'll negotiate for our release, or they'll send in Delta Force and rescue us. Either way, we'll do a lot better if we stay put."

"Shee-*it*!" Zabelsky said with some passion. "We're supposed to wait for Washington to move its ass for us?"

"They'll probably disavow all knowledge of our actions," someone said.

"Hell, they forgot all about us already," another said.

"I don't think so," Coyote said. "Someone in Washington had us deploy to look for you guys, and it's hard to disavow a dogfight."

"So where's that leave us?" Bailey asked. His eyes were bleak. "Sit around and watch our people kick off, one by one?"

"Y'know, they negotiated with the gooks for almost a year for the *Pueblo* crew," Bronkowicz said. He rubbed his chin, making a sandpapery sound. None of them had shaved for three days.

"You mean we could be stuck in this hole for a *year*?"

"Easy, men," Gilmore said. His breath rasped. "You idiots start panicking and we'll do the Koreans' work for them!"

"The Captain's right," Coleridge said. "We've got to be patient, watch for our chance."

"And don't sign their damned confessions," Gilmore said.

"Yeah. Article Five of the Code," Bronkowicz added. He was referring to the U.S. Fighting Man's Code, a list of six articles learned by every American serviceman since the Korean War. Article Five included the statement "I will make no oral or written statements disloyal to my country and its allies or harmful to their cause." Many of the men in the Wonsan Waldorf had already, like Coyote, been threatened or beaten and ordered to sign unspecified papers or confessions for their captors.

So far, no one had given in, but Coyote had the distinct impression that the North Koreans were going to bear down hard on them. The gomers were impatient, even frantic to win their prisoners' cooperation within the shortest time possible.

Coyote wondered why that was so.

"We still oughta start working on weapons for ourselves," Chief Bronkowicz said. "Just in case. I mean, if we see an opportunity—"

"Sssst!" one of the lookouts warned, dropping down off his bucket and righting it. "Company!"

". . . an' there I was, see?" Bronkowicz bellowed, slapping his ample belly. "Right there in the room with both these chicks stark naked, see? An' me with my—"

Keys rattled at the lock across the room, and the door banged open. Two soldiers in mustard-colored uniforms stepped inside, threatening the prisoners with their AK rifles. An officer, a squat, stocky little man, strode between the guards and stopped, hands on hips, surveying the room.

"I Major Po, *Nyongch'on-kiji*." The voice was flat, nasal, and so heavily accented Coyote had to concentrate hard to follow the words. "You *sonabichi* spies! Imperialist provocateurs! You admit! Tell world, sign paper! Now!" He gestured, pointing at a sailor near the wall. One of the guards strode forward, jabbing the seaman with his AK barrel and motioning the man toward the door. The major pointed to another. "An' that *sonabichi*." He strode down the length of the room, his boots clumping hollowly on the wooden floor. "An' that! An' that!" He reached the escape committee's circle, reached out, and grabbed Zabelsky by the collar of his dungaree shirt. "You, *sonabichi*! You too!"

"Don't start any good escapes without me, fellas," Zabelsky muttered as the major yanked him out of the circle. Coyote counted eight of *Chimera*'s enlisted men being lined up.

Then they were gone, marched away at gunpoint. The door slammed shut behind them.

1148 hours (2148 hours EST)
Situation Room, the White House

The latest set of photographs from the KH-12 were on display on the rear projection screen at one end of the room.

"These were taken where?" the Chief of Naval Operations asked.

"Shithole called Nyongch'on," Marlowe replied. "Five miles south of Wonsan." He looked up from the brief prepared by the analysts at the NPIC minutes before. "There's a pass through the mountains there and the main road south to Anbyon. There's a village, Nyongch'on-ni, and a military base, or *kiji*. It's one of several in the area. Barracks, motor pool, a small airstrip."

"Damn," the President said. The poster-sized photograph showed part of a quonset-hut-type building of sheet tin, and another which looked like a concrete block warehouse, photographed from an oblique angle as though from an aircraft passing overhead. A line of eight men stood halfway between the two buildings, shepherded by other men holding weapons. While the features of individual faces hovered just beyond the tantalizing edge of visibility, there was no mistaking the uniforms: blue dungarees on the POWs, mustard brown NKPA uniforms on the guards. "Damn," the President said again. The advances in the intelligence field, just in the last few years—

"The boys over at NPIC say they'll be able to bring up more detail with computer enhancement," the DCI added. "Maybe even manage an ID on the faces. But I think what we have here is conclusive."

The President looked away from the photo. "Just what the hell do you mean by conclusive, Victor? Do they have all our people here, or just these? We have to know!"

"No way to tell, Mr. President," the CIA chief said. "We can see those eight. We can suppose they have more in one or more of those buildings. But . . ." He shrugged.

"Well, I don't know how we can even consider a military option, Mr. President," the Secretary of State said. "Especially when we could hear from the Chinese at any time now."

Schellenberg had met with the Chinese ambassador that afternoon and again during the evening. An hour earlier he'd left Deputy Secretary of State Frank Rogers at the Chinese embassy and returned to the White House, there to wait as electronic messages bounced from Earth to satellite and back to Earth again, bridging the distances between Washington, Beijing, and P'yongyang.

"If the Chinese come through, I'll be delighted," the President said. "But we have to be ready if things go the other way." He examined the picture again. "Okay, so they have eight of our people in . . . where the hell is it?"

"Nyongch'on, Mr. President."

"Yeah, right. So . . . Winged Talon. Can that do it for us, do you think?"

"It'll show the bastards we mean business," Caldwell said. "Go in hard and fast—"

"And risk lighting off the Korean Police Action, Round Two," Schellenberg said. He shook his head. "With all respect, Mr. President, we *can't* cowboy this one!"

"Come off it, Jim," Admiral Grimes said. "Hell, they're already mad at us. We can't make them much madder!"

"We'd be backing ourselves into an indefensible position," Schellenberg insisted. "Look, what if they start shooting our people one at a time until we call off our planes? How could we respond to something like that from a position of strength? Isn't it better to talk first, see where things are going?"

"You can't talk with *barbarians*," Grimes said.

"And maybe it's time we tried! Besides, if our people are scattered all over, we might hit some of them."

"And wouldn't *that* look grand on page one of the *Washington Post*?" Phillip Buchalter said. The Presidential advisor chuckled. "'Hostages killed by U.S. air attack.' Hell, we need to have people left alive before we can get them out!"

"There's no better intel than this," Marlowe said, jerking a thumb at the screen. "Not without HUMINT sources on the ground."

"Could be we already have some of those on the way in," Grimes said. HUMINT—Human Intelligence—normally meant agents in place in a foreign country. But there were alternatives. "We've got SEALs out there now."

Marlowe frowned. "Maybe. Risky, though."

"I'd recommend against a covert op like that," Caldwell said. An old Army man, Amos Caldwell had always resented the concept of elite special forces—Rangers, Green Berets, even the Marines—units which stole funding from the Army's share of each military appropriations bill. "I don't care how stealthy they are, Occidentals are going to stand out over there like bugs on a plate. No place to hide, y'know?"

"Not SEALs, General Caldwell," the CNO said coldly. "*Not* SEALs."

Schellenberg pursed his lips. "If our people are caught in North Korean territory—"

"That's just the point, Mr. Secretary," Grimes continued. "We need intelligence from the ground. If anybody can get it without being caught, SEALs can."

The President nodded slowly. He remembered a briefing in this same room years before, when Reagan decided to launch an air strike on Libya. SEALs had been on the ground in that one too, using laser designators to help American F-111s target their smart bombs. And then there'd been the SEAL raids in the Gulf . . .

"When will they be in position, Fletch?"

Grimes glanced at one of the clocks on the wall. "They should be on board *Jefferson* now, Mr. President. Give them time for last-minute planning and preparation . . . they could go in tonight."

"Our ace in the hole, Fletcher," the President said quietly. "If the North Koreans don't yell uncle as soon as we send in our planes, we're going to need hard intel fast. It looks to me like your SEALs are the best way to do it."

The CNO's face broke into a wintry smile. "I would have to agree, Mr. President."

CHAPTER 13

"That should do it, gentlemen." CAG's face grinned at them from the television screen. "Good luck, and God bless you all!"

"Let's saddle up!" Tombstone's voice came from across the ready room. The Vipers were already rigged out in their pressure suits. Outside, on the flight deck, their aircraft were waiting. The squadron pilots and their RIOs began filing through the door.

Batman Wayne rose from the leatherette chair and cocked a grin at Malibu. "Oh, what a thrill . . ." he began.

Malibu joined him in the chorus. "Gonna get us a *kill!*" Their hands collided in a high-five.

"Batman!"

"Yo!" He turned and saw Tombstone approaching. Adrenaline was boiling in his blood. He felt as though he were riding a billowing, thundering wave of excitement. *Combat!* "You called, oh fearless leader?"

"You guys stick tight this time, right? No hotdogging."

Batman swallowed his irritation. *Nothing* was going to spoil this for him! "Sure thing, Skipper. Strictly steak-and-potatoes."

Tombstone had already given the two of them a dressing down for hotdogging with the Bear. Further reprimands, Batman thought, were uncalled for.

"Hey, Skip," Malibu said, grinning. "You wouldn't be just the least little bit afraid that the Batman here's gonna beat your one kill, would you?"

"I just want to know he's going to be where I want him, when I want him," Tombstone replied. The expression on his face was unreadable, a mask.

Batman gave Tombstone a tight salute. "Yes, *sir*, squadron leader *sir!*"

Tombstone looked worried. Well, Batman thought as he pulled on his helmet, why wouldn't he be? The squadron—hell, *Jefferson's* entire air wing—was being flung against the North Koreans with almost indecent haste. The final orders had come through only hours before. Tombstone's work on the squadron's op orders must have put him up against the old problem faced by every military commander since Nimrod: *Good men are going to die today, and I wrote the orders that killed them.*

Batman liked Tombstone, though he couldn't claim to know him all that well. The guy was a real pro, steady, quiet, always certain about his next move. Batman especially appreciated the fact that Tombstone never made a big deal about having been to Top Gun school. You had to listen close to his lectures even to pick up the fact that he'd been to Fightertown. He had the righteous stuff, no question.

Batman didn't want to lose him.

They filed through the passageway, emerging from the base of the carrier's island onto the flight deck. The entire deck was a maze of aircraft and men, alive with motion and bustling activity.

A major carrier launch was a complex process, the arming, the fueling, the movement of aircraft between hangar deck and flight deck a colossal ballet of men and machines. The Deck Handler—the Mangler, as he was called—would be at his table just off the flight deck, shifting cutouts about on a scale model of the carrier in order to orchestrate each movement as planes were shuffled about preparatory to launch, or brought topside on one of *Jefferson's* four huge deck elevators. Everywhere, men in color-coded jackets moved with purpose and skill. Yellow shirts were directing aircraft, one after another, into line behind the catapult blast screens forward. Close by the island, purple shirts—"grapes" in carrier parlance—were clustered about a line of F/A-18 Hornets attaching fuel hoses to their bellies, while red-shirted ordnancemen checked through the racks of bombs and missiles slung from wing pylons.

Batman had mingled feelings as he looked at the sleek Hornets with their red spear tail markings identifying them as planes of VFA-161, the Javelins. The Hornet was superb, the hottest, most modern of all Navy aircraft. Pilots for the Javelins and their sister squadron, the Fighting Hornets, consistently took the honors on the big chalkboard on the 01 deck which tallied each of

Jefferson's aviators on their skill at carrier landings. Those standings were normally a source of constant, fierce competition among the pilots, but the Hornet drivers were always at the top because their aircraft handled so well. Batman was looking forward to the day when he could strap·on one of those babies.

At the same time, though, Batman was glad he was riding a Tomcat today. The Hornet served a dual role, air superiority and ground attack. On today's raid they'd be hauling eight or ten thousand pounds of bombs all the way in. While the F/A-18s might have a chance to dogfight coming out, the F-14 Tomcats would be aloft today for one reason and one reason only: to kill enemy MiGs.

And that was what Batman wanted to do, more than anything else in the world.

The piercing whine of engines revving up to full throttle shrilled from the forward deck, followed by the *slam—pause—slam* of a double catapult launch as a pair of A-6F Intruders clawed for sky. The raw noise was painful even through Batman's helmet. A carrier flight deck is so noisy during a launch that a man without ear protectors can *die* in minutes, killed by the intensity of the sound alone.

The water-cooled JBD blast shields dropped back to the deck as the Intruders dwindled into the distance and the next two planes were hauled into position for launch. A number of *Jefferson*'s aircraft were already aloft, a pair of E-2C Hawkeyes, three of her four KA-6D tankers, several Intruders.

Batman found his Tomcat parked on the far side of the Hornets, Number 232, her tail emblazoned with the blue snake emblem of the Vipers. The crew chief signaled one of the yellow, flat-topped tractors called mules into position to hook her up. He looked over his shoulder as Batman mounted the boarding steps, grinned, and gave him a thumb's-up. "Kill us a MiG, Lieutenant," the chief yelled above the roar of another pair of Intruders vaulting off the catapults forward.

"That's why we're here," Batman replied. He swung into the cockpit and began fastening the harness. "Time to earn our pay." Malibu climbed in behind him.

Batman thought about the coming combat and felt the excitement grow.

For most of his adult life, Batman had been training and practicing for one thing and one thing only: combat! Everything— the practice ACMs, Tombstone's lectures, the hours of study, his

training at Pensacola, and later flying Tomcats with a RAG—
everything had been preparation for the moment when he would
vault into the sky to face some enemy pilot one on one. He was
ready, *knew* he was ready as he felt the jerk of the tractor pulling
his aircraft forward toward its position in line aft of the catapults.

1602 hours
Tomcat 205, Point Whiskey

The KA-6D filled the sky, a huge gray whale seemingly only
yards in front of and above Tombstone's cockpit. The F-14 looked
like a fish hooked on the tanker's line as the KA-6D topped off the
fighter's tanks.

"Roger, Fox Echo Two," Tombstone radioed the larger aircraft.
"Casting off and breaking to starboard at three . . . two . . .
one . . . *break!*"

The Tomcat detached its fueling probe from the tanker's basket
and gently dropped away to the right. Each of the fighters was
taking its turn refueling over Point Whiskey, waiting the final
signal to go in.

The staging area for the attack was over Yonghung Bay, one
hundred miles east of Wonsan Harbor. There was nothing below
the slowly circling aircraft to mark the spot but empty water. It
was identified as Point Whiskey. From his vantage point at thirty
thousand feet, Tombstone could just make out the gray blur of
Korea's east coast mountain spine, the Taebaek Sanmaek, through
a low-lying, hazy murk. At this altitude, the weather was perfect,
with scattered clouds below at ten thousand feet and visibility
unlimited. A high, thin layer of wispy clouds rushed past
overhead, close enough to touch. Tombstone ignored the specta-
cle.

It wouldn't be long now.

The two Intruder squadrons circled halfway between Tombstone's position and the sea. He could make out their stub-winged,
cruciform shapes far below. They'd been launched first since it
had taken them longer to make the almost one-hundred-fifty-mile
flight from the *Jefferson*.

Not counting the KA-6Ds, the Hawkeyes circling farther out at
sea, and the electronic warfare EA-6B Prowlers now jamming
Korean radars, there were forty aircraft in the attack, five
squadrons minus six planes with maintenance downchecks. The

Alpha Strike, designated "Marauder" and composed of two Intruder squadrons and two Hornet squadrons, would go in with bombs and missiles. They would be covered by eight of VF-95's Tomcats flying TACCAP under the call sign Shotgun.

The remaining F-14 squadron, the War Eagles of VF-97, had drawn Homeplate BARCAP, sitting out the raid while they protected the carrier, much to their vociferous and energetic disgust. Their skipper, "Made it" Bayerly, had been furious when he'd heard. "That just goes to show what having an admiral for an uncle will do for you!" Bayerly had said to Tombstone.

The words might have been spoken in jest, but Tombstone had heard the sting behind them. Was he *ever* going to get clear of that Jonah?

"We're getting a good vector from the Hawkeyes, Tombstone," Snowball said over the intercom. "It's a straight shot into Wonsan from here."

"Sounds good to me, Snowy."

He was glad that Snowball Newcombe had decided to stick it out as his RIO. To have quit before this op would have been an admission of cowardice, and the decision could have finished the man's career. Snowball's next assignment would have been at the radar console of a Hawkeye . . . if he was lucky.

"So," Tombstone said. "Any sign of the bad guys?"

"Lots of radar fuzz," Snowball replied. "The EA-6Bs are jamming them, but they know we're here. No clear targets yet."

"Keep an eye on them. I imagine it'll get pretty busy soon."

He checked the F-14's weapon load: two Phoenix, one Sparrow, and four Sidewinder missiles, plus 676 rounds for the six-barreled M61 Vulcan cannon.

Two days ago the sky had seemed to be filled with MiGs, turning and burning above the Sea of Japan. They were probably waiting now, somewhere ahead beyond the twelve-mile limit, or spooling up their engines on the airfield outside of Wonsan. He wondered if the Tomcats' combat loads would be enough when the time came.

He turned his mind away from the thought and concentrated on his flying. It was Batman's turn to refuel now. In minutes, they should be getting the word to proceed.

Tombstone was surprised to realize that he wasn't afraid. He'd thought, after losing Coyote, that he would be.

An aide held up a telephone. "Mr. Secretary? For you. Priority and scrambled."

The Secretary of State got up from the table and walked to where the aide waited. The President watched in silence as Schellenberg identified himself, then listened.

"Right, Frank. Good work," he said after a moment. He returned the phone, then turned to face the President. "That's it." His manner was jubilant. "It came through ten minutes ago. They've agreed to talk!"

"Where?" Caldwell asked. "When?"

"Special MAC meeting this Friday. Kim's top men will be there."

"Well, that's something, anyway," the President said. The words sounded hollow in a room strangely empty. Besides the few aides and the Air Force major carrying the football, only the President, the Secretary of State, and General Caldwell remained in the Situation Room. The others were asleep or, as was probably the case with Marlowe and Grimes, working late at their own offices, waiting for word.

"Hell," Caldwell said. "A MAC meeting isn't going to settle anything."

"It's a start, General," Schellenberg replied. "We have to start *somewhere*."

The Military Armistice Committee had been created at the end of the Korean War, its purpose to keep lines of negotiation open with the PDRK. For almost forty years, though, it had served as little more than a conduit for P'yongyang propaganda and a forum for complaints by both sides.

There'd been plenty to complain about over the years. Since July of 1953, 89 American servicemen had been killed in various incidents along Korea's DMZ, and 132 wounded.

And now, for the second time in history, the seizure of an American intelligence ship in international waters. Nearly five hundred MAC meetings had been called over the years. Little had ever been resolved, and the President doubted that this one would be any different. The Americans would protest, the PDRK representatives would bluster and threaten and probably walk out.

"Jim, our planes are ready to go in." He looked at the clock on the wall showing Tokyo time. If Winged Talon was on schedule, the American planes were fifteen minutes from Korean airspace. "They're on the way *now!*"

The grin dropped from the Secretary's face. "Mr. President! You can't let them continue the attack. Call them off!"

"Good God, Jim . . ."

"Mr. President, this is an extraordinarily delicate situation. I told the Chinese ambassador personally . . . I gave him my *word* that we wanted a quick and honorable end to this . . . incident. If we attack now, we'll have lost the confidence not only of the North Koreans, but of the Chinese as well!"

"Just like the bastards to wait until the last minute," Caldwell said, glancing up at the Tokyo clock. He didn't make clear whether he was referring to the Chinese or the North Koreans. "You think they want us to attack?"

A dreadful suspicion rose in the President's mind. If the North Koreans could tell the world that the United States had launched a bombing raid after promising a negotiated settlement . . .

Caldwell looked alarmed. "Mr. President! You can't call them back! Not—"

"Damn it, Amos, I have to!" World opinion would not be kind if the bombers went in. The President turned to an aide. "Get me on the satellite net. I want a direct line to Admiral Bainbridge. *Now!*"

As he was waiting, the President closed his eyes and thought about the pilots already closing on the North Korean coast. After this, they'd be mad enough to vote Democratic in the next elections.

The aide held out a telephone. "Admiral Bainbridge on the line, Mr. President."

He accepted the receiver. "Wesley? This is the President. . . ."

1612 hours
Hornet 301, off the North Korean coast

Commander Marty French, CO of VFA 161 and Deputy CAG of *Jefferson*'s air wing, touched his gloved fingers to his helmet, not quite believing what he'd just heard. "Homeplate, this is Marauder Leader. Say again your last, over."

"Marauder Leader, Homeplate," Marusko's voice crackled in his ears. "RTB. I say again, RTB."

"Return to base?" Another voice had cut in over the frequency.

The other aviators would be listening in. "What in the frigging hell are they pulling?"

"Hey, I think my radio's bad," someone else said. "Don't think I can hear any—"

"Clear the air!" French's voice snapped. His right hand tightened on the stick of his F/A-18 Hornet, feeling the nimble aircraft's responsiveness. *Damn it to hell!* "All Marauders, cut the chatter! The orders are: abort mission, return to base, execute immediate!"

He heard the radioed acknowledgments from each squadron leader, some sulky, some puzzled. With a new and swelling anger, Frenchie French pulled his stick left and dropped into a broad, slow turn to port.

The Korean coast receded behind him.

1615 hours
Tomcat 205

"Hey, Skipper? We got company!"

Tombstone's eyes automatically flicked along the horizon. "What do you have, Snowball?"

"Multiple bogies at two-zero-three, range three-two miles. Angels twenty. Closing in excess of five hundred."

"*Two*-zero-three . . . ?" That bearing put them southeast of Alpha Strike, coming in from the side instead of from behind. Tombstone had halfway expected that MiGs out of Wonsan might come out after the American strike force, but these bogies were coming from a different direction entirely.

"It's Kosong, Tombstone!" Snowball said. The edge of raw excitement was back in the RIO's voice. "They're coming from Kosong!"

"What's the count?"

"I make it . . . eight bogies, two-zero-three at three-zero!"

Thirty miles. Two and a half minutes at Mach 1.

"Marauder Leader, this is Shotgun Leader—"

"We have them, Shotgun!" Marty French replied. "Homeplate has been informed. Heads up, people, the gomers want to come out and play!"

"Shotgun Leader to Shotguns," Tombstone said. "Form on me for a break to starboard. Ready . . . break!"

Eight F-14s dipped their starboard wings in unison, swinging off their southeasterly course to align themselves with the distant, oncoming bogies, between the bombers and the oncoming MiGs.

"Target lock!" Snowball said.

"Hold on, Snowball. Let's do it by the book. Marauder Leader, this is Shotgun. We have target lock. Request clearance to fire, over."

"Shotgun, Marauder Leader. Wait one."

The ROEs for this mission had been to return fire if fired upon, but that had been assuming that they would be attacked over Korea. Things were suddenly a lot murkier since they'd been called off before entering Korean airspace.

Tombstone listened in on the crackle of radio chatter as the Deputy CAG passed on the request for ROE clarification back to the *Jefferson*. He heard the answer come through seconds later. "Marauders, this is Homeplate. ROEs stand as given. You are clear to fire if fired upon. Over."

"You heard the man, Marauders," French said. "All units, hold your fire."

"Hey, Tombstone," Snowball said. "This ain't funny! I'm reading twelve bogies now, twelve bogies inbound, one-eight miles, five hundred twelve knots!"

"Tombstone, this is Batman!" He sounded excited. "What gives, Skipper? These guys mean *business*!"

"Hold position, Batman."

"I'm holding! Like a sitting duck I'm holding!"

"Shotgun, Shotgun Leader." He was surprised at how calm his own voice was. "Let's get into combat spread. Move out!"

The aircraft began drifting apart. In the loose deuce formation favored by American Naval aviators, each pair of F-14s became a team of "shooter" and "eyeball" during a head-on combat approach, flying one and a half miles apart and separated by five thousand feet of altitude.

Tombstone glanced out the right side of his cockpit. Batman's Tomcat, the number 232 prominent on its nose, drifted a few yards off his wingtip.

"Batman? Tombstone."

"The Batman copies, Tombstone."

"You take the eyeball."

There was a moment's silence. "Hey, Stoney! You got your kill—"

"Can it, Two-three-two." Tombstone had wrestled with the question already. Batman was too eager. That all-important first shot couldn't be screwed up by a too-eager shooter. "Take your position."

"Two-three-two, affirmative."

The aircraft slid apart, Tombstone dropping back behind his wingman and drifting off to the left.

"How you want to do this, Tombstone?" his RIO asked.

"Sparrow first," Tombstone replied. It was an almost automatic decision. At five hundred pounds, Sparrows were a lot heavier than the Sidewinders, and the Tomcat picked up a weight bonus each time it loosed one. Phoenix missiles were bigger and heavier still . . . but expensive, and best saved for targets at longer range.

And like most Tomcat pilots, Tombstone did not fully trust the cranky Sparrows and wanted to hold his more reliable Sidewinders in reserve.

"Target," Snowball said, as Tombstone heard the warble of a target lock tone in his headset. "Lead bogie now at one-three miles."

"Batman, Tombstone. Let's sweep around to the left a bit."

"Two-three-two, affirmative." Batman's Tomcat, visible now as a tiny gray toy against the sky a mile up and almost two miles ahead, began slipping sideways across Tombstone's line of flight. Tombstone matched the maneuver, maintaining the separation between the two aircraft.

So he's in a snit, Tombstone thought. Let him be. He'll have targets enough any moment now.

The range closed like lightning.

"I got visual!" said Price Taggart, in the 203 Tomcat. "Blue bandits! Blue bandits! Here they come . . . !"

"Launch, launch!" Batman said. "Two-three-two has visual on bandit launch."

"Confirmed," Malibu chimed in. "Two missiles inbound. Two-three-two, one-zero miles."

"Shotgun Leader to Homeplate. We have been fired upon. TACCAP engaging."

"Homeplate copies, Shotgun Leader," a voice replied. "You have weapons free—"

"Bandits! Bandits!" someone yelled over the radio. "We got new bandits, closing from three-one-one!"

"What . . . *new* bandits?" Tombstone asked.

"He's right, Stoney! I got 'em too! I make it . . . ten bogies at three-one-one, angels twenty, nine-zero miles. Closing at five hundred plus!"

"Three-one-one? Hell, that's behind us?"

"That's what I mean, Stoney! It's our friends out of Wonsan!"

In one blinding instant of realization, Tombstone saw the trap. Twelve North Korean fighters had vectored northeast out of Kosong to engage the American planes on their way back to the carrier. And while the F-14s were dogfighting with the Kosong group, those MiGs waiting over Wonsan had followed, coming in from the rear.

The odds had suddenly turned much worse.

CHAPTER 14

Only minutes remained before the North Korean reinforcements would arrive. Tombstone listened for the warble of the Sparrow in his headphones. "I have tone."

"Shotgun Leader, Two-three-two!" Batman's voice carried the excitement now. "You have launch clearance. You're clear for launch."

Tombstone's finger came down on the firing button. "Fox one!"

The Sparrow dropped from the Tomcat's belly. To Tombstone it felt as though the aircraft was leaping into the sky. The missile had the appearance of a dazzling flare weaving toward the horizon on the end of a twisting column of white smoke.

"Good luck," Snowball said. "He's breaking right! Stay on him. . . ."

Tombstone moved the stick right. The worst thing about Sparrows was their passive homing system; the firing aircraft had to keep the enemy spotlit by its AWG-9 radar so that the Sparrow could track the target.

"*Shit!*" Snowball snapped. "Break left, Stoney. *Left!*"

The Tomcat rolled to port, right wing clawing the sky. Tombstone glimpsed a pinpoint of light, wavering as it streaked toward him.

"They've got radar lock!" Snowball yelled.

Tombstone held the Tomcat's rolling plunge, trading altitude for speed. The numbers on his HUD's altimeter reading trickled away . . . fifteen thousand feet . . . thirteen . . . eleven . . .

Firing the chaff dispenser with a vicious one-two-three stab of his thumb, he hauled back on the stick. Blackness closed in on him, narrowing his vision to a tiny blob of light as the 8-G pull-away drained the blood from his head. Something streaked past his starboard wing, moving too fast to focus on.

"Snowy!" He had to grunt hard to force each word out against the G-force. "Where's . . . missile?"

There was no answer from his RIO. The maneuver must have put Snowball to sleep. Tombstone rammed the throttles forward to full afterburner and clawed for altitude once more.

"Snowball! Wake the hell up back there!"

"Uh! I'm here! I'm here. What—"

"Where's that missile?"

There was a pause as the RIO worked his controls. "Gone! He missed us! Take bearing . . . take three-one-zero!"

Tombstone swung onto the new heading, still climbing. Above him the two squadrons, MiGs and Tomcats, were merging, interpenetrating, filling the sky with aircraft and the white crisscross of contrails.

1618 hours
Tomcat 232

Batman swung right, picking up speed in a shallow dive. The MiG he'd been eyeballing for Tombstone jinked hard to the left, falling away in a barrel roll as the Sparrow missile streaked toward it. The Sparrow missed wide and vanished into the blue, its lock broken by Tombstone's maneuver.

Other MiGs exploded past Batman's F-14, each pair locked in a rigid side-by-side formation the Americans called the welded wing. There was no time to line up a shot now, not with the targets so close, moving so fast. The best he could hope for was to slide past the enemy planes and come down behind them. In a dogfight, every pilot's goal was to get on the other guy's six, square in the rear and looking up his tailpipe.

He saw the flash as one of the oncoming MiGs launched a missile, saw the burning pinpoint of the missile's exhaust as it dipped, then began climbing toward him.

At close range, it would be a heat-seeker. Batman triggered a flare, then pulled back on the stick, hauling the F-14 into a vertical, twisting climb straight up.

"Where is it, Malibu?"

"It went ballistic! We're clear!"

"All *right*! Let's rock 'n' roll!"

"Where's Tombstone, man?" Malibu shouted. "I lost him!"

"I don't know! Right now we have other things to worry about!" He brought the F-14 out of its climb, completing the Immelmann with a half-twist that brought them out two thousand feet above the Korean aircraft . . . and behind them.

"Wheeooo!" Malibu shouted. "This is what I call a target-rich environment!"

"Roger that!"

MiGs were everywhere, twelve of them now against eight American aircraft. The F-14s were swinging around behind the MiGs, locking on with heat-seeker AIM-9L Sidewinders, engaging in earnest now that the Koreans had upped the ante. There was a radioed chorus of "Fox two! Fox two!" from several of the pilots, and white contrails scrawled themselves across blue sky.

"Let's get in the game, Batman!"

"Right, Malibu. Can you see Tombstone?"

"Negative, negative. Was he hit?"

Ahead, there was a flash, and the delta wing shape of a MiG sprouted flame and a writhing coil of black smoke. The left wing crumpled, spilling fragments in a fiery spray. "Splash one MiG!" someone called over the radio. "Two-oh-four, splash one!"

"Watch it, Price. Two on your five!"

"Whatcha waiting for, Batman?" Malibu asked.

"I want to know where our wingie is!" Batman was twisting from side to side in the cockpit, searching the sea below. "Shotgun Leader, this is Tomcat Two-three-two. Where the hell are you, Tombstone?"

"Twelve K and climbing, Batman," Tombstone's voice replied. Batman felt an inner surge of relief. For a moment he'd wondered if the gomer missile had connected. "Comin' back in."

"Roger that, Tombstone. Do you want assist? Over."

"Negative." The word was a grunt against high-Gs. "Engage . . . on your own!"

"Music to my ears." Another MiG burst into flame as a Sidewinder connected. "Right, Malibu! Let's goose it!" Batman said.

"We got at least ten more bogies inbound, three-one-oh at seven-zero miles."

"Then we've got time to lower the odds a bit more before they get here. Hang on!"

After the first pass, the MiG formation had scattered in every direction. Delta shapes twisted and turned in the cold, blue sky.

Contrails crawled like scrawled writing far above the sea as aircraft jockeyed for position.

Batman heard the sharp, sometimes shrill bursts of the Americans' radio calls. "This is Two-two-one!" That was Tom Hoffner, running name Snake. "I got two on my tail! Two on my tail!"

"Hang on, Snake!" Dragon Ashly was Snake's wingman. "I'm on him!"

"Get him off, Dragon! Get him off!"

"Too close for missiles! Goin' for guns!"

"I got one," Batman told Malibu. The F-14 nosed over, picking up speed as it entered the twisting cloud of fighters. "Lining him up!"

"Batman!" Hoffner yelled. "Help get this guy off me!"

"No joy! No joy!" Army's voice threatened to break with excitement or frustration. "Guns jammed! Break left, Snake! Break left!"

The chaos ahead resolved itself as Batman closed. An American F-14, tail number 221, rolled away to the left, a MiG-21 matching him roll for roll. A second Tomcat overshot the MiG, sweeping past both aircraft in an effort to line up for a shot.

Batman dropped into the slot above and behind the MiG just as the MiG fired. A white contrail arced forward from under the MiG's wing, sliding up the F-14's starboard tailpipe and detonating in a fiery blast. Batman saw fragments of the Tomcat's engine spraying in all directions as the aircraft dropped into a hard, spiraling roll.

"I'm hit! I'm hit!"

"Mayday! Mayday! Tomcat Two-two-one is hit and going down!"

"Shit, Batman!" Malibu called. "They got Snake!"

"And we'll nail the bastard who did it!" He slammed the engines to afterburner and rolled in for the kill.

1619 hours
Tomcat 205

It took Tombstone less than a minute to reenter the fight, but in aerial combat even thirty seconds was an eternity. He'd just dropped into swept-wing, high-speed configuration and was rocketing back into the battle when he heard the mayday call for Snake.

"This is Shotgun Leader!" he called. "Did our boys get clear?"

"Tomcat Two-oh-three." That was Ron "Price" Taggart's

aircraft. "Affirmative! I see one . . . correction! I see two chutes! Good chutes! Good chutes!"

"Copy, Two-oh-three! Homeplate, Homeplate, this is Shotgun Leader. We have two men down, good chutes. Request SAR, over."

"Copy, Shotgun Leader. Be advised ready helo has been deployed."

Tombstone banked left and looked down toward the sea. He could see the chutes himself now, a pair of white flecks drifting toward their own shadows on the blue-gray water.

"Ho, Tombstone!" Snowball yelled. "We got a pair of blue bandits, zero-four-five, range one mile!"

He whipped his head around. "I see 'em. How much longer before the gomer cavalry gets here?"

"Range now five-one miles, Tombstone. Maybe four minutes."

Four minutes. Tombstone was genuinely torn. He could take a shot at the MiGs approaching from Wonsan now with his long-ranged Phoenix missile. But lining up the shot and locking on would take time, and his squadron needed help *now*.

His second decision was harder. Snake and his RIO Zombie were in the drink. Memories of losing Coyote and Mardi Gras surfaced, painful and sharp. Should he rejoin the squadron or circle the downed flyers until the SAR helo arrived?

Rugged as the choice was, he actually had little option. His running mates were outnumbered and needed every weapon they could muster for the fight. As had been the case with Coyote and Mardi Gras, there wasn't much he could do for Snake and Zombie now.

"Okay, Snowy! First things first!" He swung the Tomcat into a broad turn, sweeping in on the tails of the pair of MiGs to the northeast. "C'mon . . . c'mon . . ." The pipper on his HUD drifted toward the right-hand MiG. Both Korean aircraft were turning now, twisting to starboard in an attempt to cut past Tombstone's line of flight and spoil his shot. "*Lock*, damn you . . ."

1620 hours
Tomcat 232

Batman held the stick hard over, tracking the MiG as it tried to turn away from him. The square of his targeting pipper slowly tracked across the HUD until it closed with the target. There was a flicker as the square became a circle, ringing the fleeing MiG and tagging it with a small "M" for "missile."

"Yeah!" Malibu shouted. "Target lock . . ."

Batman heard the warble in his headset. "Got him. Surprise, you gomer son of a bitch." He touched the launch trigger. "Fox two!"

The Sidewinder dropped from the Tomcat on a trail of white smoke, hung suspended beneath the wings for a moment, then rocketed ahead with a rush which left Batman's F-14 standing still. Warned, possibly, by his wingman, the North Korean aircraft began pulling up, but too soon, too soon. . . .

"He's jinking, Batman!"

"Yeah, he screwed it. You can run, son, but you cannot hide!"

"Watch it, man. I think you made him mad!" The MiG pilot kicked in his afterburner.

It was exactly the wrong thing to do.

1620 hours
CIC, U.S.S. *Thomas Jefferson*

"The Wonsan group is closing, Admiral," CAG said. "At least ten aircraft . . . probably more if they're using welded wing. Looks like it was a setup."

"I agree. They figured to catch our bombers while our TAC-CAP was engaged to the south."

"Admiral, I recommend we let the F/A-18s engage."

"The A-6s still need cover."

"We could detach one squadron. VFA-173 can shepherd the Intruders home. VFA-161 can drop their loads and mix it up."

"Approved. Your show, CAG."

Marusko nodded. An aide handed him a microphone, which he held to his mouth. "Marauder Leader, Marauder Leader, this is Homeplate. Do you copy, over?"

Commander Marty "Frenchie" French's voice came over the CIC speakers. "Hornet Three-oh-one copies, Homeplate. Go ahead."

"You've got friends coming in from Wonsan. Javelins are clear to execute ordnance release and engage."

"Copy, Homeplate. We'll show the turkeys how it's done."

CAG and Admiral Magruder exchanged smiles. "Turkey" was a less than complimentary Naval aviator's slang term for the large and heavy F-14 Tomcats.

There was nothing the Hornet pilots would enjoy more than showing up their Tomcat rivals.

1620 hours
Hornet 301

"Okay, Javelins," Deputy CAG French said. "Let's declare war on Greenpeace!"

French touched the weapons release switch and felt his Hornet leap into the sky as ten thousand pounds of ordnance dropped away, "bombing whales" as aviators referred to it, which explained the jibe at Greenpeace. The international conservation group had crossed swords and lawyers with the U.S. Navy more than once over issues like Trident missile tests and nuclear weapons aboard ships, and dropping bombs into open ocean was jokingly viewed by Naval aviators as retaliation.

"Damn the whales!" Lieutenant Gary Grabiak misquoted. "Full speed ahead!"

Jettisoning the Hornets' stores was wasteful necessity. The F/A-18s, faster, smaller, and more maneuverable than the Tomcats flying cover, had been loaded down with two-thousand-pound Mark 84 bombs, Maverick missiles, and Rockeye ordnance clusters which made ACM impossible. By dropping all of their air-to-ground weapons into the sea, however, they could now engage in the dogfight that was developing above and behind them. Each Hornet carried only two Sidewinders in wingtip pylons, but those, together with their M61 20-mm cannon, would be more than enough to even the odds against the outnumbered American aircraft. The A-6 Intruders, relatively helpless in a dogfight, would continue flying low and slow on a straight line back toward the *Jefferson* with the F/A-18s of VFA-173 as escort.

One by one, the Hornets of VFA-161 reported their ordnance cleared.

"Right, Javelins," Marty said. "Time to turn and burn!"

The nimble, twin-tailed single-seater vaulted skyward under his touch, afterburner flaring.

1621 hours
Tomcat 205

Tombstone was concentrating so hard on the MiG symbol crawling just ahead of the targeting pipper on his HUD that he almost didn't see the second MiG, barreling in at him head to head. In a flash, a dot hovering at the edge of visibility to his left suddenly swelled into the delta-winged angles of a North Korean MiG.

"Yow!" Snowball yelled into the intercom as Tombstone broke hard to the right. The two aircraft passed each other a scant hundred feet apart with a combined speed of better than Mach 2. Though the encounter lasted but a fraction of a second, Tombstone had the feeling that time was dragging out in a surreal slow motion. He had time to observe every detail of the other plane as it passed, wing down and cockpit dipped toward him, the twisting patterns of the green and brown camouflage paint scheme, the red star on a red-and-blue-bordered white disk on wings and tail. Tombstone could see the other pilot, head twisted around to look back at him. For that frozen instant, two pilots stared at each other across a narrow gulf, the shock of recognition, of unreality almost palpable.

"Tally-ho!" Tombstone yelled. "I'm on him!"

He'd lost his chance at the first MiG, so now he went for the second, holding the Tomcat in its hard-right twist, dropping his right wing sharply until he was in a hard six-G inverted turn. Snowball's breath rasped at him over the intercom in short, hard puffs. He lost sight of the enemy MiG for a moment, then reacquired it as he came out of the turn. The North Korean plane was a tiny speck over a mile away, turning hard from right to left across Tombstone's nose.

He let the F-14 drop, hauling the stick back to the left as he slipped into a split-S to bring him around and onto the MiG's tail. He concentrated on his heads-up display, watching the pipper close with the HUD's target symbol. The enemy MiG was trying to duck inside Tombstone's turn. The guy had almost made it too, but he'd put just a bit too much space between Tombstone's aircraft and his own before he made his move.

"Bad move, pal." Tombstone thumbed the firing switch and a Sidewinder streaked from under his port wing. "Fox two! Fox two!"

"Aw, fer cryin' out loud, Tombstone! You didn't have a lock . . . !"

Tombstone realized the mistake the instant his finger closed on the firing switch. Too eager, he'd triggered the Sidewinder just an instant before its sensors had locked on the target. The heat seeker streaked into the cold air now, passing well behind the MiG and into emptiness.

1621 hours
Tomcat 232

For Batman, it seemed to take forever for the burning contrail of his Sidewinder to crawl the distance between his Tomcat and the targeted MiG. When the enemy pilot cut in his afterburners, though, Batman knew he had him.

Twisting as he climbed, the MiG pilot was attempting to break contact with the missile with an Immelmann, flipping onto his back and then righting with a half roll. The missile followed with grim and inhumanly precise determination.

The Korean pilot must have known that death was stalking him. At the last possible moment, a dazzling pinpoint of light dropped away from the fleeing MiG, trailing behind on a streamer of smoke and falling. The Sidewinder, racing up from below, wavered for an instant as though trying to make up its tiny electronic mind. . . .

But the MiG's afterburners decided the matter. The Sidewinder ignored the flare and slid smoothly up the MiG's tailpipe.

There was a flash, and then flames were boiling from the rear half of the stricken Korean jet. The tail vanished in a fireball of exploding fuel. The remnants of the aircraft were transformed into a tumbling mass of flaming wreckage, arcing out of the sky on the end of a billowing pillar of black smoke. There was no parachute, no sign that the pilot had been able to eject.

"Splash one MiG!" Batman yelled, the excitement welling up from inside as sharp, as intense as a sexual release. *"Splash one MiG!"*

Malibu screeched a rebel yell on the tactical frequency. "Way to go, compadre! You hear that, everybody? Chalk one for Two three-two! Ol' Batman got his kill!"

Batman spun his Tomcat into a tight roll, a *victory* roll, and watched sun, sea, and sky whip around him.

1622 hours
Tomcat 205

The MiG was breaking left, slipping clear of Tombstone's targeting pipper and circling inside the F-14's turning radius. Tombstone still couldn't believe he'd missed.

"Tombstone!" Snowball called. "What's the matter? Tombstone!"

"Nothing!" He pulled the F-14 left. The MiG was trying to get on his six, and Tombstone went into a tight turn to counter the move.

"Shotgun Leader, this is Homeplate," CAG's voice called over the radio. "Be advised that the Javelins have dropped their stores and are joining the party."

"Roger that," Tombstone replied. Where was that MiG? *Damn,* that guy could turn! "Listen up, Shotguns," he said. "We've got friendlies inbound. Don't get trigger happy and mistake them for MiGs."

"Shotgun Lead, this is Two-five-one."

Tomcat 251 was Lieutenant Gary "Dragon" Ashly's aircraft. Snake had been his wingman. "Go ahead, Two-five-one."

"Leader, I have Snake and Zombie spotted. Request permission to drop to the deck and cover them."

Tombstone checked with Snowball before replying. The radar picture was confused, and made more so by the Americans' own jamming efforts, but it appeared that the Tomcats were holding the Kosong squadron and could continue to do so until the Hornets arrived.

And the Hornets and Tomcats together would be able to take the Wonsan squadron once they arrived. "Roger, Two-five-one." It was what he'd wanted to do himself as soon as Hoffner had been shot down. His own guilt over Coyote was still riding him. "You're CAP for Snake and Zombie until SAR gets here."

"Much obliged, Tombstone. Two-five-one is going on the deck."

Tombstone checked his clock. It would be another twenty minutes before the SAR helo arrived, and 251 could refuel off a Texaco if he started to run dry.

If he could keep from screwing up again, Tombstone thought, they might just pull out of this thing in one piece.

1622 hours
MiG number 444, Star Leader

Major Pak Dae-Lee scowled through his visor at the smeared, green-on-black hash on his radar screen. The MiG's radar, what the Americans called Jay Bird, was rugged and reliable but not particularly powerful. There were American electronic warfare aircraft in the area, the EA-6B aircraft called Prowlers, which could lay down a blanket of electronic interference that was almost impossible to see through unless you were right on top of the target.

Getting right on top of the target was precisely what Pak planned to do.

Major Pak represented the elite of his country's air force. Two years at Dushanbe and Moscow as a student, two years more with a training cadre instructing Libyan pilot trainees, and thousands of hours flying with his own countrymen had made him the very best of his country's air warriors.

He had proven that two days earlier, when his flight had jumped the American Tomcats off Wonsan. It was his missile which had opened the dogfight, his missile which had downed a Yankee interceptor. The memory of that victory drove him forward now, as Star Attack Group rocketed across the Yonghung Man in pursuit of the American planes.

As much as anything else, Pak craved recognition. He pictured the smug self-assurance, the patronizing smiles, the condescending attitudes of his Soviet instructors during his tour at Dushanbe. The unspoken, often the *spoken*, assumption of his Russian instructors had been that "foreign slant-eyes" like Pak were adequate as pilots . . . but nothing more.

Adequate! How many Soviet pilots could lay claim to flaming an American F-14? He looked to left and right, noting that the other aircraft of the attack group were still with him. Airspeed was close to six hundred knots now, their altitude eighteen thousand feet. Somewhere ahead, very close now, were the American aircraft, pinned against the sky by Moon Attack Group out of Kosong to the south.

This part of the plan had been his. The MiG-21 was inherently inferior to the Yankee F-14s, which could out-climb, out-run, out-last, and carry more ordnance than the smaller Soviet-designed, 1950s-era aircraft. The only way the MiGs could win was to gain an overwhelming numerical superiority, preferably by isolating part of the American strike force. And this Pak had proceeded to do once it was clear that the Americans were not going to penetrate North Korean air space. It had been his suggestion to launch the Kosong strike force to engage the enemy's tactical air patrol, drawing them off so that his force could hit either the bombers or the American fighters, whichever gave the Koreans the best odds. Outbound from Wonsan, he'd decided that the F-14s made the best target. From what little he could see through the Yankee jamming, the F-14s were already outnumbered in their dogfight against the Kosong MiGs.

And he could grab one other advantage as well. "Star Group, this is Leader. Prepare to execute Plan Dagger." He listened for a moment to acknowledgments from three of the other aircraft. Then, "Execute!"

Pak pushed the stick forward, and his MiG-21 nosed over, picking up speed as it headed for the Sea of Japan. His wingman and eight other aircraft, half of the entire group and the best pilots in his command, followed.

It was always dangerous dividing one's forces in the face of the enemy, and splitting into two sections risked defeat in detail. But the situation demanded daring. The Americans knew the Wonsan MiGs were coming, but their exact numbers would still be uncertain. It was just possible that ten of the Wonsan MiGs could be lost by approaching at wave-top height, hidden from the American radar planes in the scatter from the ocean surface. Perhaps this way, Pak thought, his force could retain a small edge of surprise. Then they would isolate some of the American aircraft. . . .

CHAPTER 15

1623 hours
Tomcat 232

Batman's RIO opened the intercom. "Here they come. I read twelve bogies inbound at angels eighteen, eight miles, speed six hundred plus."

Still too far for Sidewinders, but that would change soon enough. "Let's drop our Sparrow. Get a lock, Malibu."

"I'm working on it. . . . Target lock, bearing two-eight-five. You got tone."

"I hear it." He brought the aircraft five degrees right. Malibu's targeting radar covered a wide swath ahead, but he wanted to keep it simple and point his Tomcat dead on at the enemy target. His finger touched the firing switch and the heavy Sparrow jolted free of the F-14. "Fox one!"

1623 hours
Tomcat 251

Lieutenant Gary Ashly pulled up one hundred feet above the gray chop of the ocean, his Tomcat's wings extended straight out from the fuselage. The air was so heavy with water at this altitude that thick curls of vapor bled from his wings and tail as he circled at low speed, searching for the downed men. His RIO, Snoops Whitridge, saw the dye marker first, a yellow stain on the water half a mile to starboard.

"Shotgun Leader, Tomcat Two-five-one. We have a dye marker in sight."

"Roger that, Two-five-one," Snowball Newcombe's voice replied. "Homeplate says SAR is on the way."

"Copy, Leader." Dragon opened the intercom channel. "Snoop? Let's see if we can raise anything on the SAR channel."

"I'm on it, Dragon. This is . . . *shit!* Kick it, Dragon! *Kick it!*"

The Tomcat's afterburners roared in instinctive response to the RIO's shout. "Talk to me, Snoop!"

"Bandits at two-eight-five on the deck. *They're on the deck!*" There was a flash as one of the MiGs launched . . . then another. "Launch, Dragon! I have visual on a launch!"

Sluggishly, the Tomcat's nose came up. . . .

1624 hours
MiG number 444, Star Leader

Major Pak could not have asked for a better shot if he'd planned it out in advance. Skimming in across the sea practically at wave-top height, he'd not gotten a clear radar return from the American F-14 until he was a mile and a half away. He'd been lucky on two counts. The Yankees still seemed unaware of his group's presence, and it was pure chance which put the lone American Tomcat directly in his path.

From a mile away, Pak could easily see the F-14's large body, could clearly see the wings in their full-forward, low-speed configuration as it banked in a turn from right to left in front of Pak's MiG.

Pak had thoroughly studied American aircraft and tactics during his training assignments in the Soviet Union. Tomcats, he knew, had the attitude of their wings controlled by the aircraft's computer. While this could be overridden by the pilot, usually it was the computer which determined when the wings would be extended, a decision based almost entirely on the aircraft's speed and attitude.

While it was an efficient way of gaining extra lift in low-speed, low-energy maneuvers, this high-tech application carried with it a significant drawback. He could glance at a Tomcat's wings and take a good guess at the size and placement of the aircraft's maneuvering envelope—that invisible cone of air in front of the plane determined by speed, lift, and handling characteristics where the aircraft would be within the next few seconds. The American aircraft was in a hard, left-hand turn at less than three hundred knots, its pilot holding it just short of a stall in a mushy, nose-up loiter.

Pak squeezed the firing trigger and an Atoll missile slid off the wing in a rush of smoke and flame. A fraction of a second later, Pak's wingman triggered a second missile. Ahead, the American fighter rolled, aware now of its sudden peril.

Too late. Pak's missile arrowed into the Tomcat squarely between the two upright tailfins. A flash sent chunks of metal spinning as flame ballooned from ruptured fuel lines. Then the entire aircraft was a mass of flame as the fuel tanks blew; the second Atoll vanished into the firestorm and exploded, completing the destruction, scattering tiny fragments of debris across a mile-long footprint of ocean. Seconds later, Pak's fighters howled through the boiling trail of smoke which marked their second kill of the day.

"Victory to the Fatherland!" Pak yelled over the radio. The raw adrenaline throb of combat fury throbbed in his veins. "Now . . . with me, comrades!" Afterburners shrieking, the North Korean aircraft angled up to join the dogfight overhead.

1624 hours
Tomcat 232

"That's two!" Batman exulted as orange flame blossomed in the distance and Malibu abruptly lost the tracking lock on the AWG-9. In the next second, though, the savage joy was wiped away as a pair of MiGs dropped onto his tail, forcing him to cut left, then right, weaving madly.

"They're right on our six, Batman," Malibu yelled. The Tomcat's airframe shuddered and roared with its twistings. "Time to get out of Dodge."

"We're outa there!" He cut in the Tomcat's afterburners and pulled up sharply, rocketing straight up in a twisting Immelmann. The MiGs fell behind but kept following, trying for a lock. "This is Tomcat Two-three-two," Batman called over the radio. "I've got two on my tail! Two on my tail!"

"No sweat, Two-three-two," a voice replied. "The cavalry just arrived."

Batman saw the Hornet flash past half a mile to starboard, a Sidewinder already coming off the rail.

Batman cut his burners and dropped the Tomcat onto its back. He could see the MiGs half a mile below, splitting left and right as the Hornet's missile rocketed toward them, tracking the right-hand MiG. Moments later there was a flash and one of the Korean jet's wings crumpled in flame and scattering fragments. Batman saw a smaller flare of light as the MiG's cockpit blew free and its pilot ejected.

"Chalk up one for the Javelins," Batman announced. "I see a chute. Good chute."

"We have more blue bandits closing, Batman," his RIO said. "I'm reading ten bogies coming at us from down on the deck."

"What're they doing, launching them at us from submarines?" He let the Tomcat's inverted fall accelerate. Another explosion in the distance, and the excited shout of "Splash one MiG!" marked another kill. The Hornets were arriving in force now. The MiGs, already scattered by the dogfighting, were being caught alone or in pairs. The battle was about to become a slaughter.

But the fresh wave of MiGs could change everything. "Give me a vector, Malibu!" he yelled. Blood lust sang in his ears as he accelerated.

1625 hours
MiG number 444, Star Leader

Major Pak knew the fight was hopeless even as his MiGs closed with the Americans. The dogfight had already scattered across ten miles of sky, a fight which the Americans with their better radars and better weapons were certain to win. His squadron might be able to overwhelm one more F-14 with numbers, maybe even two . . . but it was definitely time for the MiGs to retire. Aircraft and trained pilots alike were valuable resources in the PDRK, and to squander either without good cause—or a clear advantage—was criminal.

"One more pass, comrades," he told the other pilots tucked in close behind his aircraft. "One more pass, then scatter and make for home. I doubt that the Yankees will have the stomach to pursue."

The irony of using Mao's guerrilla tactics from the cockpit of a combat interceptor was delicious. Hit-and-runs raids were designed for people's armies, untrained peasants with inadequate weapons facing a superior foe. It was strange to see the same theory applied to dogfighting with modern jet aircraft.

He was close enough to the Yankees now that his radar was burning through their jamming with ease, tracking a target ten thousand feet above him at a range of nearly four miles. He heard the tone of a weapons lock and released another missile.

He didn't see the American Hornets until they were right on top of him.

1626 hours
Hornet 301

Marty French twisted his Hornet over in a tight, inverted turn, tracking the flight of MiGs rising up from the sea. The pipper on his HUD crawled across one of the target symbols, then flashed ACQ as the warble sounded over his headset. Lock!

A Sidewinder hissed off his port wingtip. "Fox two!" he called.

"I see your fox and raise you, Skipper," Lieutenant David McConnell called from the Hornet tucked in off Frenchie's left wing. "Fox two!" Tigershark McConnell triggered a second missile an instant later. "Fox two!"

One of the MiGs in the Korean formation exploded, transformed into unfolding blossoms of smoke and orange flames as the first missile struck; the second missile hurtled through the fireball. The MiG pack scattered then as if blown apart by a bombshell. French pulled his Hornet around, maneuvering onto the six of one of the fleeing MiGs. "Okay, people," he called over the radio. "Let's show 'em how it's done."

1626 hours
MiG number 444, Star Leader

Major Pak rolled his MiG hard. Sea and sky chased one another across the curve of his canopy, and then he cut in his afterburner and the kick slammed his seat into his back with pile driver force.

His wingman's voice was shrill in his headphones. "Yankee devil on my tail!" Captain Song Tae-Hwan shouted, panic in his voice. "Help me! Help me!"

Pak brought his aircraft right, searching the sky. There! One of the American Hornets had slipped into position behind Song, closing now for a kill. Pak knew it was too late for Captain Song, but perhaps there was an advantage here for himself. Still on full burner, he closed with the American Hornet from below and behind.

1626 hours
Hornet 301

"I'm on him." The MiG filled Frenchie's HUD display, the delta form twisting wildly in an attempt to break free. The Hornet closed relentlessly. "Too close for missiles. I'm going for guns."

He flicked the weapon selector and the gunsight reticle replaced the targeting symbol on his HUD. The MiG was already well inside the outer circle which marked the cone of vulnerability. He continued to pull back on his stick, working to bring his Hornet's M61 cannon dead on target. His lead computing optical sight—LCOS in fighter parlance—drew a line which showed him exactly how far ahead of the target to fire.

"Almost there . . ."

He cut his afterburner, then popped the Hornet's airbrakes. For a moment, the F/A-18 lagged, and the fleeing MiG drifted squarely into his gunsight. French squeezed the trigger and felt the muted thunder as 20-mm shells tore into the enemy MiG.

1626 hours
MiG number 444, Star Leader

Pak saw the orange-colored tracer rounds drifting from the F/A-18 toward the wildly twisting Captain Song, smashing into the fuselage and tail. Bits of metal chipped and scattered, and then the canopy itself seemed to explode in fragments of plastic and glass. Flame licked from a gash at the root of the left wing; Song was done for, but he'd held the American's attention just long enough.

The Hornet grew in the circle of his target reticle. The only radar input to his HUD was range, but Pak had calculated the deflection perfectly. He squeezed the trigger and the roar of his MIG's GSh-23 cannon filled the cockpit, filled Pak with a surging, drunken joy.

The American's braking maneuver almost caught Pak by surprise as he found himself closing on the Hornet much faster than he'd anticipated. He had an instant's glimpse of tracer fire tearing into the American aircraft's tail and belly, and then he was hauling the stick hard to the right to avoid colliding with the Hornet from astern. His MiG shuddered as it rode across the buffeting wake of the F/A-18.

Then he was in the clear, rolling past the stricken American aircraft.

1627 hours
Hornet 301

Marty French felt the shock of the 23-mm rounds slamming into his F/A-18's hull and pulled his stick hard to the left. Orange tracers seemed to float past his starboard side as he rolled clear, and then he was plunging toward the sea.

"Hornet Three-oh-one," he said with a calmness he did not feel. "I've been hit."

He held his breath as he pulled back on the stick. If there'd been severe damage to controls or control surfaces, this was where he'd find out. . . .

The F/A-18 leveled off. The controls felt a bit mushy, but he was still flying, still in control. He took a quick look around. He'd not even seen the guy who nailed him, so intent had he been on the target.

"Hornet Three-oh-one, this is Homeplate," a voice said over his headset. "What is your condition, over?"

Gingerly, he experimented with his stick. The aircraft was sluggish, but it responded to the touch. Red and amber telltales flickered on his console. Compressor power was down slightly, but he could compensate. He might be losing some fuel—

"Homeplate, Hornet Three-oh-one. I've been holed, but she's manageable." He worked the controls some more until he was satisfied that everything was still working. He watched the numbers flicker on his fuel readout for a moment. "I'm losing some fuel. It's not serious yet."

"Three-oh-one, do you feel it advisable to eject?"

"Negative! Negative! Anticipate no problem with a normal trap."

"Copy that, Three-oh-one. Bring her on home."

Frenchie did a fast calculation in his head. Range to the *Jefferson* was one hundred twenty miles . . . about eighteen minutes at this speed. He balanced time against the rate of fuel loss. Fine. He could hold her that long, and get her safely down on deck.

French was determined to land the Hornet. Once, three years before, he'd been catapulted off the bow of the *Nimitz* and something had gone wrong. The cat had failed to deliver the needed steam pressure and he'd pitched off the carrier's bow at seventy knots . . . far too slow to remain airborne. Endless hours of training and practice had paid off; he'd ejected . . . but his parachute had snagged on the tail of an A-6 parked along the port side of the flight deck, and he'd spent ten nightmarish minutes dangling between sea and sky before they'd been able to haul him in.

Only later had he discovered that he'd broken his arm during the ejection.

Commander Marty French would never have admitted that he was afraid to eject . . . but he knew with passionate conviction that he didn't want to ever have to go through it again. He was a man who believed in odds, who believed that it didn't pay to tempt fate by pressing those odds to the limit. Yeah, he'd hold his bird together and keep her in the air long enough to get back.

Then he'd land the bitch and walk away.

1628 hours
MiG number 444, Star Leader

It was time to leave. Fuel was running low, and sooner or later more Yankee aircraft would arrive to swing the odds back in the Americans' favor. The battle had dragged individual aircraft farther and farther apart, until it was less a dogfight than it was many widely scattered one-on-one engagements. That was the sort of fight which MiGs could never win against F-14s and Hornets.

With a final roll, Major Pak broke clear of the contest and swung his MiG onto a bearing with Wonsan. The air, the sky were wonderfully clear, and Pak savored the heady excitement, the sheer joy of being alive. He'd *survived* . . . and shot down at least one more American aircraft as well . . . with a second kill that would almost certainly be listed as probable. This day's exploits would enshrine him as a hero of the PDRK. His training, his dedication to his craft had paid off at last.

Now it was time to savor the fruits of those labors.

"Star Group! Moon Group! Disengage and retire!" he snapped over the radio. "We have *beaten* them!"

The North Korean aircraft were fewer in number now, and several were limping as they formed up for the homeward leg of their flight. There was no sense of defeat in their retreat, however. The Yankee aircraft were already drawing off, bloodied by the encounter. The Americans liked to boast about the ten-to-one ratio enjoyed by their flyers . . . ten opponents shot down for every plane they lost. Today they'd lost two, possibly three aircraft if Pak's last target had been hit as seriously as he thought . . . and downed only eight North Korean planes in return.

Yes, the People's Air Force had much to be proud of this day. In combat, victory was not always awarded to the side which suffered fewer casualties. Against the Americans, this battle counted as a decisive victory.

Major Pak hoped that his superiors would see the action in the same light.

1630 hours
Tomcat 205

The North Korean aircraft were drawing off, breaking free from the dogfight and heading northwest, back toward Wonsan. "Tomcat Two-oh-five," Tombstone radioed. "It looks like the hostiles are disengaging."

"Roger that," Batman said over the tactical channel. "What say we go get 'em?"

"Negative, negative," Tombstone replied. "Check your fuel."

"Uh . . . understood. Looks like it's back to the bird farm for us."

Tombstone's fuel stood at just over six thousand pounds, enough to get back to *Jefferson*, but not enough for further combat. Sustained maneuvers on full afterburner drank fuel at an impossible rate.

Moments later a call from the carrier confirmed his decision. Homeplate wanted the attack group on deck before sundown, and that meant an RTB *now*.

"Hey, Stoney?" his RIO called over the ICS. "We're going home empty, no kills!"

"So?" Tombstone's response was harsher than he'd meant it to be. "What do you think this is, Snowball, some kind of *game*?"

"No, Tombstone. I just thought—"

"Just keeps your thoughts to yourself and let me fly."

"Aye aye, sir." Snowball sounded defensive.

Let him, Tombstone thought. After today, it wouldn't really matter.

Tombstone Magruder could not remember screwing up this badly since he'd forgotten to release the brakes on the trainer at Pensacola and managed to wreck the aircraft's nose gear steering mechanism. He'd made one decision after another, and every one of them had turned up wrong.

He'd let himself be suckered by the MiGs coming up from behind and on the deck while his Tomcats were tangling with the Kosong bandits. He'd sent Dragon and Snoops in to cover Snake and Zombie when they were shot down . . . putting them squarely in the path of those unexpected MiGs. He'd let himself get so rattled he'd loosed a missile without getting a target lock; hell, that little display was a damned nugget trainee's goof, not the sort of thing expected of a squadron skipper fresh out of Top Gun school.

Somehow, the dogfight had reinforced his earlier doubts and fears, had left him wondering if it wasn't time to pack it in. He was getting too old to let himself get shot off the nose of aircraft carriers, too old to play cowboy in the sky, competing day in and day out with young guys like Batman Wayne.

Responsibility, that was what it was all about. He sighed. Maybe it was all true what they said about him. His promotions had come so easily. Having an admiral for an uncle could do great things for your career . . . but when men's lives began riding on the decisions you made, maybe those promotions weren't such a great idea. Tombstone wondered if maybe it wouldn't be better for himself, the men under him, and the Navy if he didn't find something else to do.

The image of himself as a COD pilot or hunting subs in a Viking came to mind, and he shuddered.

1645 hours
Hornet 301

Marty French had first shot at the *Jefferson's* flight deck. For a second time he'd been given the option of ejecting, but he elected instead to ride his Hornet in. The controls were still a bit mushy and his left flaps sticky. He'd also lost a bit of hydraulic pressure, and that was worrisome but not critical. He'd clearly taken some damage, but not enough to warrant ejecting and ditching the plane. The rest of the attack group would wait in a marshall stack, a holding pattern twenty-one miles astern of the *Jefferson* while he made his approach. Once he was down and clear, the rest of them would be brought in.

"Three-oh-one," he said, identifying his aircraft. He could see the *Jefferson's* ball clearly now as he drifted down the approach glide path. "Hornet ball, one-point-six." Fuel loss was his only serious problem. If he missed on this pass he'd have to refuel before he managed a second try, and that would be more time lost . . . more time for something to go wrong with an aircraft which was already on the verge of falling apart.

"Roger ball," the LSO replied. "Don't get too low."

He took the gentle hint, already responding as the glowing yellow eye of the Fresnel lens system began drifting below the horizontal line of green lights, indicating he was low. Gently, he nudged the throttles forward, increasing power, speed, and altitude. *Jefferson*'s deck expanded to fill Frenchie's HUD.

Too much! The ball went high and he caressed the throttles back. The Hornet was responding slowly, too slowly. . . .

"Deck coming up," the LSO reported. "Power down."

The deck rushed to meet him. He cut back on the throttles to keep from overshooting the arrestor cables. A last check showed the Fresnel lens was still green.

He felt the arrestor hook grab. At the same moment he rammed the throttles to full military power and retracted his speed brakes in case he missed his trap. The wheels slammed onto the deck. . . .

A damaged hydraulic line blew and French's starboard landing gear collapsed. He felt the Hornet lurch to the right, then go nose down and tail high in a savage pancake, still burning at full power as the starboard wing crumpled with the impact, scattering fragments and fuel. Dimly, he heard the LSO's voice over the radio screaming "Eject! Eject! Eject!" His hands was grabbing for the ejector handle when the universe exploded in searing flame, erupting for a split second into indescribable brilliance before darkness engulfed him. . . .

CHAPTER 16

Tombstone was loitering in the marshall at six thousand feet when Snowball interrupted his thoughts. "Oh, God! Tombstone, did you hear that?"

"Hear what?" He'd not been paying attention to the radio chatter.

"They just called a fire on the deck."

Tombstone's blood went cold. Frenchie had been first in line for his trap. Had the damage been that bad?

"Ninety-nine aircraft!" The voice was that of the Air Boss back in *Jefferson*'s Pri-Fly, and the call code meant the message was directed at all airborne planes. "Recovery operations are suspended until further notice. We have a fire on the deck."

"What are we gonna do, Stoney?"

"Hold in the marshall until they tell us, I guess. Just stay cool, Snowball."

"Fuel's down to thirty-two hundred."

"There's a Texaco up. We'll get a drink when we need it."

Inwardly, Tombstone suppressed a shudder. It was one thing to tell Snowball to stay cool, another thing entirely to accept that advice himself.

This is it, he told himself. I don't need this. If I get back on that flight deck today, I'm turning in my wings.

1650 hours
Pri-Fly, U.S.S. *Jefferson*

Within ten seconds, the burning wreck had been surrounded by *Jefferson*'s crash crew, men armed with fire hoses and foam dispensers. They hit the F-14 with water first to hold back the fire, then attacked the flames with foam, attempting to smother them.

"Get that wreckage cleared away, and I goddamn mean now!" Commander Dick Wheeler, *Jefferson*'s Air Boss, held the microphone to his mouth, his face a dark mask of anger and urgency. It is an oft-stated maxim that any fire on board an aircraft carrier which lasts more than forty seconds means serious trouble. Commander French's Hornet had hit hard enough to smash the right wing and breach the fuel tank. He'd been running nearly empty when he hit, but enough JP-5 remained to ignite the fireball as the F/A-18 went tail-over.

"We're bringin' Tilly across now!" Chief Kuchinski's voice was unnaturally shrill and harsh over the Pri-Fly speaker. The damage control party chief was using one of the radio helmets called a Mickey Mouse for obvious reasons. The device transmitted words but filtered out the surrounding noise, which made it sound as though the person speaking was shouting himself hoarse against complete silence. "Fire's out. Afraid the pilot's dead, though."

Wheeler raised a set of Zeiss binoculars to his eyes, watching as the Tilly—a combination crane and forklift—hooked onto the wreckage and began dragging it toward the side. With Commander French dead, all that remained now was to get the flight deck back in operation. There was damage to the arrestor gear, and they would need to wash down the deck and check it for loose debris that could damage incoming planes. It would be an hour . . . maybe an hour and a half before they could start bringing them in again.

Urged on by the Tilly, French's Hornet teetered on the edge of the flight deck, then vanished over the side. Wheeler lowered the binoculars and looked up toward the sky. Under a rapidly thickening ceiling of clouds, the sun was casting a gold-orange smear of sunset glory across the western horizon. It would be dark in an hour, and those boys would be jittery, having endured an aborted bombing mission and a dogfight. Now they would be circling in the marshall for another hour while the damage to the flight deck was repaired, with nothing to do but think about one of their own, dead.

It was going to be a long evening.

**1802 hours
Tomcat 205**

It grew dark quickly once the sun slipped below the horizon. Tombstone watched the golden light fade as he continued to loiter at six thousand feet twenty miles behind the carrier. The marshall stack was a complex aerial racecourse, with each plane a thousand feet below the plane behind, and a mile ahead. There was nothing much to do but feed Air Ops with updates on fuel and time . . . and think.

"Hey, Tombstone?" Snowball asked over the intercom. "Whatcha thinking?"

Tombstone didn't answer immediately. It wouldn't do to admit he'd already decided to turn in his wings. "Just going over the checklist again, Snowy. I—"

"Oops, hold it, Skipper. Message coming through."

Tombstone listened in. *Jefferson*'s Air Ops was ordering them to begin circling out of the marshall and come on in. "Sounds like the deck is clear," he said.

"Yeah, I wonder—"

"I don't really want to think about it, Snowy. We'll find out soon enough."

One by one, the aircraft began to leave the marshall and head for the carrier, Intruders first, then the Hornets as the carrier began recovering aircraft at forty-five-second intervals. It was pitch black by the time Tombstone got the signal to begin his approach, with only a few stars showing through patchy, high-level clouds.

At five miles out, Air Ops handed him over to *Jefferson*'s Air Boss. Commander Wheeler sounded tired as he announced the take-over. Tired and . . . and shaken? Tombstone shook the thought from his mind. Of course Wheeler would be shaken, along with everyone else in the recovery team, but they were professionals.

And so are you, old son, he told himself. At least until you walk in to see CAG tonight. Right now, think about this being your last night trap.

Tombstone had never liked night landings. Once during the Vietnam War, he'd heard, some doctor types had carried out a series of tests on aviators flying combat missions off carriers. They wired them up with devices to monitor breathing, heartbeat, blood pressure, and perspiration, then recorded the biological reactions as those pilots were catapulted into the sky, refueled in midair, carried out bombing runs, engaged in dogfights, and engaged in routine carrier operations. Time after time, one thing pegged out every needle, showing a level of stress which even one-on-one air combat could not match: night carrier landings.

The *Jefferson* was lit for the occasion, with lights outlining her flight deck, and a vertical line strung down her stern over the fantail. This was designed to create a three-dimensional effect, almost like a wire-box image on the display of a computer video game. Without it, a pilot could suffer a particularly terrifying optical illusion . . . the sensation that the carrier's deck was rising up vertically in front of him, an invisible wall in the sky.

At that moment, *Jefferson* was tiny against the sea, an impossibly small target adrift in blackness, with no other visual clues to the position of sea or sky at all.

"Roger ball," Tombstone heard over his headset. That was Lieutenant Commander Ted Craig, the Vipers' LSO, telling him that he had Tombstone's aircraft in sight, that he was controlling the approach, that it was time to call the ball.

Tombstone found the meatball, an orange light in a row of green on *Jefferson*'s port side. "Tomcat Two-zero-five," he said. "Ball. Three-point-one."

"Looking good, Tombstone."

Normally, the LSO would say nothing unless he saw something to correct. The pilot was busy during the last ten seconds of an approach, and chatter wasted time. Those words were a measure of the stress on the flight deck . . . and among the pilots.

Tombstone could feel his heart pounding in his chest, as it always did during a night trap. The meatball wavered above the line of green, then below. *Damn!* The thing was all over the place. The black hulk of the *Jefferson* swept up to meet him.

He was low. "This doesn't look good," he said to no one in particular, aware of the strained silence from the backseat as his RIO held his breath.

Tombstone checked the meatball again as he corrected. It was dangerous to fasten all of your attention on the Fresnel lens, especially in a night landing. He was still low. "It's no good. . . ."

1835 hours
Landing Signals Officer's platform, U.S.S. *Jefferson*

Burner Craig had flown F-14s for five years and had served as VF-95's LSO since the cruise began. He stood on his platform just forward of the Fresnel lens system, behind a HUD and console, complete with TV screen, speaker controls, and telephone, that was raised behind a windowed barrier for landing operations. A small crowd had gathered around him, other LSOs and LSO trainees who had come to watch.

He ignored them, his attention divided between the lights of the approaching aircraft and the TV, which was tuned to the ship's pilot landing aid television. The PLAT could see in the dark and showed more detail of the approaching F-14 . . . but like all experienced LSOs, Craig preferred his own eyes. The TV image was two-dimensional and could fool you; eyes were hotwired to instincts and were far more reliable.

Mentally, Craig kicked himself after he told Tombstone he was looking good. Aviators were a touchy breed, and there was an inborn love-hate relationship between every Navy flyer and his Landing Signals Officer.

The LSO's primary responsibility was to grade each landing. "Okay" was best, followed by "fair." A "no grade" was dangerous to the pilot or his and other aircraft, while "cut" meant the approach could have ended in disaster. In peacetime, each pilot's standing relative to all of the other pilots in the wing was a matter of fierce pride and fiercer competition, and the aviators' frustrations could often be directed at the LSO who'd marked them down for some minor deviation on their recovery. Pilots could be incredibly defensive about their standings . . . and about any criticism at all, real or perceived, of their abilities.

Tombstone was an old hand and a pro, with no need for an I'm-okay-you're-okay talk-down. *The best I can do,* Craig told himself, *is keep quiet and let the man do his—*

Shit! The Tomcat was low . . . *way* low! "Power up," he snapped into his microphone. His fingers tightened a bit around the control box in his hands, the "pickle" which would light up the red wave-off display around the meatball and tell the pilot to go around for another try.

The roar of the Tomcat's engines rose in pitch and the aircraft's running lights seemed to float higher . . . higher . . .

No! Too high! Craig's finger closed on the pickle. "*Wave off! Wave off!*"

1835 hours
Tomcat 205

Tombstone swept in above the carrier's roundoff, knowing he'd missed. A circle of red lights flashed on, a ruby bulls-eye with the meatball in the center. "Wave off!" the LSO shouted in his ear. "Wave off!"

His wheels hit the deck, but too far forward for the arrestor hook to snag any of the four cables stretched across his path. Tombstone rammed the throttles forward, going to full burner as he fought to build up airspeed once more. For an instant he was aware of the carrier's deck lights on either side of his cockpit, of the shadowed island streaking past his right wing. Power roared, shoving him back in his seat.

Then he was in the open sky once more, the carrier's deck lights a dwindling glow on the black face of the sea behind him.

"Tomcat Two-oh-five, bolter," he heard in his headset. There was nothing *wrong* with missing a trap, save the embarrassment and the ribbing he'd take from the other members of his squadron, but the extra stress on top of what he was feeling already rose like a storm cloud in Tombstone's mind.

He felt an odd sensation in his right hand, the hand holding the Tomcat's stick, and he looked down. His hand was trembling, *shaking*, and there was nothing in the world he could do about it.

1838 hours
Landing Signals Officer's platform, U.S.S. *Jefferson*

Craig chewed at the end of his mustache as he watched Tombstone's second approach shaping up. He wasn't so worried about the pilot's pride now as he was about simply getting the man and his RIO down intact.

He'd been aware of Tombstone's moodiness during the past few days, ever since Coyote and Mardi Gras had bought it. That sort of thing was especially hard when it was your buddy who cashed in. And now, with four more people in the drink this afternoon, plus French's crash-and-burn on the deck . . .

"Come on, Tombstone," Craig said over the radio. He knew others were listening in, CAG and the Air Boss and anyone else tuned into the PLAT channel, but his words were for Tombstone alone. "No sweat. Silky smooth, just like a virgin's ass."

"I'm okay." Tombstone sounded tight. His red and green navigation lights hovered off the stern of the carrier, three miles aft.

"Call it, son. Call the ball."

"Tomcat Two-oh-five. Ball. Two-point-seven."

"You're lined up great. Bring her on in!"

The lights descended, wavered, corrected. He held his breath as they began to drop. *Too fast!* Craig felt a sinking sensation in his gut. Again, he stabbed the switch.

1838 hours
Tomcat 205

If he'd been embarrassed after his first bolter, Tombstone felt stark terror now. *Jefferson's* stern looked like it was all over the sky as he raced toward the carrier at 150 miles an hour. The red bulls-eye around the meatball lit up again and he heard the shouted command to abort. *"Wave off! Wave off!"*

He rammed the throttles forward. With a shattering roar they skimmed above the flight deck, not even touching this time as they whipped past the island. *Damn!*

"Hey, Stoney, this isn't looking too good."

Tombstone guided the Tomcat into a gentle left turn. "You want to get out and walk? I can do without the backseat driving!"

The next several minutes passed in silence. Tombstone focused all his concentration on controlling the ship and himself as he circled a few times. Finally, he began circling back toward the break, lining up for another pass.

"Tomcat Two-oh-five, this is Two-three-two," a familiar voice said. "What's the story, Tombstone?"

"I keep missing the goddamned carrier." He swallowed behind his mask, trying to control his twisting gut. "I think they're moving the bastard on me."

"Well, shitfire, you know what I think? I think you just don't want to face me tonight when I talk about my two kills. You don't want to admit that I'm the new hotdog of the squadron. What do you say to that, fella?"

He recognized the banter for what it was, an effort to break the tension, to get him to laugh at himself long enough to get the Tomcat down. As psychology it was a bit primitive, but Tombstone laughed. "If I land this bitch, you'll eat your words, old son."

"Okay, Tombstone," Craig's voice said. "Let's do it this time! Call the ball!"

Tombstone swallowed a hard, cold lump. The carrier's lights wavered in front of him, tiny in the dark and the distance. His hands were sweating. "Two-oh-five. Tomcat ball," he said mechanically. "Two-point-one." Another pass and he'd need to retank before trying again. *Don't let me screw it up! Not again!*

Not with Batman watching. Not with his *uncle* watching! He realized that the trembling, strength-sapping fear had been replaced by anger. *This bitch isn't going to beat me! Not now! Not when I'm goddamned through!*

The lights swelled in front of his cockpit. "Real slick, man," Snowball said, but Tombstone scarcely heard him. His hand was no longer shaking.

His wheels touched steel and he rammed the throttle to full power. There was an eye-rattling jolt as the hook grabbed wire, and the Tomcat slowed from one-fifty to zero in two seconds. For an instant, Tombstone hung suspended in his harness. . . .

Then he was throttling down, backing the aircraft to spit out the wire, following the waving yellow wands of a deck manager guiding him to a parking slot.

It's over! The thought was exultant. *It's over!*

Tombstone felt as though he'd never been so alive as he was at that moment.

DAY FOUR

CHAPTER 17

The SEAL team consisted of Lieutenant Brandon Sikes and thirteen men, operating under the call sign "Bushmaster." They sat crowded shoulder to shoulder on narrow seats, facing outward, bathed in a dim red glow barely sufficient to illuminate the helicopter's cabin. Anything like normal conversation was impossible under the hammering of the SH-3H Sea King's five-bladed rotors, so there was no talking. Each man, his face and hands heavily blackened, wore a wetsuit, life preserver and harness, and a facemask. Each man held swimfins, letting them dangle between his knees. At his feet was a waterproof rucksack holding weapons and equipment.

They'd boarded the Sea King over an hour earlier, watched only by a few curious sailors on *Jefferson*'s flight deck. Now they were approaching the Korean coast, skimming the waves at one hundred fifty miles per hour.

Several possible plans had been discussed for inserting the team. The most common means for getting SEALs ashore was to release them from the diving trunk of a submarine, but the nearest U.S. sub equipped for SEAL ops still a day's sailing time away, and the shallow waters east of Wonsan were risky haunts for subs in any case. Both HALO—a parachute drop from high altitude with the chute opening delayed until the last moment—and HAHO—a drop from high altitude with the chute opened immediately and steered across dozens of miles to the drop zone—had been considered and discarded. *Jefferson*'s Prowlers were busily jamming North Korean radar, but it was still possible that parachutists, especially high-flying, long-ranged HAHO jumpers, would be spotted coming in. Besides, the North Korean landscape was a rugged jumble of mountains, woods, villages, and industrial complexes. Without pathfinders to secure and mark the DZ, a parachute landing was extremely risky.

The solution, to insert by helocast into the sea and make the final approach to shore by raft, was risky too, but it offered several advantages. North Korean radars—those that could burn through the American jamming—had been picking up *Jefferson*'s SAR helos all evening. Helicopters had been deliberately overflying the area for hours now, even deliberately penetrating the twelve-mile limit. By now, one more helo wouldn't attract undue attention . . . if it was seen at all against the scattered returns from the waves.

Too, in a helocast, the possibility of one or more jumpers injuring themselves was smaller, and this was an op where even one casualty would seriously weaken the team's chances.

Lieutenant Sikes held one hand to the communications helmet he wore. "Three minutes!" he heard the aircraft commander say over the headset.

Sikes picked up his equipment bundle and padded barefoot across the cabin to the big sliding door on the starboard side, feeling the deck vibrate beneath his feet. A Navy helicopter crewman grinned at him and gave a jaunty thumbs-up, then undogged the door and slid it back. Wet air thundered past the opening.

The blackness outside was complete. The SEAL lieutenant took his position by the door, turned, and gave his men a hand signal. "Get ready!"

Sikes removed the communications helmet and handed it to the sailor as the team members unstrapped themselves and gathered up their gear. The stick leader, Boatswain's Chief Manuel Huerta, helped the lieutenant drag a black-shrouded bundle weighing more than three hundred pounds and fitted with safety lines and flotation collars, across the deck and position it near the door.

He signaled again. "Stand up!"

The men unbuckled themselves and shuffled into line, Huerta taking his place at the head, facing Sikes. Wind tugged at the lieutenant's life vest, but its force was lessening. The Sea King was slowing now as it approached the drop zone.

"Check equipment!" As for a parachute jump, each man checked the gear of the man in front of him, rucksack snap-linked to harness, fins looped over one arm, knife, flare, first-aid kit, and pistol secured to web belt. Sikes double-checked them all, and Huerta checked him.

The sailor, hearing a warning from the aircraft commander over his com helmet, held up his forefinger, crooked over to show half. Thirty seconds.

"Stand in the door!"

The lieutenant could make out the oily flash of wave tops in the blackness below the helo, could taste air-flung salt as the rotors lashed spray from the surface. The Sea King had slowed now to less than twenty knots, coasting a bare fifteen feet above the water. The seaman gave a signal. . . .

"Go!"

The bundle went out first, already unfolding as its CO_2 valve triggered. Huerta was next. Earlier that evening, a metal bar had been welded to the helo's side, just ahead of the door and extending three feet from the hull. Huerta reached out the door and grabbed the bar, swung clear of the cabin with his body angled slightly forward and his gear bag dangling below, then let go. The splash was lost in the roar of the engines.

One by one, the SEALs shuffled forward and repeated the procedure. When the last man had vanished into the spray-whipped night, Sikes grinned at the sailor, took his own place at the bar, then let go.

The water was cold, engulfing Sikes in a numbing grip. By the time he resurfaced, the Sea King had already picked up both speed and altitude, its roar dwindling into the night. The lieutenant slipped his fins on, cleared his mask, then began closing with the rest of the team. He could hear them nearby, gathering at the black rubber raft riding the heavy sea swell. The IBS—Navyese for Inflatable Boat, Small—could carry fourteen men and up to one thousand pounds of gear. It took only minutes for the SEALs to get themselves and their gear on board, to unship the waterproofed electric engine and secure it to the motor mount. Sikes checked his compass and indicated a direction. Land was *that* way . . . about five miles off if the helo had put them in the right place. The IBS began moving silently through the night.

0005 hours
Me Jo, U.S.S. *Thomas Jefferson*

One of the bunkrooms reserved for six of the wing's junior officers was affectionately known as a Me Jo, a humorous acronym which stood for Marginally Effective Junior Officers. The quarters belonging to six of VF-95's lieutenants and j.g.s had been taken over by pilots and RIOs from half a dozen of the wing's squadrons.

The party was in full swing when Batman arrived, at least twenty men crowded into the bunkroom, talking, laughing, and making the inevitable "there I was right on this guy's tail" motions with their hands as they described again and again their specific engagements during the dogfight. Snake Hoffner and Zombie Callahan were enjoying the attention as they talked about their fish-eye view of the battle and their long, cold wait until a SAR Sea King had reached them. They'd been released from sick bay only moments earlier, arriving just before Batman.

Since liquor was strictly prohibited aboard ship, refreshments were limited to Kool-Aid and coffee served from a pair of silver ten-gallon urns set on a cart in the corner. Food ranged from chips, pretzels, and other assorted gedunk from the ship's exchange to "autodog," soft ice cream so-called because of what chocolate ice cream was supposed to look like as it was extruded from the automatic dispenser.

Batman was late, having spent several hours debriefing and several more with paperwork. There'd also been his fruitless search for Tombstone. Pulling a succession of bolters was rough, and he wanted to know how the Vipers' skipper was doing.

"Attention on deck!" Tigershark McConnell shouted, grinning broadly, as Batman walked in. "Gentlemen, our day's high-scorer has just arrived!"

A coffee mug bearing *Jefferson*'s name and number was pressed into his hand. "Thanks, Tiger. Frenchie also scored two, you know."

McConnell raised the paper cup he was holding. "Fallen comrades," he toasted. "They were the best."

Batman sipped the amber liquid in his mug . . . and nearly choked on the smoky bite of scotch. "That's . . . good," he managed.

"We got different flavors," Army Garrison Murcheson said from the refreshment table. "Scotch, rum, vodka, wine, Michelob, Black Label, Lowenbrau . . ."

"Not to mention Kool-Aid," Malibu added. "Name your poison, compadre."

Batman raised his mug. "This'll do . . . just fine."

He was mildly surprised at the ebullient mood. Somehow,

Batman had thought that the tone of the gathering would be more subdued after the deaths of Dragon, Snoops, and—perhaps most shocking of all—the Deputy CAG. In some ways, the party had the aura of nostalgia, good humor, and fellowship that Batman imagined must characterize an Irish wake, a celebration of good comrades bravely gone, made light by the forced bravado of "the same thing can't possibly happen to *me*."

If there was anything dampening the gathering's mood, it was the knowledge that someone up the chain of command had "screwed the pooch," aborting the Alpha Strike minutes before it was due to go in. Somewhere along the line there'd been a failure of nerve, and the men of *Jefferson*'s air wing had paid for it that afternoon. Though casualties might well have been higher had Operation Winged Talon gone in, the deaths of French, Ashly, and Whitridge were perceived as the results of the bungling of an uncaring and impersonal bureaucracy. Morale was down, and more than one officer could be heard discussing the mental and moral shortcomings of "those Washington REMFs."

"So, compadre," Malibu said as Batman drained his mug. "You ever corral Tombstone?"

"Negative." Batman shook his head. "I was hoping to find him here."

"Fat chance. Y'know, dude, I think the man's layin' low."

Snake Hoffner became part of the conversation through the sheer press of the crowd. It seemed unlikely that the Me Jo could hold even one more man. "Hey, I heard old Tombstone pulled a couple bolters," he said. "Was it bad?"

Malibu shrugged. "He's been wired since Coyote and Mardi Gras bought it."

Batman studied his empty mug. It was not something he particularly wanted to talk about. Hoffner was young, one of VF-95's nuggets. His dunking in the Sea of Japan that afternoon had done nothing to dampen his youthful exuberance. He hadn't yet learned all the social graces of the aviators' fraternity.

Like the fact that you didn't talk about a man who might have lost the stuff that made him part of the brotherhood.

" 'Tention on deck!"

This time the alert was for real. Captain Fitzgerald stepped into the room and the men rose, awkwardly attempting to keep drinks and paper plates from spilling as they stood at attention.

"Carry on, gentlemen," he said, smiling broadly. Batman thought he looked . . . older now, or perhaps it was just the effects of exhaustion. Fitzgerald had rarely been absent from either the bridge or CIC during the past three days, and the beginnings of blue smudges on the pouches beneath his eyes were showing.

"Just wanted to drop in and tell you men 'well done,'" the Captain said, "And to let you all know that *Jefferson* has been officially credited with eight blue bandit kills today. That's one each for Lieutenants Taggart, Garrison, McConnell, and Grabiak. *Two* kills for Commander French." He sobered for a moment, then brightened again as he turned and looked Batman in the face. "And two for this hotdog here! If we keep this up, the NKs aren't going to have one goddamned fighter left!"

There was an answering explosion of applause and laughter.

"I know I speak for all of us . . . and for Admiral Magruder as well, when I say that Commander French and Lieutenants Ashly and Whitridge will be sorely, sorely missed. They were good men, all of them, good aviators and good shipmates. But they gave their lives in the service of their country, and no man can ask for a better epitaph than that." He looked around, noting coffee mugs and paper cups. "Well now, I don't suppose anyone's saved some of that Kool-Aid for me?"

"Comin' right up, Captain." Someone handed him a paper cup. He sipped at it appreciatively, made a sour face, and looked at it.

"Lemonade," he said, sounding disappointed. He looked up at Batman. "You know, Wayne, too much sugar can be bad for you, especially when you have to fly the next day. Screws up your metabolism."

"Yes, sir."

"That goes for all of you. Not too much sugar. Well . . ." Fitzgerald tossed off the rest of the cup. "That's all, men. Have a good evening. Thanks for the . . . Kool-Aid."

"Good night, Captain."

Batman stared dubiously into his own mug. "What did you give him, Tiger? Lemonade, or . . . ?"

"I'll never tell," Tigershark replied primly.

The laughter and easy conversation picked up again moments after the Captain had gone. Malibu took Batman's mug. "Let me get you a refill. What's your flavor?"

"More of the same," Batman replied. "But with ice this time."

"You think Tombstone'll be okay?" Hoffner asked.

"They don't make 'em any better, Snake," Batman said. "He'll do just fine."

Another junior officer crowded close. Lieutenant j.g. Peter

Costello was about the same age as Snake but looked even younger. "Hey listen, Batman, I wanted to say congratulations on your kills! Real smooth work, y'know?"

Batman smiled. "Thanks, Hitman." Costello's running name, it was said, was derived from the tough Italian street-kid manner he affected at times.

"I saw it, man," Army Garrison said, leaning over Hoffner's shoulder. "Watched his first missile goin' in smooth as silk . . ." He slapped the palm of one hand across the other. "Kapow! Fireball city!"

"No shit?" Costello shook his head. A nugget pilot with VF-97, he'd missed the fight. He looked positively wistful.

Batman wasn't certain what to say. A modest answer didn't seem to be in character somehow, but a cocky reply would have been out of place. Malibu gave him an excuse to turn away by returning with his drink. "Great timing, Malibu. Thanks."

"Hey, Batman?" Costello persisted. "I was wantin' to ask you. What's it feel like, killing a man?"

The question took Batman completely by surprise. He blinked. "What?"

"I was just wondering how it felt, killing a human being like that. You feel different? Anything?"

The words hit Batman like a hammer blow. He'd always considered himself to be a professional, hard and detached. That the question should rock him so badly surprised him as much as the question itself.

"Hey, Batman?" Malibu laid a hand on his shoulder. "You okay?"

"Fine. I'm fine." He made himself swallow the rest of his scotch, letting the liquid fire mingle with the fire in his stomach. A new emotion mingled with the others. Shame. He was ashamed of letting the others know how he felt.

Suddenly he had to get away. He handed his mug to Hoffner, the ice cubes tinkling merrily. "Stow this. I think I'm going to turn in."

He pushed his way through the crowd, ignoring the backslaps and shouted congratulations as he went.

Batman wanted to be alone with thoughts grown suddenly black.

Surf hissed and thundered, the breakers faintly luminescent under the glimmer of lights from the oil refinery on a bluff overlooking the bay to the south. Chief Huerta let the waves carry him toward the beach in a succession of rushes. He held his rucksack in front of his body with his left hand, using it as shield and flotation device. His right hand held a Colt XM177E2 Commando braced across the top of the rucksack. The SMG, barrel-heavy because of the custom suppressor affixed to the muzzle, tracked in his hand as he watched the blackness of the shore.

Another wave picked him up and slid him forward until rough sand grated under his legs and swim vest. He waited as the outgoing water sucked at his body, leaving him for the moment exposed on the beach. There was no movement at all, no sound save the repetitious roar of the surf.

Huerta sensed motion to his left. Machinist's Mate First Class Brian Copley was all but invisible in the darkness, but Huerta could make out the flicker of a hand motion, questioning. He replied with a hand sign of his own. *"Go!"*

Minutes earlier, the two of them had dropped from the raft fifty yards offshore. Lieutenant Sikes was waiting now with the others while they checked out the beach.

A low whistle, barely heard through a lull in the surf, told him the way was clear. As the next wave picked him up and slid him forward again, Huerta rose to a low crouch and loped forward. He ran twenty yards up the beach, then threw himself down at Copley's side. Working quietly, they pulled night-vision goggles from waterproof pouches and put them on. Switched on, the goggles enhanced the available light enough that the SEALs could see a man-sized target at three hundred yards.

They exchanged more hand signals. The SEALs split up, checking a hundred yards up and down the coast.

The beach was narrow, with a steep, boulder-strewn slope rising like a wall in front of them. There were buildings close by, a seaside resort and the ramshackle huts of a fishing village, but this stretch was empty.

Huerta met Copley once more, signaled him to mount guard, and made his way back to the water's edge. He switched off his starlight goggles and raised them up on his head to conserve battery power. Taking a penlight, he aimed it out past the surf and pressed the switch once . . . twice . . . three times. There was no response—no sense in alerting other watchers along the shore—but minutes later Huerta glimpsed the subdued flash of a black paddle dipping against a wave. The IBS had motored in from the drop point, stopping only once when a North Korean torpedo boat had growled past on patrol. Though their DZ had been well inside the twelve-mile limit, the team had still been forced to motor a long way to reach this portion of the coast, and speed was essential. For the final approach silence and invisibility were the watchwords, so they'd come into the beach with the motors off, using paddles to keep from broaching to in the surf.

Figures materialized out of the night, carrying the dripping rafts. Lieutenant Sikes touched his shoulder, a silent "well done." Huerta led the rest of the SEAL team back up the beach to where Copley was waiting with his suppressed Smith and Wesson M-760 SMG, prone behind his rucksack.

They worked swiftly, half mounting guard while the other half stripped off wetsuit tops and donned camouflaged combat suits, boots and web gear. Headgear, like weapons, was largely a matter of personal choice. Most of the men wore boonie hats. Some, like Huerta, preferred a simple sweat band of camo cloth.

The SEALs took another fifteen minutes using paddles to scoop out holes above the beach's high-tide line where they buried the rafts and motors, paddles, wetsuits, fins, and goggles. Whatever happened now, they would not be needing them again. They spent minutes more checking themselves and each other, making certain that exposed skin was covered with camo greasepaint, that snaps and swivels on rifles and equipment were secured with black tape, that no one wore anything which might shine or clink or rattle and thus give their presence away to the enemy. Rucksacks, lighter now with only ammo, rations, and survival gear, were strapped to backs and loose buckles and ends secured. Each man also donned night-vision goggles which gave him an oddly mechanical appearance, like a robot in a cheap SF horror film.

Huerta and Sikes checked a waterproof map. The SEALs had arrived precisely on the strip of beach chosen from the satellite photos they'd studied at Coronado and during their trip across the Pacific. The North Korean Army camp where at least some of the prisoners had been sighted lay four miles inland, near the village of Nyongch'on-ni. Other features were marked on the map, possible targets for air raids, possible locations of American prisoners, but the team's first priority was to check the camp identified as Nyongch'on-kiji.

Huerta pulled back the velcro seal of his luminous watch and checked the time. It was 0240 hours. They could be there in an hour or two if nothing delayed them.

Each man already knew his place in patrol formation. Huerta, as assistant squad leader, took position behind Vic Krueger, who was lugging one of the team's two M-60 machine guns. With another silent hand motion from Sikes, the team began moving, treading up the slope as silently as ghosts in the night.

CHAPTER 18

Huerta lay flat on his back in the muddy ditch, moving in tiny increments beneath the chain-link fence which surrounded the inner compound of the North Korean base. Runoff from repeated rains had carved this channel beneath the fence unnoticed by its builders, and now the SEAL was using it to gain entrance to the area suspected to be where the Koreans were holding the crew of the U.S.S. *Chimera*.

He was unarmed save for a knife and his Mark 22, a silenced, custom-made 9-mm first used against guard dogs in Vietnam and subsequently known as the "hush puppy." Those were for use as a last resort only, of course. The last thing he needed at the moment was a dead guard; if he killed someone, he would have to drag the body out of the camp and hope the sentry's superiors thought he'd deserted while on watch.

He'd left his night-vision gear with the others as well; it was too easy to become reliant on those technological wonders, too easy to lose touch with the night.

And now Chief Huerta was the night, a black shadow among shadows, edging silently under the fence through the runoff gully.

He'd already traversed the first, outer fence, using bolt-cutters to snip through a few links of the fence in the shadow of a guard tower next to a pole. The rest of the team waited for him outside.

The camp identified as Nyongch'on-kiji lay in a high saddle in the ridge line some seven miles south of Wonsan's waterfront district, surrounded on two sides by rugged escarpments which climbed higher still. A highway passed through the saddle, connecting Wonsan with the town of Anbyon ten miles to the south. At this hour there was little traffic.

The SEALs had reached the eastern slope overlooking the camp after an hour's hike from the coast. From the vantage point of their OP amid boulders, brush, and the scraggly, stunted pines that clung to the rocky slopes in this region, they'd surveyed the camp, identifying the building which was their prime target. One of the long, single-story structures inside the inner fence was the building in the satellite photo which had first confirmed the presence of Westerners inside the Nyongch'on compound the previous day.

That building was Huerta's target now. He'd been lucky so far: no encounters, no guard dogs, and only isolated glimpses of sentries doing their rounds in the distance. If he could get close enough to the suspect building to confirm that Americans were being held there now . . .

0410 hours
Nyongch'on-kiji

Coyote heard it first, a muffled thump as though something had landed on the roof of the hut. He'd been lying awake on the straw ticking which served as a mattress, and the sound seemed to originate beyond the wooden timbers of the ceiling directly over his head. He sat up. Commander Wilkinson, lying nearby, sat up as well.

"What is it?" Wilkinson's whisper was harsh in the near-darkness. The room's interior was dimly illuminated by the indirect light from the compound's streetlights spilling through the narrow windows high along the two long walls.

"Something on the roof," Coyote replied. His heart pounded in his chest. The night's quiet had seemed as much a torture as the beatings he'd endured earlier. Their captors had taken many of the men out in small groups, beaten them, threatened them with torture or death, demanded their signed confessions, then returned them to the Wonsan Waldorf. The sudden end to the routine was ominous. The uncertainty was as much an instrument of torture as North Korean boots and rifle butts.

Coyote heard a faint, scuffling sound. Something heavy was sliding down the roof now, making its way from the peak of the roof toward the south wall. He followed the movement in the near darkness, then rose, tiptoeing past sleeping or unconscious men toward the wall and its line of windows. Several other men, aware now that something was going on, rose and followed him.

The faint light from the sky was suddenly blotted out. Straining against the darkness outside, Coyote realized he was looking at the silhouette of a man's head, lowered over the edge of the roof and peering into the window upside down. A sudden, unreasonable hope flared in Coyote's chest. "Who's there?"

"What was the monster killed by Bellerophon?" a muffled voice replied.

Wilkinson, standing on top of an overturned bucket at Coyote's shoulder, stiffened. *"Chimera,"* he said, leaning against the open window.

"Well, either you people are round-eyed North Koreans with a classical education, or you're just the guys I'm looking for," the upside-down shape whispered. "Chief Huerta, USN SEALs."

Coyote sensed the excitement spreading through the room, heard the hasty, whispered words as more and more of the men of *Chimera*'s crew awoke.

"Is it a rescue?" Coleridge asked.

"Not yet," the SEAL replied. "We've got a team in place outside the camp. I'm just here to make sure you're you. How many guys are in there?"

In quick, terse exchanges, Wilkinson answered the SEAL's rapid-fire questions, giving him the numbers he needed: 170 prisoners, including 18 badly wounded men who would need stretchers and special care if they were to be moved.

"You mean all of you are being held in one place?" the SEAL asked.

"Yeah," Wilkinson replied. "I think they're still trying to decide what to do with us . . . and it's easier to guard all of us together."

"Well, that's good, anyway," Huerta said. "Makes it easier to get you all out."

"When?" Wilkinson asked. "When's the rescue?"

"Can't say yet, sir," the SEAL replied. Evidently, there was light enough at his back for him to recognize Wilkinson's uniform and rank bars. "First thing is to let people know you're okay." There was a pause. "You got a place in there to hide some weapons?"

Coyote thought about a corner tucked away among the rafters he'd noticed earlier, a spot someone could reach by getting on someone's shoulders. "Yeah!" he said. "There's a place!"

Huerta hesitated, as though thinking it over. "Okay. Somebody reach through the window."

The windows were too narrow for a man to squeeze through—the reason, perhaps, why they weren't barred or screened over—but Chief Bronkowicz helped Coyote up so he could stretch his arm over the sill. It was a long reach. The eaves of the roof extended well beyond the wall, but Coyote felt something cold and heavy placed in his open palm. He pulled it back inside. Light gleamed from the parkerized finish of a .22-caliber pistol, the barrel swallowed by the heavy cylinder of a long suppressor.

Two times more, Coyote reached into the night, retrieving a Marine Kabar combat knife and two fully loaded magazines for the pistol.

"Listen up now," the voice at the window said. "It's vital that those weapons not be seen by the gooks, get me? They see those, they'll know we're in the area."

"You can count on us, Chief," Wilkinson said.

"I'll try to slip back in here tomorrow night, same time, and let you know what the word is. No promises. If I don't show, just hunker down and sit it out. Those weapons are in case things get too tight and I can't make it."

"Wait a minute," Coyote said. "Won't you need these?"

"Not to worry, pal. I won't have time to stop and play with our NK friends, and those things'd just slow me up anyway. I don't care what the bastards do to you, you keep them hidden until you hear a rescue op going down, get me?"

"Right, Chief."

"When you hear the fun and games begin—explosions, helicopters, American voices, anything like that—that'll be the time. Use them to protect yourselves until the cavalry arrives." Huerta paused. When he spoke again, his voice carried the whip crack of command, even at a whisper. "Until then, keep 'em out of sight. You guys start playing cowboy and you'll get all of us killed, get me? Don't even load the damned thing until it's time to use it! I don't want an accidental shot giving the whole damn thing away!"

"Count on it, Chief," Wilkinson said.

Coyote felt the heavy authority of the pistol in his hand. The SEAL was taking a terrible chance by leaving the gun and knife with the prisoners, but it might be their one chance of survival if their captors started slaughtering them during a rescue attempt.

"Okay," Huerta said. "I trust you. Don't do nothing crazy. I'll try to make contact again tomorrow night, let you know what's happening."

Abruptly, the head pulled away. There was a whisper of noise from the ceiling as the SEAL climbed back toward the roof ridge, then silence.

For the first time since his capture, Coyote allowed himself the luxury of hope.

0630 hours
In the hills east of Nyongch'on-kiji

"Those poor bastards don't have a chance," Huerta said. "Not unless we go in fast and pull them out. I mean like tonight!"

It was two hours since he'd made contact with the prisoners inside the compound. Unwilling to approach the building's wall on the ground and in the open, he'd used his line and grapnel to get up on the roof, then secured himself by the waist so he wouldn't fall and crept spiderwise to the overhang so he could reach the window.

The prisoners' description of the North Korean questioning had convinced him that they were in serious danger. Their captors might be expecting an American attack, and it was unlikely that they would keep the prisoners together or in one place for very long. The likeliest move would be to transport them to P'yong-yang. When that happened, rescue would be out of the question.

Sikes looked at the map Huerta had drawn, then compared it with the actual camp, spread out below them in the golden light of the dawn. The SEAL team had created a hide for itself, an OP sheltered behind a blind of brush and loose rock overlooking the base and well away from the nearest roads. The lieutenant pointed to something that looked like apartment buildings beyond a motor pool garage and a cluster of supply sheds. "Barracks?"

"Yes, sir. Two sentries there." Huerta pointed out notations on his map. On his way out, he'd scouted the compound. "Also here, and here. Roving patrols here . . ."

"Too big a job for fourteen men," Sikes said. His mouth quirked in a passable imitation of a smile. "Too big even for fourteen SEALs."

"No such thing, Lieutenant," Larry Gordon said, crouched behind the OP's blind nearby. He patted his M-60 machine gun affectionately. "We can take 'em!"

"What do you think?" Sikes asked. "A battalion inside the compound?"

"About that." Huerta thought about what he'd seen. Security inside the camp was not all that good. "Securing the prisoners won't be the problem," he said. "We can handle the bad guys inside the camp. But we're going to have to bring in helos to get us out, and holding out against NK reinforcements from outside is gonna be a bitch."

Sikes studied the map a moment longer. "Agreed," he said at last. He pointed toward the airfield, sprawled across the ridge-top spine of the peninsula to the north. The valley between that ridge and this one was filled with the regular outlines of fenced-in compounds, military-looking buildings, massed trucks, and military vehicles. "We've got hostile air based there . . . and a major Army base of some kind down there in the valley." He dropped his arm. "Shit. Ten minutes after it goes down, we could have half the North Korean Army on our asses."

"We could bring in some cavalry," Huerta pointed out. "Just enough to hold on until we could evac the hostages." Already, he was thinking of the op like a hostage rescue, something he'd trained for intensively during a tour with SEAL Team Six.

They discussed the situation for another fifteen minutes, suggesting alternatives, planning, revising. Finally, Sikes looked across the hide to where Tom Halliday was unfolding the compact satellite dish and aligning it with a nondescript piece of the southern sky. The unit could assemble a burst transmission and hurl it to a Navy comsat hanging in a stationary orbit 22,000 miles above the equator, then on to Washington and to the Navy ships waiting beyond the eastern horizon.

"Well, the decision won't be ours," Sikes said at last. "Thank God. But if we can get some help, we'll go in."

The SEALs crouched lower over the map as they went over their options, composing the message they would transmit.

0740 hours
Flag Plot, U.S.S. *Thomas Jefferson*

Admiral Magruder let his finger slide across the stretch of blue labeled Yonghung Man on the map. Hundreds of close-spaced numbers gave depth readings. The finger came to rest on the outthrust slash of the Kolmo Peninsula. Symbols on the map marked the airfield at the peninsula's base, the tangled maze of

Wonsan's streets across the narrow gut between peninsula and mainland, the red-flagged triangles of known SAM and radar sites along the coast. "This stretch of beach looks clear," he said.

The man in camouflage fatigues opposite the plot table from the Admiral was Colonel John Caruso, commander of the MEU's Marines. Next to him was Admiral William E. Simpson, CO of the four ships of the amphibious squadron. They'd heloed in from the *Chosin* only an hour earlier and stood now in Flag Plot with Magruder, studying the map of the North Korean coast.

Admiral Simpson traced narrow corridors on the map, between the islands which interrupted the approaches to Wonsan. The islands bore exotic names: Yo-do, Sin-do, Su-do. *Do*, Magruder remembered, was Korean for island. "These stretches could be mined," Simpson said thoughtfully. "Gun emplacements on these islands . . ."

"We have plenty of Mark 106 sleds to take care of the mines," Magruder said.

"Air strikes can take out the gun emplacements," Caruso added. "And any NK air out of this airstrip will have to be neutralized before my boys go ashore."

"We can handle that," Magruder said. "This'll be Winged Talon all over again, except this time we'll carry it out!"

The brief message from Bushmaster had electrified the staff and senior officers of TF-18. Here was a real chance to rescue the men of *Chimera*'s crew—all of them—from a single compound four miles from the coast. There would not be a better chance than this. Bushmaster had warned that the prisoners might be moved soon. When that happened, they would be beyond the carrier group's reach forever. A rescue, if it was to be attempted at all, would have to be mounted within the next day or two, and that meant getting a start on the planning *now*.

"Do you think your people can pull it off?" Magruder asked Caruso at last. "Two thousand men against . . . God knows. Ten thousand? Twenty?"

"More'n that if we're not in and out, chop-chop." The colonel frowned. "I gave you my recommendations the other day, sir. I thought we could do it then. I think we can do it now. But the show's gonna be yours."

"I know."

Caruso's plan, submitted as one of the options the task force had been examining two days before, had been for a Marine landing to secure a base on the mainland, with recon teams ranging inland to secure the American prisoners . . . assuming that preliminary reconnaissance could locate them. At the time, no one knew where *Chimera*'s crew was being held, and the plan had been shelved in favor of Winged Talon.

But now . . .

The real question was what Washington would think. Winged Talon had been aborted minutes before the Navy aircraft had hit Korean air space, and since that time there had been no explanation, no word at all save that the SEALs should be sent in and that TF-18 should hold station at Point November. It seemed unlikely that they would approve a full-fledged Marine landing one day after calling off a far simpler, far cheaper air strike.

Magruder was still angry about that call, angry with a simmering, barely restrained resentment which needed little to boost it to white-hot fury.

"Recap it, then," Magruder said at last. "Air strikes to take out KorCom radar, SAM sites, and guns. A heliborne Marine assault on Nyongch'on to support the SEALs and secure the prisoners. Marine assault at Kolmo to give us a secure base from which to support the Nyongch'on op. Why not just go straight in from the task force with helos? Why have the Marines go ashore at all?"

"Too many things could go wrong, with nothing in reserve," the Marine colonel said. "We only have two large flight decks, *Jefferson*'s and *Chosin*'s . . . and *Jefferson* is going to be busy with CAP and ground strikes. We have no guarantee that all of our helos will arrive at Nyongch'on intact, and we might have to reinforce before we evacuate. It'll help to have a shore-based helo pad, and the airfield will provide us with just that. Any helos that are damaged on the ground at Nyongch'on will have a friendly place to set down and offload only a few miles from the DZ and won't have to make it all the way back to *Chosin*, eight, ten miles out at sea."

Magruder nodded. "Makes sense."

"Besides, the beachhead will help divert enemy attention away from Nyongch'on. Our boys are gonna have their hands full in there, no matter what, but we can help 'em take some of the heat off."

"Okay. Bill? How long before you have a detailed working plan?"

Simpson pulled at his lower lip. "My staff's already working on it. I can have a preliminary on your desk in three hours. Your boys'll have to work out the air ops and fire control."

"A preliminary's all I'll need for right now . . . to sell Washington on the idea."

Simpson grinned. "I'm glad that's your department, Tom, and not mine. I'd get mad and want to kick bureaucratic ass."

"Who says I won't?" He looked at the map again, at the small forest of red triangles, SAM sites and hardpoints. This was going to be lots more expensive than Winged Talon, in men, money, and aircraft. But then, from the look of things, Washington was going to ignore the military option in favor of the diplomatic one.

And how long, he wondered, before those boys at Nyongch'on came home? How many wouldn't come home at all? He wondered if Washington would even let them take the first, necessary steps. He felt a stab of fire in his gut, an old ulcer flaring anew.

Sometimes it was hard to know who the real enemy was.

CHAPTER 19

Batman queued up with other officers to buy a meal ticket from the cashier, picked up a tray, and started down the cafeteria-style line. It wasn't that he was hungry—quite the contrary, in fact—but the mechanical actions of moving through the chow line were a piece of mindless routine that allowed him to put off the thoughts that had been troubling him since the party the night before. Finding an unoccupied table in the corner of the wardroom, he slumped at the seat and began picking at his food without interest. His thoughts kept returning with a kind of morbid fascination to the subject of death.

Kill or be killed. There was no other way to look at aerial combat. All of his training, all of his preparation, all of the lectures and classes and maneuvers he'd gone through during his Naval career had been directed to one end and one end only: to place Lieutenant Edward Everett Wayne on the six of an enemy combat aircraft so that he could destroy it. During the actual dogfight, he'd not thought of the MiGs as anything other than targets in a kind of video game in the sky where machines exploded in flame and debris, jacking up the victor's score.

The sudden shift in his mind, from thinking of them as targets to thinking of them as men with families, wives, children . . .

Through much of the previous night, he'd wrestled with those thoughts, wondering if he should go talk to one of *Jefferson*'s three chaplains. There was an inner reserve which made him hold that idea at arm's length. He respected the chaplains, respected their experience and the Navy traditions which stood behind them, but what could they tell him that he didn't already know? None of

173

the carrier's sky pilots were aviators themselves, none had been in combat.

How could they address what he was feeling now?

Besides, Batman had heard stories of chaplains who'd gone to the ship's captain with what otherwise would have been considered confidential information . . . if that information was potentially dangerous to the man, the ship, or the crew. He suspected that CAG would ground him so fast it would make his head spin. Navy combat aviators had to have their heads screwed on straight at all times.

So maybe he should ground himself . . . or turn in his wings. Every part of Batman's background, his whole being rebelled against that idea. It would be an admission of weakness, of failure. An admission that he no longer had the right stuff.

But Batman felt that if he didn't talk to someone he'd blow his stack. The only people with whom he had enough in common were other aviators, the very men for whom he had to maintain the facade, the band-of-brothers act that all was well.

There was no one, not even Malibu. . . .

Across the wardroom, an officer in khakis rose from his table and carried his tray toward the galley window. Batman recognized the lanky gait, the pale, pale blond hair of Tombstone's RIO.

Tombstone! There was a man who had never made a point of maintaining the *machismo* of the aviator brotherhood. The guy's got problems of his own, Batman thought . . . but possibly it was the fact that Tombstone was having problems that made him seem like the right man to see.

Batman picked up his unfinished breakfast and hurried from the wardroom.

1120 hours
Flag Plot, U.S.S. *Thomas Jefferson*

A lieutenant informed him that CINCPAC was on the line. "I'll take it here," Admiral Magruder said. He picked up the handset and stabbed a button. The hollow-sounding hiss of a satellite-relayed signal sounded in his ear. "Task Force Eighteen," he said, using the time-honored Navy tradition of identifying himself by the name of his command.

"Tom?" the voice at the other end said. It had the faintly artificial quality of a security-scrambled transmission. "This is

CINCPAC. I'm afraid the answer is . . . sit tight. Washington wants you to take no action at all until further notice."

Magruder had expected as much, but the disappointment was keen nonetheless. "Understood, Admiral," he said.

"We appreciate your situation, Tom," the voice continued. Magruder had spoken with CINCPAC several times during the past few days and knew Admiral Bainbridge shared his own feelings of helplessness . . . and anger. What did Washington think it would accomplish, screwing around this way?

But to voice those feelings would be unprofessional and would change nothing.

"A diplomatic initiative is under way," Bainbridge continued. Even through the scrambling it sounded as though the words had a bad taste in his mouth. "The White House crisis team has high expectations for a successful resolution."

"Very well, sir."

"Your plan has been codenamed 'Righteous Thunder.' It is to be held in reserve, pending a breakdown in negotiations . . . or the decision by the Command Authority to proceed with a *full* military option."

CINCPAC's stress of the word "full" meant an all-out invasion, Magruder knew. They could all well be standing at the verge of a new Korean War . . . and with 1990's weapons, this one would make 1950 look like kindergarten.

Hell. Washington couldn't want that.

But the alternative didn't sound promising either. For P'yong-yang, negotiation was simply another form of warfare. The North Koreans might hold *Chimera*'s crew for months, for years, with nothing being settled. They would hold show trials, parade "confessions" extorted from their captives, promise a release and then change their minds in response to some imagined or contrived slight by American authorities. The anguish would go on and on.

"I am not optimistic about the promise of negotiations with these people," Magruder said.

"That's putting it mildly, Admiral. It'll be *Pueblo* all over again, only worse."

"What about Bushmaster, sir?" Even on a scrambled line, Magruder didn't want to make a direct reference to the SEAL team already ashore.

"Bushmaster remains in place. They will be a positive asset for Righteous Thunder . . . if it comes to that."

"Understood."

"Hang in there, Tom. Seventh Fleet is already deploying, so you'll have plenty of backup in another day or two. Until then, it's up to you to keep an eye on the bastards."

"Aye aye, Admiral."

"CINCPAC out." The line went dead.

Magruder replaced the handset. Colonel Caruso would be proceeding with the final preparations for a landing in any case. In a situation like this one, the Marine motto of *Semper Fidelis* was best reinforced by the Boy Scouts' *Be prepared*.

They would be ready to go in, no matter what happened. And as much as Magruder felt that Washington was making a mistake, he would be ready as well, ready to carry out the President's orders.

But the frustration he felt was almost tangible, like the thundering shudder in the air on the flight deck during a cat launch. He turned to an aide. "I'll be on the Flag Bridge."

The waiting was always the hard part.

1400 hours
Nyongch'on-kiji

The lookouts gave warning seconds before the door banged open. Coyote watched in silence with the men of *Chimera*'s crew as Major Po walked in, flanked by guards with AK-47 rifles.

There'd been no more interrogations since the day before, no attention from their captors at all save for the arrival several hours before of a squad of silent peasants who replaced full honey buckets and left behind a washtub containing the midday meal: an unsavory mash of rice and chunks of raw fish.

"All you, kneel down!" Po shouted. The Americans stirred uneasily. This was something new in the routine. "All down, *sonabichi*! All down!" the major screamed. A guard slammed his rifle butt into the shoulders of the nearest American sailor, driving him to his knees. Reluctantly, other sailors began, facing the Koreans in a thickly packed semicircle.

Coyote knelt with the others, sharply aware of the hostility among the prisoners. The SEAL's pre-dawn visit had instilled a fierce new hope in all of them. They'd not been abandoned, whatever their captors might say.

The Koreans felt it too, Coyote thought. They looked nervous and wary of the Americans. He thought of the pistol and knife, hidden away among the rafters in the back of the room. All we need to do is hold out a little longer, he thought.

"Where *sonabichi* captain!" Major Po snapped. He looked among the Americans until he found Gilmore. "You! You!" He indicated two sailors. "You bring!"

Goaded by blows and snarled orders, the sailors dragged the Captain to the center of the semicircle and propped him up. Gilmore was weaker today. Coyote wasn't even certain the man was aware of his surroundings.

The major surveyed the scene, then turned to face the door. *"Turo ose yo!"* More soldiers spilled into the room, followed a moment later by Colonel Li. The man exchanged several low-voiced phrases with the major, then surveyed the gathered Americans. "We will try something different," he said, the words cold and without accent. "Captain Gilmore, I hold you responsible for the lives of your men. You can order them to cooperate, or watch them die one by one."

"Go . . . hell . . ." Gilmore said. His voice was very weak, his face pale and drawn.

Li shrugged. "As you will." His gaze passed across the Americans once more. Again, his eyes locked with Coyote's, then passed on to a sailor kneeling nearby. He pointed. *"Paro ku kot!"*

Two North Korean soldiers slung their rifles and advanced on the sailor, who tried to back up, tried to rise, but was grabbed before he could get to his feet. They grabbed him, one holding each arm, and dragged him to the wall next to the door. Colonel Li nodded to the major, who drew his pistol and snapped back the slide with a loud *snick-clack*, chambering a round.

They made the American kneel again, his face against the wall. The major stood behind him, the muzzle of the pistol pressed against the back of the sailor's head.

"Captain?"

"Don't do it, Captain!" the sailor screamed. "Don't—"

One of the men holding him slammed an elbow against the side of his head. *"Kae!"* the soldier snapped. *"Choyong hi!"*

Struggling, the Captain tried to rise. Coyote felt the tension, the sheer rage among the Americans building, felt his own heart hammering under the assault. He remembered the staged firing squad, the fear and the sheer relief he'd felt at the unexpected reprieve, and wondered if this was the same thing again.

"Hang on, Sobieski!" someone shouted. "The bastards don't mean it!"

Li looked at the major. "*Kot hasipsiyo!*"

The shot was like a physical blow, unnaturally loud inside the bare-walled room. A splash of scarlet appeared on the wall in front of the sailor's face. The two soldiers released Sobieski's arms and he sagged to the floor. There was a gaping red cavity where his forehead had been.

"Two hours, Captain," Li said. His voice was scarcely above a whisper, but every man heard it in the ringing silence which followed the shot. "In two hours I shall return. You and your men will sign the confessions we have prepared for them, or in two hours another of your men will die. Until then, Captain . . ."

The silence remained long moments after the Koreans departed.

1545 hours
Hangar deck, U.S.S. *Thomas Jefferson*

The immense hangar deck occupied fully two-thirds of *Jefferson*'s 1,092-foot length, two levels below her flight deck and extending from just forward of her number one elevator almost all the way aft to the fantail. The deck was covered by the same dark-gray, non-skid surface as the flight deck, while bulkheads and overhead were painted white. Hanging in row upon colorful row along the overhead were flags of countries, U.S. territories, and states, as well as Navy signal flags. The hangar deck echoed with voices, the metallic clangor of tools and hand carts banging and squeaking in the vast, almost subterranean space.

Tombstone picked his way carefully across the deck. It was busy, a maelstrom of purposeful confusion. The room was crowded with aircraft, so much so that navigating in a straight line was impossible, for the planes, wings folded, were parked so close together that each nearly touched its neighbors. With over eighty aircraft in a carrier air wing, there never seemed to be space enough on board ship to store them all. Indeed, even during launch and recovery operations, some had to be kept topside on the flight deck. Tombstone found himself wondering again how the Mangler could possibly work out the intricate geometry of moving them from hangar deck to flight deck and back without becoming hopelessly mired in an aircraft carrier's version of gridlock.

He'd been heading aft toward the fantail but found that route blocked. *Jefferson*'s boats and launches were stored in the aft end of the hangar bay, close by the passageway leading to the fantail, stacked two-high on spidery wheeled cradles, and the way through was a narrow one. This afternoon it was walled off by a row of flat-topped mules. Crews were moving among the parked aircraft on preflight inspections, readying them for combat in case Operation Righteous Thunder was given a go, and spare equipment had been wheeled back out of the way.

Tombstone decided to get his view of the sea at an elevator instead.

Jefferson had four elevators, three to starboard, one to port, flat deck sections which moved between the hangar deck and the flight deck along rails on the outside of the hull. They were accessed from the hangar bay through broad, oval openings in the bulkheads which were normally left open for ventilation below decks, though they could be sealed off with massive sliding doors in cold weather. Dodging blue shirts and their mules, Tombstone made his way to the elevator portside and aft.

Like the fantail, the elevators offered unobstructed views of the sea rushing past the ship some twenty feet below. Walked into the light spilling into the hangar bay from outside, Tombstone had to stop and fish in his jacket pocket for his sunglasses. A mule and several blue shirts were manhandling an F-14 onto the elevator, and he moved out of their way, leaning against the elevator's safety netting.

Musing, he looked at the sunglasses before putting them on. They were the teardrop pilot's model with gold wire frames . . . like his leather flight jacket, very much in keeping with his image as a Navy aviator.

The image he was no longer able to maintain.

"Ho, Tombstone. I've been looking for you."

He turned and saw Batman advancing across the red and yellow warning stripes painted on the deck. Like Tombstone, Batman wore sunglasses and jacket, his hat cocked at a rakish angle. He acknowledged the lieutenant with a nod and hoped the man didn't want a conversation. Tombstone didn't feel like talking just now.

"Listen," Batman said. "I've been trying to find you all day."

Tombstone smiled. *Jefferson* was a small city with a population of over six thousand. Usually it was easy to get lost in her, but somehow, this time, he'd failed. "Well, looks like you found me."

"Yeah . . ." Batman looked uncertain . . . even embarrassed. "Look, I know this might not be the best time, Stoney, but I don't know who else to talk to. I'm . . . I'm wondering if I can do it again." With a sharp motion, Batman pulled the sunglasses off and looked into Tombstone's eyes. "I killed two guys yesterday. You shot down your MiG and it didn't even faze you. I . . . I need to know how you handle a thing like that."

So that was it. Several sharp or sarcastic replies rose in Tombstone's mind, but he pushed them aside. The openness, the vulnerability in Batman's expression was something he'd not seen there before.

"I don't think I have any answers," he said, shaking his head. "I didn't . . . *handle* it. I have a feeling it's going to stay with me for a long time."

When Batman didn't answer, Tombstone continued. "That was what all the training was for, right? ACM? Making the kill?"

"Making the kill . . . right. But it was always . . . you know. A target. Not a *man*."

"I doubt very much that the enemy pilot would have extended you the same courtesy, but that's beside the point. You strap on an F-14 for one purpose only, to engage the enemy, to shoot him down before he shoots you down . . . or before he kills friends and shipmates. If there's a better reason than that, I've never heard it."

"I keep wondering if those guys I nailed had families."

"Of course they did." Bitterness edged Tombstone's voice. "*Coyote* had family. Mother, father. A wife I'm going to have to go see when we get back to the World."

"Is that all there is to it? Revenge? They hit you, you hit them back?"

"Hell, no. I'll leave that to the politicians." Tombstone's fists clenched. "But I might lock and fire remembering what a hell of a fine guy Coyote was."

As he said it, for the first time since his bolters the night before, Tombstone pictured himself going up again, pictured himself once more bringing the HUD pipper into line with an enemy MiG.

Tombstone was an aviator. There was no escaping that part of him.

A warning klaxon sounded, a harsh bray above the noises of machinery and sea. The elevator gave a lurch, then began rising up the side of the carrier.

"You know you can't have any doubts about it once you're up there, right?" said Tombstone.

"I'm realizing that now."

"You remember the Top Gun motto?" The other aviator

nodded, but Tombstone pressed ahead. "'Fight to fly, fly to fight . . . fight to *win!*'"

"Fight to win. Yeah."

Tombstone shrugged. "The decision is yours, son, but if you don't mean business, you've got absolutely zero reason to be up there."

"So how about you?"

"What do you mean?"

"Coyote and Mardi Gras. Frenchie . . . Losing those guys was a real shock. I thought, well, some of the guys were wondering if you'd lost it, know what I mean? Lost the edge."

It was not the edge that he'd lost so much, Tombstone realized now, as the will to push that edge, to see how far it would stretch. To do what he did, to be who he was, meant accepting a measure of responsibility which he'd never yet been able to shoulder comfortably.

"I haven't lost it, Batman. Not yet." He was surprised to discover he meant it.

With another lurch, the elevator arrived topside, meshing perfectly with a round-cornered gap cut from the carrier's flight deck. It was as frantic here as it had been below. Red-shirted ordnancemen were arming the parked aircraft for their next mission. At several points on the deck, red lines delineated the bomb elevators where missiles and other munitions were being brought up from the ship's magazines for loading. Other men crawled over and under each aircraft, giving them their pre-flights.

No longer masked from the wind by the curve of *Jefferson's* hull, Tombstone had to lean over and shout to make himself heard. "You're the one with the responsibility," Tombstone yelled. "For yourself and your shipmates! You have to *know* why you're up there, and that's to fight to win. If you don't, you let yourself down, and your shipmates!"

They started across the flight deck, keeping clear of hurtling mules and ordies hauling bomb carts.

"Hey, Stoney. You won't . . . I mean . . ."

Tombstone grinned. "I won't tell a soul, Batman." Together they walked toward the island.

1600 hours
Nyongch'on-kiji

"*Kot hasipsiyo!*"

The shot rang out, splattering more blood across the wall.

Seaman Jacobs crumpled as the soldiers released him and he fell, collapsing to the floor across Sobieski's body. Coyote felt the horror of the death, of the methodical *murder* of a helpless man.

Li faced the ring of stunned Americans. "A death every two hours, Captain, until you and your men cooperate." He gathered his men with a gesture. "*Kapsida!*"

Bailey, the corpsman, was the first to move when the Koreans left, hurrying to Jacobs's side and feeling the man's throat for a pulse. "He's dead."

"We've got to do something," Zabelsky said. The words were a low murmur, almost a litany. "We've got to *do* something."

"Nothin' . . . we can do," Gilmore said. "Nothing . . ."

"We've got a gun—"

"Belay that right now!" Bronkowicz growled. "We won't help the SEALs . . . we won't help *ourselves* if we give it all away now."

"Yeah," Wilkinson said. "What are you going to do, son, shoot your way into the compound out there? Then what?"

Zabelsky whirled, his face a mask of rage. "Jacobs was my buddy!"

"And our shipmate," Bailey said softly. He laid a hand on Zabelsky's shoulder. "We don't help him by getting ourselves shot too."

A clattering sound from outside caught their attention. "Hey, guys!" one of the lookouts called. "It's a helo!"

"Not one of ours," Zabelsky said.

"Shit no. Commie job, looks like. Red star on the tail."

Coyote joined the lookout, balancing atop a bucket to see out. The helicopter was settling to earth amid whirling dust, landing at the small airstrip on the far side of the compound. "Mi-8 Hip," he announced, recognizing the type. "Military transport. Looks like we have visitors."

"What kind?" Wilkinson asked.

"VIPs," Coyote replied. He could just barely make out several men climbing from the bulky machine's side door, walking doubled over beneath its still-turning rotors. One wore an officer's uniform ornate with medals and gold braid. The others looked like aides or junior officers. They were met by Li and Major Po, both of whom saluted the newcomers with crisp military precision. "Looks like high-ranking brass."

"I don't think I like this," Wilkinson said.

Coyote had to agree.

CHAPTER 20

"Kot hasipsiyo!"

This time a third class radioman named Heatley died, slammed forward off his knees as the major's automatic pistol barked, and adding his blood and brain tissue and chips of bone to the dark splatter of gore on the wall next to the door.

In the silence which followed, Colonel Li turned and smiled at his kneeling audience. "I'm sure you all are aware of the helicopter which arrived not long ago. You will be interested to know that orders have arrived from my superiors in P'yongyang directing that you be sent there for, shall we say, further debriefing."

There was a stir among the prisoners. Coyote kneeled with the rest, trying to control the hammering in his chest. The torture of watching men being shot in cold blood with clockwork regularity was worse than any beating he'd suffered so far.

"I feel it is only fair to warn you that you cannot expect such . . . *lenient* treatment in P'yongyang as you have enjoyed here," the colonel continued. "General Chung Sun-Jae, who has come here from the capital to take charge of you, is a man interested in results but with little concern for the time it takes . . . or the means employed to get them." He shrugged, a deliberately Western gesture. "I had hoped that some of you at least would be willing to cooperate with me first. Any persons here who wish to do so, of course, have only to ask to see me, Colonel Li. Perhaps you can yet be spared the uncertainties that a prolonged stay in P'yongyang would bring."

"Screw you, flatface," someone in the back ranks of the Americans muttered.

Li ignored the interruption. "At dawn tomorrow, all of you will be loaded onto trucks and transported west to special camps in the P'yongyang area. Those who decide to cooperate with me will receive special privileges . . . better food, medical aid . . . and a chance to avoid General Chung's more creative approaches to prisoner interviews. Certainly, we should be able to spare you the pain and humiliation of a trial, as well as whatever punishment the court chooses to hand down. For the rest of you, well . . ." The officer looked down and nudged Heatley's body with the toe of his boot. "Perhaps you will come to envy these men who have already given their lives. They might well be the lucky ones, yes?"

"And until then?" Gilmore asked. He seemed stronger now, with a new will born of anger. "Is it your intention to continue murdering my men until dawn?"

Li pursed his lips, as though weighing his words. "Let us simply say that six more of your men will have the opportunity to escape socialist justice between now and the time when I must turn you over to General Chung." He gave the Americans a final contemptuous glance, then departed, followed by Major Po. His guards slammed the door shut behind them.

"This whole setup stinks," Bronkowicz said after they'd gone. "The bastards are violating every rule of prisoner interrogation going."

"What'd you expect, Chief?" one sailor asked. "The Geneva Convention?"

"Shit, no. But they're going about this thing all wrong. You want to brainwash a prisoner, you isolate him, don't let him talk to his buddies. You sure as hell don't try to get him to break in front of his shipmates. That just makes it harder."

"Sounds like you know something about brainwashing, Chief," Zabelsky said.

"Hell, these are the sons of bitches that *invented* it. I just can't figure what they're up to, goin' about it this way!"

"They're after me, Chief," Captain Gilmore said. There was anguish behind the eyes. "They got *Pueblo*'s captain to cooperate by threatening to shoot his men, remember? I guess this time they're actually doing it just to prove they mean business. They want me to see you, to *feel* you dying, one by one, until I agree. . . ."

"You don't agree to nothin', Skipper," Bronkowicz said roughly. "Ain't none of us going to break for those bastards, and you shouldn't either."

"As long as we're together, ain't none of us going to break," Zabelsky said. He glanced meaningfully toward the corner where Lieutenant Novak sat alone.

"That's not going to last, sailor," Wilkinson said thoughtfully. "He said 'camps,' plural. They're splitting us up. Just to make a rescue harder, if nothing else."

"They're never going to let us go," one sailor said, a low murmur in the silent room. "They're never going to let us go. . . ."

And Coyote had to agree. Added to the horror of the systematic killings was the chilling certainty that the North Koreans could never let any of them go now, not if the People's Democratic Republic feared the storm of world opinion the stories of *Chimera's* crew would raise once they won their freedom. Either P'yongyang didn't care about world opinion, or . . .

Or they did not plan on releasing them.

He faced the possibility that he might be forced to spend the rest of his life here, cut off from world and family and Julie. . . .

"So what're we gonna do?" Bronkowicz asked. He glanced toward the door, as though uncertain whether he should say more. There'd been considerable speculation among the prisoners that the North Koreans might have listening devices hidden in the building walls, but since there'd been no search for the hidden weapons, no indication that they knew their base had been infiltrated that morning, it seemed safe.

But that could change at any moment.

"We have to make contact with the SEALs," Coyote said. He forced the image of Julie from his mind. "One of us has to get away, tell them what's happening."

"Maybe they know."

"How? They're watching, I bet, probably saw that Hip land. But we have to get word out that we're being moved at dawn tomorrow."

Coleridge nodded. "If a rescue *is* being planned, they have to know. Remember Son Tay."

There was no need to say more. Son Tay was the name of the North Vietnamese prison camp twenty-three miles from Hanoi which had been the target of an American raid in November 1970, a raid aimed at releasing American POWs held there. The operation had been a spectacular success in every way but one.

The POWs held at Son Tay had been moved elsewhere shortly before the raid.

It would be ironic indeed if an American rescue mission mounted to free *Chimera*'s crew likewise arrived at the prison, only to find the place empty.

"I'll go," Coyote said quietly. He glanced up at the windows. The late afternoon light was rapidly fading. "As soon as it's dark."

"Why you, son?" Wilkinson asked.

Coyote shrugged. "Any of the rest of you guys had survival training?" Several men nearby shook their heads. "E and E courses? No? Well, I guess I'm elected."

He'd known from the start that he was the logical candidate. Ordinary Navy training included staying afloat and survival at sea, but touched little if at all on the practical aspects of living off the land. As an aviator, Coyote had suffered through more than one survival course. He knew how to evade enemy patrols, how to trap small animals for food, how to find water, how to . . .

But then, what he was really counting on was finding the SEALs. There was no point in escaping at all if he had to face a sixty-mile hike to South Korea afterward. He would never make it past the patrols and minefields of the DMZ.

Besides, any would-be rescuers had to be warned about the impending move.

"You'll want to take the pistol, then," Bronkowicz said.

"Coyote shook his head. He'd already thought about that and discarded it. "No way. If I'm caught, the KorComs'll know we had outside help."

"Hey, guy, you can't just—"

"It'll be okay! You guys keep the gun, like Huerta said. You may still need it if . . . *when* things go down."

"Good God, man, how do you expect to get out?"

For answer, Coyote walked over to a wooden beam, one of a dozen along the walls of the building which supported the roof. He ran his hand over the age-roughened, splintered wood and smiled. "Someone get that SEAL knife and I'll show you."

1922 hours
On a slope above the Nyongch'on camp

Huerta pressed his eye to the rubber eyepiece of the starlight scope. "They're taking someone now." The whisper did not carry beyond the confines of the SEAL hide. Four other men, including Lieutenant Sikes, lay in the hollow, watching the camp below them through night sights and IR gear. The other SEALS were invisible in the rapidly gathering darkness, spread out along the hillside.

Sikes took his turn at the scope. "One man, two guards. Think he broke?"

Huerta shrugged silently. They'd not been able to hear what was going on in the camp, but it was clear something out of the ordinary was happening. A sentry outside the POW building had vanished inside for a moment, then left at a run, returning minutes later with help. Now a prisoner was being escorted across the compound toward the structure already identified as an HQ.

Jerry Kohl, one of the team's two snipers, shifted, following the men through his G3 rifle's Varo image-intensifier sight. "They're taking him past the fence."

"Keep cool, everyone," Sikes reminded them. "There's nothing we can do for the poor bastard now."

1923 hours
Nyongch'on-kiji

Coyote deliberately slowed his pace as he passed the ten-foot, concertina-wire-topped chain-link fence which ringed the camp. It was almost fully dark now, but he could see the lights of a village in the valley below the ridge-top saddle in which the camp was built, and the dark masses of surrounding mountains rising on either side, still faintly visible against the darkening sky.

"P'palli!" one of the guards barked. The order to hurry needed no translation

Now what, Coyote asked himself. His pleas to see Colonel Li had been answered at once. Presumably, that was where they were taking him now, flanked by two flint-eyed North Koreans with AK assault rifles dangling from slings over their shoulders and Soviet-manufactured hand grenades on their belts.

And Coyote's only weapon was surprise, and the wooden stake he had tucked up his left sleeve.

It hadn't taken long to carve the makeshift blade from a flat sliver of wood peeled from one of the Wonsan Waldorf's roof supports, whittling it to wicked sharpness. With no cutting edge the thing wasn't much as a knife, but it would be deadly as a stabbing weapon if aimed at a soft target. It would give Coyote a single strike, no more, and a few seconds of surprise and confusion.

He would have to get it right the first time.

But it appeared he had overestimated his own chances . . . or underestimated the alertness of his guards. The camp perimeter was well lit here, and Coyote could see the shadows of guard towers behind the lights. Everything depended on surprise.

Deliberately, he staggered, clutching himself across his belly. The guards turned, then closed in. *"Irona!"* one snapped. *"P'palli ose yo!"*

Coyote straightened, the improvised knife firmly grasped in his right hand as he drew it from his sleeve, slashing out and up. The stake entered the guard's throat at the angle beneath his jaw and rammed through into the back of his mouth. The man gave a strangled cry and clawed at his face. Coyote's thrust hadn't been deep enough to kill, but the guard lost all interest in Coyote.

And Coyote was already grabbing for the guard's rifle.

Coyote had guessed that the rifle would be charged—no guard walked into a room occupied by almost two hundred angry prisoners without chambering a round first—but with the safety on. He didn't bother to take it from the Korean, but dragged his hand down over the selector switch, then closed his finger over the trigger while the weapon was still slung from its screaming owner.

He fired, a flat burst that stabbed flame into the night and shattered the silence of the camp with hammering autofire. Driving his left shoulder into the guard's chest, he pivoted gun and man together, dragging the flashing muzzle into line with the second guard. The man pitched backward, arms spread, as Coyote smashed the first guard with all the strength at his command before he could pull the wooden knife free. The soldier went down, stayed down.

Coyote could hear excited shouts as he untangled the AK-47 from the guard's body. He had his surprise. Now he needed to make the most of it.

Stooping, he unhooked one of the grenades from the guard's belt. It was a Soviet RGD-5, bright apple-green in color with an oversized cotter pin ring and a tall, thin detonator rising from the round body. He yanked out the pin, sent the grenade bouncing toward the fence, and hit the dirt facedown.

"Chogi!" someone yelled. Searchlights swept across the compound now, and the thin, ragged howl of a siren was starting to

wail. There was a brief stab of gunfire from the darkness, then another. "*E yop e ult'ari!*"

A long burst of autofire blasted from one of the towers a hundred yards away. Coyote felt something like a hammer blow in his leg, halfway up his thigh. The impact was hard enough to slap his leg aside but, strangely, there was no pain.

Then the night erupted in flame.

1924 hours
On a slope above the Nyongch'on camp

"What in the hell is that crazy bastard doing?" Sikes pressed his eye to the night-vision device, straining to gather more information from the oddly flattened, monochrome image it gave him. The flash of the grenade had scared the device's optics for a moment, leaving a fuzzy blind spot which slowly cleared. He could see the bodies of two guards on the ground, could see the American POW scrambling forward on his belly, an AK clutched in his arms. The grenade had twisted the chain-link fence, punching it out from the base enough to offer a determined man a way out.

"He's making a break!" Kohl said, his face still pressed close to his Pilkington scope's eyepiece. "He's trying to wiggle under the fence!"

"Shit!" Huerta said, "He's *hit* . . . !"

Sikes had only seconds to make a decision which could well spell disaster for his team. If the SEALs tried to help the POW, there was every possibility that the North Koreans would discover their presence.

But he also knew there must be one god-awful important reason for the man to be trying to escape.

That decided him. "Kohl! Give him cover!"

The G3 was fitted with a sound suppressor, and the shots would not be heard over the shouting, gunfire, and sirens sounding in the camp now. The wound inflicted by the 7.62-mm NATO round would be close enough to that caused by an AK-47 round that the Koreans would never know the difference—certainly not without an autopsy.

By the time the KorComs got around to that it would be too late.

Kohl held the sniper rifle steady on its bipod for a moment, then squeezed the trigger. Even with the suppressor, the shot sounded unnaturally loud among the rocks, and Sikes had to tell himself again that, if the camp guards heard it, they would never be able to tell where it came from.

In the camp, a guard pitched headlong from one of the wooden guard towers. Kohl selected a new target and fired again. A North Korean guard, running full-tilt toward the disturbance, staggered and dropped.

"Huerta!" Sikes snapped. When the SEAL faced him, the lieutenant signaled, pointing down the slope. Huerta nodded and slipped over the rim of the hide.

Kohl took aim once more. . . .

CHAPTER 21

Coyote fired the AK-47 again, a wild spray directed in the general direction of the gunfire probing toward him from the advancing Korean soldiers. He had no idea whether he hit any or not. His single hope was to make them keep their heads down long enough for him to get through the gap under the fence.

Bullets tunneled into the clay close by, sending up spurts of wet earth almost in his face. The rifle clicked empty and Coyote tossed it aside. Lying on his back, he began wiggling under the skirt of the chain-link fence.

His plan had already gone sour. He couldn't feel much of anything in his left leg, but there was a deadness there, a gone-to-sleep numbness. When he touched it, his hand came away slick with blood.

How far could he get, in the dark, in hostile country, with gomers on his heels, and him not even able to *stand* on his leg, much less run on it.

But there was no turning back, not now. He kicked out with his right leg, pushing himself backward under the fence. A fresh burst of gunfire splattered the ground close by, and something *spanged* off the metal of the fence a few feet above his head. A ragged edge of fencing caught his flight suit, pinning him. Nearly panicking, he kicked harder.

Out of the corner of his eye, he caught sight of a Korean soldier thirty feet away. Illuminated by the beam of a searchlight, the man was moving forward relentlessly, AK raised, his eyes already locked with Coyote's. The AK came up, aiming. . . .

The top of the Korean's head exploded in a spray of blood and chips of bone and the man lurched heavily to one side, then collapsed. A moment later, the searchlight flared and went out, leaving Coyote in near darkness.

He kicked again and felt his flight suit tear free. The ground outside the fence dropped away sharply, and Coyote rolled down the hill into the brush at the bottom.

It was then that the pain hit him, a searing fire in his thigh, midway between hip and knee. He grasped his leg between both hands, squeezing hard. The bone, miraculously, did not seem to be broken, but the wound throbbed and ached like hell. He found he could stand on it—barely—that he could hobble forward if he didn't put too much weight on his left leg.

Coyote's eyes were still dazzled by the camp's lights and he could see little of his surroundings. There were rocks and trees nearby, though, and the black shape of a hillside facing him. He could make out the trees in the illumination spilling from the camp and decided that they offered him his best chance of hiding. Continued shouting from the other side of the fence suggested that the Koreans had lost him, but that wouldn't last for long. Soon they'd be on his trail, possibly with dogs.

How was he going to find the SEALs before he was run to earth?

He was limping past the gnarled trunk of a pine tree when hands snaked out and grabbed Coyote's collar and mouth, yanking him to the ground. The shock jarred his leg and he bit his lower lip hard to keep from screaming.

"You stupid, sorry son of a bitch!" a voice snarled in his ear. "What in the hell do you think you're trying to pull!"

And Coyote nearly burst out laughing, so sharp was the shock of relief.

2003 hours
Flag Plot, U.S.S. *Thomas Jefferson*

Admiral Magruder looked at the hard copy of the comsat from Bushmaster and swore. The situation ashore, it seemed, was rapidly getting out of hand.

The message had not mentioned who it was that had escaped from the North Korean army camp—coding and the need to keep burst transmissions short precluded such mundane chitchat—but it sounded to Magruder as though the man must be one of the spooks, someone with James Bond-style delusions. He could well have wrecked everything by alerting the North Koreans to Bushmaster's presence. As it was, the SEALs must be going into deep hiding to avoid enemy search parties.

On the other hand, the information was certainly timely. If TF-18 was going to do anything, it would have to act now, this night . . . or watch *Chimera*'s crew whisked forever out of reach.

"Ron?"

An aide snapped to attention. "Yes, Admiral!"

He handed him the message. "Copies of this to Admiral Simpson and Colonel Caruso. And Captain Fitzgerald."

"Yes, sir."

"And fire up TAC COM. Priority CRITIC."

"Aye aye, sir."

Americans were being shot over there. *Damn!*

He wondered what the Washington appeasers and negotiators would think of this. If they didn't get their asses in gear *now* . . .

2044 hours (0644 hours EST.)
White House Situation Room

The President looked at the copy of the message relayed from Admiral Magruder and felt the weight of his office pressing down on him. He looked up, his eyes meeting Schellenberg's. "So, Jim, we're going to negotiate with these people? Sit down and talk things out?" He felt his blood pressure rising. He closed his fist and smashed it down on the table. "My God! Three of our sailors murdered in cold blood . . . and we're going to *negotiate* with them sometime next week?"

"I . . . don't have an answer, Mr. President. Possibly there are communication problems between P'yongyang and Nyong-ch'on."

"Communications problems." He sighed and looked away. The others watched him anxiously from around the table.

Caldwell licked his lips. "Sir, we can't deploy through South Korea before—"

"Not an option, General. Not now. The point is to get our people back, and if they're in P'yongyang . . ." He shrugged. "They might as well be on the moon. Hell, I think they'd be easier to reach on the moon! I can*not* go before Congress or the American people and justify starting up the Korean War all over again for . . ."

He let the words trail off. Where was the moral line in the dust across which an American President could step while balancing American lives against the risk of war? Would he commit combat troops to save two hundred men? For ten? For one?

The same decision had been faced time and time again by the White House, and the answer had never been clear-cut. Gerald Ford had sent the Marines into Cambodia to free the *Mayaguez*, sacrificing forty-one dead to rescue thirty-nine American merchant seamen. The Marines hadn't complained at the time. They would have said that putting their lives on the line to preserve American lives and property was their job.

But the guy who sent them in had some major questions to settle in his own mind first. When is the use of troops as an expression of U.S. foreign policy justified?

He turned to one of the aides hovering in the background. "Get me a direct line to Admiral Magruder."

No one spoke. No one met the President's eyes, knowing that the time for advisors—and for debate—was past. The silence lay heavy in the room as technicians worked to patch through to the *Jefferson* directly, each man, for the moment, alone with his thoughts. The President thought about Admiral Magruder. He'd never met the man, but the speed with which he'd assembled a workable operational plan earlier during the crisis spoke well of him, and of the efficiency of those under him.

The minutes dragged by. Getting a working communications linkup and going with a spot halfway around the globe was not always as simple as dialing long distance.

"Mr. President?" The aide extended a telephone handset. "Admiral Magruder, TF-18. It's scrambled."

He raised the receiver to his ear. "Admiral Magruder, this is the President."

"Good morning, Mr. President." The line was scratchy with static, but the admiral's voice was firm and distinct.

The President glanced up at the clock showing Tokyo time. It was evening in the Sea of Japan. "Admiral, do you feel that Operation Righteous Thunder, as currently planned, has a chance to succeed?"

There was a long pause on the other end of the line. "If we move fast, yes, sir. We have a good chance."

"It's a big operation. Things could go wrong."

"Things *always* go wrong, Mr. President. We just have to allow for it in the plan."

"And your recommendation is . . . ?"

"That we go for it, sir." Static crackled on the line. "My God, Mr. President, they're shooting our people in there. If we have the chance to pull them out, we'd damn well better take it."

"If things go wrong, we could lose a lot of people."

"And if we do nothing, Mr. President, the hostages could all die."

"Yes." The President looked across the table at the others, cabinet members and advisors. He felt quite alone. "Yes, of course. Admiral, please hold."

The President depressed the privacy button on the handset. "Gentlemen, I have no other option." He expected protest, but got none. Caldwell nodded slowly. Schellenberg stared at his hands, folded on the tabletop before him.

He released the button. "Admiral, I'm giving you a conditional go on Righteous Thunder."

"Conditional, Mr. President?"

"I'm putting the ball back in your court. I have no choice but to order a military response to this situation. If you believe that you have a chance of securing the release of *Chimera*'s crew before they are moved—if the level of risk is acceptable in your opinion—then you have my authorization to go in."

"Yes, sir."

He locked eyes with Caldwell as he continued. "If you do not move on your own, we will begin mounting a major military response out of South Korea, probably within two days." He hesitated. Schellenberg was still not meeting his gaze.

"I understand, Mr. President." A burst of static hissed over the line.

"Good luck, Admiral."

He handed the phone back to the waiting aide.

"Mr. President— " the Secretary of State began.

"Not now, Jim." The President pressed his hands over his eyes. "Gentlemen, we're committed. Possibly to a new war with North Korea."

"Do you think Magruder has a chance?" Hall asked.

"If he does, God knows he'll have a better crack at it if we're not trying to run things from here. Magruder's a good man. All we can do now is delegate and pray."

Abruptly, the President stood up, eliciting a flurry of squeaking chairs as the others did so as well. "And now, if you'll excuse me, gentlemen, I have to go work out what I'm going to tell the

American people." And what he would tell the wives and families later. There would be body bags coming home from this one.

How many, only God knew.

2049 hours
Flag Plot, U.S.S. *Thomas Jefferson*

Admiral Magruder replaced the phone in its cradle. Captain Fitzgerald stood beside him, hands on hips. "They bought it?"

He nodded. "It's a go." Magruder took a deep breath. His heart was hammering in his chest as hard as it ever had during any carrier landing. He was under no illusions about the limits of the authority that had just been handed to him. If Righteous Thunder failed, not even the President would be able to save his career. He would be the admiral who'd tried—and botched it.

Magruder found himself thinking about one particular failure of American arms in recent history, the debacle at Desert One, during Operation Eagle Claw in Iran.

The situation there had been similar in some ways, a large number of Americans held hostage by a hostile regime, an attempt to reach them by helicopters flown off a U.S. carrier. Eagle Claw had been unthinkably complex, much more so than Righteous Thunder. The chances for success in Iran had been slim to begin with.

But contributing to the disaster had been Washington's efforts to micromanage the entire affair. President Carter had been trying to direct the entire operation by satellite link from the White House, and a disaster had happened.

Magruder reached over to the plot table and picked up the latest TENCAP stat. It showed the inner harbor of Wonsan, *Chimera* tied up at the dock, close alongside the Russian warship. At least this President was giving his man in the field his head. The admiral knew that his career would stand or fall by his own decision.

"Lieutenant," he snapped, gesturing to an aide. "Get Admiral Simpson on the horn. Now."

"Aye aye, sir!"

Magruder grinned suddenly as he turned to face Fitzgerald, the first real smile to crease his face in several days. "By God, Jim. This time we're going to *take* them!"

2130 hours
In the hills above the Nyongch'on camp

Coyote shook his head in amazement. "You guys can't be for real."

Lieutenant Sikes grinned, his teeth startlingly white against the blacking on his face. "That's the way we earn our pay."

"Yeah, but fourteen men against three hundred . . ."

"Don't worry, fly-guy," one SEAL said, caressing his silenced Uzi SMG. "We'll get 'em to surround us . . . then kill them all. No sweat."

Coyote decided he did not understand SEALs and never would. They looked . . . *dangerous* was the only word that came to mind.

They spoke in whispers, careful not to disturb the night. The compound had been in a frenzy ever since Coyote's escape, with groups of men hurrying about inside and patrols filing through the front gates and into the surrounding darkness. More than once, the SEALs had heard men thrashing through brush in the distance, searching for the missing prisoner, but so far no one had come close to the hide. The Americans would be safe until the enemy started using dogs or infrared gear—which would take time to organize for a small base like this—or until daybreak.

And by then it would be too late.

Coyote's leg throbbed, a pounding agony beneath the bandages. One of the SEALs, a black guy named Robbins, had cleaned and dressed his wound. He'd been lucky. The AK round had torn through the fleshy part of his thigh, missing both bone and major blood vessels. There'd been a lot of blood, though, and the leg hurt like hell now that the initial shock had worn off. Whatever happened tonight, he'd be staying put, at least until he could find something he could use as a crutch.

"Okay," Sikes said, gathering the small circle of men with his eyes. "Here's the way we'll play it. Kohl, you stay put with the fly-boy. Your first responsibility is the POWs. You see what looks like a major move on the *Chimera*'s guys, get me on the TAC COM. Depending on where we are at the time, I might have you start taking them down . . . or sit tight while we deploy. No way to call it at this point."

"Right, Lieutenant."

"Rest of you guys are with me. You all know your targets?"

There was a chorus of nods and affirmative grunts. "Good. We'll lay low until midnight. You guys have until then to check your weapons, get your demo packs ready . . . and get some sleep. It's gonna be a long night."

Coyote's guts churned. The SEALs had been taking an almost bloodthirsty zeal in their last-minute planning, ever since word had come through on their compact satellite receiver from *Jefferson* that the rescue op was on for tonight. In general, the SEAL team's part in Righteous Thunder was simple: secure the prisoners and an LZ within the Nyongch'on compound, then send the message "Sunrise Blue." Reinforcements, codenamed Cavalry One, would arrive shortly after that. Zero hour had tentatively been set at 0200 for the SEAL assault and 0400 for the arrival of Cavalry One, though those times were flexible, subject to immediate change.

If Sunrise Blue was not transmitted, Cavalry One would come in anyway, but no one wanted to think about what that would mean. A helo assault into a hot LZ with an alerted enemy would not be pretty.

Coyote's real fear was that he had been responsible for this whole operation . . . and if things went down bad, it would all be his fault. His escape had aroused the North Korean camp with the thoroughness of a stick thrust into a hornet's nest, and with about the same result. Enemy patrols continued to wander through the darkness nearby, and the single sentry outside the POW compound had been replaced by an armed band of at least ten soldiers, armed with AKs and a Russian-made RPD machine gun.

If the SEALs couldn't infiltrate the enemy camp, if *Chimera*'s crew was spirited away somewhere out of reach before the op could be launched, it would be *his* fault.

2345 hours
Tomcat 205, U.S.S. *Thomas Jefferson*

Tombstone felt renewed.

The excitement extended to every man on the flight deck crew, visible in the crisp motions, signals and gestures, the jaunty grins, the two-fingered V-for-victory signs raised above their heads in salute. One yellow shirt stood in a pool of light from a nearby work lamp, looked up at Tombstone, and rammed his fist into the air. Tombstone grinned and returned the greeting with a thumbs-up as the yellow shirts began breaking down his Tomcat, releasing the chocks and chains which held her to the deck. Morale aboard the *Jefferson* had never been higher. We're going in this time, Tombstone thought. And this time nothing's going to stop us!

"How you feeling back there, Snowball?"

"Never better," his RIO replied. He sounded self-assured, businesslike. "Radio frequencies set, nav guidance punched in. We're ready to roll, skipper."

"Here she goes." He started up the Tomcat's engines, first the left, then the right, feeling the surge of power shudder through the airframe. Gently, he set the gray-white throttle handles by his left hand to idle, waiting until the breakdown was complete. A yellow shirt waved his colored wand, directing Tombstone out of his parking space.

Slowly, the F-14 moved toward the catapult. Above the thrumming roar of his engines, Tombstone heard the sudden, howling thunder of an A-6 Intruder's twin Pratt and Whitney turbojets revving to full throttle, then the shuddering blast of sound as a catapult hurled the aircraft out over the ocean. The building excitement was tangible. This was it!

The order to assemble for a briefing had come through from CAG less than three hours earlier. As before, Tombstone would be leading the tactical CAP for the ground attack aircraft, Hornets and Intruders. The Alpha Strike would be going in low, hard, and fast, skimming the waves almost all the way in; their primary targets included most of the objectives of the aborted mission of the day before, SAM sites and coastal radars, AA batteries and communications centers, as well as the airfield at Kolmo across the bay from the Wonsan waterfront.

It was imperative that the Strike, codenamed Desperado, knock out the SAMs and radar. If it didn't, the entire op would almost certainly fail. For the first few hours, the operation's success would be riding on the A-6 Intruders of VA-84 and VA-89, the Blue Rangers and the Death Dealers. The Hornets of VFA-161 and VFA-173, the Javelins and the Fighting Hornets, would be following close behind, taking down what the Intruders missed.

Meanwhile the F-14s, codenamed Shotgun, would provide cover for Desperado.

As CAG had laid it out at the briefing, Righteous Thunder would go down in a series of stages. The air-to-ground strikes were Phase One. Phase Two would begin approximately two hours later with CH-53E Super Stallion helicopters in their minesweeper role, using towed sleds to clear the approaches to the landing beaches for the Marines. At about the same time, a special flight of four RH-53D Sea Stallion helos designated Cavalry One would depart from the U.S.S. *Chosin*. The Marine landings were scheduled to begin with high tide, at approximately 0545 hours in the morning.

Tombstone checked his cockpit clock. Two hours to go before the helo ops began, six until the landings began. *Jefferson*'s air wing had that long to open the way for the Marines. It was a tall order.

In the darkness of the flight deck, colored lights probed and clustered, darted and winked, like workers attending a queen bee. Blue shirts checked flaps and control surfaces. A red shirt held high the red-tagged wires which had safed the Tomcat's air-to-air missiles until he'd removed them. Tombstone checked the wires, verifying the count. This time his load mix was six Phoenix and two Sidewinders. The rules of engagement for this mission were to hit the other guy before he hit you . . . which meant the long-range Phoenix could be used to best advantage.

What surprised him most was the realization that he had no questions about his own part in things, despite his failure the night before. He felt the familiar, rapid hammering of his heart beneath his harness, sure, but the doubts were gone. It was strange how his talk with Batman had steadied him.

Fight to fly, fly to fight, fight to win. He owed it to the other men in the squadron to see the Top Gun slogan through. He owed it to himself.

And to Coyote.

The F-14 moved into place on catapult one. A green shirt standing to the left of the aircraft held up the lighted board: 68,000. Tombstone unclipped a penlight from the clipboard on his thigh and held it against the cockpit canopy, describing a circle which indicated that he agreed with the figure for the Tomcat's weight.

The familiar succession of clanks, rattles, and thumps followed as the hook-up men clipped the launching bar on the Tomcat's nose gear to the catapult shuttle riding in its slot on the flight deck. The catapult officer waved his green-filtered flashlight horizontally, signaling Tombstone to bring his throttles up to military power.

He checked the control stick and rudder pedals: Father, Son,

Holy Ghost, Amen. All correct. The cat officer signaled again, up and down this time. Tombstone responded by sending the throttle the final notch forward to full burner, then switched on his navigation and running lights. The green light shone from the carrier island.

"They're givin' us the word, Stoney!" Snowball said.

"Hang onto your stomach, Snowball. It's go. *Go!*"

The deck officer touched his light to the deck, then raised it, pointing off the bow. There was a second's pause, and then the Tomcat slammed forward into the night.

DAY FIVE

CHAPTER 22

0052 hours
Yo-do

The first blow fell against the island of Yo-do, a rocky islet twelve miles off the Korean coast. There was little of interest there: a fishing village, a small military base—and the seaward-facing radar arrays for Yo-do's SAM sites.

At 0048 hours, the base went on full alert. The jamming which had been fogging Yo-do's radar for the past several days had cleared, and in the unaccustomed clarity a number of targets could be made out to the east, crossing into North Korean airspace.

Word was flashed back to Wonsan, and from there to P'yong-yang. Uncertainty about American reactions to the Wonsan crisis was now resolved. It was evident now that the Yankees planned to strike at North Korea with a seaborne air strike, similar to the nightmare F-111 raid they'd mounted against Libya in 1986.

Yo-do's main radar arrays tracked the oncoming Americans. The smaller tracking radars used to direct the SAM batteries switched on, picking their targets,

Minutes later death fell, unheralded and unsuspected, from the skies, shredding the concave latticeworks of the Korean radar antennae in the searing detonation of missile warheads, each packing 145 pounds of high explosive.

The HARM AGM-88A had been launched from Navy carrier aircraft against Libyan radar sites in 1986, where it had proved its worth against Qaddafi's SAMs. Each HARM—a High-speed Anti-Radiation Missile—was over thirteen feet long and weighed nearly eight hundred pounds. The only weapon ever carried by the Navy's EA-6B electronic warfare Prowler, it had a range of eighty nautical miles and a radar profile so narrow the Korean operators literally never knew what hit them.

Minutes after the destruction of Yo-do's radar eyes, similar outposts on the Kolmo Peninsula, on Sin-do outside of Wonsan Harbor, and on the rugged coasts north and south of Wonsan itself all vanished in savage explosions as their own radar emissions called down the death which hurtled in at nearly Mach 1.

The explosions were still echoing across the waters of Wonsan Harbor when the air armanda assembled above the Yonghung Man completed its refueling from orbiting tankers and began descending on the Korean coast.

0110 hours
Tomcat 232, off the North Korean coast

"Coming up on the beach, Malibu."

"I hear you. Pickin' up some fuzz from local radars now, tryin' to burn through the Prowler jamming. Nothing serious."

"Keep watching 'em." The HARM strike would have taken out most of the main North Korean radar stations, but there were certain to be some smaller ones untouched . . . any which had been shut down and therefore not emitting a homing signal for the HARMs to zero in on. The Koreans would be in a panic now, though. With the Alpha Strike again masked by jamming, they'd be desperate to see what was coming at them.

Batman checked his speed and altitude again. The Tomcat was skimming less than eighty feet off the deck, but the ocean below was an invisible black gulf.

"Anything in the air yet?"

"No, sir. No MiGs Maybe the gomers don't do nighttime."

Batman felt the faintest of uncertain stirrings. Would he be able to line up an enemy plane, lock on and shoot? He was certain now that he could, but some irrational part of himself insisted that he would never know until the time came.

And he knew that the inner voice was right.

His talk with Tombstone had steadied him. For the first time since he'd joined VF-95, he felt truly a part of the squadron. He would do what he'd been trained to do . . . and worry about that nagging inner voice later. Gently he nudged the stick forward, keeping his eye on the altimeter as he shaved several feet from the F-14's altitude.

In any case, a strong MiG response was not expected; night

would give the technologically advanced American fighters too great an advantage over the MiG-21s, which would probably elect to sit things out until daybreak. Opposition would come from SAM sites scattered up and down the coast, especially the ones clustered along the Kolmo Peninsula near the airfield. The HARMs would have taken out the major radars, but some SAM sites would not give themselves away until U.S. planes were overhead.

And that was where the Tomcats came in, riding in ahead of the bombers, deliberately tempting the North Koreans to turn on their SAM radars. Launch sites would be plotted by the E-2C Hawkeyes circling fifty miles off the coast, and relayed to the Hornets and Intruders following in the Tomcats' wakes. Malibu had jokingly referred to their role as PPT: Paid Professional Target.

Lights shone across the water, drifting now to left and right as he approached the coast. There was a low ceiling this night, solid above five thousand feet. Light from Wonsan reflected from the clouds with an orange glow, backlighting the ridge which formed the backbone of the Kolmo Peninsula. The airfield would be to the south. He brought the stick slightly to port.

The beach flashed under the Tomcat's keel, white surf on black rock dimly seen in the night. "Two-three-two, feet dry," Batman announced over the radio. He brought the stick up to clear the rugged, boulder-strewn slope of the ridge.

"Copy, Two-three-two," Tombstone's voice replied. It sounded as though Stoney finally had all his shit in one seabag. Batman wondered what had brought him around.

Maybe he'd just finally come to grips with Coyote's death. What the hell, Batman thought. Flying is a dangerous game. There isn't an aviator in the Navy who hasn't known *someone* whose number had been called. All you could do was pick up, keep going. Or pack it in and quit.

Tombstone did not look like a quitter to Batman.

"Threat warning," Malibu said. "They've got a lock."

Batman heard the chirp in his headphones, as a red light labeled MISSILE flashed. "Plot it." He looked from side to side, hoping for a glimpse of the enemy launch.

"Got it!" Malibu snapped. "Tally-ho at two o'clock!"

Batman whipped his head around in time to catch the flash. The SAM looked like a telephone pole balanced on flame as it rose above the rocky crest of the peninsula.

The ridge flashed beneath the Tomcat, and in the next instant

Wonsan spread out in front of him like a map picked out in lights. Shipping crowded the harbor, but *Jefferson*'s aviators had carefully studied current TENCAP photos before the mission. Damage to non-Korean ships and property was to be avoided, where possible.

Batman pushed the stick forward, dropping the F-14 toward the surface of the bay. The threat warning continued to chirp in his ear.

"Another launch, Batman," Malibu said. "Five o'clock . . . by the airfield."

"Now comes the fun. Let's have some chaff."

The water of the bay, illuminated now by reflected light from Wonsan, swept up beneath the Tomcat's belly. The SAMs arced overhead, points of white fire in the night.

"Negative tone," Malibu said. "They lost us in the wave scatter."

"Shotgun Leader, Two-three-two," Batman said, his voice held level and unconcerned. "Feet wet. We are engaged."

The fight over Wonsan had begun in earnest.

0115 hours
Intruder 555, off the coast of North Korea

Lieutenant Commander Isaac Greene, "Jolly Green" to his running mates, was not particularly well-liked by the others, but then he didn't care for most of them and that, he felt, made everything even. Loud, given to outbursts which made him seem somewhat obnoxious, Greene had few friends. The other members of the squadron were convinced he had a genuine talent for picking fights.

Liked or not, however, he was respected by every man in the wing and regarded with a perverse sense of pride by the members of his squadron, VA-89's Death Dealers. When he was guiding his A-6 in for a strike, the boasting and sarcasm vanished, replaced by the ice-cold professionalism which made him a superb Intruder pilot.

Unlike the Tomcat with its front seat-rear seat configuration, the Intruder seated the pilot and the bombardier-navigator almost side by side. It took a certain icy calm to fly the A-6 in on a run. Instead of a HUD the aviator had a Heads *Down* Display, a Kaiser AVA-1 Visual Display Indicator, or VDI. An electronic picture of everything in the aircraft's path was painted on the VDI monitor, together with weapons cues and basic flight data. It was the bomber's sophisticated avionics which made it so useful in the all-weather attack role, capable of carrying out pinpoint attacks in fog, rain, or snow . . . or in the middle of a moonless, overcast night. With the VDI, Jolly could literally fly the Intruder without bothering to look forward through the canopy at all, a feat which earned him both scorn and head-shaking admiration from the fighter jocks who pretended to trust their eyes more than their avionics.

As Intruder 555, "Triple Nickle," slid into its approach vector, Lieutenant Chucker Vance, Jolly's BN, kept his face buried in the black hood shielding his radar scope from extraneous light. "Contact," he said. "Ground lock!" He switched his display to Forward-Looking InfraRed for an ID. "Looks like a SAM park on FLIR."

Jolly watched the shifting patterns on his VDI. As Chucker switched the plane's computer to attack mode, new symbols giving relative target bearing, drift, time, and weapons status flicked on. "Let's give him some rock-a-bye."

Chucker set the ordnance panel to deliver a pair of Rockeye II CBU-59 cluster bombs, each a five-hundred-pound cannister which would scatter two hundred fifty separate bomblets across an oval of death three hundred feet long.

The Intruder lurched once, forcing Jolly to correct slightly, bringing the steering bug on his VDI back into line with the nav pipper. He glanced up once, noting with mild surprise that the sky was filled with red and orange tracers, long lines of fiery dots reaching into the night sky. The plane lurched again.

"Pretty heavy triple-A."

"Uh," Chucker grunted in noncommittal answer. He kept his face buried in the radar hood. "Weapons hot, safe off. Uh-oh. Threat signal. They're tracking, Jolly."

"I don't give a rat's ass what they're doing." He opened the tactical channel. "Feet dry! Lead's going in hot!"

The A-6 hurtled in low over the Kolmo Peninsula, jagged rocks clawing for the Intruder's belly out of the darkness. With the target tagged by radar and fed into the aircraft's computer, the target appeared on the VDI as a green, computer graphic square, the bombsight as a tiny cross crawling up a straight line from the bottom of the screen toward the release point. The A-6 was slow, strictly subsonic, but even at 460 knots the Intruder shrieked toward the cluster of antiaircraft guns like a thundering cavalry charge. While he could have set the computer to release the Rockeye, Jolly preferred the feel of the stick pickle under his thumb as he mashed it down. The plane shuddered as the cluster bomb released. Jolly brought the stick back and throttled up.

Behind them, a cloud of Rockeye bomblets, each one powerful enough to cripple a tank, descended across the rocky terrain. The effect in the darkness was of hundreds of flashbulbs going off within the space of half a second. An instant later, a much brighter flash stained the night with orange and gold . . . and then another. Ammunition stores were exploding down there in a furious display of fireworks, the roar lost beneath the howl of the aircraft's engines.

"Right on the money!" Chucker craned around to see aft past the Intruder's wing. "We got secondaries!" Fresh explosions marked the disintegration of a fuel tank.

"Okay, boys and girls," Jolly announced over the tactical channel to the other Death Dealers. Inwardly he was shaking. He'd never dropped munitions on a live target before. He kept the tremor from his voice, though, and managed a dry chuckle. "That's the way it's done. Let's see you beat that!"

Behind and beneath Intruder 555, flames boiled into the night sky.

0120 Hours
In the hills above Nyongch'on camp

Coyote saw the orange glow as flames lit the clouds to the north. He found himself counting off the seconds before he heard the sound, a series of dull, faint thuds more felt than heard. Thirty-seven seconds . . . almost eight miles. Although he couldn't see the fire itself or relate it to the night-invisible landscape, that put it somewhere in or near Wonsan . . . possibly on the peninsula beyond the airfield.

Closer at hand a siren began wailing. The rescue was on, and Coyote felt a galloping excitement mixed with his worry about the odds the SEALs were facing.

"Do you think they have a chance?" he whispered.

Kohl, lying beside him in the hide, shifted slightly in the darkness. "Shh." The man kept his face pressed tightly against the night sight mounted on his rifle, careful to let none of the light from the optics escape to betray their presence.

Coyote gave a mental shrug and went back to studying the

landscape below. The SEALs were awfully particular when it came to security discipline, and Coyote was not going to be allowed to settle any of his inward doubts through conversation.

Another flash lit up the northern sky. Coyote could make out the flicker of antiaircraft tracers now, could faintly hear the thunder of jets, the sharper, harsher cracks of bombs. Someone was getting an earful up there tonight.

Coyote moved, wincing with the flash of pain in his leg as he reached for a pair of binoculars lying nearby. He could see little more through the binoculars than he could with his own eyes. The camp was still brilliantly lit, and he could plainly see soldiers moving around inside in small groups.

There was no sign of the other SEALs who had vanished into the darkness with their weapons and packs hours before. The excitement in the camp had died down somewhat, though ten men remained on guard in front of the POW compound, and the roving perimeter patrols had been beefed up.

How could the SEALs hope to infiltrate the place with the base on alert?

He was also worried about *Chimera*'s crew. Would their captors punish them for his escape? Would the general who'd arrived last evening order them all to be moved at once? He shifted his attention to the Hip helicopter, still resting on the small airstrip on the west side of the camp. Those big transports couldn't carry more than twenty-five or thirty people at a time, but suppose the Koreans decided to herd just *Chimera*'s officers aboard and fly them off? That could happen at any time, and until the SEALs got into position, there was nothing to stop the gomers from doing whatever they wanted.

Sikes had not seemed worried at all. The enemy, he believed, was unlikely to do anything so long as they were kept confused and off-balance. Coyote's first assessment of these men came back to him. *Dangerous.*

All he could do was try to stay out of their way.

The sounds of explosions in the north seemed to be stirring the enemy camp once again. Lines of men trotted out of the three-story barracks at the north end of the camp. The men standing guard outside the Wonsan Waldorf stood and shuffled about uncertainly, their eyes on the sky.

To the north, the thunder continued, increasing in intensity. Searchlights probed the clouds as tracer rounds floated through the darkness.

"They're going to think this is Libya '86," Sikes had said during the planning earlier. "That'll be our edge. They don't know they've got an invasion on their hands."

That made sense. The crash and thunder of the attack would alert North Korean troops on the ground, of course—there was no way to avoid that—but they would assume that it was *only* an air raid, and that would give the SEALs the surprise they needed.

With the suddenness of a thrown switch, the Nyongch'on camp was plunged into darkness. Someone down there had decided to black out the base to avoid becoming a target for the American planes.

Coyote smiled. Maybe the SEALs knew what they were doing after all.

0132 hours
Nyongch'on-kiji

Lieutenant Sikes held his breath, wondering for at least the hundredth time this night if the SEALs hadn't finally bitten off more than they could chew. They'd been in position for over thirty minutes, sheltered in a defile below the outside perimeter fence. Huerta had led them to the spot where he'd let himself in earlier that evening.

But it appeared that Huerta's handiwork had been discovered.

There were six of them, North Korean special-purpose troops who had come along the outside of the fence out of nowhere, apparently inspecting it carefully for signs that someone had broken out . . . or in.

Sikes had hoped the enemy would assume that the American pilot had escaped on his own by wiggling under the fence a hundred yards down the line, but it appeared that this time they were taking nothing for granted. The soldiers, carrying large flashlights, had spotted the place where the chain links had been clipped away from a fence pole, then hastily wired back into place. Now the men seemed to be talking it over in harsh, animated whispers.

Gently, Sikes reached up and pulled his M927 night-sight goggles down and in place. Wearing the things for more than ten or fifteen minutes at a time caused a temporary eye strain called "scope burn." He looked left and right, meeting the otherworldly, twin-tubed stares of the other men in the team. The lieutenant raised one hand, silently flicking his fingers: *You and you, circle around.*

On the slope above them, two of the KorCom soldiers turned their flashlights on the defile, probing its recesses with the beams. Sikes looked away. Unlike early-generation starlight goggles, his M927s didn't shut down when exposed to bright light, but he could still wreck his night vision by looking into the glare.

The fact that those soldiers had already dazzled themselves with their own lights was a factor in the SEAL team's favor. Perhaps for that reason, the beams did not linger on any of the men hiding in the defile, but passed on, sweeping uselessly across the rugged slope behind them. The SEALs lay still, waiting. The Koreans were moving now. One—possibly the leader—pointed down the defile, almost directly in Sikes's direction. *"Aphuro t'tok paro kase yo!"*

Sikes did not understand Korean, but the man's gesture and tone were unmistakable. He was sending men down to search for anything out of the ordinary. Four soldiers started forward cautiously, testing the footing with each step.

The lieutenant moved his hand again. *Get ready.* With no waste motion at all, he lowered his M-760 and quietly slipped his Mark 22 pistol from its holster. The other SEALs did the same. From this angle, the missed rounds from a submachine gun burst might strike the fence or one of the compound buildings and raise the alarm.

Even with suppressors, it was too great a risk. His grip tightened on the pistol as he snicked off the safety. They were about to be discovered and they weren't even inside the damned perimeter yet.

Silently, the SEALs waited as the Koreans drew closer.

CHAPTER 23

Huerta watched the approach of the North Koreans. They were less than twenty feet away now. One stumbled as loose stones gave way beneath his boots.

Any time now . . .

Even through the M927 goggles, the attackers rising out of the shadows near the fence were nearly invisible. The two KorComs still examining the fence never knew what hit them. Black arms encircled from behind, black hands clamped down on mouths just opening to yell, black knives sliced through skin, muscle, and vein in simultaneous thrusts as the soldiers were dragged back and down.

A slight noise—the scrape of boot heel on rock, perhaps—alerted one of the Koreans halfway down the defile. "*Muos imnikka?*"

Three feet to his left, Lieutenant Sikes raised his Mark 22 hush puppy to eye level and fired, the heavy suppressor cutting the sound to a sharp clack.

Huerta fired in almost the same instant . . . and again, and again. The other SEALs were shooting as well, the sound a chorus of hard, muffled slaps. Bullet holes appeared as if by magic in each of the KorCom soldiers, marring faces, bloodying jackets, tearing throats. One man pitched forward and rolled down the defile, his AK-47 scraping rock with a metallic rasp louder than the volley of suppressed shots.

Then the night was silent once more.

The SEALs waited, listening to the stillness. If anyone had heard . . .

One of the SEALs by the fence raised his hand in a cautious all-clear. Swiftly the other black-suited commandos hurried up the defile to the fence. Then, one by one, they lay on their backs and slid under the gap in the fence and into the compound.

The lieutenant signaled again, not risking words. Each man knew his assigned target in any case, and speech was unnecessary. The raiders divided into two-man teams: Copley and Krueger for the communications shed and microwave tower, Bonner and Smith to the airstrip where a pair of sentries were guarding the grounded Mi-8 helicopter, Halliday and Austin to the headquarters building, Robbins and Pasaretti to the motor pool, and Sikes and Gordon to the barracks and the nearby trenches which served as bomb shelters. The last three men, Vespasio, Han, and Huerta, would head for the POW compound.

Huerta checked his watch, peeling back the velcro to briefly reveal its luminous dial. It was nearly 0145, and there was a long way yet to go. Silently, he led his two partners toward the Wonsan Waldorf, retracing his steps of the night before.

0150 hours
Intruder 555, over the Kolmo Peninsula

Lieutenant Commander Greene kept his attention fixed on the VDI display as he banked the Intruder slightly west, lining up for the final run. For over thirty minutes, the Death Dealers had struck at targets up and down the Kolmo Peninsula. Flames licked at the sky in a dozen places now, where flak batteries and petroleum tank farms were burning. Intruder 555 had dropped the last of its bombs, a pair of five-hundred-pound Mark 82 GPs released over the south end of the airfield runway. There was no way to tell what had been hit, exactly, but the TENCAP photos had shown what looked like aircraft hangars in the area. Something big had gone up; flames painted the runway in lurid reds and yellows, and the glow lit up the sky.

Jolly had seen no MiGs during his passes over the field. They'd either been in the hangars—in which case they were burning now—or they'd been pulled out before the attack. No matter one way or the other; the runway had been struck again and again by Snakeeye retarded bombs and GPs, leaving the concrete cratered and broken.

"Feet wet," he announced over the radio as the Intruder swept eastward over the surf. The other Death Dealers were already heading back toward the *Jefferson*, or would be as soon as they dropped the last of their ordnance. "Take a coupla cold ones out of the fridge, guys, we're comin' home."

"Copy, Intruder Five-five-five," a voice replied. That would be Lieutenant Harkins, down in CATCC. "Come to zero-nine-eight and goose it. Can't help with the beer, but we've got a fresh load of Mark 82s waitin' for you."

Jolly looked over his left shoulder, at the fires highlighting the spine of Kolmo.

"Yeah, well, it beats hell out of target practice. Triple Nickle, coming in."

0230 hours
Over Yonghung Bay

By the time Jolly Greene was back on *Jefferson*'s flight deck, other American aircraft were again approaching the North Korean coast, helicopters this time, four monster CH-53E Super Stallions flying off the *Chosin* as minesweepers. Each helo strained against its load, a Mark 105 sled dragged through the water by a cable hung astern. Intelligence believed that the sea lanes and approaches outside of Wonsan Harbor were clear of mines—there had been no cessation of seagoing traffic in or out of the city in the past week—but the technology of mine warfare had improved at least as much as the technology used for clearing them. It was possible that there were seabed mines in place, awaiting only the throwing of a switch ashore to arm them. The sleds, mimicking the sounds and changing water pressure and magnetic profile of a warship, would trick the mines into exploding, if any were in place and active.

So far, intelligence had been proven right . . . a fact which promised healthy profits to those sailors and Marines who had bet against the odds.

Farther at sea, reveille had been called aboard the *Chosin* and her Marine Expeditionary Unit escorts, breakfast served, and inspections held for all hands with weapons and full kit.

Within the cavernous aft bay of the U.S.S. *Little Rock*, Marines were already loading themselves and their equipment onto the pair of odd-shaped vessels resting in the LPD's flooded docking well. Preparations were also underway on board the LST *Westmoreland County*, where AAVP7 amphibious tractors and LCVPs were being readied for embarkation. Farther out at sea, the rotors were already turning on four RH-53D Sea Stallions resting on *Chosin*'s flight deck, as Marines filed up an outboard ladder, moved along the catwalk, then bent nearly double for the race across open deck and up the lowered rear ramps.

And farther out still, the U.S.S. *Jefferson* maintained her heading into the wind, launching aircraft almost as quickly as she recovered them. From now until Operation Righteous Thunder ended, there would be no rest at all for her crew, especially for the men of her deck division and air wing. Two of her four tankers were kept aloft at all times, refueling the planes awaiting their turn to trap, landing only when they themselves ran low on fuel. By 0230 hours, the second Alpha Strike was airborne and heading west, searching for SAM sites and radars which had eluded the first attack.

Jefferson's flight deck was a continuing whirlwind of activity, with red shirts hauling bombs and munitions up from the bowels of the ship, with the purple-shirted grapes refueling aircraft as quickly as they could be turned around, with exhausted hook-and-cat men continuing the never-ending ballet of breakdown, ready, shoot, and trap. The aviators and RIOs, if they were lucky, grabbed a few minutes' sleep at a time in their ready rooms. Most were too excited to do so, however. At long last they were being allowed to strike back at an enemy that had struck at them, doing the jobs for which they had invested so much of their lives. Morale was good, expectations high.

And disaster was something even the most pessimistic man aboard simply refused to think about.

0320 hours
Nyongch'on-kiji

Most of the charges had been planted by now, but the SEALs wanted to wait as long as possible before springing their surprise on the unsuspecting North Koreans in the camp. The idea was to wait until 0430 hours, to give the Navy air strikes more time to hit their targets, but Huerta didn't think they'd be able to wait that long.

The truck pulled up from the direction of the HQ building, carrying two officers, a major and a captain. The four KorCom soldiers standing outside the prison compound gate stood hastily when they saw them climbing out of the cab.

The three SEALs, Han, Huerta, and Vespasio, had found cover

beneath another truck parked across the road from the Korean guards. From there, Huerta could hear their voices clearly across the thirty feet which separated the soldiers from the hidden SEALs. Silently, he signaled Han. What are they saying?

BM/1 Charlie Han was an American-born Angeleno, the son of South Korean immigrants. He was also one of three SEALs on the team who spoke Korean—the best that could be done for a team assembled with such haste. Han listened for a moment, then leaned over, cupping his hand between his mouth and Huerta's ear.

"New orders," Han whispered, his voice so low it did not travel more than inches. Something about 'get them ready to move right away.'"

Huerta licked his lips. To be so close . . ..

He reached up and switched on his tactical radio. He did not speak, both for his own safety and for Sikes's. Instead, he punched the squelch button four times in rapid succession, the prearranged click code for the situation they'd all hoped would not arise: *They're moving the prisoners. Orders?*

There was a long pause. The answer, when it came, was three clicks, a pause, and three clicks more, the answer Huerta had expected. Silently, he touched Vespasio and pointed. The SEAL nodded, slid backward on his belly, then rolled out from under the truck. In seconds he was gone, a shadow moving through the night. Huerta looked at Han and grinned. The word was *go*!

Across the road, two more KorCom sentries trotted up, members of a roving patrol about the POW compound. More orders were given, something about leaving the wounded until later. Apparently, more trucks were being readied over at the motor pool. Huerta wondered if Robbins and Pasarotti had mined them yet.

Carefully, he raised his M-760 and slipped off the safety. At his side, Han brought his Uzi up. Seconds slipped by as they waited for Vespasio to get in position.

But there was no more time to waste. Four of the guards were already going through the gate, heading toward the building *Chimera*'s crew had named the Wonsan Waldorf. It was now or never.

He squeezed the trigger, holding the weapon's barrel down and dragging the muzzle back along the line of KorCom soldiers visible through his night sight. The suppressed weapon bucked and kicked in his hand, the staccato roar muted to the sharp, *slap-slap-slap* of the bolt as it ratcheted back and forth. Empty brass cartridges spun and danced, clinking as they struck the underside of the tank inches above his head. Han opened up with the silenced Uzi, loosing precisely controlled three-round bursts into the enemy troops.

The Koreans walking toward the POW building twisted, spun, and fell, or collided with one another as it registered on them that they were under fire. One man gasped, a sound more of surprise than of pain, and then a second round spun him about and slammed him to the ground seconds before one of his comrades dropped across his body. The captain staggered as three rounds stitched up his spine, marking his back with spreading patches which looked black through the starlight goggles. A soldier next to the officer turned and stared, mouth open, not realizing the man had been shot until one 9-mm round punctured his throat and a second crushed his skull. The smash and tinkle of shattered glass was louder than the gunfire. In the cab of the truck, the driver threw hands over face, then tumbled sideways out the open door.

Huerta ceased fire long enough to drop an empty magazine and slap in a fresh one. Vespasio's Colt Commando opened up from across the street at the same moment, chopping into two soldiers who had taken cover behind the truck. One man screamed, a sharp, shocking yell above the hammer of 9-mm rounds striking the truck's side.

"*Chosim!*" the major shrieked, and then he went down as well. The last soldier managed to unsling his AK-47 and drag the bolt back as he searched wildly for a target. Rounds slammed into his chest and knocked him down.

And then it was over, the North Koreans sprawled dead behind the still-idling military truck. The entire firefight had lasted less than four seconds, so brief a time that the KorComs had not even been able to shoot back. Huerta rolled out from under the tank, stood, and raced across the street, drawing his hush puppy as he ran. By the time Vespasio and Han joined him, he was already putting silent mercy rounds into the skulls of the men sprawled on the ground. There was no time now for prisoners, and the risk of taking them was too great.

Huerta didn't know if the men he shot were still alive or not. Han helped finish the job with a silent, thin-lipped ferocity, while Vespasio stood guard.

The street was deserted, except for the three SEALs and the bodies. Even the Wonsan Waldorf was silent and dark. Despite the yells, the clatter of falling weapons, the thump of rounds striking the side of the truck, no one seemed to have noticed the brief and savage firefight which had just taken place. Perhaps they'd just bought the op a precious few minutes more.

Huerta gave orders to the other two. Swiftly, they began picking up bodies and tossing them one by one into the back of the truck. He stepped aside and kept his eye on the surrounding, darkened buildings as he opened his radio's tactical channel. "Bushmaster One, this is Bush Five," he whispered, using the codename which would identify him to Sikes.

He received two clicks for answer: *Go ahead.*

"Sentry point secure. No alarm."

"Keep it that way," the lieutenant replied. "We need more time."

"I'm leaving Han on guard here. I want to check the motor pool with Vespasio." He was thinking about the trucks the KorCom officers had mentioned. "Things may be going wrong over there."

Sikes clicked the squelch twice for answer and Huerta signed off. Han had already found a jacket and pants unmarred by bullet holes or blood and was pulling them on over his combat blacks. An AK-47 and a soft, shapeless cap with a red star above the brim completed the impromptu disguise. He was still wearing black combat boots instead of the soft, high-topped boots usually worn by KorCom soldiers, but it was unlikely that anyone would get close enough to him to notice. Han should pass any casual inspection for the few minutes that Huerta and Vespasio would be away, and his knowledge of Korean and his Oriental features should let him field questions by anyone wondering where the small army guarding the POWs had gone.

"I'll tell them that everybody else went to get the trucks," Han said, grinning.

Which was exactly what Huerta had in mind. Nine bodies—six guards, a driver, and two officers—lay on the truck's flatbed, concealed by a roll of camouflage netting found in the back. The SEALs would park the vehicle near the motor pool, where the bodies should remain undiscovered until it was too late.

Without another word, Huerta brushed broken glass from the driver's seat and climbed in behind the wheel, ignoring the blood splattered across the upholstery. Vespasio got in on the passenger's side.

The motor pool was less than a hundred yards across the darkened compound. Huerta gunned the motor to life and turned into the road. Behind them, Han waved once and took the position of a lone sentry on a boring night watch.

0338 hours
Outside Anbyon, PDRK

Anbyon was a fair-sized city in the mountains south of Wonsan, and the location of an important military reserve depot located on the single highway running south across the Taebaeks toward the Demarcation Line, seventy-five kilometers away. Captain Sun Dae-jung of the People's Air Defense Forces climbed onto the aft deck of his ZSU-23-4 and scanned the darkness of the northern sky.

Wonsan was twenty kilometers away and he didn't really expect to see any sign of the air attacks which the port city had reported. Still, his orders carried a sense of raw urgency. Every available reserve unit in the area was to be mustered for the defense of the city.

The four ZSU's of Sun's company could get there within the hour. Sun had been born and raised in Wonsan, and he knew the area well. From the hills south of the harbor, where the road from Anbyon joined the coastal highway, they would have a splendid command of the skies over the harbor.

And he knew his vehicles, deadly looking antiaircraft vehicles which Sun knew by their Russian name: *Shilka*. Their quad-mounted 23-mm cannon would be only marginally effective against supersonic aircraft such as the American Tomcats and Hornets, but their radar-controlled precision, their sheer volume of fire would spell doom for any helicopter or subsonic ground attack that came within range.

The engine spat and roared as the driver cranked it to life. Behind him, the other three *Shilkas* shuddered and rumbled, exhaust fumes roiling across the pools of light cast by the Anbyon base's lights. Elsewhere, trucks and small military vehicles scurried about like insects. Every soldier in the People's Democratic Republic would be awake by now, Sun thought, armed and ready to defend the fatherland.

But his company would be on the spearpoint of that defense.

"*Kapsida!*" he shouted over the engine roar to his driver. "Let's go!"

With a lurch, the tracked vehicle thundered ahead, making Sun grip the edge of the open hatch to keep from being thrown.

He hoped the American aircraft were still over Wonsan by the time he reached the city. In the pre-dawn darkness, his squat vehicles would be next to impossible to see—a real surprise for the overconfident Imperialists.

Sun smiled to himself as his column clanked ahead toward the mountain pass at Nyongch'on.

0352 hours
Inside the Nyongch'on camp

Boatswain's Mate First Han heard the approaching Korean soldier an instant before he saw him, a confident swish-click of boots on the pavement a few yards away. He did not unsling his AK-47. A burst from the unsilenced weapon would awaken the entire compound. Instead, his right hand fished for the Mark 22 hush puppy he'd tucked into his web belt at the small of his back.

He faced the newcomer. "*Kogi nugu'se yo?*" he said, his tone challenging. "Who's there?" If there was a password or counter-sign he was dead, but if he could take the initiative before the other man's suspicions were aroused . . .

The Korean was close enough now that Han could see his features in the dim illumination from a light outside the darkened camp. He was a typical-looking soldier, with a sergeant's rank tabs and an AK slung muzzle-down, a pail in one hand. Han caught the sour tang of *kimchi* . . . dinner for the squad on duty.

The soldier glanced about once, then looked hard at Han, his eyes hardening with sudden suspicion. "*Nuku'simnikka?*" the North Korean snapped. "Who are you? Where are the others?"

Han knew at once that his carefully prepared story would not convince this man. The KorCom soldier's free hand was already going for the pistol grip of his AK-47, snapping the selector switch to full auto, dragging the muzzle up in a one-handed attempt to shoot Han before the SEAL could react.

But Han already had his hush puppy out, whipping the pistol around and squeezing the trigger. The heavy-barreled weapon thumped once . . . twice. The Korean stumbled, his feet tangling with the bucket of *kimchi* as he fell.

The blaze of autofire stabbing into the sky from the soldier's AK-47 shattered the camp's silence. Across the compound, lights were coming on . . .

"*Saram sallyo yo!*" the wounded guard screamed. He'd emptied half his magazine into the sky. "Help! Intruders!" He struggled to aim the AK at the SEAL.

Han fired again and again until the screams were silenced, but it was already too late. He could make out running figures farther down the street, and more and more lights were coming on, bathing the area in pools of harsh brilliance.

He dropped the hush puppy and unslung his stolen AK. Gunfire barked from a building across the street, and a bullet sang off the chain-link fence at his back. Close by, men ran past the truck parked at the side of the road, racing in his direction.

"*Koman!*" a voice shrilled. "Halt at once!"

Han spun. Gunfire crashed once more from the shadows beside the truck. Rounds slammed into the SEAL's chest and side, hammering him to the ground.

For a dizzying, pain-clouded eternity, there was silence. Han lay facedown on the ground, gasping for each breath against the hot blood he felt welling up in his throat. He tried reaching for the AK he'd dropped. . . .

Then rough hands knocked the AK aside and rolled him over. Someone kicked him in the side, then probed his clothing for hidden weapons as rifle muzzles pressed against his head. A face, a Korean face, grinned down at him from inches away. "So!" the man said. "South Korean Special Forces, I presume?" The face puckered, then spat.

The KorComs thought he was a ROK commando. Somehow, the irony seemed impossibly funny. Laughter turned to agony, though, as his breath rattled in his chest. Han knew he was drowning in his own blood.

"*Palli!*" the KorCom officer snapped. "Quickly! Get the prisoners!"

Then the darkness closed in and BM/1 Charlie Han died.

CHAPTER 24

HM/1 Bailey's whisper was harsh. "They're coming!"

They'd heard the disturbance outside half an hour earlier, sounds like silenced gunfire, sharp yells, the hammer of bullets striking metal, the crash of broken glass. Then, the sound of a truck being driven off, followed by a silence so complete it might never have been broken. Sailors at the windows could see nothing. The entire camp was blacked out. Searchlights swept the clouds in the distance, and the wail of sirens, the yap of barking dogs could be faintly heard.

Then, suddenly, the Americans had heard a Korean challenge, harsh voices . . . and then the ear-shattering yammer of an automatic weapon firing in the night. The firefight had lasted only seconds, but the silence was truly ended now by the slap of boots on pavement, shouted orders, and the sound of vehicles arriving outside.

"Something's going down," Chief Bronkowicz added. "Sounds like someone's stirred 'em with a stick!"

"We can't let 'em take us," Zabelsky said. He clenched his fists, his eyes on the door as guttural voices sounded just beyond. "Those bastards are never gonna let us go . . . you guys know that, right?"

"Where's the gun?" Commander Wilkinson asked. In the back of the long room, one sailor climbed onto another's shoulders, searching by feel among the rafters for the hidden weapon.

Gunfire inside the camp could only mean that the SEALs had been discovered. Anything could happen now . . . including the wholesale massacre of the American prisoners.

"Bailey!" someone shouted. "Where are you, Doc?"

"Here!" The ship's senior hospital corpsman seemed an unlikely choice as gunman for the group. In wartime it would have been against the rules of the Geneva Convention for him to carry a weapon, though plenty of corpsmen had violated those rules in Nam two decades earlier. A quiet canvassing of all the men of *Chimera*'s crew, however, had revealed that HM/1 Herb Bailey had been a member of the IPSC before he joined the Navy, had even qualified for the Bianchi Cup pistol shooters' match, though he'd never participated. He knew handguns and how to use them.

Perhaps most important, he *wanted* to do it and knew he could. A sailor passed Bailey the Mark 22 and its magazines. He took them without a word, snicked the magazine into the pistol grip, and dragged the slide back to chamber a round. The rattle of keys in the lock was already sounding through the room as he took his position to one side, ten feet from the door, the pistol concealed behind one of *Chimera*'s men.

The door banged open and three Koreans burst into the room. They were angry and shouting, gesticulating with their AK-47s. None spoke English, but their demands were unmistakable. *Hands up! Move out! Obey!*

Bailey heard Gilmore's quiet voice just behind him. "Bailey? Let's do it, son."

Outside, he heard other soldiers shouting to one another. Killing these three would only delay the inevitable. But better for them all to go down fighting than the slow horror of watching shipmates being shot, one by one.

He shoved the sailor aside and raised the silenced pistol.

0357 hours
Inside Nyongch'on-kiji

Sikes had heard the AK fire from across the compound and knew that the party had just begun in earnest. He exchanged a look with Larry Gordon, the first class torpedoman who had accompanied him to the area outside the North Korean barracks.

Earlier, during the air raid to the north of the camp, several hundred men had poured out of the three-story barracks and clambered into a system of trenches dug near the base perimeter, a crude but relatively effective air raid shelter. Once things grew quiet again, most of the KorCom troops had filed back into the barracks, though a large number had been reorganized into patrols and sentry bands. Sikes and Gordon had been busy since then, planting the claymore mines they'd carried in their packs.

Claymores were curved, rectangular boxes that were placed upright and set to detonate in any of a number of ways, from electric circuits to tripwires. Behind the neatly stenciled lettering which spelled FRONT TOWARD ENEMY, each claymore packed a pound and a half of C4 plastic explosive and seven hundred steel marbles. The device could be aimed, with the end effect a kind of gigantic shotgun.

"Looks like it's time, Lieutenant," Gordon said.

"Right." He opened his tactical radio. "All units, this is Bushmaster One. On my signal, rock and roll. Acknowledge!"

"Bush Two, acknowledge!"

"Bushmaster Three, acknowledged!"

"Bush Four! Affirmative!"

"Bushmaster Five, acknowledged. We're with Bush Six. We've left Han outside the POW command."

Another burst of gunfire echoed from the direction of the compound. Sikes couldn't know for sure, but it sounded as though it might be Han who was in trouble. The original idea had been to stay clear of the POWs until the last minute. When they saw the SEALs, they might make a lot of noise and it would be difficult to control them.

But now was the time.

"Copy, Bush Five. Take Six and get back to your target on the double. Secure the prisoners."

"Roger that."

"Okay." Sikes took a deep breath. "Take 'em down!"

There was a pause, and then the sky lit up orange in the direction of the airstrip as a fireball roiled into the night from a gasoline storage tank. An instant later there was a flash like the popping of flashbulbs, and the microwave antenna over the communications shed shuddered, sagged, then toppled slowly toward the fence. The crash was submerged in the ratcheting blast of plastic explosives detonated in a daisy chain under the bellies of trucks and other vehicles parked in the motor pool. The Mi-8 helo added the contents of its fuel tanks to the conflagration, transforming the camp into an inferno of flames and light and wildly shifting shadows.

The camp's siren began its mournful wail, and soldiers raced once more out of the barracks building, yelling and shouting to one another as they pulled on articles of clothing, stopped to lace boots, or worked the actions on their rifles. Sikes and Gordon lay still behind a hummock of earth, each man holding a small firing device connected to a battery. Men began leaping into the air raid shelter ditches.

Someone touched a tripwire carefully hidden in the ink-black bottom of one of the trenches, and claymore mines set into either end of the ditch triggered simultaneously. A hell of noise and smoke and shrill screams rose above the shouts of running soldiers. Claymores in a second ditch triggered, followed closely by a third. The soldiers still outside of the ditches became a mob, surging back toward the barracks.

Sikes flipped the safety bail on his firing trigger and squeezed hard. A claymore nestled into the shadows near the barracks fired, cutting a bloody swath through the mob. Gordon fired a second mine an instant later. The yells and shouted orders were gone now, replaced by the shrieks and screams of the wounded. Bodies lay in front of the barracks in cordwood stacks, mowed down by repeated scythes of steel ball bearings. By the time Gordon opened up with his M-60, only a few Koreans remained standing.

The morning's festivities were off to a great start.

0358 hours
Inside the POW compound, Nyongch'on-kiji

The first explosion rattled the walls on the POW building and silenced the angry shouts of the Korean guards. As the second explosion roared in the near-distance, HM/1 Bailey squeezed the trigger on the Mark 22 and the weapon bucked with a sharp *chuff* submerged by the far louder thunder outside. The soldier's head jerked back, suddenly bloody. The corpsman was already tracking his second target . . . and then his third.

A fourth Korean screamed in the door, then leaped backward, out into a night suddenly afire. Chief Bronkowicz scooped up one of the AK-47s, checked it, and handed it to one of the men. "The SEALs!" he yelled. "Now's the time!" The prisoners now had three assault rifles besides the pistol, and a chance to fight back.

The hand grenade sailed into the room through one of the windows high up along the north wall. It was one of the Soviet-made, apple-green RGDs and it skittered across the floor, bounced off the south wall, then spun in the middle of the floor.

"*Grenade!*" Coleridge screamed, and men dropped to the floor or tried to crowd back. There was a blur of motion as someone in khaki leaped *toward* the grenade instead of away, sprawling on top of it, gathering it in against his stomach.

The explosion was deafening, though the flash was smothered. The body of the man who had thrown himself across the grenade jerked a foot into the air, and bloody gobbets spattered across the floor. There was a lot of smoke, and a harsh mingling in the air of seared meat, blood, and feces.

The men crowded close. "Oh, God!" "Who is it?" "Did you see that?" "Is he alive?"

Bailey knelt at the man's side, gently rolling him over. Lieutenant Novak's eyes met his for a moment, then glazed over. Much of his abdomen had been blasted away. The shredded remains were spilled across the floor and blood was gushing from the emptied cavity.

The lieutenant was dead in seconds.

Explosions continued to echo and reverberate from outside, and a flickering glow from the west spoke of fuel tanks going up in flames. Inside the room there was a momentary silence, reaction to the horror that was Novak's mangled body, reaction to the knowledge that the man had blamed himself for what had happened.

Seconds later the spell was broken by the yammer of AK fire from close by. Zabelsky had climbed up to the window through which the grenade had come and was firing short bursts into the night.

"Come on, you guys!" Chief Bronkowicz said. His eyes were locked on Novak's gory corpse and the spreading pool of blood. "Let's make it count for somethin'!"

Bailey rose, still gripping the pistol. Everyone had been so sure that Lieutenant Novak was a coward . . .

Bailey went to the door, a new and dangerous rage boiling inside. He half expected a blaze of autofire from outside, but events seemed to have thrown the Koreans into as much confusion as their captives. He spotted movement in the darkness and snap-fired, his shot rewarded by a groan and the clatter of a dropped rifle. Bronkowicz stepped past him, brandishing an AK, closely followed by half a dozen sailors armed with nothing but their fists. "Go, *Chimeras*!" someone yelled. Another sailor let out a spine-chilling rebel yell.

The corpsman looked back at Gilmore, who grinned weakly and gave him a salute from his makeshift bed. "Those SEALs are going to need help, son."

Bailey grinned, saluted, then joined the crowd running into the night.

Coyote turned his binoculars on the camp. "God, the whole place is going up!"

Kohl pressed the nightsight of his rifle to his eye. "The guys have been busy." His rifle cracked once. Even with the suppressor, the sound was uncomfortably sharp and loud. On the camp perimeter, a KorCom soldier pitched headfirst out of a guard tower, struck the barbed-wire topping of the compound fence, and hung there, head down. Kohl shifted targets and fired again.

In the lurid, wavering illumination from a burning fuel dump, Coyote could make out individual figures spilling from the Wonsan Waldorf. The chatter of automatic fire carried across the distance, almost lost in the rising cacophony of fire, explosions, and yelling voices. A building exploded in white flame and collapsed, burning fiercely. The wall of the siren was chopped off as though by a descending ax blade. "There goes the HQ," Kohl said softly. Coyote could only watch and marvel at the slaughter. The SEALs, it appeared, were efficient killing machines.

Minutes passed. Coyote knew from the final briefing earlier that night that Sikes's team was counting on a quick kill and a quick seizure of the camp. The battle for Nyongch'on couldn't be allowed to go on for more than a few minutes, or inevitably SEALs would start dying.

If there were three hundred troops inside Nyongch'on, there were another three thousand in other bases close by . . . possibly more. By blowing the radio tower, Sikes's men had cut the camp off from its neighbors; with luck, nearby KorCom Army posts would assume Nyongch'on had been hit by another American bomber raid and delay an immediate investigation.

The SEALs could not rely on luck for long, however, or even on the disorganization of the enemy. When North Korean troops arrived at Nyongch'on, they would come in strength, and fourteen SEALs, even reinforced by *Chimera*'s crew, would not be able to hold out for very long.

Though the SEALs would never have admitted it, they needed help. That help had already been factored into the rescue plan.

"Bushmaster Seven, this is Bush One," Sikes's voice said from the backpack radio which had been left in the hide. "Do you copy? Over."

Coyote picked up the handset. Kohl was still busy picking off Korean sentries who had escaped the general slaughter in the camp. "Copy, Bush One. Go ahead."

"Make signal: Sunrise Blue."

That was it! The code message which meant that Nyongch'on and the prisoners were secure! "Copy, Bush One. Sunrise Blue!"

"After you secure the transmitter, get your tails on down here. We've got a way to go yet before we collect our paychecks."

"Roger that." Coyote glanced at Kohl, who was already slinging his rifle. "We're packing up now."

"Bush One, out."

The diminutive satellite dish was already set up, aligned with an invisible point in the southern sky. Coyote flipped switches on the backpack radio as he'd been shown earlier, listening to the hiss and crackle of static over the handset speaker.

"Homeplate, Bushmaster," he said. "Homeplate, this is Bushmaster."

After an eternity, a static-charged voice replied, "Bushmaster, this is Homeplate. We copy."

"Sunrise Blue! I say again, Sunrise Blue!"

"Copy, Bushmaster. Sunrise Blue. The cavalry's on its way!"

Coyote had never heard such beautiful words.

0403 hours
Over the Yonghung Man

The four RH-53D Sea Stallions of Cavalry One had been orbiting their marshall point for several hours, refueling once from one of *Jefferson*'s KA-6D tankers. The noise in the cargo cabin was deafening, too loud for normal speech. When the word came through over his headphones from the pilot that Sunrise Blue had been received, Lieutenant Victor A. Morgan merely turned and gave a thumbs-up to the waiting, watching Marines crowded into the compartment.

The answering roar momentarily drowned out the Sea Stallion's engine noise, as forty Marines shouted in unison, *"Gung-ho!"*

Morgan rested one hand against the Sea Stallion's bulkhead and patted it fondly. Eight Sea Stallions had been part of the Eagle Claw operation in 1980, the Delta Force attempt to rescue fifty-three American hostages in Iran, and the hydraulic failure of one of them in the harsh desert conditions over the Dasht-e Kavir had been largely responsible for the abort on that mission. The task force had been in the process of pulling out when another helo collided with a C-130, capping the raid with disaster. Two of the eight dead at Desert One had been Marines.

This morning, though, the Marines were giving the old Navy workhorse a chance to redeem herself. Cavalry One consisted of four RH-53Ds; three carried forty-two-man rifle platoons, a fourth a weapons platoon and headquarters element. Altogether, the cavalry for this particular rescue made up a complete Marine rifle company under the command of Captain Samuel L. Ford.

Upon receiving the Sunrise Blue code, the four aircraft dropped to wave-top height and raced toward the Korean shore at 160 mph. By this time, all identified SAM sites and antiaircraft batteries had been hit by the hunting packs of *Jefferson*'s Hornets and Intruders. Lone North Koreans wandering around on the ground with shoulder-launched Grails or machine guns still posed a threat, but not a large one. By contour flying, hugging the shape of the ridge-broken terrain, the helos would give little warning of their approach, and at low altitude they would not be in sight for more than a few seconds. Tomcats circling overhead would provide cover against enemy MiGs, but it was surprise and speed which would get the Sea Stallions to their landing zone.

Getting them out would be another problem entirely, but Lieutenant Morgan was more than happy to leave that worry to the operation's planners. For the moment, his only thought was to get his platoon to the Nyongch'on LZ fast, before the SEALs found themselves facing more than they could handle.

It would be his first time in combat.

With the shriek of GE turbines and the heavy clatter of rotors, the cavalry thundered toward the beach.

0411 hours
Outside Nyongch'on-kiji

It took several long minutes to dismantle and fold the satellite dish and stow it with the radio in its pack. The gunfire from the camp had entirely died away. So far, there was no sign that the capture of Nyongch'on-kiji had been noticed by any of the other PDRK Army commands in the area.

That wouldn't last for long.

"You going to be able to make it with that leg?" Kohl asked.

"I'll make it." Coyote was already wondering if he could. The pain was much worse. It felt like his left knee would buckle if he put any weight on it at all.

"Here." Kohl unslung his G3 rifle and handed it to Coyote, exchanging it for the radio pack which he shrugged onto his back. "Safe's on. Don't lean on the suppressor." He stooped and unscrewed the night sight, which he packed away into a padded tube which looked like a camera lens case. Coyote found that by planting the butt of the weapon on the ground and leaning against the foregrip he could stand. Most of the trip would be downhill, a cautious series of sideways steps using the rifle as a cane.

"You get dirt in my receiver and you'n me are gonna have words," Kohl added, but his grin robbed the threat of its sting. "Let's get down there ASAP."

"Right with you."

Their progress was painfully slow. Kohl led the way, his Mark 22 drawn, his night goggles down over his eyes as he picked out a relatively clear path down the slope. Coyote did not have goggles, but by now he could see well enough by the gasoline-fueled blaze which was roaring in Nyongch'on. Halfway down the hill, loose rocks slid from beneath Coyote's good foot and he hit the ground with a thump that brought tears to his eyes, so sharp was the pain from his wound.

"You okay, guy?"

Coyote gasped down a deep breath. "Yeah. You go ahead."

"Okay, but don't get lost. I'd hate to have to explain how I mislaid you."

The SEAL vanished into the darkness down the slope as Coyote struggled to his feet again. How had he made it this far before? Finding a relatively flat spot next to an outcropping of rocks, he paused to catch his breath.

He heard a thrashing noise in the brush to his left. At first he assumed it was Kohl, but then he realized that, so far, he'd not heard any of the SEALs make a single unnecessary sound. Someone was running through the brush, heading his way.

Coyote froze. He didn't have a radio, and to shout warning would be to broadcast his location to every Korean soldier in range. In his hands, his cane became a rifle once more as he let himself sink to the ground. Where was Kohl? The SEAL had vanished into the darkness just ahead. . . .

"*Nuku'simnikka?*" a harsh voice challenged.

Coyote heard the harsh *chuff-chuff* of Kohl's hush puppy firing twice, followed by a piercing scream. Then the night came alive with the roar of unsuppressed autofire.

He saw a tongue of flame exploding from the darkness to the left, spraying wildly back and forth as an unseen Korean soldier sprayed the night. Coyote raised Kohl's G3 rifle, thumbed off the safety, and fired at where he thought the soldier must be, behind the lashing flame, and high.

In his haste, he'd thumbed the selector to full-auto, but the suppressor on the barrel muted the roar and muffled the flash.

Then there was silence.

Cautiously, Coyote limped forward, probing the darkness with the muzzle of the rifle. Ten feet away he found a North Korean soldier, sprawled on his back with a line of bloody holes stitched from left hip to right shoulder. He was very dead.

Not much farther down the slope he found two more bodies, another dead Korean and Kohl, both torn by rounds from the first Korean's AK. Coyote guessed that Kohl had wounded one KorCom with the hush puppy, and that the second man had killed them both with his indiscriminate hosing of the underbrush. Both Koreans, he decided, had been fleeing the massacre in the Nyongch'on camp.

He went back to Kohl and sat down heavily. His leg, he noticed, was no longer hurting as badly. Adrenaline—or shock—had numbed it once again.

Coyote found himself thinking back to a small eternity ago, riding the heavy swell of the Sea of Japan, holding Mardi Gras's body in his arms. Once again, death had brushed close. He'd not known those three sailors murdered in the camp, but he'd been talking with Kohl, joking with him only moments ago.

He felt contaminated, as though Death itself had marked him. The people he got close to tended to die suddenly. . . .

There seemed to be no point in going on.

0425 hours
On the Anbyon Road

Captain Sun Dae-Jung ducked down inside the hatch of his ZSU and took the headset from the vehicle's gunner. He held it to his ear. "*Cho Sun imnida!*" He had to shout to be heard over the roar of the engine. "This is Sun!"

"This is Major Nung, Wonsan Defense Force. What is your position, Captain?"

Sun did a fast estimate. "Sector four-seven! Anbyon Road, three miles south of the coast highway! Coming up on Nyongch'on!"

"Excellent, Captain. I want you to deploy along the ridge, immediately."

Sun felt excitement thrill within. "Is it another air raid, Major?"

"We have reports of enemy helicopters in your area."

Helicopters! Those slow, thin-skinned aircraft would be no match at all for the quad 23s of his command.

"We believe the enemy has been homing on our radar emissions, Captain," the major continued. "Use your radar sparingly."

"Understood, Comrade Major." Sun had interviewed Libyan officers who had lived through the American attacks on their country in 1986. He knew what HARMs could do. "We are deploying now."

"The Fatherland is counting on you, Captain. Our intelligence believes the object of the Yankee raid may be the release of American criminals being held at Nyongch'on-kiji. If so, those helicopters could be headed for your position."

"And we will be ready!"

The lumbering tracked ZSUs spread out along the roadside, maintaining the approved two-hundred-meter interval between each vehicle. Minutes later, Sun ordered the turret-mounted B-76 radar to be switched on for a quick scan toward the north.

ZSUs carried a four-man crew: commander, radar operator, gunner, and driver. The driver was sealed into his own compartment in the chassis, but the other three occupied the fairly roomy turret. "Four targets, Comrade Captain!" the radar operator reported. "Bearing zero three-five, range twelve thousand!"

It took only a moment more to confirm that the targets were approaching, flying at low altitude and low speed. With a smile, Sun ordered the radar switched off.

His prey was only minutes away now. . . .

CHAPTER 25

Coyote wasn't certain how long he'd been lying on the hillside above Nyongch'on, but it was the sound of heavy equipment, like tractors, which stirred him. The illumination from the fires in the North Korean base was fading; he could see lights in the direction of the road which passed Nyongch'on through the saddle in the ridge off to the west, on the far side of the base, but he could not make out what they were.

Overcoming the emotional paralysis which gripped him, he made his way back to Kohl's body. The SEAL's night-vision goggles were smashed—one round had struck them squarely between the twin optic tubes and gone on to smash his skull—but the heavy rifle scope was still in its case, slung from his black web gear. He extracted the M938 starlight scope, found the switch to turn it on, and held it to his eye.

He recognized the squat, boxy shape of the ZSU at once: the broad turret which covered most of the full-tracked chassis; the outsized radar mount behind the commander's hatch; the four 23-mm rapid-fire cannons angled skyward. Those guns each fired at a rate of nine hundred rounds per minute, faster than most machine guns; in combat, the quad mount could spew out sixty explosive rounds every second, which made it rapid-fire death for anything slower than a supersonic interceptor. The fire control radar could pick up bogies twelve miles out, could lock on and track at a range of five miles, could knock thin-skinned targets out of the sky from almost two miles away.

And this monster was squatting just outside the gate to the camp, less than five hundred yards from Nyongch'on's airstrip, engine idling. Through the starlight scope's optics he could make out the commander, peering through binoculars toward the north-east.

Coyote scanned along the road with the sight. There was a second ZSU parked two hundred yards behind the first . . . a third two hundred yards beyond that. Other vehicles were hidden by a bend in the road and steep-sloped terrain, but it was fair to assume there were at least four of the deadly antiaircraft vehicles, perhaps more.

And Cavalry One's helicopters could not be more than a few minutes away.

Galvanized by the realization that the helos were flying into a trap, Coyote scrambled for the pack on Kohl's body. The radio unit was the latest in electronic communications technology, a twenty-kilo man-portable base station which could serve at a TAC COM set in the field, or establish long-range communications through the folding dish and a geosynchronous communications satellite.

The problem was who to call. He knew he could reach the SEALs in Nyongch'on, but there was little they could do at the moment. They'd have their hands full with *Chimera*'s crew and North Korean survivors without having to take on KorCom armor as well. The satellite dish would give him a direct line to the *Jefferson* at her station somewhere over the horizon, but Coyote didn't know how to acquire the satellite—an invisible point somewhere in the southern sky—and he didn't know the codes which would let him get a message through. Without the proper electronic passwords, the computers which switched and operated the system would assume he was enemy jamming and block him out. He didn't know the channel being used by Cavalry One . . . and had no way of making them believe anything he had to say. The SEALs in the camp would know the right codes, would even know how to reach Cavalry One, but there wasn't time to get their help. Already Coyote thought he could hear the faint throb of helicopters in the distance; if that was Cavalry One, the Marine reinforcements had only minutes now, possibly seconds.

But there would be tactical air cover up, possibly from Coyote's own squadron. He knew the radio frequencies they'd be on . . . and chances were they'd be in line of sight and therefore within range of his UHF transmitter. At the very least, his signal might be picked up by a Hawkeye circling somewhere out at sea and patched through to where it would do some good.

By the faint illumination of the fires dying in the camp, Coyote switched on the radio and began checking channels. He wasn't sure where the set's tuning range would overlap that used by the aircraft. He heard nothing on the first channel he tried, or the second. Combat frequencies were changed frequently as a matter of course to avoid enemy jamming or eavesdropping.

He decided to try the SAR frequency. "Mayday! Mayday! This is Bushmaster with urgent message for anyone on this frequency! Please respond! Mayday, mayday, this is Bushmaster! Any station, come in, please! This is an emergency!"

The response was silence, but Coyote kept trying. After an endless moment, he heard a faint voice over the headset. "Bushmaster, this is Hawkeye Tango Two-one. What is the nature of your emergency, over?"

Coyote felt a warm thrill, an irrational surge of hope. "Tango Two-one, this is Bushmaster! I need a line to whoever is flying CAP for Cavalry One!"

The static-crackling silence told him his message was being considered. His initial elation was dampened somewhat by the knowledge that the Hawkeye crew would not take what he said at face value. They might think that Coyote was an English-speaking Korean, one who had picked up the appropriate call signs by eavesdropping and was using them now to trick the Americans.

"Bushmaster, Tango Two-one," the voice replied after what seemed like years. "We cannot comply without authentication codes. Can you authenticate, over?"

Oh, God. "Tango Two-one! This is Lieutenant Willis Grant, VF-95, U.S.S. *Thomas Jefferson!* I was shot down four days ago and taken prisoner, but I was rescued by the SEAL team called Bushmaster! The SEALs have the codes you want, but they're not available right now! Do you hear me? I can't give you the codes!"

"Bushmaster, Tango Two-one. Wait one while we confirm, over."

The silence dragged on and on. Coyote could definitely hear the sound of helicopters in the distance. He held the starlight scope to his eye once more, and saw the turrets of the visible ZSUs swinging around, bringing the guns to bear on the approaching sound. They would probably hold their radar until the last possible second, to avoid alerting their prey.

Maybe he should have tried to talk to the SEALs first, to get the proper codes and call signs from them. . . .

"Bushmaster, Tango Two-one," the emotionless voice said

after an eternity of waiting. "Can you tell us your wife's maiden name?"

"Wilson!" he screamed into the handset. "Her maiden name was Julie Wilson!"

The thaw in the Hawkeye radio operator's voice was immediate. "Good to hear from you, Lieutenant. Maybe we won't have to file that AWOL report on you after all."

"Never mind that!" Coyote was frantic with the need to hurry. "Patch me through to Cavalry One CAP! I'm looking at three ZSUs sitting right where the helos are coming in any minute! For God's sake, hurry!"

"Bushmaster, switch to three-three-eight-point-eight. Squadron call sign 'Shotgun.'"

"Copy, Two-one! Switching to three-three-eight-point-eight. And thanks!"

He punched in the new numbers on the digital display and immediately heard the terse crackle of fighter pilot conversation. "Shotgun Three, Shotgun Leader. Come to one-eight-zero, angels twelve, on my mark—"

"Breaker, breaker! Shotgun, this is Bushmaster! Emergency! I have three Zulu Sierra Uniforms parked on the road next to Cavalry One LZ. I say again, three ZSUs and the choppers are inbound!"

There was a stunned pause. Then, "Who the hell was that?" The voice sounded like Price Taggart's.

"Price! It's me, Coyote!"

"Coyote!" That voice was Tombstone's, sharp and unmistakable. "Coyote, you bastard, if that's you . . . ! What's the name of the girl who chose the worst man?"

"Julie Wilson, you son of a bitch! Now get your ass in here and give us a hand before I shoot you down myself!"

0431 hours
Tomcat 205, over Nyongch'on

The sound of Coyote's voice over the radio caught Tombstone completely by surprise, but he managed to control the surge of excitement he felt. "Roger that," he said, his voice all business now. "What's your situation?"

Coyote filled Tombstone in, giving him the landmarks he needed to locate the ZSUs on a map of the op area clipped to his thigh pad. At least three antiaircraft vehicles were strung out along the north-south road directly adjacent to the Nyongch'on LZ. Tombstone didn't know if their position was calculated or accident, but they could not have chosen a better site from which to ambush Cavalry One.

"Copy, Coyote," he said at last. "Hold one."

"I've got Cavalry One's channel," Snowball said over the ICS, anticipating Tombstone's order. "You're on."

"Cavalry One, Cavalry One," Tombstone said. He had his F-14 in a steep inverted dive now as he dropped toward the invisible North Korean mountains. "This is Shotgun Leader. Wave off on your Lima Zulu. Repeat, wave off . . . !"

0432 hours
On the Anbyon Road

"Radar!" Captain Sun snapped from the open turret. "Nearest target!"

"Target bearing zero-three-four!" the radar operator replied. "Elevation fifteen, range six-five-zero-zero! Comrade Captain! They are changing course!"

Sun smashed his gloved fist down on the turret deck. *Ai ch'am!* Close enough for a radar lock, but too far for a hit. The Americans must have picked up his radar emissions and guessed he was waiting for them!

"Very well," Sun said. "We will wait!" If the Yankees were trying to rescue the criminals at Nyongch'on, his ZSUs were perfectly positioned. He considered sending his vehicles into the camp. On the road he was vulnerable to enemy air strikes. Inside the camp, though, they wouldn't dare attack him

"Comrade Captain!" the radar operator shouted. "New targets, high speed, inbound at twelve thousand meters!"

"Shut down!"

"Yes, Comrade Captain!"

"Radio the others! We will enter Nyongch'on-kiji!"

The driver gunned the engine and the ZSU swung off the road, heading east.

0433 hours
Tomcat 205

Tombstone pulled out of his dive at two hundred feet and rocketed south, following the road which climbed sharply toward the gap in the mountains. He eased back on his stick, bleeding off airspeed until his wings extended in the max-lift, minimum-speed configuration. For once, he needed to go *slow*; ground targets simply couldn't be seen at Mach 1. "Desperado Leader, this is Shotgun Leader! Do you copy?"

"This is the Triple Nickle, Shotgun," Jolly's voice replied. "What can we do for you?"

"We have ground targets in Sector Hotel niner-seven. Multiple Zulu Sierra Uniform, two-three mike-mike quads!"

"Roger that, Shotgun. Descending."

"Skipper!" Snowball cut in. "I had something there for a moment, but it's gone."

"Keep looking!" The ZSUs were playing it cagey. Their radars, codenamed "Gun Dish" by NATO, were difficult to pick up at the best of times, and it would be worse here with the clutter of rugged terrain and buildings. If the ZSUs' commander was using his radar only intermittently, it would be impossible to lock on with anti-radar missiles.

And an area attack with bombs would be risky because of the proximity of the SEALs and POWs at Nyongch'on.

"Cavalry One reports they are holding four miles northeast of the LZ."

"Right." He reopened the channel. "Desperado, this is Shotgun. Follow us in."

"We're right behind you, Shotgun. Three Desperados, range four miles."

The ridge heaved skyward just ahead, outlined by patches of fire to one side. That would be the base. Tombstone could just make out the shape of the road rising beneath the F-14's nose. His thumb nudged the weapons selector switch on his stick, and the glowing reticle for his cannon floated on his HUD.

Tomcats were not really built for strafing runs, but the only other weapons he carried were air-to-air missiles, and there was no way to effectively lock them on a ground target. All he could do was open fire with his Vulcan cannon and hope for a lucky hit. Sharp in his mind was the knowledge that Nyongch'on camp lay only a few hundred meters east of the road. If he got the deflection wrong, he could pump six thousand rounds per minute into the SEALs and the rescued prisoners.

There was no time to think of any of this. He saw a squat something moving off the road ahead and squeezed the trigger.

The thunderous hammer of the Vulcan Gatling gun filled the Tomcat's cockpit.

0433 hours
On the Anbyon Road

Captain Sun heard the roar of the jet an instant before he saw it, a pale gray, cruciform shape against the night sky. Then the aircraft was gone, trailing thunder.

He could hear the rattle of an automatic thunder above the engine noise, the sound of explosive rounds striking the road a few hundred meters behind him.

"Driver! Come left!"

The ZSU wallowed across a ditch at the side of the road, then slewed around, turret traversing. It was too late to fire at the lead jet, but there would be others.

"Comrade Captain!" the radar operator shouted. "Two and Three report they are being strafed!"

"Have they been hit?"

"No casualties, sir!"

"Have all units switch on their radars." There was nothing to be gained by hiding now.

"Three targets, Comrade Captain. Incoming, range three thousand . . ."

"Lock on!"

The turret traversed slowly, the quad guns rising to firing position.

"Target locked! Tracking!"

"Chigum!" Sun shouted. "Now! Fire!"

The firing of the four 23-mm cannons sounded like paper tearing or a buzzsaw, but impossibly loud. A shower of empty shell casings arced golden into the night, and the ZSU's turret shuddered with the force of the gunfire.

Brilliant green tracers streamed into the night.

0433 hours
Tomcat 205

Tombstone pulled back on the stick. His chances of hitting anything were practically nil, but his pass might have broken the gomers' concentration.

"Three Intruders coming down behind us," Snowball reported. "They report target lock. They're into their run."

"Hang tight, Snowy. We'll loop back and give them cover."

0433 hours
Intruder 555

Jolly saw the tracers arcing toward him from the ground, intermittent streams of green pinpoints which swelled to grapefruit size as they snapped past his cockpit. Instinctively, he hauled the stick right and kicked in his rudder, standing the A-6 on its right wing to avoid the wall of fire.

A glance back at his VDI showed the targeting pipper almost on the target. They were already committed.

Then the Intruder buffeted wildly as something slammed into the hull. *Shit!*

Jackhammer blows crashed along the starboard side of the aircraft, and there was a searing, metallic ricochet sound that felt suspiciously like a turbine blade chopping through paper-thin hull metal.

"We're hit!" Chucker yelled.

"Damn it, don't you think I know that?"

Power died on his starboard engine. The VDI was dead, the computer off-line. The annunciator panel was lit up like a Christmas tree with warning lights: hydraulic pressure; right generator; right engine; fuel pumps two, three, and four.

Almost without thinking, Jolly switched the weapons release to manual and jettisoned the entire load. They'd swung east of their attack path and had lost the target now. The one consolation was that they were no longer near the Nyongch'on LZ. With a thump, the bomb rack broke free and tumbled into the night. There was a flash from somewhere behind, and Jolly hoped their bomb rack had landed on something important. The aircraft leveled off at eight hundred feet, still in a shallow turn to port. They had to buy some altitude. The coast was only a few miles away. If they could just reach the sea . . .

The fire warning light for the right engine glared at him. He shot out his hand and snapped off the master fuel switch to the starboard engine. The Intruder's fuel readings were plummeting anyway. Jolly could imagine raw fuel spraying into the damaged right engine.

"Jolly," Chucker said, twisting in his seat to look aft. "We got real problems."

Jolly leaned forward, looking past his BN. He caught the yellow glare of open flames licking from the root of the wing. The wing itself had half a dozen holes punched in it, and he could see liquid streaming aft from the punctures.

"That's it," Jolly said. The Intruder could explode any second. "Punch out!"

Chucker leaned back in his seat, reached up over his head, grabbed the primary ejector handle, and yanked it down.

There was a blast, a whirlwind storm of raw noise and shattered Plexiglas. Emptiness yawned at Jolly's right side as he reached for his own ejection handle and pulled it down with a hard, clean motion.

The universe exploded in a thunderclap.

CHAPTER 26

Lieutenant Sikes heard the thunder of the first jet, heard the ratcheting fire from the ZSU. Moments later, the second jet roared overhead farther to the west. There was a flash beyond the road and to the south, and he felt the concussion of high explosives seconds later.

ZSUs! Damn! That was just what they did not need at the moment. From his position at the Nyongch'on airstrip, he could see the ZSU's green tracer fire streaming into the sky in short, precisely targeted bursts, but he couldn't locate the vehicle itself.

He reached for his tactical radio. "Bushmaster Seven, this is Bushmaster One!" There was no answer. "Bush Seven, Bush Seven! Kohl, come in! Over!"

And still there was silence. Kohl and the Navy flier would have shut the big radio down before leaving the hide, but Kohl ought to be picking him up on his tactical set. Something bad was going down out there, though. He'd lost his radio link with the outside world . . . and that included Cavalry One, which ought to have arrived by now. ZSUs sitting on top of the LZ could blow the whole op. The Navy would have warned Cavalry One off before attacking the Korean armor . . . which explained why the Marines were late in touching down.

But how much later would they be?

"Bushmaster Five, this is Bushmaster One. Do you copy, over?"

"One, this is Five," Huerta's voice replied. "Go ahead."

"Situation report!"

"Bush Six is with us, Lieutenant. POW compound secure and we've got the prisoners. We're sorting them out now."

"Any casualties?"

"One POW dead, three wounded. The bad guys tossed a grenade before we got there."

"How about your force?"

"Han is dead. And Vespasio's wounded. One of the POWs winged him when we moved in."

Sikes frowned. In any combat action accidents were bound to happen, but he needed every man now. If the Marines didn't come in damned soon . . . "Okay, Five," he said at last. "You know the drill. Ask for volunteers and pass out AKs. Things could be getting rough here pretty quick. Bushmaster One, out."

Operation Righteous Thunder was teetering on the brink between success and disaster. It didn't matter that the SEALs had freed *Chimera*'s crew. If an NK counterattack overwhelmed them in the next few minutes, if half of *Chimera*'s sailors were killed while defending themselves in what was supposed to be their rescue, it would look nasty in the news headlines.

Of course, that wouldn't matter to Sikes personally, because he would be dead, along with his entire command. The SEALs had only their personal weapons, what little equipment they'd been able to haul in on their backs, and whatever they could scrounge from the base. They had no Dragons or TOWs or even LAWs with which to attack enemy armor. Things were getting serious.

He could hear the shriek of another Navy plane, coming in low. If they didn't clear those ZSUs fast, there was going to be one hell of a butcher's bill.

0436 hours
Intruder 537

Lieutenant Jake "Blondie" Shaw squeezed the commit trigger and watched the display change on his VDI. "Desperado Two, comin' in hot!" he announced on the radio. Behind him, Intruder 532 was falling into line for its attack run.

"Left three degrees," Timmons said, his face buried in the radar hood. "I think we're getting a buzz from a Gun Dish."

"ZSUs," Shaw said. He pronounced it *zoos*. "Can you get a lock?"

"No way," the BN replied. "You're on manual release."

A blazing line of green fire rose dead ahead, so close it seemed impossible that they would miss. Shaw jinked left, then right, his eyes fixed now on the pipper crawling toward the target graphic on his screen. One mile now, less than ten seconds . . .

Something hit the Intruder's wing with a dull thump, forcing Shaw to correct. "Left two!" Timmons shouted.

"I've got it!" The pipper reached the target box and he pickled the bomb release.

The A-6 shook with a succession of small bumps as the Rockeye cannisters fell away, two at a time. Shaw rammed the throttles home and hauled back on the stick.

He'd been deliberately conservative in the approach, not wanting to scatter Rockeye bomblets into the Nyongch'on compound. Of course, that could mean missing the lead tank in line.

0436 hours
On the Anbyon Road

The ZSU shuddered, overwhelmed by the wall of sound trailing behind the enemy plane. Captain Sun rose cautiously in his hatch just as a rapid-fire succession of brilliant white flashes began popping away in the night several hundred meters from his vehicle. The roar of explosions continued second after second, but fading into the distance; the Yankee had released a string of cluster bombs, each strewing hundreds of bomblets south along the road. One particularly savage blast shook the air, and an orange fireball roiled into the sky. Streamers of fire arced through the darkness as ammunition boxes detonated, rippling and flashing like Chinese firecrackers.

The thunderous bombardment continued, but the explosions were erupting farther and farther to the south. Sun had already decided that he was out of the line of fire. The enemy bombardier had delayed his release a split second too long; the other three *Shilkas* in his command might have been hit, but his was safe.

Or would be if he could get off the road and into Nyongch'on. No American aircraft would attack him there and risk the lives of his own countrymen.

"*Kapsida!*" he shouted at the driver. "Go! Go! Go!" The ZSU lurched forward.

**0438 hours
Inside the Nyongch'on perimeter**

Lieutenant Sikes heard the growl of the approaching vehicle and knew at once what it must be. It would be too much to ask of Lady Luck for the Navy ground attack planes to get all the KorCom ZSUs with one pass. Flames seared the night toward the southwest, but at least one of the Soviet-made AA wagons had escaped and was heading toward the camp. It sounded as though it were approaching the main gate, which was facing the road on the south side of the camp.

"Krueger," he snapped. "Austin. With me!"

The two SEALs materialized seconds later. The entire team, except for Robbins, Pasaretti, Vespasio, and Huerta, had rendezvoused at the airstrip. They waited now in the shadows cast by the burning wreckage of the Mi-8.

"Yessir!" Austin said. He carried a silenced H&K MP5. Krueger was the team's second machine gunner, a blond giant who carried the bulky M-60 slung over his shoulders, and wore crossed ammo belts which gave him the air of a muscle-bound hero of some paramilitary movie epic. To his teammates he was known as "Hulk."

"Either of you guys see any RPGs laying around?" Sikes asked.

"Yeah, Boss," Krueger said. "Armory, up by the communications shack. Brian took out some guy with a 'G after we blew the com tower."

"Okay. I need your '60 with me. Austin, get the RPG. Meet us by the motor pool."

"On my way." The SEAL with the MP5 turned and vanished into the shadows again. Sikes touched Krueger's shoulder. "Let's go, Hulk."

The two men ran south, toward the roar of engines.

**0439 hours
Outside the Nyongch'on main gate**

"Hold it here!"

The *Shilka* drew to a shuddering halt just outside the main gate as Captain Sun studied the camp through narrowed eyes. Something was decidedly wrong here. He could see the flames from several spots beyond the barbed-wire-crowned chain-link fence.

The camp might well have been bombed before his arrival, but that seemed unlikely, given that American POWs were being kept here.

A pair of bodies caught his attention, lifeless forms in mustard-colored jackets sprawled near the gate, AK-47s at their sides. A third body lay farther inside the camp.

So, Nyongch'on had already been attacked by ground troops—American Special Forces or Rangers, possibly, or even South Korean commandos. Those incoming helicopters were probably intended to ferry out the POWs once they were freed.

A peal of thunder reminded him that there were still killers near, invisible in the sky. More Yankee bombers could be overhead at any time. He dropped down into the turret and banged the hatch shut. "Forward!" he barked.

The *Shilka*'s tracks chewed at the earth, and the vehicle ground forward. There was a rattling jar, and then the chain-link fence parted like cloth before the heavy machine's advance. Something whanged off the hull, followed by a staccato drumroll of metal striking metal. Machine gun! The *Shilka*'s turret armor was thin—only nine millimeters—and was easily pierced by .50-caliber machine gun fire. From the sound, he guessed that these were .223 rounds, M-16s possibly, or an M-60.

He peered into the gunner's periscope. Nothing . . . no! There! He spotted the telltale flicker of a muzzle flash close beside the wreckage of a motor pool garage.

"Turret traverse!" he yelled. The gunner worked the turret control, swinging the quad guns into line. The *Shilka*'s quad mount was extremely versatile, able to engage any target between eighty degrees high and minus seven degrees low. In Afghanistan, the Russians had used them to great effect against guerrilla ground forces. "Depress fifteen!"

He switched to the weapon sight. Crosshairs centered above the muzzle flash, bouncing with the ZSU's forward motion. Machine gun fire continued to hammer at the turret. The loader checked the receiver. "Ready to fire!"

"Fire!"

The quad guns roared.

0440 hours
The motor pool, Nyongch'on-kiji

"Hit the deck!"

Explosions shrieked and howled, filling the air with whirling splinters and chips of stone. Sikes rolled to the left, sheltering

behind the concrete block foundation wall of the motor pool
garage as 23-mm shells tore through the wooden side slats like
bullets through paper. He'd been hoping to find a point on the
ZSU's armor thin enough that the M-60 could penetrate it, but
Krueger's volleys hadn't seemed to have any effect at all. The
quad turret swung back and forth in short arcs, the cannons rattling
away in short, sharp bursts as hell exploded inches above Sikes's
head.

"Pull back!" he yelled, wondering if his voice would carry over
the storm of noise. Explosive shells chewed into the foundation
blocks, spraying chunks of concrete into the garage. "Krueger!
Pull—"

He stopped when he saw Krueger, slumped over the stock of the
now-silent M-60. Most of the big SEAL's head was gone.

The stuttering howl of the AA tank's guns fell silent, replaced
by the roar of its engine as the driver throttled up. Sikes reached
down to his harness and detached a grenade. The ZSU was still
way too far for a throw, but the monster was grinding closer.

And closer . . .

0441 hours
Near the motor pool, Nyongch'on-kiji

Captain Sun pressed the radio handset to his ear. "Yes, Comrade
General!" he shouted. The *Shilka* had ceased fire, but the engine
was thundering now as they rumbled forward. "Yes! Enemy
commandos had infiltrated Nyongch'on-kiji!"

"How large a force, Captain? Have you made contact yet?"

"We have silenced one machine gun, Comrade General. Enemy
strength unknown. We have not yet made contact with our own
troops."

"What of your own force, Captain?"

Sun had already called the other *Shilkas*. He'd been unable to
raise Numbers Two and Three, and Number Four had thrown a
tread. "Two out of action, one damaged, Comrade General. I have
moved my vehicle into the camp, where the Americans cannot get
at me without bombing their own people."

"Good thinking, Captain. Continue your operation. Flush out
the Americans in the camp. Reinforcements are on the way to
support you."

"Very well, Comrade General. I—"

The *Shilka* rocked wildly, as though recoiling before a blow from a gigantic sledgehammer. The radar operator was slung from his seat and smashed against the turret's steel bulkhead. White smoke boiled out of nowhere, fouling the air, burning Sun's eyes. "Comrade General!" he screamed into the handset. "Comrade General!"

No answer. The set was dead.

"We must get out, Captain!" the gunner said, his eyes wide with fear.

"Don't panic!" Undogging the hatch above his head, he drew his pistol, a Chinese Type 59—a copy of the Soviet Makarov—then flung the hatch open.

Flames licked at the *Shilka*'s engine compartment. By the light, he could see the jaggedly twisted metal on the starboard skirts where a high-explosive round had smashed the drive wheel. Of greater concern was the fire. If the flames reached the fuel supply or the ammo stores, they wouldn't find enough of Number One's crew to bury.

He hitched himself out of the hatch and swung his legs over the side. Thunder rolled once more. To the southwest, green tracers arced skyward until a fireball rolled into the heavens.

So, Number Four was gone as well. Captain Sun felt tears burning his eyes, and not just from the acrid smoke. These Americans—or their ROK allies—had invaded his country, murdered his countrymen. If he could reach them . . .

Movement caught his eye and he turned. He saw men—big men, too tall to be South Koreans—moving out of the shadows. One braced a familiar-looking, meter-long tube over his right shoulder, an RPG-7. A tank killer . . .

"*Ani!*" Sun screamed. "No—"

0442 hours
Motor pool, Nyongch'on-kiji

The M-760 bucked in Sikes's hands, the rounds pinning the Korean officer back against the hull of his ZSU. At the same moment, Austin triggered the RPG for a second shot. The booster charge ignited and kicked the five-pound grenade clear of the launcher; the rocket fired an instant later, lifting the grenade in a swiftly rising trajectory which sent it arrowing straight toward the target, just as a second crewman clambered out of the turret.

Austin's first shot had nearly missed. SEALs trained regularly with foreign weapons like the RPG-7, but that was the first time he'd tried to fire one in combat, in the dark, and against a moving target.

This time his target was stationary, well-lit by the flames rising from the rear deck. The rocket-propelled grenade hissed into the ZSU's broad turret and struck a foot above the dying Korean's head. The flash lit up half the compound. Austin and Sikes ducked as exploding ammunition banged and thumped. Fire engulfed the vehicle with a roar.

There was no trace at all left of the ZSU's crew.

Austin lowered the tube from his shoulder. "You think that's all there were?"

"Better be. We need to get Cavalry One down here pronto. I'm betting those boys called for help."

"Oh, shit . . ."

"Shit is right. C'mon. Let's get back to the airstrip."

0446 hours
Intruder 537

Lieutenant Shaw turned in his seat, peering out of the cockpit as his Intruder banked over the compound. He could see the funeral pyres of four ZSUs, three on the road and one fifty yards inside the main gate. Ground fire seemed to have ceased.

"Shotgun Leader, this is Desperado Five-three-seven. I think we've cleared up your little difficulty for you."

"Roger that, and thanks," Tombstone Magruder's voice replied. "We're passing the word to Cavalry One."

"Any sign of Jolly and Chucker?"

"Negative on that." There was a small hesitation. "We have people monitoring the SAR frequencies. If they made it out, we'll extract them."

"Damn right we will," Shaw replied. Like most of his running mates, he did not particularly care for Jolly's obnoxious attitude, but Chucker was a good guy . . . and this time around *no one* was going to be left behind to enjoy the North Koreans' ideas of justice and mercy.

Not even Jolly Greene.

0452 hours
Near Nyongch'on

The flame and horror of the whirlwind attack at Nyongch'on-kiji had seared themselves into Colonel Li Il-Sung's mind. He'd been asleep in the officers' quarters when the first explosion had rocked the building; he'd gotten dressed and into the compound in time to see the headquarters building in flames, to hear the screams of soldiers cut down outside the barracks.

Many had escaped. Colonel Li had joined a group of twenty or thirty men, scrambling across the wreckage of the east perimeter fence where a watchtower had collapsed and dragged the wire down. For hours now, he and the ragged band of soldiers had wandered around on the dark slopes southeast of the camp. From there he had a clear view of the pass, lit now by burning ZSUs and the torches of Nyongch'on's fuel-storage tanks. There might be another hundred survivors, possibly more, scattered among the rocks and barren slopes beyond the perimeter fence.

This night would be the end of his career. He knew that, accepted it in a fatalistic way. It had already ended General Chung's career rather abruptly. He'd seen the general outside the headquarters building, nearly cut in half by one of those devilish American claymore mines.

Other heads would roll because of this. The American prisoners should have been separated into small groups on the first day and scattered across the breadth of the People's Republic. It had been folly to keep them together in one place . . . a folly which could only have been born of overconfidence. The weakness of American will in the face of strength was preached so often and so loudly that, perhaps, there were those in the halls of power in P'yongyang who had come to believe in it.

How many Yankee commandos were there, anyway? There was no way to be certain; fifty, at least, Li thought. No smaller group could have done so much, so quickly. Some of the men thought the attackers were the dreaded South Korean Special Forces, but Li did not believe that. No, these were Americans, seeking their own.

"Comrade Colonel!" one of the men said urgently. "Comrade Colonel! Listen!"

He heard nothing at first, but then the sound grew, swelling rapidly on the night air, a deep-throated clatter which could be only one thing.

"Helicopters!" He turned sharply, searching among the soldiers with him. He had seen one with a Type 80 machine gun, a Chinese copy of the Soviet PKM. There he was. "You! Set up your weapon, quickly!"

The Type 80 was belt-fed, with a bipod under the muzzle. It

took seconds to prop the weapon on a rock as the thunder of rotors grew louder. "Stand ready! They're coming!"

Li's only hope to salvage anything out of this was to win a major tactical victory . . . and he just might accomplish that if he could bring down an American helicopter.

Then he saw it, a gray shape low above the ridge top, sweeping overhead toward the camp. Below, inside the perimeter fence, he saw red flames burst into ruby pinpoints, outlining the south end of the airstrip. "Fire!"

With a roar that drowned the thunder of rotors, the machine gun yammered, scattering spent castings in a storm of noise. The helicopter staggered, stricken. . . .

0455 hours
Helo Cavalry One-Three

Lieutenant Morgan felt the helicopter shudder, then lurch violently to port. Something shrieked through the red-lit confines of the Sea Stallion's cargo deck, and Morgan remembered hearing somewhere that the skin of a helicopter was so thin it was possible to punch a screwdriver through it with your hand.

"Cav One-Three, declaring emergency!" The pilot was using an emergency radio frequency, but Morgan was hearing the yell over his intercom plug. The helicopter lurched again and Morgan grabbed for a handhold. It felt as though the huge machine was spinning, dipping wildly to one side.

"Mayday! Mayday!" the pilot continued to call. "Cavalry One-Three hit by ground fire. Engine hit, repeat, engine hit! I'm going in!"

"Hold on!" Morgan screamed into the inferno of smoke and noise and darkness. "Brace for a crash!"

0500 hours
Flag Plot, U.S.S. *Thomas Jefferson*

Nearly one hundred miles at sea, Admiral Magruder listened to the radio messages relayed by one of the orbiting Hawkeyes. Intruder strikes appeared to have cleared the ZSUs, but at least one of the Cavalry One helos had been badly hit and gone down, well short of Nyongch'on. One Intruder had been shot down, its crew lost among the night-shrouded ridges of North Korea, and the SEALs were out of touch with Homeplate.

Commander Neil leafed through a small stack of TENCAP photos. They showed flames and scars, smoke palls and wreckage. One close-up of Nyongch'on showed bodies sprawled on the ground outside the POW compound.

"You know, it's still not too late to call off the main landings, Admiral," Neil said quietly. His eyes had a glassy, faraway look.

Magruder looked up from his half-full coffee cup. "You sorry son of a bitch . . ."

Neil blinked rapidly. "Admiral, I didn't mean—"

"You're as bad as those fuzz-brains in Washington, boy. We started this. We're going to finish it."

"Yes, sir."

"We're not leaving our people in there to die."

"No, sir."

"We're not leaving *Chimera*'s crew, we're not leaving the SEALs and Marines, we're not leaving our aviators. Hear me?"

"Yes, sir."

"They all come home, or none of us do."

"Absolutely, Admiral. I . . . I just thought I should mention the options—"

"Options." He turned away, angry with himself for having lost his temper. "Take a hike, Neil. Get the hell out of my sight."

The staff intelligence officer dropped the stack of TENCAP photos on the table and quietly left the room.

Leaving Admiral Magruder alone with the loneliness, the inner doubts which had threatened to overwhelm him ever since he'd given the order to go.

Everything depended now on the Marines of Cavalry One . . . and on the Marines about to storm ashore at Kolmo. The issue could still go either way, and there was nothing he could do now to affect the outcome except order an abort.

And that would mean failure.

For Magruder, the waiting was always the hardest part.

CHAPTER 27

One engine had failed, but the second GE T64 turbine kept turning, lowering the Sea Stallion to an undignified but relatively gentle touchdown in the rugged country southeast of Nyongch'onkiji. The helo struck the ground with a lurch, which threw the Marines against one another, but no one was hurt.

Lieutenant Morgan was already standing on the sharply tilted deck as the rear ramp began lowering. A blast of cold air penetrated the cabin. "Move them out, Gunny!"

But Gunnery Sergeant Walters was way ahead of him, grabbing each Marine by the sleeve and propelling him toward the ramp. "On your feet, Second Platoon! I want to see nothing but amphibious green blurs! Go! Go! Go!" With a thunder of boots on metal gratings, the Marines stormed down the ramp clutching their weapons and field gear. Morgan checked to make sure the chopper's crew was out, then followed himself.

Outside, the darkness was relieved by fires burning in the distance. Gunnery Sergeant Walters handed him an M-16. He took it and snicked back the charging handle to chamber a round. "Well, Gunny?"

Walters consulted a map and compass with a small penlight, then pointed. "That way, Lieutenant. Other side of that ridge."

"How far?"

"Two miles, maybe three. Not bad, considering."

Morgan agreed. He studied the map a moment longer. "We took fire from this area here."

"I'd say so, Lieutenant."

Morgan looked up, scanning the darkness. The platoon was

252

clear of the downed helo now, forming up by squads. Northwest, a steep ridge bulked against a sky only just becoming visible in the pre-dawn light. The sun would be up in another ninety minutes. "Hostiles between us and Nyongch'on, then," he said. He sighed. This wasn't going to be easy. "Okay. Have the men saddle up. I don't want to get caught out here in daylight."

"Right."

"Next, ring up Cavalry One-One. Give them our posit and tell them we're coming in. Oh, and you'd better take care of the helo too."

"Already done, sir." There was a dull thump, and flames began washing from the helicopter's cabin.

They would leave nothing behind that the enemy could use.

0510 hours
Nyongch'on airstrip

The Marine captain stepped off the ramp and extended his hand. "Captain Ford, Lieutenant," he said, shouting above the rotor noise. "U.S. Marines."

"Welcome, sir." Sikes took the hand. "Good to have the grunts aboard."

"Our pleasure, Lieutenant." The two turned and made their way off the tarmac in a bent-double stoop beneath the slowing blades of the RH-53D. "Always ready to come in and help you Navy pukes out."

Sikes laughed. "We may have bitten off more than even Marines can chew, Captain. What's the situation with Second Platoon?"

"They're down and safe, Lieutenant." He jerked a thumb over his shoulder toward the helicopter. "I was just talkin' to them on the horn. A few cuts and scrapes, but no casualties." He pointed southeast, toward the hills above the camp. "Far side of that ridge, about two miles. They should be here in another forty mikes."

Unless they run into trouble on the way, Sikes thought. Well, perhaps it was just as well to have another forty-some Marines on the loose outside the perimeter.

Three of the four choppers of Cavalry One had touched down safely at the helipad. The ramps were down, and the Marines of the first and third rifle platoons and a weapons platoon— altogether over one hundred thirty men—were spilling out across the flame-illuminated tarmac to establish their perimeter. Scattered gunshots and short bursts of fire from the perimeter fence marked skirmishes with the North Koreans still lurking just outside the captured military base.

"Let's have a look at your situation," the captain said as they reached the hangar building that Sikes had commandeered as headquarters. Ford's Marines were already setting up commo gear and a map table. "The KorComs are going to hit us hard, and we have to be ready for them."

"How long until Cavalry Two comes in, Captain?"

Ford gave a tight smile. "Long enough. *Jefferson*'s A-6s are still hammering SAM sites, and we have to make sure there are no more surprises like those ZSUs." He looked at his watch. "And our boys'll be hitting the beaches in another fifty minutes or so. We'll have to hold at least that long."

"Fair enough, Captain. I've got a map over here."

Together, they began planning the defense of Nyongch'on.

0515 hours
Off the Kolmo Peninsula

Of all the tasks the U.S. Navy is called on to perform, an amphibious assault is without question the most complex, requiring exhaustive planning, perfect timing, and a degree of coordination and cooperation between forces at sea, on shore, and in the air more exacting than in any other arena of modern warfare. As H-hour approached, Admiral Magruder could only watch the ponderous uncoilings of the many-headed beast he'd released, and pray that each head, each movement followed the plan worked out by Colonel Caruso, Admiral Simpson, and himself. With so many men and so much equipment involved, anything could cause disaster: a forgotten bit of planning, the failure of a timetable, or something as ignominious as a traffic jam on the beach.

Task Force 18 was scattered now, covering an area hugging Korea's east coast over one hundred miles across. Most far-flung of all the ships were the frigates *Gridley* and *Biddle*, charged now with backing up the antisubmarine cordon of LAMPS III helos, HS-19s Sea King helicopters, and the S-3A Vikings of VS-42. North Korea had a number of submarines, mostly older, ex-Soviet *Whiskey*-classes, and it was imperative that they be kept well clear of the American ships—especially the Marine-laden transports and the *Jefferson* herself.

The U.S.S. *Thomas Jefferson*, flagship of the task force,

cruised slowly thirty miles off Wonsan, accompanied by the guided-missile cruiser *Vicksburg* and her Combat Air Patrol umbrella of F-14 Tomcats.

Much nearer the coast, eight miles off Wonsan's harbor mouth, the Marine contingent held station: *Chosin, Little Rock, Texas City,* and *Westmoreland County.*

Closer inshore still, the destroyers *Lawrence Kearny* and *John A. Winslow* turned five-inch guns on the spine of the Kolmo Peninsula, pounding away at the heights above the beach as they covered the approach of Marine amphibious craft. And over the entire area, A-6 Intruders, F/A-18 Hornets, and F-14 Tomcats prowled, stooped, and struck. Every SAM site that could be found along the coast had been neutralized already. Because Wonsan Harbor itself was crowded with the shipping of many nations, North Korean vessels in port were largely ignored, but those which attempted to sortie were quickly spotted by Hawkeye radar planes and pounced upon. So far two Osa-class missile boats— each carrying Styx anti-ship missiles—had been discovered and sunk as they tried to motor clear of the harbor. Other Korean casualties included five patrol boats which might have posed a threat to the landing craft, and the North Korean frigate *Glorious Revolution,* run aground by her crew after sustaining a hit by an Intruder-launched Harpoon missile. Smoke from the fires still raging in her engine room stained the sky over the Kolmo Peninsula as dawn approached.

H-hour was set for 0545 hours, the time of high tide this morning along the east Korean coast. By 0515, the LPD *Little Rock*'s stern doors were open, and the first of her two LCACs began nosing onto seas made choppy by a stiff, northwesterly breeze.

Neither aircraft nor boat, each was a squat, curious-looking vessel eighty-eight feet long and forty-seven feet wide supported on cushions of air. LCAC hovercraft—the designation stood for Landing Craft Air Cushion—were one of the more recent developments in amphibious operations. Capable of carrying over one hundred twenty tons of payload twenty miles at forty knots, LCACs were such a new twist to modern warfare that the experts were still arguing over just how they should be integrated into conventional beach assault tactics.

Wonsan would be their first combat test. LCAC 53 and LCAC 55 swung clear of *Little Rock*'s stern, churning up clouds of wind-whipped spray as thick as smoke screens. Driven by twin, aft-mounted turboprops, outsized versions of the aircraft propellers which drove flat-bottomed swamp buggies in the Everglades, the LCACs accelerated toward the coast.

0529 hours
Southeast of Nyongch'on-kiji

The encounter was more accident than ambush, blind probes by opposing forces which blundered into one another just below the ridge crest on the rocky slopes a mile from Nyongch'on. Second Platoon was advancing by squads, with one thirteen-man team moving while the other two provided overwatch. Third Squad had the point when they encountered the North Korean position.

Gunfire barked and cracked, the muzzle flashes visible as rapidly strobing pulses of light against the blackness of the ridge. The Marines returned fire at once and the morning was filled with the hammering thunder of autofire.

Lieutenant Morgan was with First Squad when the pre-dawn stillness shattered. Like tens of thousands of junior Marine officers before him, Lieutenant Victor A. Morgan had originally joined the Corps during peace time, with no serious thought of ever having to go into combat. A modern Marine officer could well serve his entire career without once hearing a shot fired in anger.

It had taken OCS at Quantico, a course tougher in most respects than that meted out to enlisted recruits at Paris Island and San Diego, to give him a more realistic view of the modern world. Marines had died in Iran, Beirut, Grenada, and a score of other places around the world during "peacetime." And the war to liberate tiny Kuwait had come out of nowhere. Now Morgan found himself on a hill in North Korea, with someone up there doing his best to kill him. He was scared, but the shouted orders of the platoon's sergeant, the sure movements of his men, the memories of his own training quickly steadied him.

"Ryan!" he snapped, grateful for the hours he'd spent memorizing the names and histories of the men in his platoon. "Take your squad to the left. Van Buren! Close up and support Third Squad!"

"Aye aye, sir!"

"And use your two-oh-threes!" Sergeant Walters added. "Move it!"

"Right, Gunny!"

Gunfire continued to crackle through the night. One rifleman in each squad carried an M-203 grenade launcher clipped beneath the barrel of his M-16 assault rifle.

The lieutenant heard the hollow thump of an M-203 off to the right, followed by another. The first 40-mm grenade burst near the top of the ridge, the flash so brilliant it hurt the eyes. The second exploded close by the first. Morgan could hear someone screaming somewhere up there on the hillside. Seconds later, the firing redoubled as Second Squad reached the crest of the ridge and began flanking the enemy.

"Let's move, Lieutenant," Walters said. "Up and over."

"Right you are, Gunny." His initial fear was still with him, but controlled. He felt a swelling excitement, an urgency to close with the unseen enemy. He raised his voice in a bellow which shook his entire frame. "Marines!"

With an answering roar his platoon surged up the slope. Gunfire from the crest was sporadic now as North Korean soldiers began filtering back down the other side.

A Marine officer leads by example. The phrase from OCS was stuck in Morgan's mind, playing itself over and over as he took the lead.

"Marines!"

0535 hours
Southeast of Nyongch'on-kiji

The Yankee troops had materialized out of nowhere, and Colonel Li was faced with the very real prospect of having his entire command trapped between the Marines in Nyongch'on kiji and those who were coming up the ridge toward him from the area where that one damaged helicopter had gone down. It had been bad luck that the aircraft had managed to make a soft landing, bad luck that their blundering advance through the darkness had caught his own battered command scattered and unready. Li saw almost from the beginning that his men were not going to stand against the Yankees. With the first grenade explosion, a dozen men turned and ran.

So much, he decided, for Communist patriotic solidarity. Despite continuing clashes with the puppets in the south, few of his men had actually seen combat. The reality was like being doused by a bucket of ice water.

"You!" he snapped, pointing at the man with the Type 80 MG. "With me!"

"*Chucksiro!*" the soldier replied. He looked terrified. "At once, Comrade Colonel!"

Two hundred meters down the northwest slope of the ridge, Colonel Li and the machine gunner came to an outcropping of boulders dimly visible now in the growing light. The base lay spread out below him. From here, Li could easily see the buildings, the dying fires, and three large American helicopters sitting on the tarmac on the west side of the camp. There were well over a hundred Americans in the camp now; he could see them moving in groups among the buildings, setting up a defensive perimeter.

They would keep, he decided. His first task was to stop the Imperialist Marines coming over the top of the hill behind him.

"*Chogi!*" He pointed. "Over there. Behind those rocks!"

"*Ne*, Comrade Colonel!" The soldier propped the Type 80 on a rock, the muzzle probing back up the slope.

The sky to the south and east was well along toward dawn, growing lighter almost minute by minute. Last night's overcast appeared to have broken up, and a few of the brighter stars were shining against the royal blue patches that showed through rents in the clouds.

Colonel Li looked up the hill. The crest of the ridge was clearly visible against the sky; anyone who came over that ridge would have to show themselves, and when they did . . .

His hand closed on the machine gunner's shoulder. "*Chunbi toesyossumnikka?*" he asked, his voice scarcely raised above a whisper. "Are you ready? They will be coming soon."

The gunner nodded hard, his eyes narrowing over the weapon's rear sight, his finger tightening on the trigger.

Pin them down, then run. Bleed them with pinpricks until they bleed to death. That was the way of guerrilla war.

Any moment now . . .

0537 hours
Southeast of Nyongch'on-kiji

Coyote saw the two Korean soldiers take cover behind the rock some fifteen yards from his position, setting up a machine gun to face back up the ridge. He'd heard gunfire on the far side of the slope a few moments ago. That meant friendlies were coming, his ticket off this hill.

It seemed like he'd lain there on the ground for hours, his leg throbbing so hard he was afraid to even try to attempt the walk down the uneven slope to the camp. Crawling on hands and one knee, Coyote had taken the radio, Kohl's pistol, and some fresh magazines for the rifle back to a hide in the tangled brush near the clearing. More than once in the past hours, bands of Koreans had passed him, most heading up-slope and away from the camp, and he'd remained silent and hidden, praying that they would not stop.

The growing light as dawn approached was raising the chances of him being discovered. If someone didn't come out from the camp to get him, some gomer with nothing better to do was going to find him . . . and if it came to that, Coyote was determined not to let the bastards capture him again.

Once on this cruise was enough.

Besides, it was quickly clear to him that the Koreans were setting up an ambush. One of them appeared to be an officer, though their backs were to him and he could make out no details on the rather plain uniforms.

Only slowly did the realization that he could take both of them with Kohl's G3 rifle make its way through the shock and pain which had numbed Coyote's brain. The selector switch was set to full auto; if he emptied what was left of the magazine at them he would almost certainly hit them both.

Slowly, so as not to make a sound, he raised the rifle. As he'd been taught in survival school, he took in a deep breath, released half, and held it, centering the sight over the back of the machine gunner. His finger closed on the trigger. . . .

A single shot rang out . . . but only one. The machine gunner leaped up as though stung, scrabbled with one hand at his back, then fell. The officer whirled about, clawing for a holstered pistol. With a slow-motion sense of arrested time, Coyote saw the gleaming gold cartridge stuck in the G3's mud-caked ejection port, saw the Korean officer drawing his pistol and raising it in both hands. . . .

He recognized him. *Li!*

Coyote hurled himself to one side, gasping as fresh agony seared his leg from ankle to hip. Li's pistol barked and the aviator heard the bullet's snap inches from his ear. Coyote reached for Kohl's pistol, lying on the ground a foot away. Li fired a second time, and a pile driver struck Coyote high in the left shoulder, knocking him back.

He lunged, his fingers closing on the hush puppy's checkered grip. His left arm refused to obey orders, but he managed to heave the pistol up one-handed and squeeze the trigger. The softened blast of the suppressed weapon was drowned by the crack of Li's pistol. Dirt spat, stinging Coyote's face, but he held his wavering hand as steady as he could and kept firing, three shots, four, five, six. . . .

The hush puppy's slide locked open, the magazine empty. Colonel Li remained standing, his automatic still clutched in his right hand. The man took a step, the pistol coming up once more.

Then he toppled forward, hitting the ground with a thump, face-down. The SEAL pistol fell from nerveless fingers. Coyote was not sure how much time passed before hearing returned to his ringing ears.

"Hey, fella! Fella!"

Someone was shaking him. He opened his eyes and found himself looking up into a hideously green-painted face under a steel helmet. "Lieutenant Morgan, U.S. Marines," the face said. "Hang on. We'll have a corpsman up right away."

Then night returned and Coyote slipped away into oblivion.

0545 hours
P'yongyang-East Airbase, PDRK

Pak stood at attention in front of the general's desk. It was almost dawn, light enough that he could look through the window behind General Yi and see the line of MiG-21s lined up on the tarmac outside.

He was still angry. Hours after his return to Wonsan two days ago he'd been summoned to P'yongyang, then grounded with no reason given. Pak had spent the better part of thirty-six hours waiting, fuming . . . and now listening with increasing despair to reports of American attacks near Wonson. He should be out there, leading his squadron against the Imperialist enemy!

"So you still believe your Plan Dagger was a success, Major?" the general asked.

Pak swallowed. "Sometimes, Comrade General, success or failure cannot be measured solely by the number of kills—"

"I read your report, Major! It happens that I do not agree with your conclusions! Your so-called ambush of the American aircraft was a waste of precious national resources . . . worse, a waste of good pilots!"

Pak decided that it would be better to keep silent. He remained at attention, his eyes fixed on the MiGs in the window at Yi's back.

"Nevertheless," the general continued. "It seems you are to be given another chance, whatever my own reservations on the subject." He handed Pak's orders across the desk. "Please note the signature."

Pak did so. His eyebrows arched. "I . . . I am honored, Comrade General."

"Yes, I imagine you are. It seems there are those at Party Headquarters who agree with your notions on tactics." He sighed and looked away. "They are, apparently, more interested in politics than in the realities of men and machines."

So, the conflict here was one of politics. Pak had thought as much. "It is not our place to question the wisdom of our superiors, Comrade General."

Yi shot the major a look of pure venom, and Pak wondered if he'd gone too far. He was, after all, a very low-ranking piece in the chess match unfolding between the leadership in P'yongyang and factions within the North Korean military itself. If he overstepped his authority, the general could still crush him, with or without the signature on those orders.

"You have been given a new mission, Major," Yi continued. "A mission vital to the success of this . . . this plan devised by our Beloved Leader." He used the common euphemistic title for North Korea's president.

The plan, called *Saebyok Chosumnida*—the Fortunate Dawn—had been conceived as a way to humiliate the United States on the world stage. Initially, it had involved only the capture of the American spy ship; the Party leaders believed that espionage confessions by the ship's crew would bolster North Korean prestige . . . especially with the Soviet Union. The PDRK's Russian allies, mired in the legacies of *perestroika*, had drastically cut their military aid packages to socialist countries around the world . . . especially to those that could not pay. In the People's Democratic Republic, this new austerity had resulted in especially severe shortages of parts and spares. Many MiG-21s had already been cannibalized just to keep the others flying.

Chance had given Major Pak his opportunity to shoot down an American F-14, but the government had seized on that victory, added it to *Saebyok Chosumnida*'s promise. P'yongyang had authorized Pak's Plan Dagger two days earlier for that reason; the more aircraft and pilots the Americans lost in their attempts to punish North Korea, the more foolish and helpless they would appear to the rest of the world, especially in Moscow and Beijing.

And now that the Americans were attacking Wonsan in force, there was an even greater opportunity. Suppose they lost not just aircraft, but one of their *warships*.

Pak glanced through his orders. "I am directed to escort a flight of fighter bombers, Comrade General. The target . . ." He looked up. "The American amphibious forces off Wonsan Harbor."

Yi jerked a thumb over one ornate shoulder board. "Correct. We are loading four Nanchang Q-5s with AS-7 missiles. The American amphibious ships will be loaded with aviation gasoline, with ammunition, with troops. A solid hit by a one-hundred-kilo warhead coming in at Mach 1 . . ."

"A triumph, Comrade General!" Pak's heart pounded in anticipation.

Yi's mouth twisted unpleasantly. "Perhaps. The mission will be codenamed Plan Vengeance. You will brief the men of your squadron, then ready your aircraft. You should be cleared for takeoff within two hours."

"Yes, Comrade General!"

Yi nodded toward the papers in Pak's hand. "You have your orders from our government, Major. I will add one of my own. You have shown a disturbing tendency, these past few days, toward an independence of thought and action unbecoming to one in your position. I am thinking of your attack on the American F-14s five days ago. Your mission this time will be to escort the Nanchangs, *not* to engage in aerial dogfights. Victory this time will be measured by the survival of the fighter bombers, and by nothing else. Defeat is unthinkable. Do you understand me?"

"Perfectly, Comrade General." Yi was telling him to get the Q-5s through to their targets . . . or not return. The implied threat did not worry him. Already he thought he saw a way to slip the Q-5s past the American defenses. "Our Beloved Leader will have his victory, I swear it!"

CHAPTER 28

Dawn came to the rugged hills of North Korea in blue and gold, accompanied by the thunder of explosions and the howl of LCACs drifting across the rocky beach, a barren stretch of coastline designated Blue Beach.

The hovercraft came ashore at Blue Beach less than a mile from Wonsan's large airport and military airfield, climbing well beyond the surf line before settling to the sand on deflating skirts. LCACs were designed to carry troops and vehicles well inland on flat terrain, but the Kolmo Peninsula presented the MEU with a special problem: narrow beaches backed by rocky slopes too steep for hovercraft to climb. Ramps dropped across the LCACs' fore and aft skirts, and Marines pounded across the sand, taking cover along the base of the slope. Overhead, AH-1J SeaCobra gunships swooped and darted like dragonflies, seeking targets called in by Marine aviators serving as forward observers on the ground.

But there were no targets on the beach, no organized resistance at all. Within ten minutes of coming ashore, Marines had seized the dirt roads on the seaward face of the peninsula leading to the airfield which lay on the level ground above.

The slope was too steep for LCACs, but not for the amphibious tractors which followed them. Scores of them were swimming ashore in the wakes of the hovercraft, trailing smoke to hide their numbers. They were ugly, snub-nosed craft officially designated AAVPs for "Armored Assault Vehicle, Personnel," but known more descriptively to the Marines who rode them as "tuna cans." Each carried twenty-one riflemen as well as a squat turret mounting a machine gun, 40-mm cannon, or TOW missile launcher. By H plus 1, foot patrols had reached the airport, the AAVs close behind.

Or most of them. Sergeant Calvin Peters slammed his fist into the side of the AAVP's hull. "Okay," he growled. "Which of you dickheads has been eatin' apricots?"

"Not me, Sarge." The driver blinked at him owlishly through Marine-issue glasses. "Shit, we all know better than that!"

"Oh, come on, Polaski!" The AAV's gunner was fresh out of boot camp, obviously too raw to understand the realities of Marine Corps physics. "You don't believe that apricot curse stuff, do you?"

Peters's eyes narrowed. He pointed one camo-smeared finger at the gunner. "It ain't crap, puff, and don't you forget it. One of these babies throws a track, there's only one thing it could be. God damn it to hell!" He slammed the amtrack's green-and-brown-painted hull again in disgust. "Okay, Marines! Fall out! We walk from here!"

It was an article of faith among Marine Corps officers and men alike that if you ate apricots on a tank or an amtrack, that vehicle was going to break down. Any track driver could recite an endless list of incidents where vehicles had been crippled by the "apricot curse."

The Marines piled out of the amtrack as the driver shut the engine off. The AAV had crested the ridge near the south end of the airport, wallowing up the rocky slope like some massive, high-snouted, prehistoric beast, when the portside tread let go with a crash and a grinding clatter.

"Cover us," Peters shouted to the gunner. The track's turret slewed about, its 40-mm cannon probing the smoke which hung like thick fog across the top of the ridge. "The rest of you guys, c'mon! By fire teams!"

Three by three, the Marines advanced into the fog. Their mission had been to check out the south end of the airport, but the smoke was so thick there there was nothing to check. Reaching a bomb crater, Peters waited while five other men dropped in behind him. Off to the left, Peters could make out the charred skeleton of an aircraft—a MiG-21, it looked like, its back broken.

"Navy pukes sure flattened this place," one of the men said.

"They could sink the whole stinking country," Peters replied. "Wouldn't bother me at all! Weber! Gould! Take point!"

"Right, Sarge!" The two men rose and clambered over the lip of the crater. The smoke was clearing now, revealing the tattered outline of structures ahead, buildings, and a stone tower. That must be the traffic control tower, Peters thought.

A flash of light winked from the tower platform, accompanied by the chatter of an assault rifle on full-auto. Stone chips and sparks gouted from the tarmac. Weber, arms outstretched, toppled backward into the crater.

The other men opened fire, pumping round after round toward the tower, the building, and anything else they could see through the thinning smoke. The AAV opened up as well, its cannon adding a deep-throated thunder to the gunfire.

Explosions gouged chunks of concrete from the tower. "Go!" Peters yelled. "Move it! Move it!" The Marines rolled out of the crater and charged, moving in short rushes until they reached the building.

Peters used his tactical radio to signal the AAV. "Cease fire! Cease fire!"

They found the sniper behind the tower, what was left of him. The airport buildings appeared to be deserted.

"My God, Sarge!" Gould called. "Will you look at this!"

Not sure what to expect, Peters joined the Marine rifleman. He was standing on a boulder outcropping a short distance behind the buildings, looking toward the west.

The smoke was lifting there, like smog above a city. Morning light filtered through, catching the buildings on the far side of the bay.

They were perhaps a mile and a half from the waterfront and well above it, looking down into the city. Modern skyscrapers mingled with shacks, and everywhere was the clutter of industrial plants and shipyards, factories and smokestacks. A squared-off tower rose next to the water, the Wonsan Sports Complex. Fishing boats and small craft crowded against the jetties of the commercial waterfront.

"So that's Wonsan," Peters said.

"Yeah, and that ain't all, Sarge." Gould pointed. "Take a look there. To the south, just to the left of that big gray mother."

Peters did not need binoculars to recognize that ship. He'd seen it before, during briefings on the *Chosin*. "That's *Chimera*," he said. "That's the goddamned *Chimera*!"

The captured ship now lay less than two miles away. Beside her was a warship, flying the red and white naval ensign of the Soviet Union.

"Let's get back, Gould. The choppers'll be coming in soon."

"Yeah. Right, Sarge."

They started back toward the buildings. Gunfire rattled and popped from the south, where Marines were setting up their perimeter. From the sea came the deep-voiced *whup-whup-whup* of CH-46 Sea Knights, twin-rotored, banana-shaped helos loaded with troops and weapons to reinforce the Kolmo beachhead.

He thought of the Russian ship in the harbor. What, Peters wondered, were the Russkies making of all this?

0712 hours
Tomcat 205

From five thousand feet, Tombstone could see the whole of Wonsan Harbor spread out for his inspection. Smoke still rose from the hangar buildings southwest of the airfield and from the grounded frigate to the north, but overall damage had been slight. The waters off Blue Beach were swarming with Mike boats and other Naval landing craft, as well as an armada of AAVPs making their endless churnings between shore and the Marine ships just visible on the horizon.

"Shotgun, Shotgun, this is Homeplate, do you read, over?"

"Homeplate, Shotgun. What can I do for you boys?"

"We've just had word from the beach. Kolmo Airfield is secure. Cavalry Two is now inbound. Please deploy to cover their approach, over."

"Copy, Homeplate." Tombstone banked the Tomcat, his eyes scanning the blue-gray of the ocean to the east. He saw a number of helicopters: Super Stallions still dragging their mine sleds, SeaCobra gunships working close support with the grunts, Marine Sea Knights heading for the captured airport. . . .

Then he saw them, four RH-53D Sea Stallions with Marine markings, flying in a wedge formation low over the water. According to plan, they would set down at the Kolmo Airfield and await the call from Nyongch'on. When the camp was completely secure, they would make the last short hop to the airstrip at Nyongch'on-kiji.

"Homeplate, Shotgun. I have Cavalry Two in sight. Will comply."

Batman pulled up close to Tombstone's starboard wingtip. "Well, pardner," Batman said. "Now we find out if this shindig was worth the price of admission."

"You're right there. Ready, everyone? Let's go give the grunts a hand."

The four Tomcats peeled out of formation and dropped toward the sea.

Far below, the Marines hurried to throw up their perimeter south of the airport. The runways were too pitted and cratered by the Intruder bomb runs of a few hours before to be usable by regular aircraft, but the helicopters would have no trouble finding a place to set down.

And soon, very soon, it would be the helicopters' show . . . the final act.

0720 hours
Nyongch'on perimeter

"Make smoke," the voice said over Morgan's radio.

"Roger that." Morgan nodded to Gunnery Sergeant Walters, who popped the pin on a smoke grenade. Green smoke billowed out, a cottony cloud in the morning sun.

"I see green smoke," the radio voice said. "Come on in."

Second Platoon rose and began walking the final hundred yards toward a gap torn in Nyongch'on perimeter fence. Craters marred the road, and Morgan saw the burned-out hulk of a Russian-made ZSU.

Captain Ford was waiting for him. "About time you showed up, Lieutenant." He grinned, teeth white in his camo-smeared face. The smile vanished as Marines approached, carrying stretchers. "How many casualties?"

"Two wounded," Morgan replied. "Not too bad, considering Oh . . . and a Navy guy, Lieutenant Grant." He pointed. "We found him up there, pretty badly hit. He saved our asses. We're also bringing in a KIA, one of the SEALs."

"Corporal!" The captain signaled. "See the wounded get to the Waldorf."

"Aye aye, sir!"

"Oh, yeah, we also found these." Morgan handed the captain a packet of folded papers. "Took them off a dead NK colonel. They looked important."

"Good work, Lieutenant," Ford said. "Pull up a seat and take a load off."

"Thank you, sir." Morgan savored the silence, broken only by the clink and trudge of Second Platoon coming in. The rumble of bombs sounded to the northeast. "It's quiet."

"Too quiet. They hit us three times before dawn, then broke off. We think they're gathering for a hard push."

"And Cavalry Two?"

"Waiting." The captain wiped his eyes with his hand. "At Kolmo Airfield. Hear the thunder? That's A-6 Intruders laying a carpet. When all the SAM sites are cleared, Cav Two will come on in."

Morgan smiled. "I'm glad we didn't miss *that*." He watched as the last of his men filed through the gap in the fence.

"That's for sure, Lieutenant," Ford said. "That's for *damned* sure."

0740 hours
Flight deck, U.S.S. *Thomas Jefferson*

AN/3 Dale Carter was tired. His division had been on alert and on the job for nearly sixteen hours straight now, an uninterrupted agony of work as *Jefferson*'s aircraft were launched, recovered, and launched again. Long days were the rule rather than the exception on board aircraft carriers, even during normal times. During a crisis such as this one, every man on board was expected to work around the clock. Most of the crew took this in stride, even preferring work to the boredom of below-decks routine. There was sharp pride in the certain knowledge that it was they, the men of the U.S.S. *Jefferson*, who kept the big ship going and her planes flying.

Carter, carrying a heavy lug wrench in one hand, was coming around the open door of the forward bomb elevator where red-vested ordies were jackassing a rack of Mark 82 GPs onto a hand cart for transport to a flight of waiting Intruders. Fifty yards away, his division chief waved, then pumped his fist up and down. *Double time!*

Breaking into a run, Carter ducked underneath the bulk of an A-6 already locked into the number two catapult, engines howling and ready for launch. Exhaustion, and the fact that Carter was still new to carriers, blurred his thinking. He turned sharply left, taking a shortcut in front of the Intruder.

Someone yelled a warning, but he couldn't catch the words through his ear protectors and the shriek of the Intruder's engines. Before he even had a chance to scream, he was swept from the deck, caught in a black maelstrom of wind and noise and plunged headfirst into the aircraft's starboard intake.

Carter's body was more than enough to wreck an engine, but it was the lug wrench which did the real damage, shearing off turbine blades and blasting them through the aircraft's thin skin like shrapnel. Fuel vented from a dozen punctures in the wing tank, gushing across the hot engine manifold.

Flames boiled into the sky as if from a bomb blast, and every sailor on the deck was hammered flat by the concussion. The catapult officer tumbled to his knees, his uniform wreathed in flames until a sailor, less stunned than others, knocked him down and pounded them out.

"Emergency! Emergency!" shrilled from the 5-MC. "Fire on the flight deck! Fire on the flight deck! Fire and damage control parties man your stations!"

Air operations on the *Jefferson* came to a halt.

0815 hours
Air Ops, U.S.S. *Thomas Jefferson*

"How long can we keep them up?" Admiral Magruder's voice sounded grim over the batphone.

Lieutenant Commander Mike Leahy looked at the huge, transparent status board where every aircraft not within Pri-Fly's control pattern was listed, complete with its fuel state. "Admiral, we have two KA-6Ds airborne with full loads. That's better than twenty-one thousand pounds of fuel each, but it won't last long. Four of VFA-161 Hornets are inbound now, and they'll be on bingo fuel when they hit the marshall. We were going to have to tank them up just to get them trapped."

"The deck is closed," Magruder said. "Another hour at least."

"So I see, Admiral." One of the Air Op monitors showed the flight deck from a vantage point high up on the island looking down onto cats one and two. The fire was out, the wreckage shoved over the side by the Tilly. Green shirts were working now to replace a damaged catapult shuttle, while men used hoses to wash oil and bits of wreckage from the deck. "We're not going to be able to keep our planes flying, sir. Not with only two tankers up."

"Understood." He heard the admiral sigh. "Okay. Start working out a rotation schedule between here and Ch'unch'on. I'll give them a buzz and have them get a KC-135 airborne stat."

"That'll do it, Admiral." He thought for a moment. Ch'unch'on was a South Korean air base used by the U.S. Air Force, the closest of several such bases in the country. Allowing for a detour around North Korea, it was a one-hundred-twenty-mile flight from *Jefferson*'s position. "We'll feed the Hornets from the KAs and send them back in. If they can get a tanker up out of Ch'unch'on, we shouldn't have to use any South Korean bingo fields at all."

"Okay. Great, if you can do it. Keep me posted." The batphone went dead.

Leahy considered the phone for a moment before replacing it in its cradle. Calling in South Korean-based assets could well up the ante in the escalating battle with the KorComs.

Not for the first time, Leahy was very glad he did not have the admiral's job.

0820 hours
Nyongch'on perimeter

"Here they come again!"

"Pour it on them, Marines!"

Gunfire crashed from among the rubble and grenade-smashed ruin of what had once been warehouses across the road, as men in mustard-tan uniforms spilled from holes and doorways, brick piles and shattered walls, storming toward the west side of the camp. Simultaneously, there was a deafening blast and a black mushroom of smoke and earth sprouted in the center of the captured camp, close by the burned-out motor pool. The first blast was followed by a second, this one squarely in the fire-blackened skeleton of a garage. Splinters and debris sprinkled from the sky like rain.

But the Marines were too busy to notice. M-60 machine guns and M-16s barked and chattered, cutting down the KorCom soldiers halfway across the road. Those few who reached the chain-link fence died trying to climb it—or died in heaps crowded through one of the gaps blasted through it during the night.

Lieutenant Morgan crouched behind a pile of sandbags, watching as the surviving Koreans broke off and retreated, straggling back to hidden positions among the shattered ruins across the street. The man beside him pressed binoculars to his face. "Got the bastards!"

"Rather a bloodthirsty attitude, isn't it, Carl?"

Lieutenant Carl Olivetti grinned. "Actually, it was the mortars I was talking about. Spotted the smoke that time!" Olivetti was a member of the company's headquarters unit, the company's Forward Air Controller. He unfolded a map across one knee, then picked up the handset of a radio phone. "Skyhawk! Skyhawk! This is Charlie Alpha Victor. Priority target, coordinates seven-three-five by six-six-niner." He continued to call in the target data, stopping from time to time for confirmation. Another mortar explosion showered them with dirt.

"Wish you were flying again, Carl?"

Olivetti laughed. "Hey, like they say. I'm a Marine rifleman temporarily assigned as a pilot!" It was an old joke, one with more than the usual grain of truth to it. Marine FACs were themselves pilots assigned to Marine companies as ground spotters and liaison with Marine air.

But every Marine considered himself a combat rifleman first, no matter what his specialty.

He replaced the radio handset and turned, cupping his hands to his mouth. "Hey, Captain!" Olivetti yelled. Captain Ford ran toward them, doubled over to lower his profile. Another mortar round went off, this one at the north end of the camp.

"Whatcha got, Lieutenant?"

"Strike coming in, sir. We got a fix on the mortars. It should be any—"

He was interrupted by monsters rising above the ridge behind them. They were Marine SeaCobras, two-man helicopter gunships mounting six-barreled Gatling cannons and 2.5-inch rockets. They rose above the ridge crest east of the camp in a thunder of rotor noise.

Rockets ripple-fired from their pods, streaking across the sky on trails of white smoke, smashing into the opposite hillside with an avalanche of sound. Blast followed blast, as North Korean troops scattered beneath the onslaught.

The attack was over in seconds. Silence, when it returned, was an unearthly stillness which lay across the barren ridges like a blanket. In the distance, Morgan could hear the rumble of high-flying jets, the popping of helicopters.

"I think that got 'em," Ford said. He stood up looking west, hands on hips. "At least for a while."

"I hope it's a long while, sir," Morgan said. "We're running low on five-six-two already. And forty mike-mikes too." He was referring to the ammunition used by M-60s and M-16s, and to the

40-mm grenades fired from M-203s. He pushed his helmet back on his head, feeling the exhaustion drag at him. "How much longer, Captain?"

"Not much longer," Ford replied. He sounded tired too. He paused, as though listening. "This might be our chance now. Can't get any quieter than this."

"Hell, why wait for them?" Olivetti said. "We'll walk out."

"We sure as hell won't drive." They laughed. A number of Korean armored vehicles had been captured in the camp, but few of them were in working order, thanks either to the SEALs or to mechanical problems. It was Sergeant Walters's firm conviction that the Korean mess hall had served apricots for dinner the night before.

"I just came from the Waldorf," Ford said. "The wounded are ready to move. I think it's about time to get those damned helos in here, gentlemen, don't you?"

"Sounds good to me," Morgan said. He was mildly surprised. His first combat had carried fear but no great terror . . . and no great glory either. He didn't *feel* any different, and he was almost disappointed. After all, there was nothing much to combat but fear, dirt, mind-numbing exhaustion, and discomfort. "Let's call them in."

Olivetti was already adjusting the frequency on his radio. "Homeplate, Homeplate, this is Cavalry One. Do you copy, over?" He listened to the handset for a long moment, repeating himself once. Then, "Got them!" Ford and Morgan could not hear the reply. Olivetti squeezed the transmit button on the handset. "Homeplate, Cav One. Cavalry roundup, repeat, roundup!" He listened again. "They confirm, sir."

Morgan let out a pent-up breath. Cavalry roundup. The next few minutes would spell success or failure for the whole operation. So far, things had been going remarkably well, despite Second Platoon getting lost.

He found himself looking forward to getting back to the cramped and uncomfortable claustrophobia of the *Chosin*. He wouldn't have to wait much longer.

0835 hours
West of the Taebaek Mountains, PDRK

Pak checked his radar again, then confirmed the positions of the aircraft in the group. Plan Vengeance called for thirty MiG fighters to accompany the four Nanchangs. All planes were in position, the fighters in loose formation at one thousand meters, the bombers far below, skimming the rugged uplands east of P'yongyang.

Here, he thought, was another application of the guerrilla tactics of Mao applied to the arena of air combat. The successful guerrilla fighter, Pak knew, made use of local terrain, especially terrain with which he was familiar.

And that was precisely what Plan Vengeance was about to do.

Korea's backbone was the Taebaek Sanmaek, the mountain range which separated the east coast from the rest of the country, rising in places to over two thousand meters above sea level. The search radar of the American Hawkeyes had a range of almost four hundred kilometers, twice the distance from Wonsan to P'yongyang.

That range was limited, however, by the terrain it was attempting to scan. Flying low, weaving among the ridges and rugged uplands behind the upthrust Taebaeks, the thirty-four aircraft should escape detection . . . at least until they emerged from the mountain passes at Majon-ni, a scant twenty-five kilometers from Wonsan.

And by then, it would be too late.

The North Korean fighters would suffer heavy losses in the coming battle, but Pak had already dismissed the matter from his mind. A good commander learned to accept losses in exchange for tactical advantage. The PDRK could not possibly hope to match the Americans plane for plane, and so, losses would be enormous. There was no helping that.

Pak had a single advantage, however, which should even the odds considerably, an advantage which was yet another application of Mao's strategy. When the guerrilla fighter is prepared to die to strike at an invader, then the invader has already lost.

The MiGs would come on in two groups, one high to attract the American radar, the other low, hugging the mountains, slipping through the well-mapped passes, to emerge practically on top of the American ships.

This time, the battle would be decidedly in Pak's favor.

CHAPTER 29

"Now hear this, now hear this." The voice boomed from the 5-MC speakers across the flight deck. "Commence FOD walkdown. That is, commence FOD walkdown."

On board a carrier, FOD stood for Foreign Object Damage, and it was a special nightmare for every pilot, every plane captain, every sailor who worked on the flight deck, where a scrap of metal, a wrench, a dropped bolt could get sucked into an engine intake and cripple a very expensive airplane. An FOD parade was conducted immediately before every flight operation.

The walkdown was especially vital now. Crewmen had hosed down the deck, but it was always possible that a loose bit of wreckage had been missed. A line of over two hundred men stood shoulder to shoulder across the flight deck walking aft, eyes on the deck at their feet. The men moved slowly, stooping to pick up each bit of wreckage scattered by the explosion.

Admiral Magruder watched from the Flag Bridge high above the flight deck. Operations had been suspended for over an hour now, and that had left him mighty thin in the air. Ops had been able to get a KC-135 tanker deployed north out of Ch'unch'on, and that had kept *Jefferson*'s airborne planes in the air, but the crews were getting tired now, stretched to the limit and ready to break.

Worse, an F/A-18 squadron, the Fighting Hornets of VFA-173, and an A-6 squadron, the Blue Rangers, had both been trapped on board by the accident, unable to rotate with squadrons already in the air. With the Javelins now deployed south to refuel with the tanker and the War Eagles flying CAP for the fleet, there were only the eight Tomcats of VF-95 to cover Cavalry Two over Nyongch'on and the bomber strikes still going on around Wonsan.

It wasn't enough, not by a long shot.

Disaster, Magruder knew, was less likely to come as a single, catastrophic blow than as a series of minor incidents, each contributing its little bit of Murphy's Law until things were well and truly out of control. He had the feeling now that things were beyond his reach, that the prisoners and Marines at Nyongch'on, the Marines and rescue helos at Kolmo Airfield, the eight Tomcats of Tombstone's Vipers were all game pieces, pawns at the point of being sacrificed.

And having set the game in motion, there was nothing whatsoever that he could do to set things right.

0850 hours
Nyongch'on-kiji

Thirty minutes after sending the code phrase "Cavalry roundup," they heard the second flight of Sea Stallions approaching from the east at treetop height, closely escorted by six SeaCobra gunships and four F-14 Tomcats tagging along overhead, flying cloverleafs above the camp.

For Lieutenant Morgan, the thrill of seeing those four RH-53Ds was like a dream realized, like the charge he'd gotten as a boy watching a magician produce a bowl of fire from beneath a cape. He saw it, yet he could not quite believe it. The plan, complex, demanding, was actually working.

Now all they had to do was pull off the rest of it without losing the helos to ground fire or MiGs.

The *Chimera* crewmen were already loading their wounded on the three Cav One helos grounded at the camp's airstrip. Each RH-53 had room for twenty-one men on stretchers stacked three high on the cargo deck.

According to the plan, three helos carrying *Chimera*'s wounded would depart Nyongch'on first, flying under escort straight across the Marine perimeter on the beach and on to the *Chosin*, now eight miles out at sea. *Tarawa*-class LPHs like the *Chosin* boasted enormous sickbays, with three operating rooms and bed space for three hundred patients.

The remaining *Chimera* crewmen, almost one hundred of them, plus twelve SEALs and nearly one hundred eighty Marines, would be ferried out in piecemeal fashion. They needed eight helicopters to get them all out . . . an impossibility since there simply weren't that many free passenger-carrying helos in the task force. Besides, the flight all the way out to the *Chosin* and back could take as much as thirty minutes, counting landing and turn-around time and taking into account the crowded state of the sky above the LPH's flight deck. A better scheme was to ferry the men forty at a time from Nyongch'on to the Kolmo Airfield, the four newly arrived helos each making two trips.

The first of the medevac choppers was full. A Marine on the ground signaled, the pilot saluted from the window, and the machine's rotors increased their shrill beating as it rose, clumsy now with a full load, and hovered in the sky. Then the pilot dropped the nose and the Sea Stallion's nose swung toward the northeast. The Marine perimeter at Kolmo was only about five miles away. The helo raced for the safety of the sea at top speed, skimming treetops and burned-out buildings.

"This is the part that's been makin' my mouth dry, Lieutenant."

Morgan turned and saw Gunnery Sergeant Walters standing behind him. " 'Lo, Gunny. Why's that?"

"Desert One, 1980," Walters replied. "The helo crash, remember?"

Morgan didn't know the details, but he knew the story in general. The Delta Force raiders in the Iran hostage rescue were already pulling out, their mission aborted, when a Sea Stallion identical to these had risen from the desert . . . and collided with a grounded C-130 Hercules. The crash had claimed the mission's only casualties: eight dead.

"I guess we've learned a few things since then, Gunny."

"Mebee." He did not sound convinced. "It's not the men I worry about, though. It's *never* the men. Machines, those are somethin' else."

Morgan did not agree but saw no point in arguing. Across the airstrip, *Chimera*'s unwounded crewmen were lining up to board a Cavalry Two chopper, filing up the rear ramp and into the darkness of the cargo deck. Morale was high. There was a lot of good-natured bantering between the sailors and the Marines, and few signs of the strain the Navy men had been going through for the past four days.

With a roar, the second medevac chopper lifted from the tarmac in a swirl of dust and wind. A pair of SeaCobras raced after it, passing low overhead.

"I guess it's all going pretty well," Morgan said as the noise faded. "Like clockwork, huh?"

Walters looked at him with a curious expression. "Ain't you heard, Lieutenant? *Jefferson*'s flight deck is shut down."

"What? When?"

He shrugged. "I just heard a few minutes ago. An hour, mebee."

"Is that going to slow things down here?"

"It sure as hell will make them more interesting. Way I heard it, they need lots more fighters flying cover for the hostage choppers. Now . . ." He shrugged eloquently. "There just ain't enough Hornets and Tomcats to go around, know what I mean?"

The revelation sent a cold chill down Morgan's spine. Withdrawal from this LZ was going to be damned touchy, no matter how they went about it. As soon as the Marines started pulling out, there would be fewer and fewer defenders to hold a shrinking perimeter against enemy forces.

If the task force's air ops were restricted by damage to the *Jefferson*'s flight deck, things could get very bad indeed. Without fighter cover and bombing runs by the Intruders, the Marines could find themselves overwhelmed by North Korean forces.

"Like I say, Lieutenant," Walters added. "It's not the men who let you down. . . ."

Morgan gripped his M-16 a little tighter and stared out beyond the perimeter. Behind him, a third helicopter lifted into the sky.

0855 hours
Fox Company, Blue Beach

Private Benjamin D. Ross crouched behind the wall as rifle fire gouged chips from the top. "Sniper!" he yelled, and the other men in his squad fanned out, crawling on their bellies as they closed in on the buildings.

Fox Company had been among the first on the beach that morning, coming ashore by LCAC, then pushing southeast along the coast to establish the Marine perimeter three miles south of the Kolmo airport. They'd held that line for an hour until Bravo had relieved them, then pulled back to the complex of buildings on the coast just south of Blue Beach, which was identified on the maps as a resort.

The Marines had been amused by the relative luxury of the complex, which apparently had been reserved for party leaders and visitors from other Socialist workers' paradises. There was a large swimming pool, game courts, and more trees and shrubs—all carefully manicured—than there were growing on the whole of the Kolmo Peninsula. The buildings themselves were of immaculate white stone, quite different from the ramshackle huts of clapboard and pine which clustered along the coast farther south. Like the airport, the resort was deserted when the Marines first entered it; any occupants had fled during the night bombing raids or else later when the Marines started coming ashore.

At least, it had seemed deserted. Another shot rang out, burying itself with a thud in the trunk of a tree nearby. The enemy appeared to be holed up in a two-story building perched on an overhang above the sea, a clubhouse or restaurant of some sort. A railed, wooden deck extended from the east side of the house over the side of the cliff.

"Ross! Aguilar!" Sergeant Nelson snapped from a spot farther along the wall. "Make smoke! The rest of you, give 'em cover!"

"Right, Sarge!"

The two Marines loaded the M-203s slung beneath the forward grips of their M-16s with 40-mm smoke grenades. With a silent exchange of nods, they rose together above the wall as the rest of the company opened up with a devastating fire. The double thump of the grenade launchers was drowned by the gunfire, but there was a splintering crash from downrange, and seconds later, clouds of white smoke began billowing from the clubhouse.

"Hold tight!" Nelson bellowed. "We got help on the way!"

Seconds later that help arrived in the form of a sleek-looking Marine SuperCobra rising above the trees which lined the resort's western boundary. The roar of the 20-mm cannon in its chin turret drowned out even the crack and thump of the infantry battle. The face of the clubhouse seemed to dissolve in smoke and hurtling chunks of stone and glass. Round after round slammed into and through the structure.

The cannon fire let up and the SuperCobra turned away. "Okay, Marines!" Nelson yelled. "Let's mop up!"

Ross rolled over the top of the bullet-chipped wall and ran toward the still-smoking building. He could see several bodies sprawled in the wreckage where the front wall had caved in. Apparently, this small detachment had remained hidden earlier as the Marines moved through the area, with the idea of emerging later in the American rear.

Which was precisely what detachments such as Fox Company

were to watch for. There apparently wasn't much mopping up to do; nothing was moving in the smoking, broken shell of the building.

What happened next passed too quickly for Ross to be sure of the order of events.

The sky had been filled with helicopters all morning—mostly the big, double-ended Sea Knights ferrying Marines in from the ships to the airport—but two caught Ross's attention now. Huey UH-1s, the ubiquitous "Slicks" of Vietnam, were rare over a Marine beachhead. There were only a handful in *Chosin*'s Marine air wing, reserved for command and utility service . . . or special missions where their small size and maneuverability in tight corners were assets. These were flying rapidly toward the beach, two miles to the north.

At the same instant, two men appeared ahead, bursting from the side of the ruined building and running onto the wooden deck. One was armed with an AKM; the other carried a heavy-looking tube which he balanced on his shoulder like a bazooka. They must have stayed hidden in a basement inside the house, out of reach of the SuperCobra's fire.

The man with the AKM opened fire at the advancing Marines before they had a chance to hit the ground, his weapon chattering on full auto, spent casings spraying into the air. Aguilar jerked, as though yanked back by an invisible line, then collapsed screaming. The second Korean ignored the Marines; he seemed to be concentrating on the distant Hueys, tracking them with the device on his shoulder.

Ross recognized the weapon at once: an SA-7 Grail, what its Russian designers called *Strela*, or arrow. A man-portable, heat-seeking SAM, it was often derided as a poor copy of the obsolete American Redeye, but it was effective enough to bring down a helicopter at a range of two miles.

A second Marine was hit. Ross opened fire with his M-16, three closely spaced single shots aimed at the man with the Grail, but the soldier with the AKM stepped to the left at the wrong moment. He took the rounds in his chest and fell, his rifle spitting out the last rounds in the curved, banana-clip magazine. Behind him, the man with the Grail had already locked onto his target and was completing the double squeeze on the trigger.

An explosive charge thumped, kicking the missile clear of the tube. Ross kept firing and the other Marines joined in. Bullets splintered the wooden deck railing, then cut the soldier down in a bloody spray as the rocket's motor fired out over the surf, sending the warhead arrowing into the distance at the tip of a cottony white contrail of smoke.

Ross watched with horrified fascination as the contrail merged with one of the distant Hueys. There was a flash . . . a puff of smoke . . . and then the helo was spinning wildly in a fiery plunge into the ocean.

The sound of the explosion reached the Marines almost fifteen seconds later.

0905 hours
Kolmo Airfield

Colonel Caruso had arrived by helicopter, flying out from the *Chosin* as soon as he could convince his staff that it was necessary to do so. Strictly speaking, his presence on the beachhead was not according to regs; a sniper or a mortar shell could cut him down, and—quite apart from what Caruso thought about the matter—that loss would more than outweigh any benefit to be gained by his being there in person.

But that was not the way John Caruso managed things. An old-school Marine, a mustang who had come up through the ranks against all expectations or reason, Caruso held an almost fanatical devotion to the idea that a Marine officer led best by being visible . . . and accessible.

And that also made his men accessible to him.

"You! Sergeant!" His D.I.'s bellow carried across the tarmac despite the roar of helicopter rotors close by. "What's your name?"

"Peters, sir!" the Marine snapped back.

"Who's your platoon leader?"

"Lieutenant Rolland, sir."

"Cut the 'sir' crap, Sarge. How'd you and your squad like to go on a little trip?"

The sergeant had a guarded expression as though he didn't quite know what to make of this apparition with its black colonel's eagle pinned to its camo fatigues. "Where does the Colonel want—"

Caruso pointed across Wonsan Harbor, toward the buildings gleaming in the morning sun. "Sarge, ten minutes ago one of my helos went down on the beach. One of two very important helos, with a special tactical team. I need your squad to fill in and Charlie Mike."

Charlie Mike. Continue Mission. It was as much a part of the Marine Corps' creed as *Semper fidelis*. "Aye aye, Colonel."

"Get your people, then find Lieutenant Adams and report to him, over by those Hueys. I'll let your lieutenant know where you're going."

He returned the sergeant's salute, then strode across the tarmac, looking for Rolland.

0915 hours
Over Wonsan Harbor

Sergeant Peters was stunned when he learned what the special tactical team's mission was, but that didn't slow him as he hustled his squad up through the side door of a UH-1 Huey. Another Slick was grounded nearby, its rotors turning.

The fourteen men counted off as they strapped in, and he signaled the pilot when they were ready. With a roar, the Slick lifted from the Kolmo airfield in a whirlwind of noise and dust.

The Huey's side doors were open, and Peters could look across Wonsan Harbor as they dipped to almost wave-top height. There was plenty of shipping, merchant ships, fishing boats, sampans, even oil tankers crowding the water close to shore. North Korea had become increasingly isolated in the world community during the past few years, but Peters could see the flags of numerous countries who still did business with the Stalinist state: Cuba, China, Japan, and a vertically striped red and white ensign which he thought was that of Peru.

The Huey slipped sideways suddenly, and Peters caught a glimpse of orange tracers lashing past the open door. Someone was shooting at them.

"Looks like these bozos don't know when to quit," the Huey's pilot yelled back over his shoulder. "We're pickin' up some fire from patrol boats!"

That fire did not last long. The Hueys were accompanied by a pair of sleek Marine SuperCobras, swooping in with miniguns blazing, puffs of smoke trailing from their chin turrets like lines of white periods in the sky. There was a flash . . . then another, as a pair of TOW missiles streaked toward the surface. Peters felt the concussion of twin explosions but could not see far enough forward to identify the target.

"Stand by!" the pilot yelled. "We're clear and goin' in!"

Peters tried to get a look forward over the pilot's shoulder, but the cabin partition and the Huey's crew chief blocked his view. He could see fine a moment later, however, when the Huey swung to starboard, giving him a perfect view of the Wonsan waterfront . . .

. . . and *Chimera*.

The North Koreans' prize lay port side to alongside a long, wooden pier, bow on to the city. This part of the waterfront seemed given over to the military. There were numerous harbor tugs and torpedo boats lying at other piers close by; a blazing fire and a pillar of oily smoke marked the spot where a patrol craft had just gone down, sunk by the barrage from the SuperCobras. The scene was dominated, however, by the American ship and by the sleek gray killer shape tied up at the pier off the *Chimera*'s starboard side: a Soviet guided-missile cruiser. Peters did not speak Russian, but he knew enough of the Cyrillic alphabet to let him pick out the ship's name: *Tallinn*.

"I'm sure glad they're not shootin' at us, Sarge!" a young Marine sitting at his side yelled. Peters had to agree. From where he sat, those batteries of antiaircraft missiles looked sufficient to take on a whole Marine air wing with no trouble at all.

And what *were* the Russians thinking just now? The tactical team's orders specified that property of governments other than the PDRK was not to be damaged or threatened in any way. He imagined that Moscow had been warned before the assault on Wonsan . . . but without even trying he could think of a dozen scenarios which might lead to a direct confrontation between the Russians and the Americans.

Why the hell hadn't the Russkies pulled out as soon as the crisis started?

Then he was too busy for questions. The Huey dipped, swooping low across the water as it raced toward the piers, the pilot deliberately placing *Chimera* between the helicopters and the *Tallinn*.

The helicopter slowed, then hovered. Peters stood up, grabbing a handhold on one bulkhead as the Huey drifted crabwise toward the pier.

"Let's go, Marines!" Peters yelled, jumping off the Huey's skid and dropping to the rough wood of the pier. The pilot had come in above the shoreside end of the pier just off *Chimera*'s bow. Peters could see the gray mass of the spy ship's hull looming out of the water close by. The second Huey was hovering just above *Chimera*'s helipad as Marines scrambled out and scattered down the gangways and ladders to secure the ship. Over the bay, the SuperCobras circled like sharks, menacing and hungry.

Gunfire rattled from *Chimera*'s decks, but Peters didn't look back. The pier was deserted except for a trio of North Korean sentries, sprawled beside *Chimera*'s gangway, dead. One of the gunships had made a strafing pass before the Hueys went in.

Toward the city, the pier joined a concrete wharf backed by a street and the regimented drab buildings of the military district's waterfront. A North Korean flag hung in front of one building, and a six-story-tall portrait of the country's president hung from another. The streets were deserted, however. Any enemy forces in the area had fled at the approach of the helicopter gunships. There were plenty of potential ambush sites, though: a low concrete wall, stacks of wooden shipping crates, fifty-five-gallon drums arrayed in rusty steel walls. Peters pointed them out to the squad and dispersed his men. The Koreans might have abandoned the area, but it was likely that they would be back. When they did, they would find Peters holding the near end of the pier, blocking the way to *Chimera*'s gangway.

"Johnson! Sanchez!" he shouted. "With me!" The three men trotted toward the concrete wall, part of a retaining buttress for the seawall along the sea edge of the wharf. It would make a good site for Johnson's M-249 SAW, positioned to give a clear field of fire down the waterfront street toward the Soviet cruiser, some fifty yards away.

"*Stoy!*" a sharp voice called. "*Nyeh sheveleetyes!*"

Peters skidded to a halt, his M-16 raised to his shoulder. He didn't understand the words, but the sound of spoken Russian was unmistakable.

They stepped from among the stacks of supply crates on the far side of the street, a dozen men in the blue-trimmed white of Soviet naval uniforms. Every one carried an AKM assault rifle, and every weapon was trained on the Marines.

"Sergeant Peters, United States Marines!" he called out in a clear voice that, miraculously, did not break.

The Russian weapons did not waver.

0915 hours
Tomcat 205

"Shotgun, this is Tango Three-seven." The voice crackled in Tombstone's headset. "We have multiple bogies, repeat, many bogies, bearing from you two-seven-five at angels three, range twenty-two thousand."

"I got 'em, Tombstone!" Snowball said. "I see sixteen . . . eighteen . . ."

"Uh-oh, the shit's hittin' the old fan now," Batman said.

"Can it, people," Tombstone said. "Assemble at angels five over the harbor. Let's catch them as they come down the slot."

"The slot" was the aviators' name for a valley twisting down out of the mountains northwest of Wonsan. A major road and railway wound up into the Taebaeks along that valley, heading toward the small town of Majon-ni farther west. The attackers must be coming through that pass.

"Twenty-one bogies now," Snowball called. "Coming in high, above the pass."

Twenty-one . . . and Tombstone had three Tomcats in his flight besides himself, plus four more somewhere down on the deck, riding herd on the Sea Stallions ferrying wounded out to the *Chosin*. He opened a channel to *Jefferson*. "Homeplate, Homeplate, this is Shotgun. Advise me on status, Javelins and Fighting Hornets."

"Shotgun, Homeplate. Be advised flight deck is still out of commission. Fighting Hornets will not be able to launch for another ten minutes at least. Javelins are tanking up at Point Echo and are at least fifteen minutes out."

Shit! "Copy, Homeplate. We . . . uh . . . have a problem."

"We are tracking your problem, Shotgun. We are redeploying War Eagle CAP to cover helo operations over Nyongch'on and the beach. The other four birds of your squadron will be with you in a few minutes."

Great, Tombstone thought. That makes it eight to twenty-one, just about what we had the other day.

"Shotguns, this is Shotgun Leader," he said. "Come to new heading, two-seven-five, and take 'em up to angels six. Let's see if we can get the drop on our playmates up in the mountains."

"Roger that," Batman said cheerfully.

Tombstone felt the familiar stirrings of doubt and pushed them aside. "Ready . . . *break!*"

CHAPTER 30

Tombstone pushed his F-14's stick forward and watched the mountains behind Wonsan rise in front of his canopy. He could see the valley notch in the ridge line which led toward Majon-ni. North Korean aircraft would be bursting through that opening and into the skies above Wonsan in seconds now. "Weapons armed!" he snapped. "Snowball! Gimme a range!"

"Uh . . . eighteen, no! Sixteen bogies now. Range eight thousand."

"What happened to twenty-one?"

"Lost 'em, Stoney. Lost 'em in the ground clutter!"

So some of the enemy aircraft were hedgehopping, funneling through the mountain canyons like the spaceships in a sci-fi thriller. Somebody on the opposing team had balls. Tombstone's heart was hammering now, the adrenaline flowing. He licked his lips. "Shotguns! We have some guys sneaking through the pass at low altitude. Keep your eyes peeled." In the twisted gray and dun patchwork of stone and forest, spotting low-flying fighters was going to be a bitch.

Worse, he didn't dare try for a lock with his Phoenix missiles, not if the targets were going to vanish in the ground clutter. Better to wait and be sure.

"Shotgun Leader, this is Homeplate. Come in, Shotgun."

"Shotgun here. Go ahead, Homeplate."

"Tombstone, I thought I'd better pass the word." It was Commander Barnes in *Jefferson*'s CIC. "The wounded off *Chimera* have just gone on board *Chosin*. The rest of *Chimera*'s crew is at Blue Beach, loading onto the LCACs." There was a hesitation. "Stoney, they're going to be naked out there if those MiGs break through!"

Tombstone fought the rising, ice-cold feeling in his gut. Marine LCACs and helicopters would make prime targets; hell, you couldn't miss the damned things.

If a boatload of rescued POWs died during the final leg of their flight to safety . . .

"I copy, Homeplate. Send us what help you can. We'll hold the line."

"Tombstone!" Snowball yelled. "Eight bogies, going high!"

"Tag 'em! We'll go Phoenix!"

"Locked on! Tone!"

Tombstone heard the chirp of a radar lock in his headphones. "Six missiles, six targets. Ready to launch!"

The Tomcat's AWG-9 could track six targets simultaneously, guiding a radar-homing missile to each one. It could even pick targets for itself, selecting those radar bogies which posed the greatest threat to the Tomcat.

The machines, Tombstone reflected, were getting more efficient at war than the men who used them.

"Fox one! Fox one!" His Tomcat lurched as a blunt-nosed Phoenix slid clear of the starboard wing with a gush of white smoke. Five seconds later, a second Phoenix followed the trail of the first, twisting into blue sky ahead.

"Targets are breaking, Tombstone," his RIO reported. "Solid locks. Missile three away . . . missile four away . . ."

"Target lock!" Army Garrison called. "Fox one!"

Tombstone noticed that Batman was holding back, that he had not yet launched. He wondered if Wayne was having trouble again, face to face with the need to kill another man.

He decided to say nothing. Batman would click in, *had* to click in . . . or he was dead. Anything Tombstone said to Batman over the radio might cause more trouble then it solved. He remembered how things had started going to pieces for him during the last dogfight . . . culminating with his repeat bolters on the *Jefferson*.

If Batman was having trouble, he'd have to resolve it himself.

Missiles five and six slid clear of the Tomcat and Tombstone rolled left, heading for the deck. He pulled up seconds later as concrete buildings blurred beneath the F-14's belly. Tombstone glimpsed roads, bridges, factories, and apartments. This is a hell of a place for a dogfight, he thought. I hope the civilians have already bugged out.

Orange flame blossomed ahead. "Hit!" Snowball exalted. "Splash one MiG!"

The other MiGs scattered across the sky, their contrails interpenetrating with the twisting white lines of Phoenix AAMs. Missile two steered into the side of a mountain seconds later. Several MiGs were scrambling for the deck now, attempting to lose the radar-locked hunters among the rocks and crags of the valley.

The notch in the mountains became a valley of death. A second explosion hurled flaming chunks of MiG across the canyon. Tombstone pulled up and arrowed into the valley as half a dozen silver delta-winged aircraft lashed past above his canopy heading in the opposite direction. One MiG exploded, the concussion rocking the F-14.

"Splash two! Splash three!" Snowball yelled. "Holy mother, it's raining MiGs!"

"Lining up nice . . . Fox one!"

Fire blazed in the sky. "Splash one for Two-oh-four," Army announced.

"Fox two! Fox two!" That was Taggart. If he'd gone to Sidewinders, he was close.

Tombstone pulled back on the stick, climbing from the valley in a loop which took him up to five thousand feet. MiGs were everywhere now, above him, behind him, and spilling out of the pass over Wonsan. From a mile in the air, Tombstone could see the morning sun glint off the harbor ahead, could see the black silhouettes of the big Marine amphib ships far out toward the horizon.

"Shotgun Leader, this is Two-two one. We're in the game. Where's the action?"

So Snake Hoffner had arrived, along with the three other Tomcats which had been escorting helicopters. "Two-four-four in," Nightmare Marinaro said.

"And Two-four-eight." That was Shooter Rostenkowski.

"And Two-nine-five," Paddy Padden added. "Upping the ante with Fox two!"

"Welcome aboard, guys," Price Taggart said. "Ain't we got fun?"

Another MiG blossomed into flames, the wreckage tumbling end for end as it streaked into the valley below and slammed into the face of a cliff. Atoll missiles were crisscrossing with Phoenixes and Sidewinders now. "Splash one for Two-nine-five!"

"Way to go, Paddy! Come left to two-seven-oh! Bandits! Bandits at angels three!"

"Watch it, Stoney!" Batman warned. "Three comin' in on your six!"

At least Batman sounded like he was still in the fight. "Batman! Where are you?"

"On your three at eight-triple-oh."

"I see you. Get on them! Breaking right!"

Tombstone snap-rolled his F-14 to starboard. He was well above the walls of the valley now, but rocky crags seemed to claw the sky, reaching for his aircraft as he twisted into a tight split-S. As he leveled out two thousand feet above the ground, he caught a glimpse of Batman streaking overhead, the MiGs scattering. An arrow of white fire intersected one MiG in a blaze of orange and black. "Splash one for Two-oh-three," Taggart said. "Watch out for falling MiGs!"

"Shotgun Leader! Shotgun Leader! You still have one on your tail!"

Tombstone twisted in his seat, looking back past Snowball. "He's on us!" the RIO shouted. "He's still coming!"

There he was! Tombstone saw the flash of a missile as it left the MiG's wing.

There was no radar tone, and at short range it would be a heat-seeker. "Hit the flares!" Tombstone yelled. He yanked the throttle back and over into a barrel roll while Snowball stabbed the release on the chaff/flare board on the RIO's right cockpit panel. At the last possible moment, Tombstone yanked the Tomcat onto its back and plunged toward the ground, now less than a thousand feet away.

The heat-seeker missed, a streak of fire past the canopy. Tombstone kicked the F-14 to full burner and hauled it into a brutal, vertical climb.

That was when he saw the ground attack fighters.

There were four of them, flying wingtip to wingtip in a diamond formation racing out of the valley at better than Mach 1, just above and ahead of their own shadows rippling along the uneven ground. Tombstone recognized the type: Nanchang Q-5s, a Chinese export ground attack fighter known to NATO as the Fantan. They were painted in green and brown camouflage markings and escorted by four low-flying MiGs. Each carried several dull-white missiles slung from pylons under the wings, AS-7 Kerry ASMs, most likely, with one-hundred-pound warheads.

Tombstone knew exactly what their targets would be.

"Tally-ho!" he yelled as he rolled out of his climb. "Fantans! Fantans coming out of the valley!"

Time seemed to stand still for Tombstone. As he went port wing high, he could look down and see the Fantans emerging from the mouth of the valley from Majon-ni beneath him. In another few minutes, they would be across the city and out over the water, with dozens of targets to choose from. High on their list would be the distinctive, boxy shapes of the LCACs, by now well away from Blue Beach and on the way back to the fleet. A single Kerry planted in one of those hovercraft, and the odd-looking vessel would become a deathtrap, killing every rescued POW on board.

Or worse, they might try for *Chosin* herself, now recovering, refueling, and launching Marine helicopters at a furious rate. Though it was far larger and harder to sink than an LCAC, the flight deck of the LPH was a tangle of men, machines, fuel hoses, and ammunition. A Kerry or two into *that* mix could kill hundreds, could cripple or even sink the Marine carrier, together with the more than sixty wounded sailors from *Chimera*.

And there were other targets as well: *Little Rock*, *Texas City*, and *Westmoreland County* with their flocks of AAVs and Mike boats, the destroyers closing with the Korean coast, the Sea Knight helos plying back and forth between ship and shore. . . .

A target-rich environment which would almost guarantee the Fantan drivers a hit . . . and a major blow against the American task force.

"Nightmare! Nightmare! He's on my six!"

"Break left, Shooter! Break left!"

"See if you can—"

"I'm on him! I'm on him! Fox two!"

"I'm too close for a shot! Goin' to guns!"

"Get him off me, Nightmare!"

The background radio chatter told him the rest of the Tomcats were tangling with other MiGs in a colossal dogfight which arched across the sky over all of Wonsan. He banked his Tomcat left, lining up on the Korean Fantans . . .

. . . and then the F-14 shuddered as jackhammer blows slammed into its hull. He turned to look back. One of the North Korean fighters hung there, one hundred yards off his tail.

"Shit, Stoney!" Snowball said. "Where'd he come from?"

Flashes of light stuttered at the roots of the MiG's wings, and 23-mm tracers floated past his head, scant feet from his canopy. Two more MiGs dropped into view as he watched.

"Tombstone!" Batman yelled. "Three blue bandits on your six!"

"I know! I know!"

"On my way!"

"Negative, Batman!" Tombstone went to full burner, climbing rapidly. The MiGs stayed with him, matching each twist and maneuver. "The Fantans! You've got to keep those Fantans from reaching the fleet!"

Cannon fire slashed into his Tomcat's right wing.

**0922 hours
Tomcat 232**

Batman looked up through his canopy, watching the four aircraft gleaming in the sunlight far above. Tombstone's Tomcat was dropping out of its Immelmann now, nosing over into an inverted dive.

The three MiGs stayed with him.

Below Batman, the Fantans and their escorts thundered toward Wonsan and the sea's edge.

There was no time to think, though the conflict within was cold and diamond-hard. He could save his wingman or attack the Fantans . . . but not both.

Biting off a curse, he pulled his wing over and plummeted, letting the altitude scale on his HUD rocket down the numbers, past five thousand . . . four thousand . . . three thousand . . .

"Sidewinders!" They were too close for a Phoenix.

"Yo!" Malibu said. "Watch it, Boss. We've got a missile lock on us."

He heard the tone. Somewhere, a MiG's radar was hunting for him. "Screw it!" He concentrated on the targeting pipper on his HUD, hauling the stick over as he lined up on the lead Fantan, now three miles ahead. Sun glint sparked fire from the surface of Wonsan Harbor beyond.

The target graphic changed to a circle, indicating a lock. Batman's thumb closed over the firing button. There was a pilot riding in that Nanchang Q-5 . . .

. . . and there were sailors and Marines in those ships riding black against the sunlight. "Fox two!"

The Sidewinder streaked from beneath the Tomcat's wing.

"Batman!" Malibu called. "Missile launch, on our six!"

"Chaff!"

"Done. It's still coming!"

Batman slipped the Tomcat to the side, lining up on another target. From behind the Fantan formation, their tailpipes made perfect heat-seeker targets. The escorting MiGs were all over the sky, screening the Q-5s, dogging the F-14.

"Pull up, Batman! *Batman!*"

Damn! He pulled up sharply, dumping chaff as he twisted into a hard loop. The missile followed, but too quickly to turn inside the American's arc. A proximity fuse detonated the warhead thirty yards away, a thunderous concussion which rocked the Tomcat. The escort MiGs dropped onto his tail, and searing lines of tracers burned the sky.

Then the first missile hit and the lead Fantan exploded, blossoming in a succession of savage blasts as the Kerry missiles under the wings detonated. Burning fragments rained from the sky.

0923 hours
Tomcat 205

Tombstone twisted away from the gunfire in a clockwise barrel roll, slamming on his air brakes to kill his speed. The entire point in any ACM was always, always, to get the other guy out front; most dogfighting maneuvers were designed to force the guy on your tail to overshoot and pass you, lining him up for a shot from the rear.

One of the MiGs flashed past, so close to Tombstone's port wing he could see the man looking back at him through his helmet's dark visor.

"Missile launch!" Snowball yelled. "Heat-seeker!"

"Pop flares!" His RIO would have to handle the countermeasures. He was busy.

His last dive and roll had carried him well to the northwest of the city and into the fringes of the combat area. He was down on the deck, altitude less than three hundred feet, and the roads, buildings, and powerlines whipped past him almost too quickly to be perceived.

"It's still comin', Tombstone!"

"Hang on!" He pulled up sharply and broke right. Something streaked past his canopy on a trail of fire. He whipped the F-14 into a scissors and saw a second MiG roll away. Tombstone brought his stick over; he was tempted to try for a shot at the second MiG, but he knew there was a third one back there somewhere.

"Where's number three?" he yelled.

"Still there, Tombstone. Right on our six!"

"Good night, Snowy!" He kicked in his afterburner.

0924 hours
Tomcat 232

Batman pulled out of the loop. The escort MiGs had scattered, unable to follow his high-G pull-out, and he was in the clear once more.

The Fantans . . . where were they? He spotted them eight miles ahead, riding their own shadows across the rugged ground as they streaked toward the outskirts of Wonsan. He slid back into the formation's wake, much farther astern now, but still too close for a decent Phoenix shot. The three Q-5s were still dead on course for the fleet, flashing across Wonsan's western suburbs, the sprawl of industrial plants and refineries. The taller buildings of the city rose ahead, snatching at the low-flying aircraft.

"Hey, dude, this is turnin' into an obstacle course!" They were down to five hundred feet. Batman remained intent on the three target symbols on his HUD.

"Hold on, Malibu! Just a little more . . ." The pipper crawled across the display. The Q-5s were jinking, swinging back and forth in an attempt to avoid buildings as well as Batman's lock. He could see the ships of the American task force clearly now, less than fifteen miles away. The Korean pilots would be arming their missiles now. . . .

ACQ flashed on his display, and the targeting box over the left-hand Q-5 became a circle. A tone sounded in his headset.

"I got lock! Fox two!"

A second Sidewinder slid clear of the Tomcat's rails and arrowed toward the Fantans. Two of the Q-5s broke then, swinging left and right to avoid the missile. The Sidewinder, locked onto the plane to port, swept off to the left.

Batman stayed with the remaining Q-5, which was maintaining

its dead-level course. He switched his missile system back to Search Mode. A warning came up on his HUD. "Damn!" He'd forgotten his combat load included only two Sidewinders, and both were gone now.

"You want to go for Phoenix?" Malibu asked.

His Tomcat was riding now with six of the heavy, long-range killers under his wings. They could destroy MiGs in the sky over P'yongyang a hundred miles away, but he was too close to deal with the Fantan lumbering less than two miles ahead.

"Negative!" he snapped. His left hand rammed the throttle forward as he went to burner. "I'm goin' to guns!"

The Q-5 raced across the city's waterfront and thundered out over the bay. Batman followed. He had an instant's glimpse of *Chimera* less than five hundred feet below . . . and the sinister gray shape of the Soviet cruiser.

0924 hours
Wonsan waterfront

The Marines and the Russians had stood there for an eternity, it seemed like, neither side willing to move, neither side willing to retreat. Peters had dispatched one of his men with a tense, urgent whisper to back off and radio Lieutenant Adams, who was leading the squad on board *Chimera*. It might be a while before help came, though. Peters could still hear shooting on board *Chimera*, occasional ragged bursts of autofire.

One Russian had departed as well, running toward the boarding ladder on the Soviet ship's side. Peters didn't know if he was going to report or to bring help.

"Do you speak English?" Peters called.

The Russian who seemed to be in charge had shaken his head. "*Nyeh panemayu. Gavareeti lee vih parouski?*"

Impasse.

Very, very slowly, Peters lowered his M-16. It did not look as though the Russians were looking for a confrontation. If they were, they could have fired from ambush and killed every Marine on the dock . . . could have opened up on the Huey while they were still out over the harbor. But disengaging from this eyeball-to-eyeball confrontation was going to be tricky.

The Russian, eyes narrowed, lowered the muzzle of his AKM in response. . . .

BOOM!

Peters dove forward, landing on the concrete facedown. Every man on the dock, Russian and American, was on the ground at the same moment, scrabbling for cover, certain that a bomb had just gone off. . . .

0924 hours
Tomcat 232

Kolmo Peninsula swelled larger just ahead as the two aircraft flashed low across Wonsan Harbor. Batman had a glimpse of the airport, of a multitude of vehicles, of helicopters on the runways, rotors turning. He crossed the landing beaches and hurtled on over the open ocean. *Chosin* was ten miles away. . . .

The gunsight reticle on his HUD tracked the Nanchang Q-5, his LCOS showing minimum target lead. At this range, he could actually *see* the enemy pilot, turning in his cockpit for a view aft at his pursuer. Batman could imagine the man's fear.

Chosin was eight miles away. . . .

0924 hours
Tomcat 205

Tombstone held his F-14 under control as he twisted away from the enemy MiG. Whoever this guy was, he was *good*!

The Tomcat lashed into a scissors . . . then another, as Tombstone tried to sucker the Korean into an overshoot which would put him in the American's sight, but the MiG driver was having none of it. He was staying tucked in tight.

"Still with me, Snowball?" Rugged cliffs reached for the F-14 to left and right. They were dropping into a narrow valley.

"Right behind you! Hey, how about shakin' this guy? He's gettin' on my nerves!"

"Mine too, partner. Time to get out of Dodge!"

The Tomcat stood on its tail, clawing for altitude. The MiG, anticipating the maneuver, rose with it, cannons thundering.

Hammer blows smashed into the Tomcat's hull, walking up the fuselage between the upright stabilizers. Warning lights flashed across Tombstone's console.

Tombstone twisted away from the deadly fire. This guy was definitely first string on the Korean team. He leveled out at eight thousand feet, turning hard to port.

"Stoney!" Snowball called. "Watch it! He's—"

Then the cockpit exploded in flame and smoke and the F-14 was falling, falling, the wind shrieking through a pair of holes punched through the Plexiglas inches above Tombstone's head. The MiG thundered past yards off Tombstone's left wing.

"Close one, Snowball!" Tombstone yelled. He fought for control, feeling the flaps bite air. The F-14 shuddered as he pulled up the nose. "Are you okay? Snowy? Snowy!"

A small rearview mirror was mounted on his console, positioned so he could see into the backseat. He could not see his RIO, but he could see a ragged tear in the rear part of the canopy where cannon shells had passed through the cockpit. Snowball must be slumped over, out of sight.

There was blood on the canopy, a spray of crimson.

He checked his indicator. The ship's AWG-9 was out . . . no data on the scope. The missile systems were out . . . as were electronic countermeasures.

Another shudder wracked the stricken Tomcat, and they began losing altitude.

CHAPTER 31

Water raced past hunter and hunted as the Fantan continued to
arrow toward the U.S. fleet, the F-14 closing from behind.
Batman's finger squeezed the trigger and his Vulcan cannon
howled, hurling a stream of 20-mm slugs into the Nanchang.

The Chinese ground attack fighter, a design similar to the
American F-4 Phantom, was ruggedly built. It absorbed round
after round after burning round, slowing, but not falling. Bits of
debris flaked away from the stabilizer and pinged off Batman's
canopy. He moved closer, waiting for the flash of an A-7 launch.
Chosin was six miles away, well within range of the Kerry. . . .

He squeezed the trigger again, and smoke began spilling from
the Fantan's engine, then a gush of flame. At first Batman thought
the Fantan was cutting in its afterburner, but then he realized that
fuel was spilling into the tailpipe and igniting.

The Fantan exploded, a savage eruption of burning metal and
spinning fragments. The Kerry warheads went off in a succession
of blasts, each larger than the one before, until the sky was filed
with orange flame. The F-14 roared into the fire . . .

. . . and burst through the other side, rocking with the
concussion, its wings scored by fragments.

Chosin and her consorts lay less than five miles ahead. The sea
around her was thick with AAVs, and Batman could see the
foam-lashed shape of an LCAC making its way across the water
below, making for the *Little Rock*. Farther away still, at the very
edge of visibility, Batman could see the gray shadow of *Jefferson*,
at the point where sea met sky.

Batman brought the Tomcat around in a shallow turn, passing
back across the tip of the Kolmo Peninsula. Wonsan lay spread out

before him, a gleaming city of white buildings and towers, of columns of greasy smoke hanging above burning ships, shattered buildings. . . .

"Where are they, Malibu? Where are the other Fantans?"

"One's down, Batman. You killed him. Lost the other . . . no, wait! I can get a feed from one of the Hawkeyes! Bearing . . . two-eight-five. Batman! He's running!"

"We'll take him with Phoenix! Arming . . . !"

"Hot!"

"Lock 'em!"

"Damn! He's ducked back through the pass. I think he's running for home, dude. Looks like he doesn't like the surfin' around here!"

For a moment, the killer's fury threatened to overwhelm Batman. He could have had a clean sweep, four for four. He could still go to burner, still . . .

He let out a long breath. "Let him go. Just so he doesn't circle back on us. Give me a vector to Tombstone."

"I'm on it, compadre. Two-five-nine, angels five . . ."

The Tomcat streaked toward the mountains.

0925 hours
MiG 444

Major Pak took a deep breath as he brought his MiG around in a climbing turn, positioning himself high on the wounded American's tail. He recognized that aircraft; he'd glimpsed hull number 205 once before, during the dogfight out over the Sea of Japan. He wasn't sure if American aviators always flew the same aircraft or not, but meeting this one was like meeting an old friend.

The Yankee's cockpit was shattered, and a thin trickle of black smoke was leaking from the left engine. Another burst at close range would send the American plunging into the sea.

Over his headset, Pak could hear the North Korean air assault falling to pieces. Three of the Q-5s had been shot down, and the survivor had broken off and was fleeing west. Eleven MiGs had gone down in the space of eight minutes, and the others were scattered across the sky . . . or fleeing for a friendly airfield covered by SAMs.

And there were reports of more American aircraft approaching from the east.

There was, Pak knew, no use in attempting to return to P'yongyang himself. The best he could hope for was exile to some isolated post in the Yalu Valley. The worst . . .

He didn't want to think about it. His leaders did not easily forgive failure.

His death would not atone for this disaster, but he might be able to arrange things so that the defeat was not so shockingly one-sided. Major Pak would shoot down the Tomcat, then turn east. There were American carriers out there, and transports filled with Marines. He would find a target. His MiG carried no bombs, but that hardly mattered. Fifty years before, the detested Japanese had shown how to use the aircraft itself as a bomb.

There were infinitely worse ways to die. . . .

With a grimace of determination, Major Pak dropped his MiG once again onto the tail of the damaged American Tomcat.

0925 hours
Tomcat 205

Tombstone pulled the stick left, praying his Tomcat would hold together. He'd seen the Korean MiG approach, seen the number 444 on the hull in front of the cockpit. He pulled into a sweep to get inside the MiG's turn, but indicators lit up, warning of damage to his port engine, forcing him to break and roll clear. The MiG followed.

Launch!

Tombstone saw the flash of the missile. He waited, keeping the flare of its exhaust in sight until the last moment, then popped flares and turned. The missile decoyed toward the flares and Tombstone brought the F-14 around hard for a riposte.

No good. His radar was out, and an indicator showed his weapons systems were inoperable. *Damn!* He had two Sidewinders still hanging from his wings, but no way to lock on and fire them. All he had left were his guns.

He found himself wondering about his opponent. Most Korean aviators—at least according to Intelligence—were mediocre pilots. The PDRK's air defense forces had nothing similar to Top Gun or Red Flag, schools where they could sharpen their dogfighting skills against live opponents. There were a few, though, who had received special training in the Soviet Union, men who had gone on to train the fighter pilots of other countries: Iraq, Syria, Libya.

It was hard thinking of his opponent as a person . . . as

someone who might have trained in Moscow or worked for a time in Damascus. Tombstone had an eerie sense of identity with Batman, knowing exactly the shock he'd felt after his first kill.

But it was also part of the job, a job which was quite literally kill or be killed. The Korean pilot was doing his level best to kill *him*. . . .

They were at five thousand feet now, a mile above the patchwork of grays and browns, roads and factories and buildings northwest of Wonsan. The two aircraft were traveling at over six hundred knots. The F-14's wings were folded back, but the damage to the aircraft was bad enough that Tombstone was considering overriding the control. If the wing pivots froze, he didn't want to try to maintain lift with the wings back when his airspeed started falling.

But not yet. He kept jinking his F-14, trying to avoid a missile lock by the other pilot, but the MiG kept closing in, apparently trying for another pass with his guns. He was less than a mile away now, and still closing.

A maxim he'd picked up at Top Gun came to him. When you can't outfly the other guy, you have to out*think* him. This guy had anticipated every scissors, every yo-yo, every maneuver designed to reverse their positions. But perhaps there was something else Tombstone could try.

He pulled the Tomcat into a shallow turn to port, banking the aircraft more and more as he tried to turn inside the MiG's turning radius. The MiG followed. Tombstone tightened up on the turn, wings still folded, luring the MiG closer. . . .

F-14 Tomcats had one particular weakness in air combat, a subtle weakness which could nonetheless give the enemy a powerful advantage during a dogfight. Unless the pilot hit the override, the aircraft's computer controlled the angle on the wings automatically, folding them back at high speed, opening them wide for better lift at low speed. An enemy pilot who knew what he was looking at could glance at a Tomcat's wings and make a very good guess at just how much energy the F-14 had at the moment, information which let him adjust his own speed to avoid overshooting the target.

Tombstone's speed was down to three hundred knots now, and his wings were starting to come forward. He slapped the override, keeping the wings tucked back. It was like avoiding a "goose mode" when making the break toward a carrier trap. He was losing altitude now as he lost speed and lift, but he kept the wings tucked in.

"C'mon," he told the Korean pilot. "C'mon, you bastard . . ."

0925 hours
MiG 444

Pak was still turning inside the Tomcat's circle. The American fighter's wings were still folded. Pak's Spin Scan radar was too primitive to provide him with speed data on the target, but the fact that the F-14's wings were still folded told Pak that the Yankee was maintaining the turn at better than three hundred knots. Pak's own airspeed was falling below two hundred eighty knots as he tightened his turn. The Yankee was going to slip away!

He kicked his throttle forward for a sudden burst of speed. . . .

0925 hours
Tomcat 205

He kept his eyes on the MiG floating off his portside tail, still staying inside the F-14's turn. When the MiG accelerated with a rush, Tombstone knew he'd won.

The MiG passed the Tomcat barely thirty yards to port at the same instant that Tombstone opened his wings and popped the air brakes. For an instant, Tombstone looked into the other man's face. . . .

Then he pulled the F-14 hard to the left, sliding in behind the MiG so close that the Tomcat bucked and rumbled in the other plane's jet wash. Tombstone knew he would have only a second before the other pilot went into a break. He let the gun reticle drift across the MiG's hull, squeezing the trigger as the target filled his sights.

Cannon fire hammered into the MiG from less than fifty yards away, gouging chunks of hull metal. Tracers seemed to sink into the MiG, walking up the fuselage.

The MiG was already burning, already starting to come apart as the deadly rain of high-speed cannon fire found the cockpit. The wings seemed to crumple in toward the hull, and then the entire plane was engulfed by flames. Tombstone's Tomcat bumped and shook as it rode through the fireball.

He watched the wreckage trail fire all the way to the ground.

0925 hours
Wonsan dock

Slowly, Sergeant Peters rose to his feet. There was absolute silence on the dock as U.S. Marines and Russians, in twos and threes, began getting up, looking at one another sheepishly. The thunder had receded. Long seconds passed before they realized that the near-miss blast had not been a bomb at all, but a Tomcat cutting in its afterburners less than five hundred feet overhead.

The nearest Russian marine stood slowly less than ten feet away. The front of his white trousers was wet. As he moved, Peters realized his own camo fatigue pants were wet too. The Russian looked at himself, then at Peters. Another long moment passed, and the Russian began to laugh.

The Marine joined in.

Within the next few minutes, a dialogue of sorts was worked out. After a hurried consultation, it was discovered that Private Greeley had brought along a strictly unauthorized item of equipment, a much-worn copy of *Playboy* tucked into his rucksack. The Russians obviously were interested in a trade; Greeley was convinced to part with his contraband in exchange for a Russian Naval cap . . . and the sergeant's promise to see him hauled before the skipper at mast for carrying contraband if he didn't go along with this new and promising turn in intercultural relations.

The Russians offered the Americans vodka and bread; the Marines offered them MREs. Meals, Ready to Eat—plastic packages of dehydrated food—were widely regarded by Marines as neither ready to eat nor meals, a poor substitute indeed for the canned C-rations they replaced. There was a spirited discussion over whether that particular gift would make the Russians mad. Peters broke the impasse by walking over to the Russian Marine and opening one of his MRE pouches.

The Russian looked puzzled as he sampled it. "*Shtoh eta?*"

Peters didn't understand the words, but the question in the tone and in the man's face was clear enough. He smiled. "Apricots."

"Ah-bree-kods . . . ?"

"Try 'em," Peters said, grinning. "You'll love 'em!"

At least the Soviet Marine wasn't a tank driver. Peters didn't think the apricot curse applied to ships.

0930 hours
Tomcat 205

"Homeplate, Homeplate, this is Two-oh-five," Tombstone said. He was holding the Tomcat level at four thousand feet, flying slowly east across the coast north of Wonsan. "Homeplate, this is Two-oh-five. Come in, please."

He was just beginning to wonder if his radio was out too when he heard the crisp, all-business voice of Commander Barnes. "Two-oh-five, this is Homeplate. Be advised you have friendlies entering your area. Watch you don't score an own goal."

"Glad to hear it, Homeplate." He paused to examine the sky. "It looks like the locals don't want to play anymore."

"Copy, Tombstone. That's good news."

"Listen, Homeplate, does that mean your flight deck is open for business?"

"That's affirmative, Two-oh-five. We started launching five minutes ago. We sent the call out, but I guess you were too busy to hear us."

"Roger that." He checked his instruments again. He was losing fuel . . . fast. His hydraulic pressure was failing as well, and his left engine was running hot. "Homeplate, I'm calling an emergency."

"Copy, Two-oh-five. What is your situation, over?"

He ran down the list of warning indicators. The most serious problem was fuel. At the rate he was losing it, he would be going dry in another fifteen minutes. Coming in for a trap on *Jefferson* shouldn't be too hard; his ILS appeared to be out but he'd be able to come in by eyeball, no sweat. The loss of hydraulic pressure was a nagging worry, though. He might not be able to get his landing gear down . . . and if he did, the gear might not hold when he slammed into the deck.

"Two-oh-five," Barnes said. "Suggest you approach Homeplate and eject. We have an angel standing by."

"Concur, Homeplate. I—" He heard a groan and felt his heart skip a beat. The ICS was on, and he was hearing sounds from the back seat! "Wait one, Homeplate!" Tombstone turned, trying to see his RIO. "Snowball! Snowball, are you there?"

He saw movement in the rearview mirror, caught a glimpse of Snowball's face, a mask of blood beneath his helmet. "It . . . hurts . . ."

"Homeplate, this is Two-oh-five."

"Go ahead, Tombstone. What do you have?"

"Homeplate, I thought my RIO was dead. He's not. He's alive! Can't tell his condition, but he's hurt pretty bad."

"Ah . . . copy, Tombstone. Wait one."

"Snowy? Can you hear me back there?"

"Tombstone!" The voice was weak, and Tombstone heard a wet gurgle behind each breath his RIO took. "Tombstone . . . it *hurts!*"

"That's good, buddy! If it hurts, you're still in there kicking. Stay with me, son! We're on our way back to the *Jeff!*"

"Tombstone . . . I don't . . ."

"Stay with me, Dwight! Where do you hurt?"

There was no answer, but Tombstone could still hear the ragged breathing. If they were forced to eject, if Snowball's neck or back or head were broken, if he had a rib poking through a lung . . . damn it! Ejecting from a damaged bird was dangerous at the best of times. If you were injured, your chances of survival went way, way down.

Under it all was the nagging realization that Snowball was in the backseat now because Tombstone had landed on him two days ago. Snowy had been ready to quit, and if he had, he'd be safe and whole on the carrier right now.

Of course, someone else would be in the backseat instead. It seemed that there was little purpose in trying to second-guess the universe.

"Tomcat Two-oh-five, this is Homeplate."

"Two-oh-five."

"Tombstone, do you think your RIO can eject? Over."

"Negative! Negative! We cannot eject!"

"Okay, Tombstone. Listen up. The Captain's rigging the barricade. You are clear for a straight-on approach. The Air Boss will talk you in, over."

"Roger that, Homeplate." He took in a deep breath. "I'm coming in."

"And I'm right here with you," another voice cut in.

"Batman! Where are you?"

"On your five and low, Boss. Looks to me like you're bleeding."

"Roger that." The hydraulic fluid in Tomcats had an additive which colored it red, making it easier to detect leaks. "Hydraulic pressure is way down."

"Ah, you don't need that shit. Just follow me on down, slick as a baby's ass."

"Yeah. My port engine's running hot. I'm shutting down."

They pulled into a gentle turn, coming up astern of the *Jefferson*. Two days ago, Marty French had made this same approach in a damaged Hornet. The images recorded off the PLAT system were still burned into his mind . . . the horror as Frenchie's nose gear failed and the wing tanks burst into flame.

"Two-oh-five," the LSO's voice said over his headphones. "Check your gear."

He slapped the switch. "Gear down."

"Take it easy, Stoney." That was CAG's voice, coming from Air Ops. "You've got loads of time. Captain says the ship is at your disposal. If you want to circle a few times to catch your breath, that's okay. If we can help you by maneuvering, that's okay too."

He thought of Snowball in the backseat, possibly bleeding to death. He thought about his bolters two nights before. Well, they wouldn't have that option this time around. "Negative, CAG. Thanks."

On *Jefferson*'s deck, hundreds of men from the deck crew were completing rigging the barricade, a kind of net with loose, vertical nylon straps hanging between two cables stretched across the flight deck. Tombstone had never made a net trap before, and he didn't like the thought at all. To drop toward a carrier deck on approach and actually see something *in the way* . . .

"Two-oh-five, call the ball."

"Tomcat Two-oh-five. Ball. One-point-eight." Fuel was getting critical. He wondered if there was a danger of fuel spewing over a hot engine and igniting. Well, he'd done all he could by shutting down the damaged engine. His left wing dipped and he compensated. The F-14 was sluggish; on only one engine it was like flying a boxcar.

"Watch attitude," the LSO said. "You're lined up fine. . . ."

He watched the orange ball, making tiny, incremental adjustments to the throttle. The sea was calm, and *Jefferson* was steering into the wind at less than fifteen knots. He eased up the power a bit as the ball went high. . . .

"Looks good," Batman said. The other Tomcat paced him off his left side. The deck swept up to meet him, the barricade stretched across his path. He overrode the instinct to hit the throttles as his rear wheels touched down.

The landing gear gave way with a jar and the Tomcat's belly slammed into the steel deck. Sparks showered as the aircraft skidded down the deck at one hundred fifty miles an hour. The nylon straps of the barricade seemed to engulf the cockpit, and then Tombstone was slammed forward against his harness.

Training took over as he switched off the engine, closed fuel valves, shut down power. The danger now was fire as fuel or fumes reached hot metal or an exposed electrical wire. Within ten seconds, *Jefferson*'s crash crew had surrounded the aircraft, hosing it down with fire extinguisher chemicals, using the emergency release lever to free the canopy. As the cockpit opened, Tombstone felt hands reaching in to pull him out and safe the ejection seats, while behind him corpsmen began tending to Snowball.

Only then did Tombstone's hands shake . . . this time from relief instead of fear.

They'd made it.

CHAPTER 32

Lieutenant Morgan signaled Sergeant Walters with a chopping motion of his hand. The sergeant twisted the plunger on the device he held, and a chain of explosions ripped through the compound, destroying the barracks, the few surviving vehicles, the headquarters, and the building called the Wonsan Waldorf.

"C'mon! C'mon! Let's go!" The sergeant dropped the plunger and trotted across the airstrip where the last ten Marines crouched in a circle, weapons facing outward.

Morgan was eager to abandon the place. All of the former prisoners were gone, as well as the SEALs and most of the Marines. He alone remained with a single squad.

The explosions set off another round of firing as automatic weapons opened up from the ruins across the street, followed by the heavy crump of a mortar round. The North Koreans were gathering again, had been pressing against the dwindling Marine perimeter all morning.

It was time to go.

"That's everybody!" Walters shouted.

Morgan looked up. The last helo had lifted out of the camp minutes before. The Sea Stallion circled slowly overhead, waiting as SeaCobras made a final pass across the road, miniguns blazing. The lieutenant pulled the pin on a smoke grenade and tossed it onto the tarmac.

Wind whipped up clouds of dust as the helicopter descended. The Marines stayed where they were, watching outward as a line flipped from the Sea Stallion's side and uncoiled toward the earth. When it reached them, the Marines grabbed it and stretched out the end on the ground. At Morgan's command, each man used swivel snaps to fasten himself to the line. "All secure?" he yelled, and each man in the line signaled readiness.

Morgan waved, and the helicopter began going up once more, taking the dangling rope and the ten Marines with it. The lieutenant had always thought it an undignified way to travel. It reminded him of flies stuck to a long strip of flypaper, but it was a quick means of extraction which avoided the necessity of a helo setting down in the middle of a fire-covered LZ. The only real threat was that the helo pilot would fail to allow enough clearance for his low-flying passengers.

Last man off the ground, Morgan clung to the line with one hand and gripped his M-16's pistol grip with the other. The line twisted, spinning him slowly as he rose clear of the ground. As he passed over the road, he could see a number of men in mustard uniforms spilling out of the ruins west of the camp and crossing the fence.

They were probably shooting at the helo, but he could hear nothing under the thunder of the rotors and he resisted the urge to fire into the mob. "That's okay, boys," he said under his breath. The helicopter picked up speed and he trailed behind, the wind lashing at his face. "You're welcome to the place. We're just leaving."

The twistings of the line turned him until he was facing north, and he caught a glimpse of blue sea beyond the Kolmo Peninsula and the smoke rising from the airfield.

The Sea Stallion picked up speed as it turned toward the Marine beachhead.

1114 hours
Wonsan waterfront

They were leaving.

The fight for *Chimera* had been short and sharp. There'd been only a handful of North Korean guards on board; four had died at their posts and another had dived overboard. The rest, ten in number, stood uncertainly on the pier, their hands still cuffed behind them by plastic straps brought for the purpose.

A Huey had arrived at 1000 hours and landed on the middeck helipad, disgorging a khaki-clad Navy chief and a small army of sailors in dungarees. These men vanished into *Chimera*'s bowels. Twenty minutes later, another helicopter arrived carrying more sailors, volunteers drawn from *Chosin* and *Texas City*, all under the command of Lieutenant Gerald Cole. The shipboard Marine contingent divided into smaller details, some manning the vessel's machine guns fore and aft, others joining working parties who began clearing the wreckage from the spy ship's deck and cutting away the ruin of her boat davits and mast. One Marine had brought along a large American flag. The flag of the PDRK was taken down, folded, and stowed, the Stars and Stripes tied to a makeshift mast abaft of the bridge in its place. There was no ceremony to mark the moment. For the Marines, the act itself was enough.

An hour later, the word was passed: *Chimera* was ready in all respects for sea. Cole turned to Lieutenant Adams, commanding the Marine platoon, and smiled. "Liberty's over, Lieutenant. Call your men back and let's get the hell out of here."

The Marines on the waterfront filed down the pier and up *Chimera*'s gangway. They left behind their Korean captives and a coterie of Soviet Marines and sailors. The atmosphere was friendly, even relaxed, though the Marines remained on guard. Gunshots continued to bang away in the distance, beyond the city and across the bay. The waterfront area, though, seemed deserted; at the least the inhabitants were staying well under cover. A-6 and Hornet interdictions at dozens of points around the city's road net had paralyzed traffic and prevented troop movements into the waterfront. Also, the landings across the harbor and the fighting at Nyongch'on had served admirably as a diversion.

Chimera's engines boomed into life, causing the dirty water under her stern to boil and froth. Sailors cast off lines fore and aft, and the combat-battered vessel began to slide away from the pier, moving dead slow astern. Sergeant Peters leaned on the railing forward of the helipad, watching the group of Russians and Koreans as the ship backed into the harbor.

One Russian Marine waved a packet of MREs above his head. "Peh-ters!" he yelled. "*Vsyegoh harashigah, tovarisch!*"

Peters waved back. He didn't know what Vladimir Ilych was saying, but he seemed to be wishing the Americans luck.

Machine gun fire rattled from a building somewhere to the south, but there was no telling what the target was. In reply, a single, piercing blast shrilled from *Chimera*'s horn, echoing back from city buildings. An answering blast sounded from the harbor. There, the sleek gray shape of the destroyer *John A. Winslow* made her way among the fishing boats and merchantmen. The

Winslow had been brought into the harbor against the possibility
that *Chimera* would need a tow, or support from her five-inch
guns. With her engines and steering operational, with Korean
military forces along the waterfront fled or in hiding, the destroyer
would serve as an escort of honor instead. Tomcats from VF-97
boomed low overhead, flying cover, as SeaCobras and SuperCobras continued their hungry circling. *Winslow* came about in a
broad half-circle and began churning through the gray waters
toward the north point of the Kolmo Peninsula.

Her flag flying, *Chimera* followed.

There would be no more *Pueblos*.

1130 hours
Blue Beach, Kolmo Peninsula

Private Ross followed his training, leaning *around* the pile of
rubble to look for the enemy instead of over. The resort complex,
which had been in what passed for a rear area well within the
Marine perimeter, had within the past hour become the front line
once more. Mortar fire rained down on the Marines from hidden
sites among the villages to the south, and the steady rattle of
machine guns, the bang of sniper rifles echoed from buildings and
cliff sides. Smoke, from gunfire, fires, and smoke markers, hung
like a gray pall of fog across the ground, reducing visibility to a
few yards and men to hunch-backed shadows slipping among trees
and walls.

A shrill, eerie wail sounded through the murk. Some clown
over there had found a bugle and was using it to summon another
charge. He'd heard stories about those bugles passed on from
earlier generations of Marines in an earlier Korean war. "Get
ready, guys!" he yelled. "They're coming!"

They came in a rush, not the human wave hordes he and his
squad mates had expected, but small groups of eight or ten men
each. Autofire stuttered and snapped, the muzzle flashes bright,
flickering tongues of flame in the fog. Ross chose his target, then
elevated his weapon, his right hand caressing the trigger of the
M-203, mounted just forward of his magazine. The weapon
jolted against his arm. Seconds later, the 40-mm frag burst just
behind the advancing Koreans, mowing them down like wheat.
More kept coming, firing and shrieking as they ran. Ross took
aim, sighting down his M-16's carrying handle, and began firing

single shots with careful deliberation. One Korean fell . . . and another . . . and another . . .

"Fox Company!" Corporal Charnesky yelled. Sergeant Nelson was dead, cut down by AK fire thirty minutes earlier. "Stand by to withdraw!"

"How the hell are we supposed to withdraw with gooks climbing all over us?" Private Grenoble muttered from his firing hole a few feet away. He levered himself up and loosed three quick shots at the advancing soldiers. "We must have half the damned gook army here!"

"We'll invite them out to the ship," Ross replied. He aimed again . . . fired. A North Korean clutched at his face and dropped back into the murk. "Have them join us in the mess hall. Ptomaine'll get them."

"You wish. With our luck—" He stopped himself, looking up at the low overcast. The air was quivering with a new sound, a thundering roar approaching from the sea. "*INCOMING!*"

"Down!" Ross screamed, and he did his best to burrow into the soil, his hands over ears and head.

The ground seemed to rise up and kick him in the chest and stomach. The noise . . . the noise was too vast to be described as sound, a shattering detonation which tore sky and ground apart with a concussion wave which rang like a bell.

Another express train roar followed the first . . . and the blast shook the ground and rained gravel across the backs of the huddled Marines. Explosions tore the face of the ridge, uprooting trees, collapsing buildings, splintering walls. . . .

The silence which followed was so deep Ross thought he'd gone deaf, but he heard cheering rising from the beach moments later. Raising his head, he looked out toward the sea, where a low, gray silhouette rode the waves five miles out. Even at this distance, Ross recognized the *John A. Winslow*, the old *Spruance*-class destroyer which had accompanied the Marine amphib ships close into shore. Both of her five-inch turrets were swung around to cover the shore; those seventy-pound projectiles could be laid down with pinpoint accuracy with help from spotters ashore or in the air. The barrage had slammed into the Korean attack, shattering it utterly.

"On your feet, Marines!" Charnesky ordered. Already he sounded like prime sergeant material, loud and obnoxious. "You bums miss the boat this time and it'll be a long walk home!"

Fox Company stumbled back down the hill toward Blue Beach,

sliding down a shallow ridge and jogging across sand and gravel toward the water. A trio of Sea Knights roared low overhead and out to sea, the last flight out of Kolmo Airport today . . . and probably for weeks to come, so badly had the runway been cratered.

The beach area was littered with the burned-out hulks of vehicles—AAVs, mostly, but numerous humvees and several helicopters as well—which had suffered damage and were being left behind. One working vehicle remained, one of *Chosin*'s LCACs, resting on its skirts just above the surf line with its forward ramp deployed. The beachmaster stood on the ramp, signaling Fox to hurry. "Move it, Marines!" he yelled. "You wanna be left behind?"

Ross followed the others aboard, combat boots rattling on the ramp grating. The coxswain gunned the craft's engines and the skirts inflated, lifting the air cushion vehicle clear of the beach in a storm of wind-blown sand and spray. The ramp came up, and LCAC 2 nosed around, sliding off the beach and out over the water. Mortar shells stuttered and howled overhead; geysers of water erupted to either side . . . and then the LCAC was hurtling to sea at fifty knots, the wind and sea spray clawing at Ross's face.

Only then did he realize that the shore line behind him was empty now, that he had been the *last* Marine off the Wonsan beach.

"Hey, what happened?" he asked a Marine standing next to him. "Did we get the Navy guys out?"

"How the shit should I know," the man growled. "The colonel didn't see fit to confide in me this time!"

"Yeah," another grumbled. "SOP. Never tell us anything!"

"An oversight, gentlemen," a tall Marine said. "My apologies. The last of the hostages came off the beach at approximately zero-nine-fifteen. Only one of the prisoners died in the rescue. *Chimera* has been secured and is underway, heading out to rejoin the fleet."

Only then did Ross notice the black eagle pinned to the Marine's camo fatigues and realize who was talking to him. He snapped to attention. "Excuse me, Colonel sir!"

"At ease, at ease," Colonel Caruso said, waving Ross down. "God knows, you boys earned it." The colonel's words were already spreading among the Marines crowded in the LCAC's well deck. The cheering broke out seconds later, beginning as a

murmur and swelling, growing larger, going on and on and on, so
loud it drowned out the hovercraft's roar.

Admiral Magruder held the binoculars to his eyes, peering
through them toward the west. He could see the darker shadow
that was the Kolmo Peninsula against the vaster, paler background
of the mountains, but at this distance he could see neither Wonsan
nor the beaches.

The Marine intervention in North Korea was over. All of
Chimera's surviving officers and crew were safe, the wounded in
the extensive sick bay facilities on board *Chosin*, the rest on the
Little Rock where the LCACs had carried them. By any standards,
the raid had been a spectacular success. Of *Chimera*'s original
crew of 193 officers and men, 23 had died during the original
attack at sea five days before. Three had been shot by the Koreans.
One more, a Lieutenant Novak, had died during the rescue. The
SEALs and Marines had brought out all of the rest.

But the *cost* . . .

The casualty figures weren't complete, but over one hundred
Marines had died in the landings. Add to that the casualties on
Jefferson's flight deck in the accident that morning: four dead,
fifteen injured.

Plus two SEALS, and the Navy aviators and NFOs . . .
Mardi Gras, Frenchie, Dragon, Snoops. Brave men all, who had
died for what they thought was right.

"Now hear this, now hear this," a voice boomed out from the
ship's 5-MC, faintly audible through the bridge windows. "Stand
by to receive helo." One of *Jefferson*'s Sea King SAR helicopters
was approaching from the west. The admiral watched as the
machine settled onto the deck. Through his binoculars, he could
see two men on board, lying strapped into the wire mesh baskets
of a pair of Stokes stretchers.

Jolly and Chucker. The SAR chopper had plucked them from
the sea less than a mile off shore. They looked half-frozen and too
weak to walk after spending hours adrift in the cold water, but the
helo had already radioed that they were okay. Corpsmen lowered
the stretchers to the deck, then hustled them toward the island.

Magruder remembered his nephew's outrage a five-day eternity ago. We do look after our own, he thought. When we can. When we *possibly* can. . . .

Three American planes had been downed today, but the crews had all managed to eject and been rescued. The butcher's bill this day was not as high as it could have been, perhaps, but it was high enough. The brutality of the equation was appalling, and it raised a disturbing question. How many deaths can be justified in the saving of two hundred lives?

Admiral Magruder knew the answer to that question as soon as he'd framed it in his mind. The Marines, the *Jefferson* herself and every man aboard her . . . they were there to defend American rights and American lives, at the cost of their own lives if need be. There was no particular logic to the mathematics of the question, and damned little glory. But there *was* tradition.

And honor.

And that was enough.

2200 hours (0800 hours EST.)
The Oval Office

The President swiveled his chair away from the desk and stared out past the Rose Garden toward the pinnacle of the Washington Monument in the distance. It was a glorious fall day, blue skies, puffy white clouds . . . with just a hint of autumn crispness to the early October air.

It was over. The speech, the pile of papers on his desk, said so. The last of the Marine and Naval forces had disengaged hours before and were now standing well out into the Sea of Japan, leaving the shores of North Korea behind them. *Chimera* and her crew were coming home.

He would read that speech on the special television broadcast scheduled for later that morning. He was certain the American public, at least, would support what had been done. Despite storms of controversy in the press, most Americans had cheered the Mayaguez rescue, Grenada, Panama, and the Gulf War to liberate Kuwait. They would cheer this time as well, and in the end, it was their cheers that mattered most. A former occupant of this office had once called the nation a "pitiful, helpless giant." Never again. By God, never again!

The tragedy was that things were never as neat and as orderly as they were in works of fiction . . . such as Presidential speeches. Crises were not neatly resolved when the President sent in the Marines . . . *never*. More often than not, the real problems were just beginning when the outward crisis was solved. The Marines might be out of North Korea, but the real fight was just warming up. The government of the Philippines was calling the Wonsan incursion an unjustifiable use of force to settle what was essentially a diplomatic problem; the People's Republic of China called it a serious provocation and a threat to stability in the Far East; Japan thought it an unforgivable reversion to the stupidities of gunboat diplomacy.

God only knew what North Korea would call it when they began addressing the world audience: war, murder, rape, and piracy, most likely, emotional charges which the logic of truth could never fully counter.

There was a knock at the door. "Yes?"

A secretary stepped in. "Mr. President? Secretary of State Schellenberg."

"Send him in."

Schellenberg looked drawn, and his expression was hard. The President rose from the chair and advanced to greet him.

"Good morning, Mr. President," Schellenberg said. He fumbled for a moment with an envelope in his suit coat pocket.

"That had better not be what I think it is, Jim."

"My resignation, Mr. President. I . . . think you know why."

The President folded his arms, refusing the envelope. "I don't want it."

"But, Mr. President . . ."

"No. You ought to know me better than that, Jim. We didn't agree on how to handle the Koreans, but that doesn't mean I don't need *you*, or respect your opinion."

"I was wrong." He dropped the envelope on the President's desk, then closed his eyes. "My God, when I heard they'd started shooting our people, one by one . . ."

"No. You were *right*."

"Sir?"

The President picked up a folder, stamped TOP SECRET at top and bottom, and handed it to Schellenberg. "The DCI brought this by this morning. Read it."

Silently, the Secretary of State paged through the documents inside. Marlowe had briefed the President on the translated documents and the CIA's analysis of them only hours before. Taken from the body of a North Korean officer in the field, they offered a glimpse of P'yongyang's strategy. The plan, codenamed

Fortunate Dawn, had started as an attempt to embarrass the United States by capturing and quickly breaking the crew of a U.S. intelligence ship . . . but somewhere along the line things had gotten out of hand.

"You see, Jim?" the President asked when Schellenberg looked up from the papers. "They set a trap and we almost stepped into it."

"They *wanted* us to invade?"

"I think they wanted us to get so bogged down we couldn't pull out. Then the Russians or the Chinese would have come to their aid . . . and bailed out their economy. Thing is, if Righteous Thunder hadn't worked, they might have gotten their wish. *Jefferson* and the MEU gave us the flexibility to get in, accomplish our objectives, and get out . . . fast."

"Thank God for the carrier battle group, then."

"Amen to that. If I'd ordered a full military response . . ." He shuddered. "No, you keep right on telling me what you think. Yes men I don't need, not in this job."

"Yes, sir."

The President grinned. "Besides, I'm not about to let you off the hook. Hell, man! Our Asian allies are fit to be tied over this thing . . . and I'm supposed to break in a new hand now?"

Schellenberg smiled. "Bad timing, huh?"

"Damn right it's bad timing." He plucked the secretary's resignation from the desk and tore it into pieces. "Now, I thought we should send some of State's best people over there. You know, smooth things over. I was wondering about that doctor who briefed us, what was her name . . . ?"

"Dr. Chu. Yes, I'd thought of her for something like that myself. She's not afraid to give it to people straight."

"Good. I've given you one hell of a mess over there, Jim, and I'm counting on you to clean it up."

Schellenberg's resistance weakened as they continued to talk.

Mess it might be, the President reflected as they discussed the situation, and mess it would continue to be for weeks to come. But it could have been worse . . . much worse. If it had not been for the *Jefferson* and her battle group . . .

There was a major contradiction there . . . a U.S. Navy carrier battle group as an instrument of *peace*. But without *Jefferson* and the will to use her, America would have been held hostage—again—or been forced to go to war. The challenges to freedom included not only foreign invaders, but fear, indecision, and the willingness to sacrifice principles on the altar of appeasement, of peace-at-any-price.

More often than not, the cost of appeasement was too damned high.

He hoped the men who had died on those beaches understood. Somehow, he thought they would.

EPILOGUE

U.S. Naval Hospital, Yokosuka, Japan

"So, Coyote!" Tombstone said, grinning. "Do you mean to tell me you're leaving me stuck with *this* character for a wingman?"

"Ah, you're just jealous, Stoney," Batman said, laughing. "You saw that walking dream in nurse's whites out there! She's the only reason this guy's screwing off here!"

Coyote lay in the hospital bed between them. It was three days since he'd been carried on a stretcher off the rescue helo, then medevaced to the Naval hospital here at Yokosuka. Physically, he looked only a little the worse for wear, with bandaged leg and shoulder and a needle in his arm feeding him D5W from a bottle hung on an IV stand. But Tombstone had looked into Coyote's eyes and seen something else, a hurt or a fear or some inner twisting which IV bottles could not reach.

The cure lay within the patient. Whether he could find it was still a question.

"Can't be the nurse, Batman," Coyote said. "You know I've got a ticket home."

Tombstone walked to the window, which overlooked Yokosuka Bay. The harbor was clogged with Navy ships, tugs, cargo ships, and ferries. Looming over them all was the gray steel mountain of the U.S.S. *Jefferson*, just around the headland at Uraga on her way to the anchorage. He and Batman had gotten permission for the hop to Japan ahead of the carrier the day before. They'd spent the night at the Yokosuka BOQ in order to be at the hospital at the start of visiting hours.

He'd only just learned that Coyote was due to be casevaced once more, this time to the Naval Hospital in San Diego. He was

going home, just like Snowball Newcombe, who'd been shipped
out yesterday.

"Sure, sure," Batman said. "I think you've got something
going with her!"

"Cool it, Batman," Tombstone said. "This here's a married
man!" He grinned, then shook his head in mock despair. "My
God, Coyote, you've *got* to come back! You haven't seen the
latest flock of nuggets they're sticking us with! They just flew out
to the *Jeff* yesterday."

Just before they'd strapped on their Tomcats for the flight to
Yokosuka, Tombstone and Batman had talked briefly with the air
wing replacements. Fresh-faced, raw, and new, every one of
them, full of questions about what it was like to down a MiG.

Or to kill a man.

"Shitfire," Batman said, catching Tombstone's eye. "Hotdogs,
every one of them. You know, I think we're gonna have our hands
full!"

"Yeah, hotdogs." Tombstone threw Batman a wink. "I bet they
fit right in!"

Coyote looked away, toward the window, where sunlight was
spilling across mountains, water, and the drab orderliness of
military buildings. The *Jefferson* was sliding slowly past the
harbor entrance. "Yeah . . . well, I've been doing a lot of
thinking, guys, these last few days. I don't know if I *will* be
back."

Batman, for once, said nothing, and Tombstone was grateful.
He thought he knew what the Coyote was going through.

All three of them had endured much the same test during the
past week, each facing that one choice which is the secret dread of
all Navy aviators: the decision to turn in his wings. A simple
matter, really . . . a walk down to CAG's office, a flip of the
fingers to send the gold device spinning through the air . . .

Loneliness. Strange to think of loneliness on a ship with six
thousand people aboard, in a squadron where every man knew
every other like a brother. But every man in the wing had an inner,
private place where he could no longer rely on the camaraderie,
the banter, the public *image* which each fighter pilot carried of
himself.

For Tombstone, that loneliness had been the loneliness of
responsibility, of dealing with his men's burdens while he still
carried burdens of his own. For Batman, it had been the lonely
confrontation with reality . . . and with duty.

And Coyote? He had a lonely choice too. Unlike Batman and Tombstone, he had someone waiting for him, far away in another world.

"Your choice, friend," Tombstone said softly. He found himself thinking of Snowball, of the young RIO's fear . . . and of his unwillingness to be ostracized by the brotherhood. He and Tombstone had forged a special bond facing death together in the crippled Tomcat, a *brothers'* bond. Snowball would not fly again, not as an NFO. He'd be lucky if he walked again without crutches.

But he *belonged*, no matter what happened. Just as Batman belonged . . . and the Coyote. There was a sense of family there which could not be denied.

Tombstone looked at his friend and thought he knew what he would choose. Coyote had been shaken by his experiences ashore, sure. But he was tough, tougher than Coyote himself realized right now. He needed time to work things out, but he'd be back.

"Ah, he'll be back," Batman said. "He couldn't get along without us!"

"Maybe." Tombstone put his arm over Batman's shoulders. "You know, Will, whatever happens, whatever you decide, we're with you."

Coyote grinned. "Maybe that's what I'm afraid of."

And Tombstone knew then that the Coyote would be okay. Whatever happened.

GLOSSARY

AA or AAA: Also "triple A." Antiaircraft artillery.

AAM: Air-to-air missile.

AAVP: Amphibious Armored Vehicle, Personnel. Also "AAV" or "amtrack." Amphibious Marine tracked vehicle used to ferry personnel ashore. Carries 21 Marines.

ACM: Air Combat Maneuvers. Dogfighting.

AEW: Airborne Early Warning.

Air Boss: Air Department Officer. Directs aircraft within 5 miles of carrier from Primary Flight Control.

Air Operations: Also "Air Ops." Department responsible for aircraft outside Pri-Fly's 5-mile zone.

Air Wing: All of a carrier's aircraft squadrons. A typical wing on a *Nimitz*-class carrier includes 2 fighter squadrons, 2 light attack or strike/fighter squadrons, 2 medium attack squadrons, 1 EW squadron, 1 AEW squadron, 1 ASW squadron, and 1 helicopter ASW squadron, for a total of 86 aircraft.

Alpha Strike: A number of aircraft carrying out a raid.

Angels: Expression of altitude in thousands of feet; i.e. "angels seven," seven thousand feet. Also, designation for helicopters aloft for SAR during carrier launch or landing operations.

ASW: Anti-submarine warfare.

Autodog: Soft ice cream from an automatic dispenser.

Bandit: Identified enemy aircraft.

BARCAP: Barrier Combat Air Patrol. Element patrolling between the carrier and possible enemy aircraft.

Batphone: Direct line to principal carrier departments and personnel.

Bear: NATO code for Tupolev Tu-20 bomber and several variants.

Bingo Fuel: Enough fuel remaining for a few more minutes of flight, depending on speed and payload. A "bingo field" is a shore airfield close enough for an aircraft to reach and land on if there are difficulties in landing aboard a carrier.

Blue Bandit: A MiG-21, as opposed to a "Red Bandit" (MiG-17) or "White Bandit" (MiG-19).

BN: Bombardier/Navigator. The right seat position in an A-6 Intruder.

Bogie: Unidentified radar target.

CAG: Commander Air Group. Commanding officer of a carrier air wing. The title, which rhymes with "rag," is left over from the days when carriers had air groups rather than air wings.

CAP: Combat Air Patrol.

Carrier Battle Group: One aircraft carrier and air wing, with between 5 and 7 support ships.

CATCC: Carrier Air Traffic Control Center, pronounced "Cat-see." Nerve center of Carrier Air Operations on the 0-3 level, responsible for traffic control outside Pri-Fly's 5-mile radius.

CIC: Combat Information Center. Department where combat is monitored and directed. Also called "Combat."

CINCPAC: Commander-In-Chief, PACific. The admiral in command of Pacific Naval forces.

COD: Carrier On-board Delivery. Aircraft used to carry mail, personnel, and supplies to a carrier at sea.

CVIC: Carrier (CV) Intelligence Center, pronounced "civic." An intelligence briefing room. Also where addresses by senior officers are televised for the benefit of the ship's crew.

DCI: Director, Central Intelligence. Head of American intelligence agencies, including both the CIA and the NSA.

DCO: Damage Control Officer.

DMZ: Demilitarized Zone. Refers to the no-man's-land between North and South Korea.

E&E: Escape and Evasion.

ECM: Electronic Counter Measures. Jamming and other strategies designed to interfere with enemy attempts to locate, identify, and track friendly aircraft.

Element: In fighter tactics, a two-plane unit, a leader and his wingman.

EW: Electronic Warfare.

FAC: Forward Air Controller. Officer in the air or on the ground who calls in and coordinates ground attacks by air support units.

Fantan: NATO code for Nanchang Q-5 ground attack fighter.

Feet Dry: Call from an aircraft passing from over water to over land. As opposed to "feet wet."

Fishbed: NATO code for MiG-21.

5-MC: Loudspeaker on carrier flight deck.

Flag Bridge: Bridge set aside for use of the admiral in command of a Naval squadron.

Flag Plot: Mapping and operations room set aside for use by the admiral commanding a Naval squadron.

Flight: In fighter tactics, two elements, four aircraft.

FLIR: Forward-Looking InfraRed. IR targeting system allowing bombing runs at night or in bad weather.

Fox One: Radio code for launch of a radar-guided missile such as Phoenix or Sparrow.

Fox Two: Radio code for launch of a heat-seeker missile such as Sidewinder.

Grail: NATO code name for SA-7 *Strela*, shoulder-launched SAM.

G2: Intelligence.

Homeplate: Radio code for the carrier.

HUD: Heads Up Display. System of projecting flight and targeting information on a screen between the pilot and his canopy, or, in some cases, on the canopy itself.

Hush Puppy: Slang for S&W Mark 22 9-mm suppressed automatic pistol favored by SEAL teams in covert operations. The name came from their use to silence guard dogs in Vietnam.

IBS: Inflatable Boat, Small. Rubber boat favored by SEALs and other covert forces. Sizes vary from four to fourteen men.

ICS: Intercom system aboard two-man fighters.

IFF: Identification Friend or Foe. Known informally as the "parrot," the device transmits coded signals which allow identification on friendly radar screens as an aid to traffic control.

Immelmann: A vertical ACM; the aircraft twists as it climbs straight up, exiting at the top in an unexpected direction.

JBD: Jet Blast Deflector.

KH-12: Latest in a series of extremely sophisticated spy satellites. "KH" is shorthand for "Keyhole," the security designation for the entire project.

Kimchi: Korean delicacy prepared by soaking cabbage in various spicy potions and burying it in a clay pot for days or weeks. Smells like rotten cabbage.

KorCom: Korean Communist.

LCAC: Landing Craft, Air Cushion. Marine landing hovercraft which rides above water or land on a cushion of air.

Loose Deuce: Air tactic favored by American pilots, allowing for great flexibility within individual elements.

LSO: Landing Signals Officer, responsible for monitoring incoming aircraft during carrier landings.

MAC: Military Armistice Commission. Group which oversees Korean armistice, meeting regularly to discuss incidents and violations along the DMZ.

Mangler: Deck Handler, in Flight Deck Control on the O-4 level. Responsible for moving aircraft between flight deck and hangar deck. Also "Handler."

MEU: Marine Expeditionary Unit. Formerly MAU, the smallest air-ground task force, normally built around a reinforced battalion and a Marine air squadron.

MiG: Any of a series of fighter interceptors from the Soviet design team of Mikoyan-Gurevich. Thousands have been exported all over the world, and many are built in third-world countries under license. Loosely: any Russian-made aircraft.

Mike Boat: Smallest Naval landing craft, also known as an LMC. Carries 25 Marines.

MRE: Meal, Ready to Eat. Packaged, dehydrated field rations for U.S. combat troops.

Mule: Flat-topped, yellow tractor used to tow aircraft aboard a carrier.

NFO: Naval Flight Officer. Commissioned member of an aircrew other than a pilot. RIOs are NFOs.

NPIC: National Photo Interpretation Center. Department in Washington, D.C., which receives and analyzes photographic reconnaissance.

NSA: National Security Agency. Secret organization based at Fort Meade, Maryland, and headed by the DCI which is charged with electronic signals intercepts and decoding.

1-MC: Internal loudspeakers on carrier.

O-1 Deck, O-2, etc.: Decks on a carrier are identified by their location relative to the hangar deck, which is the O-1 level. The next deck up is the O-2 level, and so on going up through the various decks in the island. The O-3 level is directly below the flight deck, while the flight deck itself is O-4. Going down, the deck immediately below the hangar deck is the first deck, the next is the second deck, and so on down toward the ship's keel.

PLAT: Pilot Landing Aid Television. Closed-circuit channel on a carrier used to monitor, record, and critique pilot landings.

Pri-Fly: Primary Flight Control.

RAG: Reserve Air Group stationed in U.S. from which new aviators are drawn.

RIO: Radar Intercept Officer. The "backseater" in a Tomcat.

ROE: Rules of Engagement. Guidelines under which fighter and bomber pilots operate in a given political situation.

SAM: Surface-to-Air Missile.

SAR: Search and Rescue.

Scissors: An ACM involving a series of sharp turn reversals.

SEALs: Acronym for SEa, Air, and Land. Naval fleet tactical unit organized in 1962 to carry out special warfare operations, including recon, sabotage, raids, and hostage rescue.

Six: On an aircraft's tail. Derived from aircraft clock positions, with "twelve o'clock" directly ahead, three o'clock to the right, and nine o'clock to the left. All dogfight maneuvers are designed to put an attacking aircraft on the target's "six."

Slick: The Huey UH-1 helicopter, employed in large numbers in Vietnam.

SOD-Hut: Special Operations Department aboard ship, always highly classified. Also called "spook shack."

Squadron: Naval aviation unit composed of aircraft of a single type. Typically, fighter squadrons (VF), strike-fighter squadrons (VFA), medium attack squadrons (VA), and antisubmarine squadrons (VS) number 10 aircraft each. Electronic warfare squadrons (VAQ) and Airborne Early Warning squadrons (VAW) number 5 aircraft each. Helicopter ASW squadrons (HS) number 6 aircraft.

TACCAP: Tactical air cover for a raid.

TAC COM: Tactical Communications.

Tally-ho: Radio call indicating visual contact with enemy.

TENCAP: Tactical Exploitation of National CAPabilities. System allowing commanders in the field to draw on KH-12 satellite reconnaissance data directly, rather than waiting to receive it from Washington.

Tilly: Large combination of crane and forklift used to lift or move damaged aircraft.

Top Gun: U.S. Navy Fighter Weapons School, NAS, Miramar, California. A training school for Navy aviators designed to expose them to ACM.

Tuna Boat: Marine slang for a loaded AAVP.

Unit Designations. Codes identifying squadrons by aircraft type. e.g. VF-95. Some examples:

VA: Medium attack squadrons, flying A-6E/F Intruders.

VAQ: Electronic Warfare (EW) squadrons, flying EA-6B Prowlers.

VAW: Airborne Early Warning (AEW) squadrons, flying E-2C Hawkeyes.

VF: Fighter squadrons, flying F-14A/D Tomcats.

VFA: Strike-fighter squadrons, flying F/A-18 Hornets.

VS: ASW squadron, flying S-3A/B Vikings.

VDI: Visual Display Indicator. Display on A-6 Intruder linked to on-board computer which displays flight and targeting information.

Vulture's Row: Railed catwalk high on carrier island overlooking the flight deck.

Welded Wing: Air tactic where an element's leader and wingman stick tightly together, as opposed to the "loose deuce."